"Daphne du Maurier's collection of short stories...leaves no doubt as to the author's talent as a crackerjack raconteuse. Each selection is a masterpiece—sometimes of suspense, chicanery, insidious evil, in other instances of sensitivity and perception, as in the case of 'The Pool'.... She takes the reader by the icy hand and leads him behind the curtain to view the characters on their ways to their own breaking points....Throughout these stories, Daphne du Maurier demonstrates her talent in ferreting out and describing the subtleties and foibles of human nature."   —*Saturday Review*

"Miss du Maurier develops her nine stories around experiences which are strange and rare and yet valid....A bright disturbing clarity, like the one that pervades the dream world of the surrealists, illuminates all the stories."
—*San Francisco Chronicle*

"Recommended to readers who yearn for some good, sound, old-fashioned story-telling."
—*Library Journal*

The Breaking Point
was originally published by
Doubleday & Company, Inc.

THE
BREAKING
POINT

Daphne du Maurier

Drawings by Margot Tomes

PUBLISHED BY POCKET BOOKS NEW YORK

THE BREAKING POINT

Doubleday edition published October, 1959

POCKET BOOK edition published August, 1961

6th printing......November, 1971

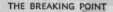

This POCKET BOOK edition includes every word
contained in the original, higher-priced edition. It is printed
from brand-new plates made from completely reset, clear, easy-to-read
type. POCKET BOOK editions are published by POCKET BOOKS, a division
of Simon & Schuster, Inc., 630 Fifth Avenue, New York, N.Y. 10020.
Trademarks registered in the United States and other countries.

L

Standard Book Number: 671-78122-7.
This POCKET BOOK edition is published by arrangement with Doubleday
& Company, Inc.

Printed in the U.S.A.

NOTE

There comes a moment in the life of every individual when reality must be faced. When this happens, it is as though a link between emotion and reason is stretched to the limit of endurance, and sometimes snaps. In this collection of stories, men, women, children, and a nation are brought to the breaking point. Whether the link survives or snaps, the reader must judge for himself.

Contents

The Alibi

THE FENTONS were taking their usual Sunday walk along the Embankment. They had come to Albert Bridge and paused, as they always did, before deciding whether to cross it to the gardens or continue along past the houseboats; and Fenton's wife, following some process of thought unknown to him, said, "Remind me to telephone the Alhusons when we get home to ask them for drinks. It's their turn to come to us."

Fenton stared heedlessly at the passing traffic. His mind took in a lorry swinging too fast over the bridge, a sports car with a loud exhaust, and a nurse in a grey uniform, pushing a pram containing identical twins with round faces like Dutch cheeses, who turned left over the bridge to Battersea.

"Which way?" asked his wife, and he looked at her without recognition, seized with the overwhelming, indeed appalling impression that she, and all the other people walking along the Embankment or crossing the bridge, were minute, dangling puppets manipulated by a string. The very steps they took were jerking, lopsided, a horrible imitation of the real thing, of what should be; and his wife's face—the china blue eyes, the too heavily made-up mouth, the new spring hat set at a jaunty angle—was nothing but a mask painted rapidly by a master hand, the hand that held the puppets, on the strip of lifeless wood, matchstick wood, from which these marionettes were fashioned.

He looked quickly away from her and down to the ground, hurriedly tracing the outline of a square on the pavement with his walking stick, and pinpointing a blob in the centre of the square. Then he heard himself saying, "I can't go on."

3

"What's the matter?" asked his wife. "Have you got a stitch?"

He knew then that he must be on his guard. Any attempt at explanation would lead to bewildered stares from those large eyes, to equally bewildered, pressing questions; and they would turn on their tracks back along the hated Embankment, the wind this time mercifully behind them yet carrying them inexorably towards the death of the hours ahead, just as the tide of the river beside them carried the rolling logs and empty boxes to some inevitable, stinking mud spit below the docks.

Cunningly he rephrased his words to reassure her. "What I meant was that we can't go on beyond the houseboats. It's a dead end. And your heels"—he glanced down at her shoes —"your heels aren't right for the long trek round Battersea. I need exercise and you can't keep up. Why don't you go home? It's not much of an afternoon."

His wife looked up at the sky, low-clouded, opaque, and blessedly, for him, a gust of wind shivered her too thin coat and she put up her hand to hold the spring hat.

"I think I will," she said, and then with doubt, "Are you sure you haven't a stitch? You look pale."

"No, I'm all right," he replied. "I'll walk faster alone."

Then, seeing at that moment a taxi approaching with its flag up, he hailed it, waving his stick, and said to her, "Jump in. No sense in catching cold." Before she could protest he had opened the door and given the address to the driver. There was no time to argue. He hustled her inside, and as it bore her away he saw her struggle with the closed window to call out something about not being late back and the Alhusons. He watched the taxi out of sight down the Embankment, and it was like watching a phase of life that had gone forever.

He turned away from the river and the Embankment, and, leaving all sound and sight of traffic behind him, plunged into the warren of narrow streets and squares which lay between him and the Fulham Road. He walked with no purpose but to lose identity, and to blot from present thought the ritual of the Sunday which imprisoned him.

The idea of escape had never come to him before. It was as though something had clicked in his brain when his wife made the remark about the Alhusons. "Remind me to telephone when we get home. It's their turn to come to us." The drowning man who sees the pattern of his life pass by as the sea engulfs him could at last be understood. The ring at the front door, the cheerful voices of the Alhusons, the drinks set out on the sideboard, the standing about for a moment and then the sitting down—these things became only pieces of the tapestry that was the whole of his life imprisonment, beginning daily with the drawing back of the curtains and early morning tea, the opening of the newspaper, breakfast eaten in the small dining-room with the gas fire burning blue (turned low because of waste), the journey by Underground to the City, the passing hours of methodical office work, the return by Underground, unfolding an evening paper in the crowd which hemmed him in, the laying down of hat and coat and umbrella, the sound of television from the drawing-room blending, perhaps, with the voice of his wife talking on the phone. And it was winter, or it was summer, or it was spring, or it was autumn, because with the changing seasons the covers of the chairs and sofa in the drawing-room were cleaned and replaced by others, or the trees in the square outside were in leaf or bare.

"It's their turn to come to us," and the Alhusons, grimacing and jumping on their string, came and bowed and disappeared, and the hosts who had received them became guests in their turn, jiggling and smirking, the dancing couples set to partners in an old-time measure.

Now suddenly, with the pause by Albert Bridge and Edna's remark, time had ceased; or, rather, it had continued in the same way for her, for the Alhusons answering the telephone, for the other partners in the dance; but for him everything had changed. He was aware of a sense of power within. He was in control. His was the master hand that set the puppets jiggling. And Edna, poor Edna, speeding home in the taxi to a predestined role of putting out the drinks, patting cushions, shaking salted almonds from a tin, Edna had no

5

conception of how he had stepped out of bondage into a new dimension.

The apathy of Sunday lay upon the streets. Houses were closed, withdrawn.

"They don't know," he thought, "those people inside, how one gesture of mine, now, at this minute, might alter their world. A knock on the door, and someone answers—a woman yawning, an old man in carpet slippers, a child sent by its parents in irritation; and according to what I will, what I decide, their whole future will be decided. Faces smashed in. Sudden murder. Theft. Fire." It was as simple as that.

He looked at his watch. Half-past three. He decided to work on a system of numbers. He would walk down three more streets, and then, depending upon the name of the third street in which he found himself and how many letters it contained, choose the number of his destination.

He walked briskly, aware of mounting interest. No cheating, he told himself. Block of flats or United Dairies, it was all one. It turned out that the third street was a long one, flanked on either side by drab Victorian villas which had been pretentious some fifty years ago and now, let out as flats or lodgings, had lost caste. The name was Boulting Street. Eight letters meant No. 8. He crossed over confidently, searching the front doors, undaunted by the steep flight of stone steps leading to every villa, the unpainted gates, the lowering basements, the air of poverty and decay which presented such a contrast to the houses in his own small Regency square, with their bright front doors and window boxes.

No. 8 proved no different from its fellows. The gate was even shabbier, perhaps, the curtains at the long, ugly ground-floor window more bleakly lace. A child of about three, a boy, sat on the top step, white-faced, blank-eyed, tied in some strange fashion to the mud scraper so that he could not move. The front door was ajar.

James Fenton mounted the steps and looked for the bell. There was a scrap of paper pasted across it with the words "Out of Order." Beneath it was an old-fashioned bellpull fastened with string. It would be a matter of seconds, of course, to unravel the knotted strap binding the child, carry him off under his arm down the steps, and then dispose of him according to mood or fancy. But violence did not seem to be indicated just yet: it was not what he wanted, for the feeling of power within demanded a longer term of freedom.

He pulled at the bell. The faint tinkle sounded down the dark hall. The child stared up at him, unmoved. Fenton turned away from the door and looked out on the street, at the plane tree coming into leaf on the pavement edge, the brown bark patchy yellow, a black cat crouching at its foot biting a wounded paw; and he savoured the waiting moment as delicious because of its uncertainty.

He heard the door open wider behind him and a woman's voice, foreign in intonation, ask, "What can I do for you?"

Fenton took off his hat. The impulse was strong within him to say, "I have come to strangle you. You and your child. I bear you no malice whatever. It just happens that I am the instrument of fate sent for this purpose." Instead, he smiled. The woman was pallid, like the child on the steps, with the same expressionless eyes, the same lank hair. Her age might have been anything from twenty to thirty-five. She was wearing a woollen cardigan too big for her, and her dark, bunched skirt, ankle length, made her seem squat.

"Do you let rooms?" asked Fenton.

A light came into the dull eyes, an expression of hope. It was almost as if this was a question she had longed for and had believed would never come. But the gleam faded again immediately and the blank stare returned.

"The house isn't mine," she said. "The landlord let rooms once, but they say it's to be pulled down, with those on either side, to make room for flats."

"You mean," he pursued, "the landlord doesn't let rooms any more?"

"No," she said. "He told me it wouldn't be worth it, not with the demolition order coming any day. He pays me a small sum to caretake until they pull the house down. I live in the basement."

"I see," he said.

It would seem that the conversation was at an end. Nevertheless Fenton continued to stand there. The girl or woman—for she could be either—looked past him to the child, bidding him to be quiet, though he hardly whimpered.

"I suppose," said Fenton, "you couldn't sublet one of the rooms in the basement to me? It could be a private arrangement between ourselves while you remain here. The landlord couldn't object."

He watched her make the effort to think. His suggestion, so unlikely, so surprising coming from someone of his appearance, was something she could not take in. Since surprise is the best form of attack, he seized his advantage. "I only need one room," he said quickly, "for a few hours in the day. I shouldn't be sleeping here."

The effort to size him up was beyond her—the tweed suit, appropriate for London or the country, the trilby hat, the walking stick, the fresh-complexioned face, the forty-five to fifty years. He saw the dark eyes become wider and blanker still as they tried to reconcile his appearance with his unexpected request.

"What would you want the room for?" she asked doubtfully.

There was the crux. To murder you and the child, my dear, and dig up the floor, and bury you under the boards. But not yet.

"It's difficult to explain," he said briskly. "I'm a professional man. I have long hours. But there have been changes lately, and I must have a room where I can put in a few hours every day and be entirely alone. You've no idea how difficult it is to find the right spot. This seems to me ideal for the purpose." He glanced from the empty house down to the child, and smiled. "Your little boy, for instance. Just the right age. He'd give no trouble."

A semblance of a smile passed across her face. "Oh, Johnnie is quiet enough," she said. "He sits there for hours, he wouldn't interfere." Then the smile wavered, the doubt returned. "I don't know what to say. . . . We live in the kitchen, with the bedroom next to it. There *is* a room behind, where I have a few bits of furniture stored, but I don't think you would like it. You see, it depends what you want to do. . . ."

Her voice trailed away. Her apathy was just what he needed. He wondered if she slept very heavily, or even drugged. Those dark shadows under the eyes suggested drugs. So much the better. And a foreigner too. There were too many of them in the country.

"If you would only show me the room, I should know at once," he said.

Surprisingly she turned and led the way down the narrow, dingy hall. Switching on a light above a basement stair, murmuring a continual apology the while, she took Fenton below. This had been, of course, the original servants' quarters of the Victorian villa. The kitchen, scullery, and pantry had now become the woman's living-room, kitchenette, and bedroom, and in their transformation had increased in squalor. The ugly pipes, the useless boiler, the old range might once have had some pretension to efficiency, with fresh white paint on the pipes and the range polished. Even the dresser, still in position and stretching nearly the full width of one wall, would have been in keeping some fifty years ago with polished brass saucepans and a patterned dinner service, while an overalled cook, bustling about with arms befloured, called orders to a minion in the scullery. Now the dirty cream paint hung in flakes, the worn linoleum was torn, and the dresser was bare save for odds and ends bearing no relation to its original purpose—a battered wireless set with trailing aerial, piles of discarded magazines and newspapers, unfinished knitting, broken toys, pieces of cake, a toothbrush, and several pairs of shoes. The woman looked about her helplessly.

"It's not easy," she said, "with a child. One clears up all the time."

It was evident that she never cleared, that she had given in, that the shambles he observed was her answer to life's problems, but Fenton said nothing, only nodded politely and smiled. He caught a glimpse of an unmade bed through a half-open door, bearing out his theory of the heavy sleeper —his ring at the bell must have disturbed her—but seeing his glance, she shut the door hurriedly, and in a half-conscious effort to bring herself to order buttoned her cardigan and combed her hair with her fingers.

"And the room you do not use?" he asked.

"Oh yes," she replied, "yes, of course . . ." vague and uncertain, as if she had forgotten her purpose in bringing him to the basement. She led the way back across the passage, past a coal cellar—useful, this, he thought—a lavatory with a child's pot set in the open door and a torn *Daily Mirror* beside it, and so to a further room, the door of which was closed.

"I don't think it will do," she said sighing, already defeated. Indeed, it would not have done for anyone but himself, so full of power and purpose; for as she flung open the creaking door and crossed the room to pull aside the strip of curtain made out of old wartime blackout material, the smell of damp hit him as forcibly as a sudden patch of fog beside the river, and with it the unmistakable odour of escaping gas. They sniffed in unison.

"Yes, it's bad," she said. "The men are supposed to come, but they never do."

As she pulled the curtain to let in air the rod broke, the strip of material fell, and through a broken pane of the window jumped the black cat with the wounded paw which Fenton had noticed beneath the plane tree in front of the house. The woman shooed it ineffectually. The cat, used to its surroundings, slunk into a far corner, jumped on a packing case, and composed itself to sleep. Fenton and the woman looked about them.

"This would do me very well," he said, hardly considering the dark walls, the odd L-shape of the room, and the low ceiling. "Why, there's even a garden," and he went to the window and looked out upon the patch of earth and stones —level with his head as he stood in the basement room— which had once been a strip of paved garden.

"Yes," she said, "yes, there's a garden," and she came beside him to stare at the desolation to which they both gave so false a name. Then with a little shrug she went on, "It's quiet, as you see, but it doesn't get much sun. It faces north."

"I like a room to face north," he said abstractedly, already seeing in his mind's eye the narrow trench he would be able to dig for her body—no need to make it deep. Turning towards her, measuring the size of her, reckoning the length and breadth, he saw a glimmer of understanding come into her eye and he quickly smiled to give her confidence.

"Are you an artist?" she said. "They like a north light, don't they?"

His relief was tremendous. An artist. But of course. Here was the excuse he needed. Here was a way out of all difficulty.

"I see you've guessed my secret," he answered slyly, and his laugh rang so true that it surprised even himself. He began to speak very rapidly. "Part-time only," he said. "That's the reason I can only get away for certain hours. My mornings are tied down to business, but later in the day I'm a free man. Then my real work begins. It's not just a casual hobby, it's a passion. I intend to hold my own exhibition later in the year. So you understand how essential it is for me to find somewhere . . . like this."

He waved his hand at the surroundings, which could offer no inducement to anyone but the cat. His confidence was infectious and disarmed the still doubtful, puzzled enquiry in her eyes.

"Chelsea's full of artists, isn't it?" she said. "At least they say so, I don't know. But I thought studios had to be high up for getting the light."

"Not necessarily," he answered. "Those fads don't affect me. And late in the day the light will have gone anyway. I suppose there is electricity?"

"Yes . . ." She moved to the door and touched a switch. A naked bulb from the ceiling glared through its dust.

"Excellent," he said. "That's all I shall need."

He smiled down at the blank, unhappy face. The poor soul would be so much happier asleep. Like the cat. A kindness, really, to put her out of her misery.

"Can I move in tomorrow?" he asked.

Again the look of hope that he had noticed when he first stood at the front door enquiring for rooms, and then—was

11

it embarrassment, just the faintest trace of discomfort, in her expression?

"You haven't asked about . . . the cost of the room," she said.

"Whatever you care to charge," he replied, and waved his hand again to show that money was no object. She swallowed, evidently at a loss to know what to say, and then, a flush creeping into the pallid face, ventured, "It would be best if I said nothing to the landlord. I will say you are a friend. You could give me a pound or two in cash every week, what you think fair."

She watched him anxiously. Certainly, he decided, there must be no third party interfering in any arrangement. It might defeat his plan.

"I'll give you five pounds in notes each week, starting today," he said.

He felt for his wallet and drew out the crisp, new notes. She put out a timid hand, and her eyes never left the notes as he counted them.

"Not a word to the landlord," he said, "and if any questions are asked about your lodger say your cousin, an artist, has arrived for a visit."

She looked up and for the first time smiled, as though his joking words, with the giving of the notes, somehow sealed a bond between them.

"You don't look like my cousin," she said, "nor much like the artists I have seen, either. What is your name?"

"Sims," he said instantly, "Marcus Sims," and wondered why he had instinctively uttered the name of his wife's father, a solicitor dead these many years, whom he had heartily disliked.

"Thank you, Mr. Sims," she said. "I'll give your room a cleanup in the morning." Then, as a first gesture towards this intention, she lifted the cat from the packing case and shooed it through the window.

"You will bring your things tomorrow afternoon?" she asked.

"My things?" he repeated.

12

"What you need for your work," she said. "Don't you have paints and so on?"

"Oh yes . . . yes, naturally," he said, "yes, I must bring my gear." He glanced round the room again. But there was to be no question of butchery. No blood. No mess. The answer would be to stifle them both in sleep, the woman and her child. It was much the kindest way.

"You won't have far to go when you need tubes of paint," she said. "There are shops for artists in the King's Road. I have passed them shopping. They have boards and easels in the window."

He put his hand over his mouth to hide his smile. It was really touching how she had accepted him. It showed such trust, such confidence.

She led the way back into the passage and so up the basement stair to the hall once more.

"I'm so delighted," he said, "that we have come to this arrangement. To tell you the truth, I was getting desperate."

She turned and smiled at him again over her shoulder. "So was I," she said. "If you hadn't appeared . . . I don't know what I might not have done."

They stood together at the top of the basement stair. What an amazing thing. It was an act of God that he had suddenly arrived. He stared at her, shocked.

"You've been in some trouble, then?" he asked.

"Trouble?" She gestured with her hands, and the look of apathy, of despair, returned to her face. "It's trouble enough to be a stranger in this country, and for the father of my little boy to go off and leave me without any money, and not to know where to turn. I tell you, Mr. Sims, if you had not come today . . ." she did not finish her sentence, but glanced towards the child tied to the foot scraper and shrugged her shoulders. "Poor Johnnie . . ." she said, "it's not your fault."

"Poor Johnnie indeed," echoed Fenton, "and poor you. Well, I'll do my part to put an end to your troubles, I assure you."

"You're very good. Truly, I thank you."

"On the contrary, I thank *you*." He made her a little bow and, bending down, touched the top of the child's head.

13

"Good-bye, Johnnie, see you tomorrow." His victim gazed back at him without expression.

"Good-bye, Mrs. . . . Mrs. . . ."

"Kaufman is the name. Anna Kaufman."

She watched him down the steps and through the gate. The banished cat slunk past his legs on a return journey to the broken window. Fenton waved his hat with a flourish to the woman, to the boy, to the cat, to the whole fabric of the mute, drab villa.

"See you tomorrow," he called, and set off down Boulting Street with the jaunty step of someone at the start of a great adventure. His high spirits did not even desert him when he arrived at his own front door. He let himself in with his latch key and went up the stairs humming some old song of thirty years ago. Edna, as usual, was on the telephone—he could hear the interminable conversation of one woman to another. The drinks were set out on the small table in the drawing-room. The cocktail biscuits were laid ready, and the dish of salted almonds. The extra glasses meant that visitors were expected. Edna put her hand over the mouthpiece of the receiver and said, "The Alhusons will be coming. I've asked them to stay on for cold supper."

Her husband smiled and nodded. Long before his usual time he poured himself a thimbleful of sherry to round off the conspiracy, the perfection, of the past hour. The conversation on the telephone ceased.

"You look better," said Edna. "The walk did you good."

Her innocence amused him so much that he nearly choked.

2

It was a lucky thing that the woman had mentioned an artist's props. He would have looked a fool arriving the following afternoon with nothing. As it was, it meant leaving the office early, and an expedition to fit himself up with the necessary paraphernalia. He let himself go. Easel, canvases, tube after tube of paint, brushes, turpentine—what had been intended as a few parcels became bulky packages impossible to transport except in a taxi. It all added to the excitement, though. He must play his part thoroughly. The assistant in the shop, fired by his customer's ardour, kept adding to the list of paints; and, as Fenton handled the tubes of colour and read the names, there was something intensely satisfying about the purchase, and he allowed himself to be reckless, the very words chrome and sienna and terre-verte going to his head like wine. Finally he tore himself away from temptation and climbed into a taxi with his wares. No. 8 Boulting Street; the unaccustomed address instead of his own familiar square added spice to the adventure.

It was strange, but as the taxi drew up at its destination the row of villas no longer appeared so drab. It was true that yesterday's wind had dropped, the sun was shining fitfully, and there was a hint in the air of April and longer days to come; but that was not the point. The point was that No. 8 had something of expectancy about it. As he paid his driver and carried the packages from the taxi, he saw that the dark blinds in the basement had been removed and makeshift curtains, tangerine-coloured and a shock to the eye, hung in their place. Even as he noted this the curtains were pulled back and the woman, the child in her arms, its face smeared with jam, waved up at him. The cat leapt from the sill and came towards him purring, rubbing an arched back against his trouser leg. The taxi drove away, and the woman came down the steps to greet him.

"Johnnie and I have been watching for you the whole afternoon," she said. "Is that all you've brought?"

"All? Isn't it enough?" he laughed.

She helped him carry the things down the basement stair, and as he glanced into the kitchen he saw that an attempt had been made to tidy it, besides the hanging of the curtains. The row of shoes had been banished underneath the dresser, along with the child's toys, and a cloth, laid for tea, had been spread on the table.

"You'll never believe the dust there was in your room," she said. "I was working there till nearly midnight."

"You shouldn't have done that," he told her. "It's not worth it, for the time."

She stopped before the door and looked at him, the blank look returning to her face. "It's not for long, then?" she faltered. "I somehow thought, from what you said yesterday, it would be for some weeks?"

"Oh, I didn't mean that," he said swiftly. "I meant that I shall make such a devil of a mess anyway, with these paints, there was no need to dust."

Relief was plain. She summoned a smile and opened the door. "Welcome, Mr. Sims," she said.

He had to give her her due. She had worked. The room did look different. Smelt different, too. No more leaking gas, but carbolic instead—or was it Jeyes? Disinfectant, anyway. The blackout strip had vanished from the window. She had even got someone in to repair the broken glass. The cat's bed —the packing case—had gone. There was a table now against the wall, and two little rickety chairs, and an armchair also, covered with the same fearful tangerine material he had observed in the kitchen windows. Above the mantelpiece, bare yesterday, she had hung a large, brightly-coloured reproduction of a Madonna and Child, with an almanac beneath. The eyes of the Madonna, ingratiating, demure, smiled at Fenton.

"Well . . ." he began, "well, bless me . . ." and to conceal his emotion, because it was really very touching that the wretched woman had taken so much trouble on what was probably one of her last days on this earth, he turned away and began untying his packages.

"Let me help you, Mr. Sims," she said, and before he could protest she was down on her knees struggling with the knots, unwrapping the paper, and fixing the easel for him. Then together they emptied the boxes of all the tubes of colour, laid them out in rows on the table, and stacked the canvases against the wall. It was amusing, like playing some absurd game, and curiously she entered into the spirit of it although remaining perfectly serious at the same time.

"What are you going to paint first?" she asked, when all was fixed and even a canvas set up upon the easel. "You have some subject in mind, I suppose?"

"Oh yes," he said, "I've a subject in mind." He began to smile, her faith in him was so supreme, and suddenly she smiled too and said, "I've guessed. I've guessed your subject."

He felt himself go pale. How had she guessed? What was she driving at?

"What do you mean, you've guessed?" he asked sharply.

"It's Johnnie, isn't it?"

He could not possibly kill the child before the mother—what an appalling suggestion. And why was she trying to push him into it like this? There was time enough, and anyway his plan was not yet formed. . . .

She was nodding her head wisely, and he brought himself back to reality with an effort. She was talking of painting, of course.

"You're a clever woman," he said. "Yes, Johnnie's my subject."

"He'll be good, he won't move," she said. "If I tie him up he'll sit for hours. Do you want him now?"

"No, no," Fenton replied testily. "I'm in no hurry at all. I've got to think it all out."

Her face fell. She seemed disappointed. She glanced round the room once more, converted so suddenly and so surprisingly into what she hoped was an artist's studio.

"Then let me give you a cup of tea," she said, and to save argument he followed her into the kitchen. There he sat himself down on the chair she drew forward for him, and drank tea and ate Bovril sandwiches, watched by the unflinching eyes of the grubby little boy.

"Da . . ." uttered the child suddenly, and put out its hand.

"He calls all men Da," said his mother, "though his own father took no notice of him. Don't worry Mr. Sims, Johnnie."

Fenton forced a polite smile. Children embarrassed him. He went on eating his Bovril sandwiches and sipping his tea.

The woman sat down and joined him, stirring her tea in an absent way until it must have been cold and unfit to drink.

"It's nice to have someone to talk to," she said. "Do you know, until you came, Mr. Sims, I was so alone. . . . The empty house above, no workmen even passing in and out. And this is not a good neighbourhood—I have no friends at all."

Better and better, he thought. There'll be nobody to miss her when she's gone. It would have been a tricky thing to get away with had the rest of the house been inhabited. As it was, it could be done at any time of the day and no one the wiser. Poor kid, she could not be more than twenty-six or -seven; what a life she must have led.

". . . he just went off without a word," she was saying. "Three years only we had been in this country, and we moved from place to place with no settled job. We were in Manchester at one time, Johnnie was born in Manchester."

"Awful spot," he sympathised. "Never stops raining."

"I told him, 'You've got to get work,'" she continued, banging her fist on the table, acting the moment over again. "I said, 'We can't go on like this. It's no life for me, or for your child.' And, Mr. Sims, there was no money for the rent. What was I to say to the landlord when he called? And then, being aliens here, there is always some fuss with the police."

"Police?" said Fenton, startled.

"The papers," she explained. "There is such trouble with our papers. You know how it is, we have to register. Mr. Sims, my life has not been a happy one, not for many years. In Austria I was a servant for a time to a bad man. I had to run away. I was only sixteen then, and when I met my husband, who was not my husband then, it seemed at last that there might be some hope if we got to England. . . ."

She droned on, watching him and stirring her tea the while, and her voice with its slow German accent, rather pleasing and lilting to the ear, was somehow soothing and a pleasant accompaniment to his thoughts, mingling with the ticking of the alarm clock on the dresser and the thumping of the little boy's spoon upon his plate. It was delightful to remind himself that he was not in the office, and not at home either, but was Marcus Sims the artist, surely a great artist, if not in colour at least in premeditated crime; and here was his victim putting her life into his hands, looking upon him, in fact, almost as her saviour—as indeed he was.

"It's queer," she said slowly. "Yesterday I did not know you. Today I tell you my life. You are my friend."

"Your sincere friend," he said, patting her hand. "I assure you it's the truth." He smiled and pushed back his chair.

She reached for his cup and saucer and put them in the

sink, then wiped the child's mouth with the sleeve of her jumper. "And now, Mr. Sims," she said, "which would you prefer to do first? Come to bed or paint Johnnie?"

He stared at her. Come to bed? Had he heard correctly?

"I beg your pardon?" he said.

She stood patiently, waiting for him to move.

"It's for you to say, Mr. Sims," she said. "It makes no difference to me. I'm at your disposal."

He felt his neck turn slowly red, and the colour mount to his face and forehead. There was no doubt about it, no misunderstanding the half smile she now attempted, and the jerk of her head towards the bedroom. The poor wretched girl was making him some sort of offer, she must believe that he actually expected . . . wanted. . . . It was appalling.

"My dear Madame Kaufman," he began—somehow the Madame sounded better than Mrs., and it was in keeping with her alien nationality—"I am afraid there is some error. You have misunderstood me."

"Please?" she said, puzzled, and then summoned a smile again. "You don't have to be afraid. No one will come. And I will tie up Johnnie."

It was preposterous. Tie up that little boy. . . . Nothing he had said to her could possibly have made her misconstrue the situation. Yet to show his natural anger and leave the house would mean the ruin of all his plans, his perfect plans, and he would have to begin all over again elsewhere.

"It's . . . it's extremely kind of you, Madame Kaufman," he said. "I do appreciate your offer. It's most generous. The fact is, unfortunately, I've been totally incapacitated for many years . . . an old war wound . . . I've had to put all that sort of thing out of my life long ago. Indeed, all my efforts go into my art, my painting, I concentrate entirely upon that. Hence my deep pleasure in finding this little retreat, which will make all the difference to my world. And if we are to be friends . . ."

He searched for further words to extricate himself. She shrugged her shoulders. There was neither relief nor disappointment in her face. What was to be would be.

"That's all right, Mr. Sims," she said. "I thought perhaps

19

you were lonely. I know what loneliness can be. And you are so kind. If at any time you feel you would like . . ."

"Oh, I'll tell you immediately," he interrupted swiftly. "No question of that. But alas, I'm afraid. . . . Well now, to work, to work." And he smiled again, making some show of bustle, and opened the door of the kitchen. Thank heaven she had buttoned up the cardigan which she had so disastrously started to undo. She lifted the child from his chair and proceeded to follow him.

"I have always wanted to see a real artist at work," she said to him, "and now, lo and behold, my chance has come. Johnnie will appreciate this when he is older. Now, where would you like me to put him, Mr. Sims? Shall he stand or sit? What pose would be best?"

It was too much. From the frying pan into the fire. Fenton was exasperated. The woman was trying to bully him. He could not possibly have her hanging about like this. If that horrid little boy had to be disposed of, then his mother must be out of the way.

"Never mind the pose," he said testily. "I'm not a photographer. And if there is one thing I cannot bear, it's being watched when I work. Put Johnnie there on the chair. I suppose he'll sit still?"

"I'll fetch the strap," she said, and while she went back to the kitchen he stared moodily at the canvas on the easel. He must do something about it, that was evident. Fatal to leave it blank. She would not understand. She would begin to suspect that something was wrong. She might even repeat her fearful offer of five minutes ago. . . .

He lifted one or two tubes of paint and squeezed out blobs of colour on to the palette. Raw sienna . . . Naples yellow . . . Good names they gave these things. He and Edna had been to Siena once, years ago, when they were first married. He remembered the rose-rust brickwork, and that square—what was the name of the square?—where they held a famous horse race. Naples yellow. They had never got as far as Naples. See Naples and die. Pity they had not travelled more. They had fallen into a rut, always going up to Scotland, but Edna did not care for the heat. Azure blue . . . made you think of the deepest, or was it the clearest, blue? Lagoons in the South Seas, and flying fish. How jolly the blobs of colour looked upon the palette . . .

"So . . . be good, Johnnie." Fenton looked up. The woman had secured the child to the chair and was patting the top of his head. "If there is anything you want you have only to call, Mr. Sims."

"Thank you, Madame Kaufman."

She crept out of the room, closing the door softly. The artist must not be disturbed. The artist must be left alone with his creation.

"Da," said Johnnie suddenly.

"Be quiet," said Fenton sharply. He was breaking a piece of charcoal in two. He had read somewhere that artists drew in the head first with charcoal. He adjusted the broken end between his fingers and, pursing his lips, drew a circle, the shape of a full moon, upon the canvas. Then he stepped back and half closed his eyes. The odd thing was that it did look like the rounded shape of a face without the features . . . Johnnie was watching him, his eyes large. Fenton realised that he needed a much larger canvas. The one on the easel would only take the child's head. It would look much more effective to have the whole head and shoulders on the canvas, because he could then use some of the azure blue to paint the child's blue jersey.

He replaced the first canvas with a larger one. Yes, that was a far better size. Now for the outline of the face again . . . the eyes . . . two little dots for the nose, and a small slit for the mouth . . . two lines for the neck, and two more, rather squared like a coat hanger, for the shoulders. It was a face all right, a human face, not exactly that of Johnnie at the moment, but given time . . . The essential thing was to get some paint on to that canvas. He simply must use some of the paint. Feverishly he chose a brush, dipped it in turpentine and oil, and then, with little furtive dabs at the azure blue and the flake white to mix them, he stabbed the result on to the canvas. The bright colour, gleaming and glistening with excess of oil, seemed to stare back at him from the canvas, demanding more. It was not the same blue as the blue of Johnnie's jersey, but what of that?

Becoming bolder, he sloshed on further colour, and now the blue was all over the lower part of the canvas in vivid streaks, making a strange excitement, contrasting with the charcoal face. The face now looked like a real face, and the patch of wall behind the child's head, which had been nothing but a wall when he first entered the room, surely had colour to it after all, a pinkish green. He snatched up tube after tube and squeezed out blobs; he chose another brush so as not to spoil the brush with blue on it . . . damn it, that burnt sienna was not like the Siena he had visited at all, but more like mud. He must wipe it off, he must have rags, something that wouldn't spoil. . . . He crossed quickly to the door.

"Madame Kaufman?" he called. "Madame Kaufman? Could you find me some rags?"

She came at once, tearing some undergarment into strips, and he snatched them from her and began to wipe the offending burnt sienna from his brush. He turned round to see her peeping at the canvas.

"Don't do that," he shouted. "You must never look at an artist's work in the first rough stages."

She drew back, rebuffed. "I'm sorry," she said, and then, with hesitation, added, "It's very modern, isn't it?"

He stared at her, and then from her to the canvas, and from the canvas to Johnnie.

"Modern?" he said. "Of course it's modern. What did you think it would be? Like that?" He pointed with his brush to the simpering Madonna over the mantelpiece. "I'm of my time. I see what I see. Now let me get on."

There was not enough room on one palette for all the blobs of colour. Thank goodness he had bought two. He began squeezing the remaining tubes on to the second palette and mixing them, and now all was riot—sunsets that had never been and unrisen dawns. The Venetian red was not the Doge's palace but little drops of blood that burst in the brain and did not have to be shed, and zinc white was purity, not death, and yellow ochre . . . yellow ochre was life in abundance, was renewal, was spring, was April even in some other time, some other place . . .

It did not matter that it grew dark and he had to switch on the light. The child had fallen asleep, but he went on painting. Presently the woman came in and told him it was eight o'clock. Did he want any supper? "It would be no trouble, Mr. Sims," she said.

Suddenly Fenton realised where he was. Eight o'clock, and they always dined at a quarter to. Edna would be waiting, would be wondering what had happened to him. He laid down the palette and the brushes. There was paint on his hands, on his coat.

"What on earth shall I do?" he said in panic.

The woman understood. She seized the turpentine and a piece of rag and rubbed at his coat. He went with her to the kitchen and feverishly began to scrub his hands at the sink.

"In future," he said, "I must always leave by seven."

"Yes," she said, "I'll remember to call you. You'll be back tomorrow?"

"Of course," he said impatiently, "of course. Don't touch any of my things."

"No, Mr. Sims."

He hurried up the basement stair and out of the house, and started running along the street. As he went he began to make up the story he would tell Edna. He'd dropped in at the club, and some of the fellows there had persuaded him into playing bridge. He hadn't liked to break up the game and never realised the time. That would do. And it would do again tomorrow. Edna must get used to this business of him dropping into the club after the office. He could think of no better excuse with which to mask the lovely duplicity of a secret life.

3

It was extraordinary how the days slipped by, days that had once dragged, that had seemed interminable. It meant several changes, of course. He had to lie not only to Edna, but at the office as well. He invented a pressing business that took him away in the early part of the afternoon, new contacts, a family firm. For the time being, Fenton said, he could really only work at the office half time. Naturally, there would have to be some financial adjustment, he quite understood that. In the meantime, if the senior partner would see his way . . . Amazing that they swallowed it. And Edna, too, about the club. Though it was not always the club. Sometimes it was extra work at another office, somewhere else in the City; and he would talk mysteriously of bringing off some big deal which was far too delicate and involved to be discussed. Edna appeared content. Her life continued as it had always done. It was only Fenton whose world had changed. Regularly now each afternoon, at around half-past three, he walked through the gate of No. 8, and, glancing down at the kitchen window in the basement, he could see Madame Kaufman's face peering from behind the tangerine curtains. Then she would slip round to the back door, by the strip of garden, and let him in. They had decided against the front door. It was safer to use the back. Less conspicuous.

"Good afternoon, Mr. Sims."

"Good afternoon, Madame Kaufman."

No nonsense about calling her Anna. She might have thought . . . she might have presumed. And the title "Madame" kept the right sense of proportion between them. She was really very useful. She cleaned the studio—they always alluded to his room as the studio—and his paintbrushes, and tore up fresh strips of rag every day, and as soon as he arrived she had a cup of tea for him, not like the stew they used to brew in the office, but piping hot. And the boy . . . the boy had become quite appealing. Fenton had felt more tolerant about him as soon as he had finished the first portrait. It was as though the boy existed anew through him. He was Fenton's creation.

It was now midsummer, and Fenton had painted his portrait many times. The child continued to call him Da. But the boy was not the only model. He had painted the mother too. And this was more satisfying still. It gave Fenton a tremendous sense of power to put the woman upon canvas. It was not her eyes, her features, her colouring—heavens above, she had little enough colouring!—but somehow her shape: the fact that the bulk of a live person, and that person a woman, could be transmuted by him upon a blank canvas. It did not matter if what he drew and painted bore no resemblance to a woman from Austria called Anna Kaufman. That was not the point. Naturally the silly soul expected some sort of chocolate-box representation the first time she acted as his model. He had soon shut her up, though.

"Do you really see me like that?" she asked, disconsolate.

"Why, what's wrong?" he said.

"It's . . . it's just that . . . you make my mouth like a big fish ready to swallow, Mr. Sims."

"A fish? What utter nonsense!" He supposed she wanted a cupid's bow. "The trouble with you is that you're never satisfied. You're no different from any other woman."

He began mixing his colours angrily. She had no right to criticise his work.

"It's not kind of you to say that, Mr. Sims," she said after a moment or two. "I am very satisfied with the five pounds that you give me every week."

"I was not talking about money," he said.

"What were you talking about, then?"

He turned back to the canvas, and put just the faintest touch of rose upon the flesh part of the arm. "What was I talking about?" he asked. "I haven't the faintest idea. Women, wasn't it? I really don't know. And I've told you not to interrupt."

"I'm sorry, Mr. Sims."

That's right, he thought. Stay put. Keep your place. If there was one thing he could not stand it was a woman who argued, a woman who was self-assertive, a woman who nagged, a woman who stood upon her rights. Because of course they were not made for that. They were intended by their Creator to be pliable, and accommodating, and gentle, and meek. The trouble was that they were so seldom like that in reality. It was only in the imagination, or glimpsed in passing or behind a window, or leaning from a balcony abroad, or from the frame of a picture, or from a canvas like the one before him now—he changed from one brush to another, he was getting quite dexterous at this—that a woman had any meaning, any reality. And then to go and tell him that he had given her a mouth like a fish . . .

"When I was younger," he said aloud, "I had so much ambition."

"To be a great painter?" she asked.

"Why, no . . . not particularly that," he answered, "but to become great. To be famous. To achieve something outstanding."

"There's still time, Mr. Sims," she said.

"Perhaps . . . perhaps . . ." The skin should not be rose, it should be olive, a warm olive. Edna's father had been the trouble, really, with his endless criticising of the way they lived. Fenton had never done anything right from the moment they became engaged: the old man was always carping, always finding fault. "Go and live abroad?" he had exclaimed. "You can't make a decent living abroad. Besides, Edna wouldn't stand it. Away from her friends and all she's been accustomed to. Never heard of such a thing."

Well, he was dead, and a good thing too. He'd been a wedge between them from the start. Marcus Sims . . . Marcus Sims the painter was a very different chap. Surrealist. Modern. The old boy would turn in his grave.

"It's a quarter to seven," murmured the woman.

"Damn . . ." He sighed and stepped back from the easel. "I resent stopping like this, now it's so light in the evenings," he said. "I could go on for quite another hour, or more."

"Why don't you?" she asked.

"Ah! Home ties," he said. "My poor old mother would have a fit."

He had invented an old mother during the past weeks. Bedridden. He had promised to be home every evening at a quarter to eight. If he did not arrive in time the doctors would not answer for the consequences. He was a very good son to her.

"I wish you could bring her here to live," said his model. "It's so lonely when you've gone back in the evenings. Do you know, there's a rumour this house may not be pulled down after all. If it's true, you could take the flat on the ground floor, and your mother would be welcome."

"She'd never move now," said Fenton. "She's over eighty. Very set in her ways." He smiled to himself, thinking of Edna's face if he said to her that it would be more comfortable to sell the house they had lived in for nearly twenty years and take up lodgings in No. 8 Boulting Street. Imagine the upheaval! Imagine the Alhusons coming to Sunday supper!

"Besides," he said, thinking aloud, "the whole point would be gone."

"What point, Mr. Sims?"

He looked from the shape of colour on the canvas that meant so much to him to the woman who sat there, posing with her lank hair and her dumb eyes, and he tried to remember what had decided him, those months ago, to walk up the steps of the drab villa and ask for a room. Some temporary phase of irritation, surely, with poor Edna, with the windy grey day on the Embankment, with the fact of the Alhusons coming to drinks. But the workings of his mind on that vanished Sunday were forgotten, and he knew only that his life had changed from then, that this small, confined basement room was his solace, and the personalities of the woman Anna Kaufman and the child Johnnie were somehow symbolic of anonymity, of peace. All she ever did was to make him tea and clean his brushes. She was part of the background, like the cat, which purred at his approach and crouched on the window sill, and to which he had not as yet given a single crumb.

"Never mind, Madame Kaufman," he said. "One of these days we'll hold an exhibition, and your face, and Johnnie's, will be the talk of the town."

"This year . . . next year . . . sometime . . . never. Isn't that what you say to cherry stones?" she said.

"You've got no faith," he told her. "I'll prove it. Just wait and see."

She began once more the long, tedious story about the man she had fled from in Austria, and the husband who had deserted her in London—he knew it all so well by now that he could prompt her—but it did not bother him. It was part of the background, part of the blessed anonymity. Let her blab away, he said to himself, it kept her quiet, it did not matter. He could concentrate on making the orange she was sucking, doling out quarters to Johnnie on her lap, larger than life, more colourful than life, rounder, bigger, brighter.

And as he walked home along the Embankment in the evening—because the walk was no longer suggestive of the old Sunday but was merged with the new life as well—he would throw his charcoal sketches and rough drawings into the river. They were now transfigured into paint and did not matter. With them went the used tubes of colour, pieces of rag, and brushes too clogged with oil. He threw them from Albert Bridge and watched them float for a moment, or be dragged under, or drift as bait for some ruffled, sooty gull. All his troubles went with his discarded junk. All his pain.

4

He had arranged with Edna to postpone their annual holiday until mid-September. This gave him time to finish the self-portrait he was working upon, which, he decided, would round up the present series. The holiday in Scotland would be pleasant. Pleasant for the first time for years, because there would be something to look forward to on returning to London.

The brief mornings at the office hardly counted now. He scraped through the routine somehow and never went back after lunch. His other commitments, he told his colleagues, were becoming daily more pressing: he had practically decided to break his association with the present business during the autumn.

"If you hadn't warned us," said the senior partner drily, "we should have warned you."

Fenton shrugged his shoulders. If they were going to be unpleasant about it, the sooner he went the better. He might even write from Scotland. Then the whole of the autumn and winter could be given up to painting. He could take a proper studio: No. 8, after all, was only a makeshift affair. But a large studio, with decent lighting and a kitchenette off it— there were some in the process of being built only a few streets away—that might be the answer to the winter. There he could really work. Really achieve something good, and no longer feel he was only a part-time amateur.

The self-portrait was absorbing. Madame Kaufman had found a mirror and hung it on the wall for him, so the start was easy enough. But he found he couldn't paint his own eyes. They had to be closed, which gave him the appearance of a sleeping man. A sick man. It was rather uncanny.

"So you don't like it?" Fenton observed to Madame Kaufman when she came to tell him it was seven o'clock.

She shook her head. "It gives me what you call the creeps," she said. "No, Mr. Sims, it's not you."

"A bit too advanced for your taste," he said cheerfully. "Avant-garde, I believe, is the right expression."

He himself was delighted. The self-portrait was a work of art.

"Well, it will have to do for the time being," he said. "I'm off for my holiday next week."

"You are going away?"

There was such a note of alarm in her voice that he turned to look at her.

"Yes," he said, "taking my old mother up to Scotland. Why?"

She stared at him in anguish, her whole expression changed. Anyone would think he had given her some tremendous shock.

"But I have no one but you," she said. "I shall be alone."

"I'll give you your money all right," he said quickly. "You shall have it in advance. We shall only be away three weeks."

She went on staring at him, and then, of all things, her eyes filled with tears and she began to cry.

"I don't know what I shall do," she said. "I don't know where I am to go."

It was a bit thick. What on earth did she mean? What should she do and where should she go? He had promised her the money. She would just go on as she always did. Seriously, if she was going to behave like this, the sooner he found himself a studio the better. The last thing in the world he wanted was for Madame Kaufman to become a drag.

"My dear Madame Kaufman, I'm not a permanency, you

know," he said firmly. "One of these days I shall be moving. Possibly this autumn. I need room to expand. I'll let you know in advance, naturally. But it might be worth your while to put Johnnie in a nursery school and get some sort of daily job. It would really work out better for you in the end."

He might have beaten her. She looked stunned, utterly crushed.

"What shall I do?" she repeated stupidly, and then, as if she still could not believe it, "When do you go away?"

"Monday," he said, "to Scotland. We'll be away three weeks." This last very forcibly, so that there was no mistake about it. The trouble was that she was a very unintelligent woman, he decided as he washed his hands at the kitchen sink. She made a good cup of tea and knew how to clean the brushes, but that was her limit. "You ought to take a holiday yourself," he told her cheerfully. "Take Johnnie for a trip down the river to Southend or somewhere."

There was no response. Nothing but a mournful stare and a hopeless shrug.

The next day, Friday, meant the end of his working week. He cashed a cheque that morning, so that he could give her three weeks' money in advance. And he allowed an extra five pounds for appeasement.

When he arrived at No. 8 Johnnie was tied up in his old place by the foot scraper, at the top of the steps. She had not done this to the boy for some time. And when Fenton let himself in at the back door in the basement, as usual, there was no wireless going and the kitchen door was shut. He opened it and looked in. The door through to the bedroom was also shut.

"Madame Kaufman . . . ?" he called. "Madame Kaufman . . . ?"

She answered after a moment, her voice muffled and weak. "What is it?" she said.

"Is anything the matter?"

Another pause, and then, "I am not very well."

"I'm sorry," said Fenton. "Is there anything I can do?"

"No."

Well, there it was. A try-on, of course. She never looked

well, but she had not done this before. There was no attempt to prepare his tea: the tray was not even laid. He put the envelope containing the money on the kitchen table.

"I've brought you your money," he called. "Twenty pounds altogether. Why don't you go out and spend some of it? It's a lovely afternoon. The air would do you good."

A brisk manner was the answer to her trouble. He was not going to be blackmailed into sympathy.

He went along to the studio, whistling firmly. He found, to his shocked surprise, that everything was as he had left it the evening before. Brushes not cleaned but lying clogged still on the messed palette. Room untouched. It really was the limit. He'd a good mind to retrieve the envelope from the kitchen table. It had been a mistake ever to have mentioned the holiday. He should have posted the money over the weekend and enclosed a note saying he had gone to Scotland. Instead of which . . . this infuriating fit of the sulks and neglect of her job. It was because she was a foreigner, of course. You just couldn't trust them. They always let you down in the long run.

He returned to the kitchen with his brushes and palette, the turpentine and some rags, and made as much noise as possible running the taps and moving about, so as to let her know that he was having to do all the menial stuff himself. He clattered the teacup, too, and rattled the tin where she put the sugar. Not a sound, though, from the bedroom. Oh, damn it, he thought, let her stew . . .

Back in the studio he pottered with the final touches to the self-portrait, but concentration was difficult. Nothing worked. The thing looked dead. She had ruined his day. Finally, an hour or more before his usual time, he decided to go home. He would not trust her to clean up, though, not after last night's neglect. She was capable of leaving everything untouched for three weeks.

Before stacking the canvases one behind the other he stood them up, ranged them against the wall, and tried to imagine how they would look hanging in an exhibition. They hit the eye, there was no doubt about it. You couldn't avoid them. There was something . . . well, something telling about the whole collection! He didn't know what it was. Naturally, he couldn't criticize his own work. But . . . that head of Madame Kaufman, for instance, the one she had said was like a fish, possibly there *was* some sort of shape to the mouth that . . . or was it the eyes, the rather full eyes? It was brilliant, though. He was sure it was brilliant. And, although unfinished, that self-portrait of a man asleep, it had significance.

He smiled in fantasy, seeing himself and Edna walking into one of those small galleries off Bond Street, himself saying casually, "I'm told there's some new chap got a show on here. Very controversial. The critics can't make out whether he's a genius or a madman." And Edna, "It must be the first time you've ever been inside one of these places." What a sense of power, what triumph! And then, when he broke it to her, the dawn of new respect in her eyes. The realization that her husband had, after all these years, achieved fame. It was the shock of surprise that he wanted. That was it! The shock of surprise . . .

Fenton had a final glance round the familiar room. The canvases were stacked now, the easel dismantled, brushes and palette cleaned and wiped and wrapped up. If he should decide to decamp when he returned from Scotland—and he was pretty sure it was going to be the only answer, after Madame Kaufman's idiotic behavior—then everything was ready to move. It would only be a matter of calling a taxi, putting the gear inside, and driving off.

He shut the window and closed the door, and, carrying his usual weekly package of what he called "rejects" under his arm—discarded drawings and sketches and odds and ends— went once more to the kitchen and called through the closed door of the bedroom.

"I'm off now," he said. "I hope you'll be better tomorrow. See you in three weeks' time."

He noticed that the envelope had disappeared from the kitchen table. She could not be as ill as all that.

Then he heard her moving in the bedroom, and after a moment or two the door opened a few inches and she stood there, just inside. He was shocked. She looked ghastly, her face drained of colour and her hair lank and greasy, neither combed nor brushed. She had a blanket wrapped round the lower part of her and, in spite of the hot, stuffy day, and the lack of air in the basement, was wearing a thick woollen cardigan.

"Have you seen a doctor?" he asked with some concern. She shook her head.

"I would if I were you," he said. "You don't look well at all." He remembered the boy, still tied to the scraper above. "Shall I bring Johnnie down to you?" he suggested.

"Please," she said.

Her eyes reminded him of an animal's eyes in pain. He felt disturbed. It was rather dreadful, going off and leaving her like this. But what could he do? He went up the basement stairs and through the deserted front hall, and opened the front door. The boy was sitting there, humped. He couldn't have moved since Fenton had entered the house.

"Come on, Johnnie," he said. "I'll take you below to your mother."

The child allowed himself to be untied. He had the same sort of apathy as the woman. What a hopeless pair they were, thought Fenton; they really ought to be in somebody's charge, in some sort of welfare home. There must be places where people like this were looked after. He carried the child downstairs and sat him in his usual chair by the kitchen table.

"What about his tea?" he asked.

"I'll get it presently," said Madame Kaufman.

She shuffled out of her bedroom, still wrapped in the blanket, with a package in her hands, some sort of paper parcel, tied up with string.

"What's that?" he asked.

"Some rubbish," she said, "if you would throw it away with yours. The dustmen don't call until next week."

He took the package from her and waited a moment, wondering what more he could do for her.

"Well," he said awkwardly, "I feel rather bad about this. Are you sure there is nothing else you want?"

"No," she said. She didn't even call him Mr. Sims. She

made no effort to smile or hold out her hand. The expression in her eyes was not even reproachful. It was mute.

"I'll send you a postcard from Scotland," he said, and then patted Johnnie's head. "So long," he added—a silly expression and one he never normally used. Then he went out of the back door, round the corner of the house and out of the gate, and so along Boulting Street, with an oppressive feeling in his heart that he had somehow behaved badly, been lacking in sympathy, and that he ought to have taken the initiative and insisted that she see a doctor.

The September sky was overcast and the Embankment dusty, drear. The trees in the Battersea gardens across the river had a dejected, faded, end-of-summer look. Too dull, too brown. It would be good to get away to Scotland, to breathe the clean, cold air.

He unwrapped his package and began to throw his "rejects" into the river. A head of Johnnie, very poor indeed. An attempt at the cat. A canvas that had got stained with something or other and could not be used again. Over the bridge they went and away with the tide, the canvas floating like a matchbox, white and frail. It was rather sad to watch it drift from sight.

He walked back along the Embankment towards home and then, before he turned to cross the road, realised that he was still carrying the paper parcel Madame Kaufman had given him. He had forgotten to throw it away with the rejects. He had been too occupied in watching the disappearance of his own debris.

Fenton was about to toss the parcel into the river when he noticed a policeman watching him from the opposite side of the road. He was seized with an uneasy feeling that it was against the law to dispose of litter in this way. He walked on self-consciously. After he had gone a hundred yards he glanced back over his shoulder. The policeman was still staring after him. Absurd, but it made him feel quite guilty. The strong arm of the law. He continued his walk, swinging the parcel nonchalantly, humming a little tune. To hell with the river—he would dump the parcel into one of the litter baskets in Chelsea Hospital gardens.

He turned into the gardens and dropped the parcel into the first basket, on top of two or three newspapers and a pile of orange peel. No offence in that. He could see the damn fool of a bobby watching through the railings, but Fenton took good care not to show the fellow he noticed him. Anyone would think he was trying to dispose of a bomb. Then he walked swiftly home and remembered, as he went up the stairs, that the Alhusons were coming to dinner. The routine dinner before the holiday. The thought did not bore him now as it had once. He would chat away to them both about Scotland without any sensation of being trapped and stifled. How Jack Alhuson would stare if he knew how Fenton spent his afternoons! He would not believe his ears!

"Hullo, you're early," said Edna, who was arranging the flowers in the drawing-room.

"Yes," he replied. "I cleared up everything at the office in good time. Thought I might make a start planning the itinerary. I'm looking forward to going north."

"I'm so glad," she said. "I was afraid you might be getting bored with Scotland year after year. But you don't look jaded at all. You haven't looked so well for years."

She kissed his cheek and he kissed hers, well content. He smiled as he went to look out his maps. She did not know she had a genius for a husband.

The Alhusons had arrived and they were just sitting down to dinner when the front-door bell rang.

"Who on earth's that?" exclaimed Edna. "Don't say we asked someone else and have forgotten all about them."

"I haven't paid the electricity bill," said Fenton. "They've sent round to cut us off, and we shan't get the soufflé."

He paused in the middle of carving the chicken, and the Alhusons laughed.

"I'll go," said Edna. "I daren't disturb May in the kitchen. You know the bill of fare by now, it *is* a soufflé."

She came back in a few moments with a half-amused, half-puzzled expression on her face. "It's not the electricity men," she said, "it's the police."

"The police?" repeated Fenton.

Jack Alhuson wagged his finger. "I knew it," he said. "You're for it this time, old boy."

Fenton laid down the carving knife. "Seriously, Edna," he said, "what do they want?"

"I haven't the faintest idea," she replied. "It's an ordinary policeman, and what I assumed to be another in plain clothes. They asked to speak to the owner of the house."

Fenton shrugged his shoulders. "You carry on," he said to his wife. "I'll see if I can get rid of them. They've probably come to the wrong address."

He went out of the dining-room into the hall, but as soon as he saw the uniformed policeman his face changed. He recognized the man who had stared after him on the Embankment.

"Good evening," he said. "What can I do for you?"

The man in plain clothes took the initiative.

"Did you happen to walk through Chelsea Hospital gardens late this afternoon, sir?" he enquired. Both men were watching Fenton intently, and he realized that denial would be useless.

"Yes," he said, "yes, I did."

"You were carrying a parcel?"

"I believe I was."

"Did you put the parcel in a litter basket by the Embankment entrance, sir?"

"I did."

"Would you object to telling us what was in the parcel?"

"I have no idea."

"I can put the question another way, sir. Could you tell us where you obtained the parcel?"

Fenton hesitated. What were they driving at? He did not care for their method of interrogation.

"I don't see what it has to do with you," he said. "It's not an offence to put rubbish in a litter basket, is it?"

"Not ordinary rubbish," said the man in plain clothes.

Fenton looked from one to the other. Their faces were serious.

"Do you mind if I ask you a question?" he said.

"No, sir."

"Do you know what was in the parcel?"

"Yes."

"You mean the policeman here—I remembered passing him on the beat—actually followed me and took the parcel after I had dropped it in the bin?"

"That is correct."

"What an extraordinary thing to do. I should have thought he would have been better employed doing his regular job."

"It happens to be his regular job to keep an eye on people who behave in a suspicious manner."

Fenton began to get annoyed. "There was nothing suspicious in my behaviour whatsoever," he declared. "It so happens that I had been clearing up odds and ends in my office this afternoon, and it's rather a fad of mine to throw rubbish in the river on my way home. Very often I feed the gulls too. Today I was about to throw in my usual packet when I noticed the officer here glance in my direction. It occurred to me that perhaps it's illegal to throw rubbish in the river, so I decided to put it in the litter basket instead."

The two men continued to stare at him.

"You've just stated," said the man in plain clothes, "that you didn't know what was in the parcel, and now you state that it was odds and ends from the office. Which statement is true?"

Fenton began to feel hunted.

"Both statements are true," he snapped. "The people at the office wrapped the parcel up for me today, and I didn't know what they had put in it. Sometimes they put in stale biscuits for the gulls, and then I undo it and throw the crumbs to the birds on my way home, as I told you."

It wouldn't do, though. Their set faces said so, and he supposed it sounded a thin enough tale—a middle-aged man collecting rubbish so that he could throw it in the river on his way home from the office, like a small boy throwing twigs from a bridge to see them float out on the other side. But it was the best he could think of on the spur of the moment, and he would have to stick to it now. After all, it couldn't be a criminal action—the worst they could call him was eccentric.

The plain-clothes policeman said nothing but, "Read your notes, Sergeant."

The man in uniform took out his notebook and read aloud:

"At five minutes past six today I was walking along the Embankment and I noticed a man on the opposite pavement make as though to throw a parcel in the river. He observed me looking and walked quickly on, and then glanced back over his shoulder to see if I was still watching him. His manner was suspicious. He then crossed to the entrance to Chelsea Hospital gardens and, after looking up and down in a furtive manner, dropped the parcel in the litter bin and hurried away. I went to the bin and retrieved the parcel, and then followed the man to 14 Annersley Square, which he entered. I took the parcel to the station and handed it over to the officer on duty. We examined the parcel together. It contained the body of a premature newborn infant."

He snapped the notebook to.

Fenton felt all his strength ebb from him. Horror and fear merged together like a dense, overwhelming cloud, and he collapsed on to a chair.

"Oh, God," he said. "Oh, God, what's happened . . . ?"

Through the cloud he saw Edna looking at him from the open door of the dining-room, with the Alhusons behind her. The man in plain clothes was saying, "I shall have to ask you to come down to the station and make a statement."

5

Fenton sat in the Inspector's room, with the Inspector of Police behind a desk, and the plain-clothes man, and the policeman in uniform, and someone else, a medical officer. Edna was there too—he had especially asked for Edna to be there. The Alhusons were waiting outside, but the terrible thing was the expression on Edna's face. It was obvious that she did not believe him. Nor did the policemen.

"Yes, it's been going on for six months," he repeated. "When I say 'going on,' I mean my painting has been going on, nothing else, nothing else at all. . . . I was seized with the desire to paint . . . I can't explain it. I never shall. It just came over me. And on impulse I walked in at the gate of No. 8 Boulting Street. The woman came to the door and I asked if she had a room to let, and after a few moments' discussion she said she had—a room of her own in the basement —nothing to do with the landlord, we agreed to say nothing to the landlord. So I took possession. And I've been going there every afternoon for six months. I said nothing about it to my wife . . . I thought she wouldn't understand . . ."

He turned in despair to Edna, and she just sat there, staring at him.

"I admit I've lied," he said. "I've lied to everyone. I lied at home, I lied at the office. I told them at the office I had contacts with another firm, that I went there during the afternoon, and I told my wife—bear me out, Edna—I told my wife I was either kept late at the office or I was playing bridge at the club. The truth was that I went every day to No. 8 Boulting Street. Every day."

He had not done anything wrong. Why did they have to stare at him? Why did Edna hold on to the arms of the chair?

"What age is Madame Kaufman? I don't know. About twenty-seven, I should think . . . or thirty, she could be any age . . . and she has a little boy, Johnnie. . . . She is an Austrian, she has led a very sad life, and her husband has left her. . . . No, I never saw anyone in the house at all, no other men. . . . I don't know, I tell you . . . I don't know. I went there to paint. I didn't go for anything else. She'll tell you so. She'll tell you the truth. I'm sure she is very attached to me. . . . At least, no, I don't mean that; when I say attached I mean she is grateful for the money I pay her . . . that is, the rent, the five pounds for the room. There was absolutely nothing else between us, there couldn't have been, it was out of the question. . . . Yes, yes, of course I was ignorant of her condition. I'm not very observant . . . it wasn't the sort of thing I would have noticed. And she did not say a word, not a word."

He turned again to Edna. "Surely you believe me?"

She said, "You never told me you wanted to paint. You've never mentioned painting, or artists, all our married life."

It was the frozen blue of her eyes that he could not bear. He said to the Inspector, "Can't we go to Boulting Street now, at once? That poor soul must be in great distress. She should see a doctor, someone should be looking after her. Can't we all go now, my wife too, so that Madame Kaufman can explain everything?"

And, thank God, he had his way. It was agreed they should go to Boulting Street. A police car was summoned, and he and Edna and two police officers climbed into it, and the Alhusons followed behind in their car. He heard them say something to the Inspector about not wanting Mrs. Fenton to be alone, the shock was too great. That was kind, of course, but there need not be any shock when he could quietly and calmly explain the whole story to her, once they got home. It was the atmosphere of the police station that made it so appalling, that made him feel guilty, a criminal.

The car drew up before the familiar house, and they all got out. He led the way through the gate and round to the back door and opened it. As soon as they entered the passage the smell of gas was unmistakable.

"It's leaking again," he said. "It does, from time to time. She tells the men but they never come."

Nobody answered. He walked swiftly to the kitchen. The door was shut, and here the smell of gas was stronger still.

The Inspector murmured something to his subordinates. "Mrs. Fenton had better stay outside in the car with her friends."

"No," said Fenton, "no, I want my wife to hear the truth."

But Edna began to walk back along the passage with one of the policemen, and the Alhusons were waiting for her, their faces solemn. Then everybody seemed to go at once into the bedroom, into Madame Kaufman's bedroom. They jerked up the blind and let in the air, but the smell of gas was overpowering, and they leant over the bed and she was lying there asleep, with Johnnie beside her, both fast asleep. The envelope containing the twenty pounds was lying on the floor.

"Can't you wake her?" said Fenton. "Can't you wake her and tell her that Mr. Sims is here? Mr. Sims."

One of the policemen took hold of his arm and led him from the room.

When they told Fenton that Madame Kaufman was dead

and Johnnie, too, he shook his head and said, "It's terrible . . . terrible . . . if only she'd told me, if only I'd known what to do. . . ." But somehow the first shock of discovery had been so great, with the police coming to the house and the appalling contents of the parcel, that this fulfilment of disaster did not touch him in the same way. It seemed somehow inevitable.

"Perhaps it's for the best," he said. "She was alone in the world. Just the two of them. Alone in the world."

He was not sure what everyone was waiting for. The ambulance, he supposed, or whatever it was that would take poor Madame Kaufman and Johnnie away. He asked, "Can we go home, my wife and I?"

The Inspector exchanged a glance with the man in plain clothes, and then he said, "I'm afraid not, Mr. Fenton. We shall want you to return with us to the station."

"But I've told you the truth," said Fenton wearily. "There's no more to say. I have nothing to do with this tragedy. Nothing at all." Then he remembered his paintings. "You haven't seen my work," he said. "It's all here, in the room next door. Please ask my wife to come back, and my friends too. I want them to see my work. Besides, now that this has happened I wish to remove my belongings."

"We will take care of that," said the Inspector.

The tone was noncommittal, yet firm. Ungracious, Fenton thought. The officious attitude of the law.

"That's all very well," said Fenton, "but they are my possessions, and valuable at that. I don't see what right you have to touch them."

He looked from the Inspector to his colleague in plain clothes—the medical officer and the other policeman were still in the bedroom—and he could tell from their set expressions that they were not really interested in his work. They thought it was just an excuse, an alibi, and all they wanted to do was to take him back to the police station and question him still further about the sordid, pitiful deaths in the bedroom, about the body of the little, prematurely born child.

"I'm quite ready to go with you, Inspector," he said quietly, "but I make this one request—that you will allow me to show my work to my wife and my friends."

The Inspector nodded at his subordinate, who went out of the kitchen, and then the little group moved to the studio, Fenton himself opening the door and showing them in.

"Of course," he said, "I've been working under wretched conditions. Bad light, as you see. No proper amenities at all. I don't know how I stuck it. As a matter of fact, I intended to move out when I returned from my holiday. I told the poor girl so, and it probably depressed her."

He switched on the light, and as they stood there, glancing about them, noting the dismantled easel, the canvases stacked neatly against the wall, it struck him that of course these preparations for departure must seem odd to them, suspicious, as though he had in truth known what had happened in the bedroom behind the kitchen and had intended a getaway.

"It was a makeshift, naturally," he said, continuing to apologize for the small room that looked so unlike a studio, "but it happened to suit me. There was nobody else in the house, nobody to ask questions. I never saw anyone but Madame Kaufman and the boy."

He noticed that Edna had come into the room, and the Alhusons too, and the other policeman, and they were all watching him with the same set expressions. Why Edna? Why the Alhusons? Surely they must be impressed by the canvases stacked against the wall? They must realize that his total output for the past five and a half months was here, in this room, only awaiting exhibition? He strode across the floor, seized the nearest canvas to hand, and held it up for them to see. It was the portrait of Madame Kaufman that he liked best, the one which—poor soul—she had told him looked like a fish.

"They're unconventional, I know that," he said, "not picture-book stuff. But they're strong. They've got originality." He seized another. Madame Kaufman again, this time with Johnnie on her lap. "Mother and child," he said, half smiling, "a true primitive. Back to our origins. The first woman, the first child."

He cocked his head, trying to see the canvas as they would

42

see it, for the first time. Looking up for Edna's approval, for her gasp of wonder, he was met by the same stony frozen stare of misunderstanding. Then her face seemed to crumple, and she turned to the Alhusons and said, "They're not proper paintings. They're daubs, done anyhow." Blinded by tears, she looked up at the Inspector. "I told you he couldn't paint," she said. "He's never painted in his life. It was just an alibi to get into the house with this woman."

Fenton watched the Alhusons lead her away. He heard them go out of the back door and through the garden to the front of the house. "They're not proper paintings, they're daubs," he repeated. He put the canvas down on the ground with its face to the wall, and said to the Inspector, "I'm ready to go with you now."

They got into the police car. Fenton sat between the Inspector and the man in plain clothes. The car turned out of Boulting Street. It crossed two other streets and came into Oakley Street and on towards the Embankment. The traffic lights changed from amber to red. Fenton murmured to himself, "She doesn't believe in me—she'll never believe in me." Then, as the lights changed and the car shot forward, he shouted, "All right, I'll confess everything. I was her lover, of course, and the child was mine. I turned on the gas this evening before I left the house. I killed them all. I was going to kill my wife too when we got to Scotland. I want to confess it . . . I did it . . . I did it . . . I did it . . ."

The Blue Lenses

THIS WAS THE DAY for the bandages to be removed and the blue lenses fitted. Marda West put her hand up to her eyes and felt the crêpe blinder and the layer upon layer of cotton wool beneath. Patience would be rewarded at last. The days had passed into weeks since her operation, and she had lain there suffering no physical discomfort, but only the anonymity of darkness, a negative feeling that the world and the life around were passing her by. During the first few days there had been pain, mercifully allayed by drugs, and then the sharpness of this wore down, dissolved, and she was left with a sense of great fatigue, which they assured her was reaction after shock. As for the operation itself, it had been successful. Here was definite promise. A hundred per cent successful.

"You will see," the surgeon told her, "more clearly than ever before."

"But how can you tell?" she urged, desiring her slender thread of faith to be reinforced.

"Because we examined your eyes when you were under the anaesthetic," he replied, "and again since, when we put you under for a second time. We would not lie to you, Mrs. West."

This reassurance came from them two or three times a day, and she had to steel herself to patience as the weeks wore by, so that she referred to the matter perhaps only once every twenty-four hours, and then by way of a trap, to catch them unawares. "Don't throw the roses out. I should like to see them," she would say, and the day nurse would be surprised

47

into the admission, "They'll be over before you can do that."
Which meant that she would not see this week.

Actual dates were never mentioned. Nobody said, "On the
fourteenth of the month you will have your eyes." And the
subterfuge continued, the pretence that she did not mind and
was content to wait. Even Jim, her husband, was now classed
in the category of "them," the staff of the hospital, and no
longer treated as a confidant.

Once, long ago, every qualm and apprehension had been
admitted and shared. This was before the operation. Then,
fearful of pain and blindness, she had clung to him and said,
"What if I never see again, what will happen to me?" pictur-
ing herself as helpless and maimed. And Jim, whose anxiety
was no less harsh than hers, would answer, "Whatever comes,
we'll go through it together."

Now, for no known reason except that darkness, perhaps,
had made her more sensitive, she was shy to discuss her eyes
with him. The touch of his hand was the same as it had ever
been, and his kiss, and the warmth of his voice; but always,
during these days of waiting, she had the seed of fear that he,
like the staff at the hospital, was being too kind. The kindness
of those who knew towards the one who must not be told.
Therefore, when at last it happened, when at his evening
visit the surgeon said, "Your lenses will be fitted tomorrow,"
surprise was greater than joy. She could not say anything, and
he had left the room before she could thank him. It was
really true. The long agony had ended. She permitted herself
only a last feeler, before the day nurse went off duty—
"They'll take some getting used to, and hurt a bit at first?"
—her statement of fact put as a careless question. But the
voice of the woman who had tended her through so many
weary days replied, "You won't know you've got them, Mrs.
West."

Such a calm, comfortable voice, and the way she shifted
the pillows and held the glass to the patient's lips, the hand
smelling faintly of the Morny French Fern soap with which
she washed her, these things gave confidence and implied
that she could not lie.

"Tomorrow I shall see you," said Marda West, and the

nurse, with the cheerful laugh that could be heard sometimes down the corridor outside, answered, "Yes, I'll give you your first shock."

It was a strange thought how memories of coming into the nursing home were now blunted. The staff who had received her were dim shadows, the room assigned to her, where she still lay, like a wooden box built only to entrap. Even the surgeon, brisk and efficient during those two rapid consultations when he had recommended an immediate operation, was a voice rather than a presence. He gave his orders and the orders were carried out, and it was difficult to reconcile this bird of passage with the person who, those several weeks ago, had asked her to surrender herself to him, who had in fact worked this miracle upon the membranes and the tissues which were her living eyes.

"Aren't you feeling excited?" This was the low, soft voice of her night nurse, who, more than the rest of them, understood what she had endured. Nurse Brand, by day, exuded a daytime brightness; she was a person of sunlight, of bearing in fresh flowers, of admitting visitors. The weather she described in the world outside appeared to be her own creation. "A real scorcher," she would say, flinging open windows, and her patient would sense the cold uniform, the starched cap, which somehow toned down the penetrating heat. Or else she might hear the steady fall of rain and feel the slight chill accompanying it. "This is going to please the gardeners, but it'll put paid to Matron's day on the river."

Meals, too, even the dullest of lunches, were made to appear delicacies through her method of introduction. "A morsel of brill *au beurre?*" she would suggest happily, whetting reluctant appetite, and the boiled fish that followed must be eaten, for all its tastelessness, because otherwise it would seem to let down Nurse Brand, who had recommended it. "Apple fritters—you can manage two, I'm sure," and the tongue began to roll the imaginary fritter, crisp as a flake and sugared, which in reality had a languid, leathery substance. And so her cheerful optimism brooked no discontent—it would be offensive to complain, lacking in backbone to admit, "Let me just lie. I don't want anything."

The night brought consolation and Nurse Ansel. She did not expect courage. At first, during pain, it had been Nurse Ansel who had administered the drugs. It was she who had smoothed the pillows and held the glass to the parched lips. Then, with the passing weeks, there had been the gentle voice and the quiet encouragement. "It will soon pass. This waiting is the worst." At night the patient had only to touch the bell, and in a moment Nurse Ansel was by the bed. "Can't sleep? I know, it's wretched for you. I'll give you just two and a half grains, and the night won't seem so long."

How compassionate that smooth and silken voice. The imagination, making fantasies through enforced rest and idleness, pictured some reality with Nurse Ansel that was not hospital—a holiday abroad, perhaps, for the three of them, and Jim playing golf with an unspecified male companion, leaving her, Marda, to wander with Nurse Ansel. All she did was faultless. She never annoyed. The small shared intimacies of nighttime brought a bond between nurse and patient that vanished with the day, and when she went off duty, at five minutes to eight in the morning, she would whisper, "Until this evening," the very whisper stimulating anticipation, as though eight o'clock that night would not be clocking in but an assignation.

Nurse Ansel understood complaint. When Marda West said wearily, "It's been such a long day," her answering "Has it?" implied that for her, too, the day had dragged, that in some hostel she had tried to sleep and failed, that now only did she hope to come alive.

It was with a special secret sympathy that she would announce the evening visitor. "Here is someone you want to see, a little earlier than usual," the tone suggesting that Jim was not the husband of ten years but a troubadour, a lover, someone whose bouquet of flowers had been plucked in an enchanted garden and now brought to a balcony. "What gorgeous lilies!" the exclamation half a breath and half a sigh, so that Marda West imagined exotic dragon-petalled beauties growing to heaven, and Nurse Ansel, a little priestess, kneeling. Then, shyly, the voice would murmur, "Good evening, Mr. West. Mrs. West is waiting for you." She would hear the gentle closing of the door, the tiptoeing out with the lilies, and the almost soundless return, the scent of the flowers filling the room.

It must have been during the fifth week that Marda West had tentatively suggested, first to Nurse Ansel and then to her husband, that perhaps when she returned home the night nurse might go with them for the first week. It would chime with Nurse Ansel's own holiday. Just a week. Just so that Marda West could settle to home again.

"Would you like me to?" Reserve lay in the voice, yet promise too.

"I would. It's going to be so difficult at first." The patient, not knowing what she meant by difficult, saw herself as helpless still, in spite of the new lenses, and needing the protection and the reassurance that up to the present only Nurse Ansel had given her. "Jim, what about it?"

His comment was something between surprise and indulgence. Surprise that his wife considered a nurse a person in her own right, and indulgence because it was the whim of a sick woman. At least, that was how it seemed to Marda West, and later, when the evening visit was over and he had gone home, she said to the night nurse, "I can't make out whether my husband thought it a good idea or not."

The answer was quiet yet reassuring. "Don't worry, Mr. West is reconciled."

But reconciled to what? The change in routine? Three people round the table, conversation, the unusual status of a guest who, devoting herself to her hostess, must be paid? (Though the last would not be mentioned, but glossed over at the end of a week in an envelope.)

"Aren't you feeling excited?" Nurse Ansel, by the pillow, touched the bandages, and it was the warmth in the voice, the certainty that only a few hours now would bring revelation, which stifled at last all lingering doubt of success. The operation had not failed. Tomorrow she would see once more.

"In a way," said Marda West, "it's like being home again. I've forgotten how the world looks."

"Such a wonderful world," murmured Nurse Ansel, "and you've been patient for so long."

The sympathetic hand expressed condemnation of all those who had insisted upon bandages through the waiting weeks. Greater indulgence might have been granted had Nurse Ansel herself been in command and waved a wand.

"It's queer," said Marda West, "tomorrow you won't be a voice to me any more. You'll be a person."

"Aren't I a person now?"

A note of gentle teasing, of pretended reproach, which was all part of the communication between them, so soothing to the patient. This must surely, when sight came back, be foregone.

"Yes, of course, but it's bound to be different."

"I don't see why."

Even knowing she was dark and small—for so Nurse Ansel had described herself—Marda West must be prepared for surprise at the first encounter, the tilt of the head, the slant of the eyes, or perhaps some unexpected facial form like too large a mouth, too many teeth.

"Look, feel . . ." and not for the first time Nurse Ansel took her patient's hand and passed it over her own face, a little embarrassing, perhaps, because it implied surrender, the patient's hand a captive. Marda West, withdrawing it, said with a laugh, "It doesn't tell me a thing."

"Sleep, then. Tomorrow will come too soon." There came the familiar routine of the bell put within reach, the last-minute drink, the pill, and then the soft, "Good night, Mrs. West. Ring if you want me."

"Thank you. Good night."

There was always a slight sense of loss, of loneliness, as the door closed and she went away, and a feeling of jealousy, too, because there were other patients who received these same mercies and who, in pain, would also ring their bells. When she awoke—and this often happened in the small hours—Marda West would no longer picture Jim at home, lonely on his pillow, but would have an image of Nurse Ansel, seated perhaps by someone's bed, bending to give comfort, and this alone would make her reach for the bell, and press her thumb upon it, and say, when the door opened, "Were you having a nap?"

"I never sleep on duty."

She would be seated, then, in the cubbyhole midway along the passage, perhaps drinking tea or entering particulars of charts into a ledger. Or standing beside a patient, as she now stood beside Marda West.

"I can't find my handkerchief."

"Here it is. Under your pillow all the time."

A pat on the shoulder (and this in itself was a sort of delicacy), a few moments of talk to prolong companionship, and then she would be gone to answer other bells and other requests.

"Well, we can't complain of the weather!" Now it was the day itself, and Nurse Brand coming in like the first breeze of morning, a hand on a barometer set fair. "All ready for the great event?" she asked. "We must get a move on, and keep your prettiest nightie to greet your husband."

It was her operation in reverse. This time in the same room, though, and not a stretcher, but only the deft hands of the surgeon with Nurse Brand to help him. First came the disappearance of the crêpe, the lifting of the bandages and lint, the very slight prick of an injection to dull feeling. Then he did something to her eyelids. There was no pain. Whatever he did was cold, like the slipping of ice where the bandages had been, yet soothing too.

"Now, don't be disappointed," he said. "You won't know any difference for about half an hour. Everything will seem shadowed. Then it will gradually clear. I want you to lie quietly during that time."

"I understand. I won't move."

The longed-for moment must not be too sudden. This made sense. The dark lenses, fitted inside her lids, were temporary for the first few days. Then they would be removed and others fitted.

"How much shall I see?" The question dared at last.

"Everything. But not immediately in colour. Just like wearing sunglasses on a bright day. Rather pleasant."

His cheerful laugh gave confidence, and when he and Nurse Brand had left the room she lay back again, waiting for the

53

fog to clear and for that summer day to break in upon her vision, however subdued, however softened by the lenses.

Little by little the mist dissolved. The first object was angular, a wardrobe. Then a chair. Then, moving her head, the gradual forming of the window's shape, the vases on the sill, the flowers Jim had brought her. Sounds from the street outside merged with the shapes, and what had seemed sharp before was now in harmony. She thought to herself, "I wonder if I can cry? I wonder if the lenses will keep back tears," but, feeling the blessing of sight restored, she felt the tears as well, nothing to be ashamed of—one or two which were easily brushed away.

All was in focus now. Flowers, the washbasin, the glass with the thermometer in it, her dressing gown. Wonder and relief were so great that they excluded thought.

"They weren't lying to me," she thought. "It's happened. It's true."

The texture of the blanket covering her, so often felt, could now be seen as well. Colour was not important. The dim light caused by the blue lenses enhanced the charm, the softness of all she saw. It seemed to her, rejoicing in form and shape, that colour would never matter. There was time enough for colour. The blue symmetry of vision itself was all-important. To see, to feel, to blend the two together. It was indeed rebirth, the discovery of a world long lost to her.

There seemed to be no hurry now. Gazing about the small room and dwelling upon every aspect of it was richness, something to savour. Hours could be spent just looking at the room and feeling it, travelling through the window and to the windows of the houses opposite.

"Even a prisoner," she decided, "could find comfort in his cell if he had been blinded first and had recovered his sight."

She heard Nurse Brand's voice outside, and turned her head to watch the opening door.

"Well . . . are we happy once more?"

Smiling, she saw the figure dressed in uniform come into the room, bearing a tray, her glass of milk upon it. Yet, incongruous, absurd, the head with the uniformed cap was not a woman's head at all. The thing bearing down upon her was a cow . . . a cow on a woman's body. The frilled cap was perched upon wide horns. The eyes were large and gentle, but cow's eyes, the nostrils broad and humid, and the way she stood there, breathing, was the way a cow stood placidly in pasture, taking the day as it came, content, unmoved.

"Feeling a bit strange?"

The laugh was a woman's laugh, a nurse's laugh, Nurse Brand's laugh, and she put the tray down on the cupboard beside the bed. The patient said nothing. She shut her eyes, then opened them again. The cow in the nurse's uniform was with her still.

"Confess now," said Nurse Brand, "you wouldn't know you had the lenses in, except for the colour."

It was important to gain time. The patient stretched out her hand carefully for the glass of milk. She sipped the milk slowly. The mask must be worn on purpose. Perhaps it was some kind of experiment connected with the fitting of the lenses—though how it was supposed to work she could not imagine. And it was surely taking rather a risk to spring such a surprise and, to people weaker than herself who might have undergone the same operation, downright cruel.

"I see very plainly," she said at last. "At least, I think I do."

Nurse Brand stood watching her with folded arms. The broad uniformed figure was much as Marda West had imagined it, but that cow's head tilted, the ridiculous frill of the cap perched on the horns . . . where did the head join the body, if mask it in fact was?

"You don't sound too sure of yourself," said Nurse Brand. "Don't say you're disappointed, after all we've done for you."

The laugh was cheerful, as usual, but she should be chewing grass, the slow jaws moving from side to side.

"I'm sure of myself," answered her patient, "but I'm not so sure of you. Is it a trick?"

"Is what a trick?"

"The way you look . . . your . . . face?"

Vision was not so dimmed by the blue lenses that she could not distinguish a change of expression. The cow's jaw distinctly dropped.

"Really, Mrs. West!" This time the laugh was not so cordial. Surprise was very evident. "I'm as the good God made me. I dare say He might have made a better job of it."

The nurse, the cow, moved from the bedside towards the window and drew the curtains more sharply back, so that the full light filled the room. There was no visible join to the mask: the head blended to the body. Marda West saw how the cow, if she stood at bay, would lower her horns.

"I didn't mean to offend you," she said, "but it *is* just a little strange. You see . . ."

She was spared explanation because the door opened and the surgeon came into the room. At least, the surgeon's voice was recognisable as he called, "Hullo! How goes it?" and his figure in the dark coat and the sponge-bag trousers was all that an eminent surgeon's should be, but . . . that terrier's head, ears pricked, the inquisitive, searching glance? In a moment surely he would yap, and a tail wag swiftly?

This time the patient laughed. The effect was ludicrous. It must be a joke. It was, it had to be; but why go to such expense and trouble, and what in the end was gained by the deception? She checked her laugh abruptly as she saw the terrier turn to the cow, the two communicate with each other soundlessly. Then the cow shrugged its too ample shoulders.

"Mrs. West thinks us a bit of a joke," she said. But the nurse's voice was not overpleased.

"I'm all for that," said the surgeon. "It would never do if she took a dislike to us, would it?"

Then he came and put his hand out to his patient and bent close to observe her eyes. She lay very still. He wore no mask either. None, at least, that she could distinguish. The ears were pricked, the sharp nose questing. He was even marked, one ear black, the other white. She could picture him at the entrance to a fox's lair, sniffing, then quick on the scent scuffing down the tunnel, intent upon the job for which he was trained.

"Your name ought to be Jack Russell," she said aloud.

"I beg your pardon?"

He had straightened himself but still stood beside the bed, and the bright eyes had a penetrating quality, one ear cocked.

"I mean"—Marda West searched for words—"the name seems to suit you better than your own."

She felt confused. Mr. Edmund Greaves, with all the letters after him on the plate in Hartley Street, what must he think of her?

"I know a James Russell," he said to her, "but he's an orthopaedic surgeon and breaks your bones. Do you feel I've done that to you?"

His voice was brisk, but he sounded a little surprised, as Nurse Brand had done. The gratitude which was owed to their skill was not forthcoming.

"No, no indeed," said the patient hastily, "nothing is broken at all, I'm in no pain. I see clearly. Almost too clearly, in fact."

"That's as it should be," he said, and the laugh that followed resembled a short sharp bark.

"Well, Nurse," he went on, "the patient can do everything within reason except remove the lenses. You've warned her, I suppose?"

"I was about to, sir, when you came in."

Mr. Greaves turned his pointed terrier nose to Marda West.

"I'll be in on Thursday," he said, "to change the lenses. In the meantime, it's just a question of washing out the eyes with a solution three times a day. They'll do it for you. Don't touch them yourself. And above all don't fiddle with the lenses. A patient did that once and lost his sight. He never recovered it."

"If you tried that," the terrier seemed to say, "you would get what you deserved. Better not make the attempt. My teeth are sharp."

"I understand," said the patient slowly. But her chance had gone. She could not now demand an explanation. Instinct warned her that he would not understand. The terrier was saying something to the cow, giving instructions. Such a sharp staccato sentence, and the foolish head nodded in answer. Surely on a hot day the flies would bother her—or would the frilled cap keep insects away?

As they moved to the door the patient made a last attempt.

"Will the permanent lenses," she asked, "be the same as these?"

"Exactly the same," yapped the surgeon, "except that they won't be tinted. You'll see the natural colour. Until Thursday, then."

He was gone, and the nurse with him. She could hear the murmur of voices outside the door. What happened now? If it was really some kind of test, did they remove their masks instantly? It seemed to Marda West of immense importance that she should find this out. The trick was not truly fair: it was a misuse of confidence. She slipped out of bed and went to the door. She could hear the surgeon say, "One and a half grains. She's a little overwrought. It's the reaction, of course."

Bravely she flung open the door. They were standing there in the passage, wearing the masks still. They turned to look at her, and the sharp bright eyes of the terrier, the deep eyes of the cow both held reproach, as though the patient, by confronting them, had committed a breach of etiquette.

"Do you want anything, Mrs. West?" asked Nurse Brand.

Marda West stared beyond them down the corridor. The whole floor was in the deception. A maid, carrying dustpan and brush, coming from the room next door had a weasel's head upon her small body, and the nurse advancing from the other side was a little prancing kitten, her cap coquettish on her furry curls, the doctor beside her a proud lion. Even the porter, arriving at that moment in the lift opposite, carried a boar's head between his shoulders. He lifted out luggage, uttering a boar's heavy grunt.

The first sharp prick of fear came to Marda West. How could they have known she would open the door at that minute? How could they have arranged to walk down the corridor wearing masks, the other nurses and the other doctor, and the maid appear out of the room next door, and the porter come up in the lift? Something of her fear must have shown in her face, for Nurse Brand, the cow, took hold of her and led her back into her room.

"Are you feeling all right, Mrs. West?" she asked anxiously.

Marda West climbed slowly into bed. If it was a conspiracy,

what was it all for? Were the other patients to be deceived as well?

"I'm rather tired," she said. "I'd like to sleep."

"That's right," said Nurse Brand, "you got a wee bit excited."

She was mixing something in the medicine glass, and this time, as Marda West took the glass, her hand trembled. Could a cow see clearly how to mix medicine? Supposing she made a mistake?

"What are you giving me?" she asked.

"A sedative," answered the cow.

Buttercups and daisies. Lush green grass. Imagination was strong enough to taste all three in the mixture. The patient shuddered. She lay down on her pillow, and Nurse Brand drew the curtains close.

"Now just relax," she said, "and when you wake up you'll feel so much better." The heavy head stretched forward—in a moment it would surely open its jaws and moo.

The sedative acted swiftly. Already a drowsy sensation filled the patient's limbs.

Soon peaceful darkness came, but she awoke, not to the sanity she had hoped for, but to lunch brought in by the kitten. Nurse Brand was off duty.

"How long must it go on for?" asked Marda West. She had resigned herself to the trick. A dreamless sleep had restored energy and some measure of confidence. If it was somehow necessary to the recovery of her eyes, or even if they did it for some unfathomable reason of their own, it was their business.

"How do you mean, Mrs. West?" asked the kitten, smiling. Such a flighty little thing, with its pursed-up mouth, and even as it spoke it put a hand to its cap.

"This test on my eyes," said the patient, uncovering the boiled chicken on her plate. "I don't see the point of it. Making yourselves such guys. What is the object?"

The kitten, serious, if a kitten could be serious, continued to stare at her. "I'm sorry, Mrs. West," she said, "I don't follow you. Did you tell Nurse Brand you couldn't see properly yet?"

"It's not that I can't see," replied Marda West. "I see perfectly well. The chair is a chair. The table is a table. I'm about to eat boiled chicken. But why do you look like a kitten, and a tabby kitten at that?"

Perhaps she sounded ungracious. It was hard to keep her voice steady. The nurse—Marda West remembered the voice, it was Nurse Sweeting, and the name suited her—drew back from the trolley table.

"I'm sorry," she said, "if I don't come up to scratch. I've never been called a cat before."

Scratch was good. The claws were out already. She might purr to the lion in the corridor, but she was not going to purr to Marda West.

"I'm not making it up," said the patient. "I see what I see. You are a cat, if you like, and Nurse Brand's a cow."

This time the insult must sound deliberate. Nurse Sweeting had fine whiskers to her mouth. The whiskers bristled.

"If you please, Mrs. West," she said, "will you eat your chicken, and ring the bell when you are ready for the next course?"

She stalked from the room. If she had a tail, thought Marda West, it would not be wagging, like Mr. Greaves', but twitching angrily.

No, they could not be wearing masks. The kitten's surprise and resentment had been too genuine. And the staff of the hospital could not possibly put on such an act for one patient, for Marda West alone—the expense would be too great. The fault must lie in the lenses, then. The lenses, by their very nature, by some quality beyond the layman's understanding, must transform the person who was perceived through them.

A sudden thought struck her, and, pushing the trolley table aside, she climbed out of bed and went over to the dressing table. Her own face stared back at her from the looking glass. The dark lenses concealed the eyes, but the face was at least her own.

"Thank heaven for that," she said to herself, but it swung her back to thoughts of trickery. That her own face should seem unchanged through the lenses suggested a plot and that her first idea of masks had been the right one. But why?

What did they gain by it? Could there be a conspiracy amongst them to drive her mad? She dismissed the idea at once—it was too fanciful. This was a reputable London nursing home, and the staff was well known. The surgeon had operated on royalty. Besides, if they wanted to send her mad, or kill her even, it would be simple enough with drugs. Or with anaesthetics. They could have given her too much anaesthetic during the operation and just let her die. No one would take the roundabout way of dressing up staff and doctors in animals' masks.

She would try one further proof. She stood by the window, the curtain concealing her, and watched for passers-by. For the moment there was no one in the street. It was the lunch hour and traffic was slack. Then, at the other end of the street, a taxi crossed, too far away for her to see the driver's head. She waited. The porter came out from the nursing home and stood on the steps, looking up and down. His boar's head was clearly visible. He did not count, though. He could be part of the plot. A van drew near, but she could not see the driver . . . yes, he slowed as he went by the nursing home and craned from his seat, and she saw the squat frog's head, the bulging eyes.

Sick at heart, she left the window and climbed back into bed. She had no further appetite and pushed away her plate, the rest of the chicken untasted. She did not ring her bell, and after a while the door opened. It was not the kitten. It was the little maid with the weasel's head.

"Will you have plum tart or ice cream, madam?" she asked.

Marda West, her eyes half closed, shook her head. The weasel, shyly edging forward to take the tray, said, "Cheese, then, and coffee to follow?"

The head joined the neck without any fastening. It could not be a mask, unless some designer, some genius, had invented masks that merged with the body, blending fabric to skin.

"Coffee only," said Marda West.

The weasel vanished. Another knock on the door and the kitten was back again, her back arched, her fluff flying. She plonked the coffee down without a word, and Marda West, irritated—for surely, if anyone was to show annoyance, it should be herself?—said sharply, "Shall I pour you some milk in the saucer?"

The kitten turned. "A joke's a joke, Mrs. West," she said, "and I can take a laugh with anyone. But I can't stick rudeness."

"Miaow," said Marda West.

The kitten left the room. No one, not even the weasel, came to remove the coffee. The patient was in disgrace. She did not care. If the staff of the nursing home thought they could win this battle, they were mistaken. She went to the window again. An elderly cod, leaning on two sticks, was being helped into a waiting car by the boar-headed porter. It could not be a plot. They could not know she was watching them. Marda went to the telephone and asked the exchange to put her through to her husband's office. She remembered a moment afterwards that he would still be at lunch. Nevertheless, she got the number, and as luck had it he was there.

"Jim . . . Jim, darling."

"Yes?"

The relief to hear the loved familiar voice. She lay back on the bed, the receiver to her ear.

"Darling, when can you get here?"

"Not before this evening, I'm afraid. It's one hell of a day, one thing after another. Well, how did it go? Is everything O.K.?"

"Not exactly."

"What do you mean? Can't you see? Greaves hasn't bungled it, has he?"

How was she to explain what had happened to her? It sounded so foolish over the telephone.

"Yes, I can see. I can see perfectly. It's just that . . . that all the nurses look like animals. And Greaves, too. He's a fox terrier. One of those little Jack Russells they put down the foxes' holes."

"What on earth are you talking about?"

He was saying something to his secretary at the same time, something about another appointment, and she knew from the tone of his voice that he was busy, very busy, and she had

62

chosen the worst time to ring him up. "What do you mean about Jack Russell?" he repeated.

Marda West knew it was no use. She must wait till he came. Then she would try to explain everything, and he would be able to find out for himself what lay behind it.

"Oh, never mind," she said. "I'll tell you later."

"I'm sorry," he told her, "but I really am in a tearing hurry. If the lenses don't help you, tell somebody. Tell the nurses, the matron."

"Yes," she said, "yes."

Then she rang off. She put down the telephone. She picked up a magazine, one left behind at some time or other by Jim himself, she supposed. She was glad to find that reading did not hurt her eyes. Nor did the blue lenses make any difference, for the photographs of men and women looked normal, as they had always done. Wedding groups, social occasions, debutantes, all were as usual. It was only here, in the nursing home itself and in the street outside, that they were different.

It was much later in the afternoon that Matron called in to have a word with her. She knew it was Matron because of her clothes. But inevitably now, without surprise, she observed the sheep's head.

"I hope you're quite comfortable, Mrs. West?"

A note of gentle enquiry in the voice. A suspicion of a baa?

"Yes, thank you."

Marda West spoke guardedly. It would not do to ruffle the matron. Even if the whole affair was some gigantic plot, it would be better not to aggravate her.

"The lenses fit well?"

"Very well."

"I'm so glad. It was a nasty operation, and you've stood the period of waiting so very well."

That's it, thought the patient. Butter me up. Part of the game, no doubt.

"Only a few days, Mr. Greaves said, and then you will have them altered and the permanent ones fitted."

"Yes, so he said."

"It's rather disappointing not to observe colour, isn't it?"

"As things are, it's a relief."

The retort slipped out before she could check herself. The matron smoothed her dress. And if you only knew, thought the patient, what you look like, with that tape under your sheep's chin, you would understand what I mean.

"Mrs. West . . ." The matron seemed uncomfortable, and turned her sheep's head away from the woman in the bed. "Mrs. West, I hope you won't mind what I'm going to say, but our nurses do a fine job here, and we are all very proud of them. They work long hours, as you know, and it is not really very kind to mock them, although I am sure you intended it in fun."

Baa . . . Baa . . . Bleat away. Marda West tightened her lips.

"Is it because I called Nurse Sweeting a kitten?"

"I don't know what you called her, Mrs. West, but she was quite distressed. She came to me in the office nearly crying."

Spitting, you mean. Spitting and scratching. Those capable little hands are really claws.

"It won't happen again."

She was determined not to say more. It was not her fault. She had not asked for lenses that deformed, for trickery, for make-believe.

"It must come very expensive," she added, "to run a nursing home like this."

"It is," said the matron. Said the sheep. "It can only be done because of the excellence of the staff, and the co-opera-tion of all our patients."

The remark was intended to strike home. Even a sheep can turn.

"Matron," said Marda West, "don't let's fence with each other. What is the object of it all?"

"The object of what, Mrs. West?"

"This tomfoolery, this dressing up." There, she had said it. To enforce her argument she pointed at the matron's cap. "Why pick on that particular disguise? It's not even funny."

There was silence. The matron, who had made as if to sit

down to continue her chat, changed her mind. She moved slowly to the door.

"We, who were trained at St. Hilda's, are proud of our badge," she said. "I hope, when you leave us in a few days, Mrs. West, that you will look back on us with greater tolerance than you appear to have now."

She left the room. Marda West picked up the magazine she had thrown down, but the matter was dull. She closed her eyes. She opened them again. She closed them once more. If the chair had become a mushroom and the table a haystack, then the blame could have been put upon the lenses. Why was it only people who had changed? What was so wrong with people? She kept her eyes shut when her tea was brought her, and when the voice said pleasantly, "Some flowers for you, Mrs. West," she did not even open them, but waited for the owner of the voice to leave the room. The flowers were carnations. The card was Jim's. And the message on it said, "Cheer up. We're not as bad as we seem."

She smiled and buried her face in the flowers. Nothing false about them. Nothing strange about the scent. Carnations were carnations, fragrant, graceful. Even the nurse on duty who came to put them in water could not irritate her with her pony's head. After all, it was a trim little pony, with a white star on its forehead. It would do well in the ring. "Thank you," smiled Marda West.

The curious day dragged on, and she waited restlessly for eight o'clock. She washed and changed her nightgown and did her hair. She drew her own curtains and switched on the bedside lamp. A strange feeling of nervousness had come upon her. She realized, so strange had been the day, that she had not once thought about Nurse Ansel. Dear, comforting, bewitching Nurse Ansel. Nurse Ansel, who was due to come on duty at eight. Was she also in the conspiracy? If she was, then Marda West would have a showdown. Nurse Ansel would never lie. She would go up to her, and put her hands on her shoulders, and take the mask in her two hands, and say to her, "There, now take it off. You won't deceive me." But if it was the lenses, if all the time it was the lenses that were at fault, how was she to explain it?

She was sitting at the dressing table, putting some cream on her face, and the door must have opened without her being aware; but she heard the well-known voice, the soft beguiling voice, and it said to her, "I nearly came before. I didn't dare. You would have thought me foolish." It slid slowly into view, the long snake's head, the twisting neck, the pointed barbed tongue swiftly thrusting and swiftly withdrawn, it came into view over her shoulders, through the looking glass.

Marda West did not move. Only her hand, mechanically, continued to cream her cheek. The snake was not motionless: it turned and twisted all the time, as though examining the pots of cream, the scent, the powder.

"How does it feel to see yourself again?"

Nurse Ansel's voice emerging from the head seemed all the more grotesque and horrible, and the very fact that as she spoke the darting tongue spoke, too, paralysed action. Marda West felt sickness rise in her stomach, choking her, and suddenly physical reaction proved too strong. She turned away, but as she did so the steady hands of the nurse gripped her, she suffered herself to be led to her bed, she was lying down, eyes closed, the nausea passing.

"Poor dear, what have they been giving you? Was it the sedative? I saw it on your chart," and the gentle voice, so soothing and so calm, could only belong to one who understood. The patient did not open her eyes. She did not dare. She lay there on the bed, waiting.

"It's been too much for you," said the voice. "They should have kept you quiet the first day. Did you have visitors?"

"No."

"Nevertheless, you should have rested. You look really pale. We can't have Mr. West seeing you like this. I've half a mind to telephone him to stay away."

"No . . . please, I want to see him, I must see him."

Fear made her open her eyes, but directly she did so the sickness gripped her again, for the snake's head, longer than before, was twisting out of its nurse's collar, and for the first time she saw the hooded eye, a pin's head, hidden. She put her hand over her mouth to stifle her cry.

A sound came from Nurse Ansel expressing disquiet.

"Something has turned you very sick," she said. "It can't be the sedative. You've often had it before. What was the dinner this evening?"

"Steamed fish, I wasn't hungry."

"I wonder if it was fresh. I'll see if anyone has complained. Meanwhile, lie still, dear, and don't upset yourself."

The door quietly opened and closed again, and Marda West, disobeying instructions, slipped from her bed and seized the first weapon that came to hand, her nail scissors. Then she returned to her bed again, her heart beating fast, the scissors concealed beneath the sheet. Revulsion had been too great. She must defend herself, should the snake approach her. Now she was certain that what was happening was real, was true. Some evil force encompassed the nursing home and its inhabitants, the matron, the nurses, the visiting doctors, her surgeon—they were all caught up in it, they were all partners in some gigantic crime, the purpose of which could not be understood. Here, in Upper Watling Street, the malevolent plot was in process of being hatched, and she, Marda West, was one of the pawns; in some way they were to use her as an instrument.

One thing was very certain. She must not let them know that she suspected them. She must try and behave with Nurse Ansel as she had done hitherto. One slip and she was lost. She must pretend to be better. If she let sickness overcome her, Nurse Ansel might bend over her with that snake's head, that darting tongue.

The door opened and she was back. Marda West clenched her hands under the sheet. Then she forced a smile.

"What a nuisance I am," she said. "I felt giddy, but I'm better now."

The gliding snake held a bottle in her hand. She came over to the washbasin and, taking the medicine glass, poured out three drops.

"This should settle it, Mrs. West," she said, and fear gripped the patient once again, for surely the words themselves constituted a threat. "This should settle it"—settle what? Settle her finish? The liquid had no colour, but that meant nothing.

She took the medicine glass handed to her, and invented a subterfuge.

"Could you find me a clean handkerchief in the drawer there?"

"Of course."

The snake turned its head, and as it did so Marda West poured the contents of the glass on to the floor. Then fascinated, repelled, she watched the twisting head peer into the contents of the dressing-table drawer, search for a handkerchief, and bring it back again. Marda West held her breath as it drew near the bed, and this time she noticed that the neck was not the smooth glowworm neck that it had seemed on first encounter, but had scales upon it, zigzagged. Oddly, the nurse's cap was not ill-fitting. It did not perch incongruously as had the caps of kitten, sheep, and cow. She took the handkerchief.

"You embarrass me," said the voice, "staring at me so hard. Are you trying to read my thoughts?"

Marda West did not answer. The question might be a trap.

"Tell me," the voice continued, "are you disappointed? Do I look as you expected me to look?"

Still a trap. She must be careful. "I think you do," she said slowly, "but it's difficult to tell with the cap. I can't see your hair."

Nurse Ansel laughed, the low, soft laugh that had been so alluring during the long weeks of blindness. She put up her hands, and in a moment the whole snake's head was revealed, the flat, broad top, the telltale adder's V. "Do you approve?" she asked.

Marda West shrank back against her pillow. Yet once again she forced herself to smile.

"Very pretty," she said, "very pretty indeed."

The cap was replaced, the long neck wriggled, and then, deceived, it took the medicine glass from the patient's hand and put it back upon the washbasin. It did not know everything.

"When I go home with you," said Nurse Ansel, "I needn't wear uniform—that is, if you don't want me to. You see, you'll be a private patient then and I your personal nurse for the week I'm with you."

Marda West felt suddenly cold. In the turmoil of the day she had forgotten the plans. Nurse Ansel was to be with them for a week. It was all arranged. The vital thing was not to show fear. Nothing must seem changed. And then, when Jim arrived, she would tell him everything. If he could not see the snake's head as she did—and indeed, it was possible that he would not, if her hypervision was caused by the lenses—he must just understand that for reasons too deep to explain she no longer trusted Nurse Ansel, could not, in fact, bear her to come home. The plan must be altered. She wanted no one to look after her. She only wanted to be home again with him.

The telephone rang on the bedside table, and Marda West seized it as she might seize salvation. It was her husband.

"Sorry to be late," he said. "I'll jump into a taxi and be with you right away. The lawyer kept me."

"Lawyer?" she asked.

"Yes, Forbes and Millwall, you remember, about the trust fund."

She had forgotten. There had been so many financial discussions before the operation. Conflicting advice, as usual. And finally Jim had put the whole business into the hands of the Forbes and Millwall people.

"Oh, yes. Was it satisfactory?"

"I think so. Tell you directly."

He rang off, and looking up, she saw the snake's head watching her. No doubt, thought Marda West, no doubt you would like to know what we were saying to one another.

"You must promise not to get too excited when Mr. West comes." Nurse Ansel stood with her hand upon the door.

"I'm not excited. I just long to see him, that's all."

"You're looking very flushed."

"It's warm in here."

The twisting neck craned upward, then turned to the window. For the first time Marda West had the impression that the snake was not entirely at its ease. It sensed tension. It knew, it could not help but know, that the atmosphere had changed between nurse and patient.

"I'll open the window just a trifle at the top."

If you were all snake, thought the patient, I could push you through. Or would you coil yourself round my neck and strangle me?

The window was opened, and, pausing a moment, hoping perhaps for a word of thanks, the snake hovered at the end of the bed. Then the neck settled in the collar, the tongue darted rapidly in and out, and with a gliding motion Nurse Ansel left the room.

Marda West waited for the sound of the taxi in the street outside. She wondered if she could persuade Jim to stay the night in the nursing home. If she explained her fear, her terror, surely he would understand. She would know in an instant if he had sensed anything wrong himself. She would ring the bell, make a pretext of asking Nurse Ansel some question, and then, by the expression on his face, by the tone of his voice she would discover whether he saw what she saw herself.

The taxi came at last. She heard it slow down, and then the door slammed and, blessedly, Jim's voice rang out in the street below. The taxi went away. He would be coming up in the lift. Her heart began to beat fast, and she watched the door. She heard his footstep outside, and then his voice again —he must be saying something to the snake. She would know at once if he had seen the head. He would come into the room either startled, not believing his eyes, or laughing, declaring it a joke, a pantomime. Why did he not hurry? Why must they linger there, talking, their voices hushed?

The door opened, the familiar umbrella and bowler hat the first objects to appear round the corner, then the comforting burly figure, but—God . . . no . . . please God, not Jim too, not Jim, forced into a mask, forced into an organisation of devils, of liars . . . Jim had a vulture's head. She could not mistake it. The brooding eye, the bloodtipped beak, the flabby folds of flesh. As she lay in sick and speechless horror, he stood the umbrella in a corner and put down the bowler hat and the folded overcoat.

"I gather you're not too well," he said, turning his vulture's head and staring at her, "feeling a bit sick and out of sorts. I won't stay long. A good night's rest will put you right."

She was too numb to answer. She lay quite still as he approached the bed and bent to kiss her. The vulture's beak was sharp.

"It's reaction, Nurse Ansel says," he went on, "the sudden shock of being able to see again. It works differently with different people. She says it will be much better when we get you home."

We . . . Nurse Ansel and Jim. The plan still held, then.

"I don't know," she said faintly, "that I want Nurse Ansel to come home."

"Not want Nurse Ansel?" He sounded startled. "But it was you who suggested it. You can't suddenly chop and change."

There was no time to reply. She had not rung the bell, but Nurse Ansel herself came into the room. "Cup of coffee, Mr. West?" she said. It was the evening routine. Yet tonight it sounded strange, as though it had been arranged outside the door.

"Thanks, Nurse, I'd love some. What's this nonsense about not coming home with us?" The vulture turned to the snake, the snake's head wriggled, and Marda West knew, as she watched them, the snake with darting tongue, the vulture with his head hunched between his man's shoulders, that the plan for Nurse Ansel to come home had not been her own after all; she remembered now that the first suggestion had come from Nurse Ansel herself. It had been Nurse Ansel who had said that Marda West needed care during convalescence. The suggestion had come after Jim had spent the evening laughing and joking, and his wife had listened, her eyes bandaged, happy to hear him. Now, watching the smooth snake whose adder's V was hidden beneath the nurse's cap, she knew why Nurse Ansel wanted to return with her, and she knew too why Jim had not opposed it, why in fact he had accepted the plan at once, had declared it a good one.

The vulture opened its bloodstained beak. "Don't say you two have fallen out?"

"Impossible." The snake twisted its neck, looked sideways

71

at the vulture, and added, "Mrs. West is just a little bit tired tonight. She's had a trying day, haven't you, dear?"

How best to answer? Neither must know. Neither the vulture, nor the snake, nor any of the hooded beasts surrounding her and closing in must ever guess, must ever know. "I'm all right," she said. "A bit mixed up. As Nurse Ansel says, I'll be better in the morning."

The two communicated in silence, sympathy between them. That, she realized now, was the most frightening thing of all. Animals, birds, and reptiles had no need to speak. They moved, they looked, they knew what they were about. They would not destroy her, though. She had, for all her bewildered terror, the will to live.

"I won't bother you," said the vulture, "with these documents tonight. There's no violent hurry anyway. You can sign them at home."

"What documents?"

If she kept her eyes averted she need not see the vulture's head. The voice was Jim's, steady and reassuring.

"The trust fund papers Forbes and Millwall gave me. They suggest I should become a co-director of the fund."

The words struck a chord, a thread of memory belonging to the weeks before her operation. Something to do with her eyes. If the operation was not successful she would have difficulty in signing her name.

"What for?" she asked, her voice unsteady. "After all, it is my money."

He laughed. And, turning to the sound, she saw the beak open. It gaped like a trap and then closed again.

"Of course it is," he said. "That's not the point. The point is that I should be able to sign for you if you should be ill or away."

Marda West looked at the snake, and the snake, aware, shrank into its collar and slid towards the door. "Don't stay too long, Mr. West," murmured Nurse Ansel. "Our patient must have a real rest tonight."

She glided from the room, and Marda West was left alone with her husband. With the vulture.

"I don't propose to go away," she said, "or be ill."

"Probably not. That's neither here nor there. These fellows always want safeguards. Anyway, I won't bore you with it now."

Could it be that the voice was overcasual? That the hand, stuffing the document into the pocket of the greatcoat, was a claw? This was a possibility, a horror, perhaps, to come. The bodies changing too, hands and feet becoming wings, claws, hoofs, paws, with no touch of humanity left to the people about her. The last thing to go would be the human voice. When the human voice went, there would be no hope. The jungle would take over, multitudinous sounds and screams coming from a hundred throats.

"Did you really mean that," Jim asked, "about Nurse Ansel?"

Calmly she watched the vulture pare his nails. He carried a file in his pocket. She had never thought about it before—it was part of Jim like his fountain pen and his pipe. Yet now there was reasoning behind it: a vulture needed sharp claws for tearing its victim.

"I don't know," she said. "It seemed to me rather silly to go home with a nurse, now that I can see again."

He did not answer at once. The head sank deeper between the shoulders. His dark city suit was like the humped feathers of a large brooding bird. "I think she's a treasure," he said. "And you're bound to feel groggy at first. I vote we stick to the plan. After all, if it doesn't work we can always send her away."

"Perhaps," said his wife.

She was trying to think if there was anyone left whom she could trust. Her family was scattered. A married brother in South Africa, friends in London, no one with whom she was intimate. Not to this extent. No one to whom she could say that her nurse had turned into a snake, her husband into a vulture. The utter hopelessness of her position was like damnation itself. This was her hell. She was quite alone, coldly conscious of the hatred and cruelty about her.

"What will you do this evening?" she asked quietly.

"Have dinner at the club, I suppose," he answered. "It's

becoming rather monotonous. Only two more days of it, thank goodness. Then you'll be home again."

Yes, but once at home, once back there, with a vulture and a snake, would she not be more completely at their mercy than she was here?

"Did Greaves say Thursday for certain?" she asked.

"He told me so this morning when he telephoned. You'll have the other lenses then, the ones that show colour."

The ones that would show the bodies too. That was the explanation. The blue lenses only showed the heads. They were the first test. Greaves, the surgeon, was in this too, very naturally. He had a high place in the conspiracy—perhaps he had been bribed. Who was it, she tried to remember, who had suggested the operation in the first place? Was it the family doctor, after a chat with Jim? Didn't they both come to her together and say that this was the only chance to save her eyes? The plot must lie deep in the past, extend right back through the months, perhaps the years. But, in heaven's name, for what purpose? She sought wildly in her memory to try to recall a look, or sign, or word which would give her some insight into this dreadful plot, this conspiracy against her person or her sanity.

"You look pretty peaky," he said suddenly. "Shall I call Nurse Ansel?"

"No . . ." It broke from her, almost a cry.

"I think I'd better go. She said not to stay long."

He got up from the chair, a heavy, hooded figure, and she closed her eyes as he came to kiss her good night. "Sleep well, my poor pet, and take it easy."

In spite of her fear she felt herself clutch at his hand.

"What is it?" he asked.

The well-remembered kiss would have restored her, but not the stab of the vulture's beak, the thrusting bloodstained beak. When he had gone she began to moan, turning her head upon the pillow.

"What am I to do?" she said. "What am I to do?"

The door opened again, and she put her hand to her mouth. They must not hear her cry. They must not see her cry. She pulled herself together with a tremendous effort.

"How are you feeling, Mrs. West?"

The snake stood at the bottom of the bed, and by her side the house physician. She had always liked him, a young pleasant man, and although like the others he had an animal's head it did not frighten her. It was a dog's head, an Aberdeen's, and the brown eyes seemed to quiz her. Long ago, as a child, she had owned an Aberdeen.

"Could I speak to you alone?" she asked.

"Of course. Do you mind, Nurse?" He jerked his head at the door, and she had gone. Marda West sat up in bed and clasped her hands.

"You'll think me very foolish," she began, "but it's the lenses. I can't get used to them."

He came over, the trustworthy Aberdeen, head cocked in sympathy.

"I'm sorry about that," he said. "They don't hurt you, do they?"

"No," she said, "no, I can't feel them. It's just that they make everyone look strange."

"They're bound to do that, you know. They don't show colour." His voice was cheerful, friendly. "It comes as a bit of a shock when you've worn bandages so long," he said, "and you mustn't forget you were pulled about quite a bit. The nerves behind the eyes are still very tender."

"Yes," she said. His voice, even his head, gave her confidence. "Have you known people who've had this operation before?"

"Yes, scores of them. In a couple of days you'll be as right as rain." He patted her on the shoulder. Such a kindly dog. Such a sporting, cheerful dog, like the long-dead Angus. "I'll tell you another thing," he continued. "Your sight may be better after this than it's ever been before. You'll actually see more clearly in every way. One patient told me that it was as though she had been wearing spectacles all her life, and then, because of the operation, she realized she saw all her friends and her family as they really were."

"As they really were?" She repeated his words after him.

"Exactly. Her sight had always been poor, you see. She had thought her husband's hair was brown, but in reality it was

75

red, bright red. A bit of a shock at first. But she was delighted."

The Aberdeen moved from the bed, patted the stethoscope on his jacket, and nodded his head. "Mr. Greaves did a wonderful job on you, I can promise you that," he said. "He was able to strengthen a nerve he thought had perished. You've never had the use of it before—it wasn't functioning. So who knows, Mrs. West, you may have made medical history. Anyway, sleep well and the best of luck. See you in the morning. Good night." He trotted from the room. She heard him call good night to Nurse Ansel as he went down the corridor.

The comforting words had turned to gall. In one sense they were a relief, because his explanations seemed to suggest there was no plot against her. Instead, like the woman patient before her with the deepened sense of colour, she had been given vision. She used the words he had used himself. Marda West could see people as they really were. And those whom she had loved and trusted most were in truth a vulture and a snake. . . .

The door opened and Nurse Ansel, with the sedative, entered the room.

"Ready to settle down, Mrs. West?" she asked.

"Yes, thank you."

There might be no conspiracy, but even so all trust, all faith were over.

"Leave it with a glass of water. I'll take it later."

She watched the snake put the glass on the bedside table. She watched her tuck in the sheet. Then the twisting neck peered closer and the hooded eyes saw the nail scissors half hidden beneath the pillow.

"What have you got there?"

The tongue darted and withdrew. The hand stretched out for the scissors. "You might have cut yourself. I'll put them away, shall I, for safety's sake?"

Her one weapon was pocketed, not replaced on the dressing table. The very way Nurse Ansel slipped the scissors into her pocket suggested that she knew of Marda West's suspicions. She wanted to leave her defenceless.

"Now, remember to ring your bell if you want anything."

"I'll remember."

The voice that had once seemed tender was oversmooth and false. How deceptive are ears, thought Marda West, what traitors to truth. And for the first time she became aware of her own new latent power, the power to tell truth from falsehood, good from evil.

"Good night, Mrs. West."

"Good night."

Lying awake, her bedside clock ticking, the accustomed traffic sounds coming from the street outside, Marda West decided upon her plan. She waited until eleven o'clock, an hour past the time when she knew that all the patients were settled and asleep. Then she switched out her light. This would deceive the snake, should she come to peep at her through the window slide in the door. The snake would believe that she slept. Marda West crept out of bed. She took her clothes from the wardrobe and began to dress. She put on her coat and shoes and tied a scarf over her head. When she was ready she went to the door and softly turned the handle. All was quiet in the corridor. She stood there motionless. Then she took one step across the threshold and looked to the left, where the nurse on duty sat. The snake was there. The snake was sitting crouched over a book. The light from the ceiling shone upon her head, and there could be no mistake. There were the trim uniform, the white starched front, the stiff collar, but rising from the collar the twisting neck of the snake, the long, flat, evil head.

Marda West waited. She was prepared to wait for hours. Presently the sound she hoped for came, the bell from a patient. The snake lifted its head from the book and checked the red light on the wall. Then, slipping on her cuffs, she glided down the corridor to the patient's room. She knocked and entered. Directly she had disappeared Marda West left her own room and went to the head of the staircase. There was no sound. She listened carefully, and then crept downstairs. There were four flights, four floors, but the stairway itself was not visible from the cubbyhole where the night nurses sat on duty. Luck was with her.

Down in the main hall the lights were not so bright. She waited at the bottom of the stairway until she was certain of not being observed. She could see the night porter's back—his head was not visible, for he was bent over his desk—but when it straightened she noticed the broad fish face. She shrugged her shoulders. She had not dared all this way to be frightened by a fish. Boldly she walked through the hall. The fish was staring at her.

"Do you want anything, madam?" he said.

He was as stupid as she expected. She shook her head.

"I'm going out. Good night," she said, and she walked straight past him, out of the swing door, and down the steps into the street. She turned swiftly to the left and, seeing a taxi at the further end, called and raised her hand. The taxi slowed and waited. When she came to the door she saw the driver had the squat black face of an ape. The ape grinned. Some instinct warned her not to take the taxi.

"I'm sorry," she said. "I made a mistake."

The grin vanished from the face of the ape. "Make up your mind, lady," he shouted, and let in his clutch and swerved away.

Marda West continued walking down the street. She turned right, and left, and right again, and in the distance she saw the lights of Oxford Street. She began to hurry. The friendly traffic drew her like a magnet, the distant lights, the distant men and women. When she came to Oxford Street she paused, wondering of a sudden where she should go, whom she could ask for refuge. And it came to her once again that there was no one, no one at all; because the couple passing her now, a toad's head on a short black body clutching a panther's arm, could give her no protection, and the policeman standing at the corner was a baboon, the woman talking to him a little prinked-up pig. No one was human, no one was safe, the man a pace or two behind her was like Jim, another vulture. There were vultures on the pavement opposite. Coming towards her, laughing, was a jackal.

She turned and ran. She ran, bumping into them, jackals, hyenas, vultures, dogs. The world was theirs, there was no human left. Seeing her run, they turned and looked at her,

78

they pointed, they screamed and yapped, and gave chase, their footsteps followed her. Down Oxford Street she ran, pursued by them, the night all darkness and shadow, the light no longer with her, alone in an animal world.

"Lie quite still, Mrs. West, just a small prick, I'm not going to hurt you."

She recognised the voice of Mr. Greaves, the surgeon, and dimly she told herself that they had got hold of her again. She was back at the nursing home, and it did not matter now—she might as well be there as anywhere else. At least in the nursing home the animal heads were known.

They had replaced the bandages over her eyes, and for this she was thankful. Such blessed darkness, the evil of the night hidden.

"Now, Mrs. West, I think your troubles are over. No pain and no confusion with these lenses. The world's in colour again."

The bandages were being lightened after all. Layer after layer removed. And suddenly everything was clear, was day, and the face of Mr. Greaves smiled down at her. At his side was a rounded, cheerful nurse.

"Where are your masks?" asked the patient.

"We didn't need masks for this little job," said the surgeon. "We were only taking out the temporary lenses. That's better, isn't it?"

She let her eyes drift round the room. She was back again all right. This was the shape, there was the wardrobe, the dressing table, the vases of flowers. All in natural colour, no longer veiled. But they could not fob her off with stories of a dream. The scarf she had put round her head before slipping away in the night lay on the chair.

"Something happened to me, didn't it?" she said. "I tried to get away."

The nurse glanced at the surgeon. He nodded his head.

"Yes," he said, "you did. And, frankly, I don't blame you. I blame myself. Those lenses I inserted yesterday were pressing upon a tiny nerve, and the pressure threw out your balance. That's all over now."

His smile was reassuring. And the large warm eyes of Nurse Brand—it must surely be Nurse Brand—gazed down at her in sympathy.

"It was very terrible," said the patient. "I can never explain how terrible."

"Don't try," said Mr. Greaves. "I can promise you it won't happen again."

The door opened and the young physician entered. He, too, was smiling. "Patient fully restored?" he asked.

"I think so," said the surgeon. "What about it, Mrs. West?"

Marda West stared gravely at the three of them, Mr. Greaves, the house physician, and Nurse Brand, and she wondered what palpitating wounded tissue could so transform three individuals into prototypes of an animal kingdom, what cell linking muscle to imagination.

"I thought you were dogs," she said. "I thought you were a hunt terrier, Mr. Greaves, and that you were an Aberdeen."

The house physician touched his stethoscope and laughed.

"But I am," he said, "it's my native town. Your judgment was not wholly out, Mrs. West. I congratulate you."

Marda West did not join in the laugh.

"That's all right for you," she said. "Other people were not so pleasant." She turned to Nurse Brand. "I thought you were a cow," she said, "a kind cow. But you had sharp horns."

This time it was Mr. Greaves who took up the laugh. "There you are, Nurse," he said, "just what I've often told you. Time they put you out to grass and to eat the daisies."

Nurse Brand took it in good part. She straightened the patient's pillows and her smile was benign. "We get called some funny things from time to time," she said. "That's all part of our job."

The doctors were moving towards the door, still laughing, and Marda West, sensing the normal atmosphere, the absence of all strain, said, "Who found me, then? What happened? Who brought me back?"

Mr. Greaves glanced back at her from the door. "You didn't get very far, Mrs. West, and a damn good job for you, or you mightn'ta be here now. The porter followed you."

"It's all finished with now," said the house physician, "and the episode lasted five minutes. You were safely in your bed before any harm was done, and I was here. So that was that. The person who really had the full shock was poor Nurse Ansel when she found you weren't in your bed."

Nurse Ansel . . . The revulsion of the night before was not so easily forgotten. "Don't say our little starlet was an animal too?" smiled the house doctor. Marda West felt herself colour. Lies would have to begin. "No," she said quickly, "no, of course not."

"Nurse Ansel is here now," said Nurse Brand. "She was so upset when she went off duty that she wouldn't go back to the hostel to sleep. Would you care to have a word with her?"

Apprehension seized the patient. What had she said to Nurse Ansel in the panic and fever of the night? Before she could answer, the house doctor opened the door and called down the passage.

"Mrs. West wants to say good morning to you," he said. He was smiling all over his face. Mr. Greaves waved his hand and was gone, Nurse Brand went after him, and the house doctor, saluting with his stethoscope and making a mock bow, stepped back against the wall to admit Nurse Ansel. Marda West stared, then tremulously began to smile, and held out her hand.

"I'm sorry," she said, "you must forgive me."

How could she have seen Nurse Ansel as a snake! The hazel eyes, the clear olive skin, the dark hair trim under the frilled cap. And that smile, that slow, understanding smile.

"Forgive you, Mrs. West?" said Nurse Ansel. "What have I to forgive you for? You've been through a terrible ordeal."

Patient and nurse held hands. They smiled at one another. And, oh heaven, thought Marda West, the relief, the thankfulness, the load of doubt and despair that were swept away with the new-found sight and knowledge.

"I still don't understand what happened," she said, clinging to the nurse. "Mr. Greaves tried to explain. Something about a nerve."

Nurse Ansel made a face towards the door. "He doesn't know himself," she whispered, "and he's not going to say either, or he'll find himself in trouble. He fixed those lenses too deep, that's all. Too near a nerve. I wonder it didn't kill you."

She looked down at her patient. She smiled with her eyes. She was so pretty, so gentle. "Don't think about it," she said. "You're going to be happy from now on. Promise me?"

"I promise," said Marda West.

The telephone rang, and Nurse Ansel let go her patient's hand and reached for the receiver. "You know who this is going to be," she said. "Your poor husband." She gave the receiver to Marda West.

"Jim . . . Jim, is that you?"

The loved voice sounding so anxious at the other end. "Are you all right?" he said. "I've been through to Matron twice, she said she would let me know. What the devil has been happening?"

Marda West smiled and handed the receiver to the nurse. "You tell him," she said.

Nurse Ansel held the receiver to her ear. The skin of her hand was olive smooth, the nails gleaming with a soft pink polish.

"Is that you, Mr. West?" she said. "Our patient gave us a fright, didn't she?" She smiled and nodded at the woman in the bed. "Well, you don't have to worry any more. Mr. Greaves changed the lenses. They were pressing on a nerve, and everything is now all right. She can see perfectly. Yes, Mr. Greaves said we could come home tomorrow."

The endearing voice blended to the soft colouring, the hazel eyes. Marda West reached once more for the receiver.

"Jim, I had a hideous night," she said. "I'm just beginning to understand it now. A nerve in the brain . . ."

"So I gather," he said. "How damnable. Thank God they traced it. That fellow Greaves can't have known his job."

"It can't happen again," she said. "Now the proper lenses are in, it can't happen again."

"It had better not," he said, "or I'll sue him. How are you feeling in yourself?"

"Wonderful," she said. "Bewildered but wonderful."

"Good girl," he said. "Don't excite yourself. I'll be along later."

His voice went. Marda West gave the receiver to Nurse Ansel, who replaced it on the stand.

"Did Mr. Greaves really say I could go home tomorrow?" she asked.

"Yes, if you're good." Nurse Ansel smiled and patted her patient's hand. "Are you sure you still want me to come with you?" she asked.

"Why, yes," said Marda West. "Why, it's all arranged."

She sat up in bed, and the sun came streaming through the window, throwing light on the roses, the lilies, the tall-stemmed iris. The hum of traffic outside was close and friendly. She thought of her garden waiting for her at home, and her own bedroom, her own possessions, the day-by-day routine of home to be taken up again with sight restored, the anxiety and fear of the past months put away forever.

"The most precious thing in the world," she said to Nurse Ansel, "is sight. I know now. I know what I might have lost."

Nurse Ansel, hands clasped in front of her, nodded her head in sympathy. "You've got your sight back," she said, "that's the miracle. You won't ever lose it now."

She moved to the door. "I'll slip back to the hostel and get some rest," she said. "Now I know everything is well with you I'll be able to sleep. Is there anything you want before I go?"

"Give me my face cream and my powder," said the patient, "and the lipstick and the brush and comb."

Nurse Ansel fetched the things from the dressing table and put them within reach upon the bed. She brought the hand mirror, too, and the bottle of scent, and with a little smile of intimacy sniffed at the stopper. "Gorgeous," she murmured. "This is what Mr. West gave you, isn't it?"

Already, thought Marda West, Nurse Ansel fitted in. She saw herself putting flowers in the small guest-room, choosing the right books, fitting a portable wireless in case Nurse Ansel should be bored in the evenings.

"I'll be with you at eight o'clock."

The familiar words, said every morning now for so many days and weeks, sounded in her ear like a melody, loved through repetition. At last they were joined to the individual, the person who smiled, the one whose eyes promised friendship and loyalty.

"See you this evening."

The door closed. Nurse Ansel had gone. The routine of the nursing home, broken by the fever of the night before, resumed its usual pattern. Instead of darkness, light. Instead of negation, life.

Marda West took the stopper from the scent bottle and put it behind her ears. The fragrance filtered, becoming part of the warm, bright day. She lifted the hand mirror and looked into it. Nothing changed in the room, the street noises penetrated from outside, and presently the little maid who had seemed a weasel yesterday came in to dust the room. She said, "Good morning," but the patient did not answer. Perhaps she was tired. The maid dusted and went her way.

Then Marda West took up the mirror and looked into it once more. No, she had not been mistaken. The eyes that stared back at her were doe's eyes, wary before sacrifice, and the timid deer's head was meek, already bowed.

Ganymede

THEY CALL IT Little Venice. That was what drew me here in the first place. And you have to admit that there is a curious resemblance—at least for people like myself with imagination. There is a corner, for instance, where the canal takes a bend, fronted by a row of terraced houses, and the water itself has a particular stillness, especially at night, and the glaring discordancies that are noticeable during the day, like the noise of the shunting from Paddington Station, the rattle of the trains, the ugliness, all that seems to vanish. Instead . . . the yellow light from the street lamps might be the mysterious glow you get from those old lanterns set in brackets on the corner of some crumbling *palazzo,* whose shuttered windows look blindly down upon the stagnant sweetness of a side canal.

It is, and I must repeat this, essential to have imagination, and the house agents are clever—they frame their advertisements to catch the eye of waverers like myself. "Two-roomed flat, with balcony, overlooking canal, in the quiet backwater known as Little Venice," and instantly, to the famished mind, the aching heart, comes a vision of another two-roomed flat, another balcony, where, at the hour of waking, the sun makes patterns on a flaking ceiling, water patterns, and the sour Venetian smell comes through the window with the murmur of Venetian voices, the poignant "Ohé!" as the gondola rounds the bend and disappears.

In Little Venice we have traffic too. Not sharp-nosed gondolas, of course, gently rocking from side to side, but barges pass my window carrying bricks and sometimes coal—the coal dust dirties the balcony; and if I shut my eyes, surprised by the sudden hooting, and listen to the rapid chug-chug of the barge's engine, I can fancy myself, with my same shut eyes, waiting for a *vaporetto* at one of the landing stages. I stand on the wooden planking, hemmed in by a chattering crowd, and there is a great surge and throbbing as the vessel goes hard astern. Then the *vaporetto* is along side, and I, with my chattering crowd, have gone on board and we are off again, churning the water into wavelets and our wash, and I am trying to make up my mind whether to go direct to San Marco, and so to the piazza and my usual table, or to leave the *vaporetto* higher up the Grand Canal and thus prolong exquisite anticipation.

The hooting stops. The barge passes. I cannot tell you where they go. There is a junction, close to Paddington, where the canal splits. This does not interest me; all that interests me is the echo of the barge's hooter, the echo of the engine, and—if I am walking—the barge's wake in the canal water, so that, glancing down the bank, I can see a film of oil amongst the bubbles, and then the oil disperses, and the bubbles too, and the water becomes still.

Come with me and I'll show you something. You see the street across the canal, that one there, with the shops, going towards Paddington Station; and you see the bus stop, half-way down, and the board with blue letters on it. Your eyes won't be able to pick it up at this distance, but I can tell you that it reads MARIO, and it's the name of a small restaurant, an Italian restaurant, hardly more than a bar. They know me there. I go there every day. You see, the lad there—he's training to be a waiter—reminds me of Ganymede . . .

2

I am a classical scholar. I suppose that was really the trouble. Had my interests been scientific, or geographical, or even historical—though history has associations enough, heaven knows—then I don't believe anything would have happened. I could have gone to Venice, and enjoyed my holiday, and come away again, without losing myself to such an extent that . . . Well, what occurred there meant a total break with everything that had gone before.

You see, I've given up my job. My superior was exceedingly nice about it all, most sympathetic in fact, but, as he said, they really couldn't afford to take risks, they couldn't permit one of their employees—and, naturally, that applied to me—to continue working for them if he had been connected . . . that was the word he used, not mixed-up but connected . . . with what he called unsavoury practices.

Unsavoury is a hideous word. It's the most hideous word in the dictionary. It conjures up, to my mind, all that is ugly in life, yes, and in death too. The savoury is the joy, the *élan*, the zest that goes with mind and body working in unison; the unsavoury is the malodorous decay of vegetation, the rotted flesh, the mud beneath the water of the canal. And another thing. The word unsavoury suggests a lack of personal cleanliness: unchanged linen, bed sheets hanging to dry, the fluff off combs, torn packets in wastepaper baskets. None of this can I abide. I am fastidious. Above all things I am fastidious. So that when my superior mentioned the word unsavoury I knew I had to go. I knew I could never allow him, or anyone, so to misinterpret my actions that they could consider what had taken place as, to put it bluntly, nauseous. So I resigned. Yes, I resigned. There was nothing else for it. I just cut myself loose. And I saw the advertisement in the house agent's column, and here I am in Little Venice . . .

I took my holiday late that year because my sister, who lives in Devon and with whom I usually spend three weeks in August, suddenly had domestic trouble. A favourite cook left after a lifetime of devotion, and the household was disorganised. My nieces wanted to hire a caravan, my sister wrote me: they were all determined to go camping in Wales, and although I would be welcome she was sure it was not the sort of break that would appeal to me. She was right. The idea of hammering tent pegs into the ground in a tearing wind, or sitting humped four abreast in a tiny space while my sister and her daughters produced luncheon out of a tin, filled me with misgiving. I cursed the cook, whose departure had put an end to the pleasurable series of long, lazy days to which I had been accustomed, when, relaxing in a chaise longue, favourite book in hand, and most delightfully fed, I had idled away my Augusts for many years.

When I protested over a series of trunk calls that I had nowhere to go, my sister said, or rather shouted over the muffled line, "Get abroad for a change. It would do you a world of good to break routine. Try France or Italy." She even suggested a cruise, which frightened me even more than a caravan.

"Very well," I told her coldly, for in a sense I blamed her for the cook's departure and the cessation of my comfort, "I will go to Venice," thinking that, if I was obliged to get myself out of the rut, then I would at least be obvious. I would go, guidebook in hand, to a tourist's paradise. But not in August. Definitely not in August. I would wait until my compatriots and my friends across the Atlantic had been and gone again. Only then would I venture forth, when the heat of the day was done and some measure of peace had returned to the place I believed was beautiful.

I arrived the first week in October. . . . You know how sometimes a holiday, even a brief one, a visit to friends for the weekend, can go wrong from the start. One departs in rain, or misses a connection, or wakes with a chill, and the thread of ill luck laced with irritation continues to mar every hour. Not so with Venice. The very fact that I had left late, that the month was October, that the people I knew were now back again at office desks, made me more aware of my own good fortune.

I reached my destination just before dusk. Nothing had gone amiss. I had slept in my sleeper. I had not been annoyed by my fellow travellers. I had digested my dinner of the preceding night and my luncheon of the day. I had not been obliged to overtip. Venice with all its glories lay before me. I collected my baggage and stepped out of the train, and there was the Grand Canal at my feet, the thronging gondolas, the lapping water, the golden *palazzi*, the dappled sky.

A fat porter from my hotel who had come to meet the train, so like a deceased member of the royal family that I dubbed him Prince Hal on the spot, seized my trappings from me. I was wafted, as so many travellers have been wafted before me, through the years and centuries, from the prosaic rattle of the tourist train to an instant dream world of romance.

To be met by boat; to travel by water; to loll upon cushions, swaying from side to side, even with a Prince Hal shouting the sights in one's ear in appalling English—all this makes for a loosening of restraint. I eased my collar. I threw off my hat. I averted my eyes from my walking stick and my umbrella and my Burberry tucked in the holdall—I invariably travel with a holdall. Lighting a cigarette, I was aware, surely for the first time in my life, of a sense of abandon, of belonging—certainly not to the present, nor to the future, nor even to the past, but to a period in time that was changeless and was Venetian time, that was outside the rest of Europe and even the world, and existed, magically, for myself alone.

Mark you, I realised there must be others. In that dark gondola floating by, at that wide window, even on the bridge from which, as we passed underneath, a figure peering down suddenly withdrew, I knew there must be others who, like myself, found themselves suddenly enchanted, not by the Venice they perceived, but by the Venice they felt within themselves. That uncelestial city from which no traveller returns . . .

What am I saying, though? I anticipate events and thoughts which no doubt I could not have had during that first half hour from station to hotel. It is only now, in retrospect, that I realise there must be others like myself who, with the first glimpse, become enchanted, damned. Oh yes indeed, we know all about the rest, the obvious rest. The people clicking cameras, the hubbub of nationalities, the students, the school-mistresses, the artists. And the Venetians themselves—the Prince Hal porter, for instance, and the fellow who steered the gondola and was thinking of his *pasta* supper and his wife and children and the lire I would give him, and all those homeward bounders in the *vaporetti* no different from other homeward bounders at home who go by bus or tube—those people are part of the Venice of today, just as their forebears were part of the Venice that is past: dukes, and merchants, and lovers, and ravished maidens. No, we have a different key. A different secret. It is what I said before, the Venice within ourselves.

"To ze right," shouted Prince Hal, "famous *palazzo* now belonging to American gentleman." Foolish and useless as his information was, it did at least suggest that some tycoon, weary of making money, had created an illusion, and, stepping into the speedboat I saw tethered at the steps, believed himself immortal.

That was what I felt, you see. I had the sense of immortality, the knowledge, instantaneous as I left the station and heard the lapping water, that time contained me. I was not imprisoned. I was held. And then we left the Grand Canal and were in the backwaters, and Prince Hal fell silent, and there was no sound except the stroke of the long oar as we were propelled along the narrow stream. I remember thinking —curious, wasn't it?—of the waters that usher us into this life at birth, of the waters that contain us in the womb. Somehow they must have the same stillness, the same force.

We came out of darkness into light, we shot under a bridge —it was only later that I realised it was the Bridge of Sighs —and there was the lagoon in front of us, and a hundred stabbing, flickering lights, and a great jostle of figures, of people walking up and down. I had to cope at once with my unaccustomed lire, with the gondolier, with Prince Hal before being swallowed up in the hotel and the paraphernalia of desk-clerk, keys, and page showing me to my room. Mine was one of the smaller hotels, basking in the proximity of the more famous, yet comfortable enough at first glance, though a little stuffy perhaps—odd how they keep a room tight closed before a guest arrives. As I threw open the shutters the warm damp air from the lagoon infiltrated slowly, and the laughter and footsteps of the promenaders floated upwards while I unpacked. I changed and descended, but one glance at the half-empty dining-room decided me against dining there, although my pension terms permitted it, and I went out and joined the promenaders by the lagoon.

The sensation I had was strange and never experienced before. Not the usual anticipation of the traveller on the first evening of his holiday, who looks forward to his dinner and the pleasure of new surroundings. After all, in spite of my sister's mockery I was no John Bull. I used to know Paris quite well. I had been to Germany. I had toured the Scandinavian countries before the war. I had spent an Easter in Rome. It was only that I had been idle of late years, without initiative, and to take my annual holiday in Devon saved planning and, incidentally, my purse.

No, the sensation I had now, as inevitably I walked past the Doge's palace—which I recognised from postcards—and into the Piazza San Marco, was one of . . . I hardly know how to describe it . . . recognition. I don't mean the feeling "I have been here before." I don't mean the romantic dream "This is reincarnation." Neither of those things. It was as though, intuitively, I had become, at last, myself. I had arrived. This particular moment in time had been waiting for me and I for it. Curiously it was like the first flavour of intoxication, but more heightened, more acute. And deeply secret. It is important to remember that; deeply secret. This sensation was somehow palpable, invading the whole of me, the palms of my hands, my scalp. My throat was dry. Physically I felt I was infused with electricity, that I had become some sort of powerhouse radiating, into the damp atmosphere of this Venice I had never seen, currents which, becoming charged with other currents, returned to me again. The excitement was intense, almost unbearable. And, to look at me, nobody would guess anything. I was just another Englishman at the fag end of the tourist season, strolling, walking stick in hand, on his first night in Venice.

Although it was nearly nine o'clock the crowd was still dense on the piazza. I wondered how many amongst them felt the same current, the same intuition. Nevertheless, I must dine, and to escape the crowd I chose a turning to the right, halfway down the piazza, which brought me to one of the side canals, very dark and still, and as luck had it to a restaurant nearby. I dined well, with excellent wine, at far less expense than I had feared, and lighting a cigar—one of my small extravagances, a really good cigar—I strolled back again to the piazza, that same electric current with me still.

The crowd had thinned and, instead of strolling, had concentrated into two marked groups before two separate orchestras. These orchestras—rivals, so it appeared—had their stance in front of a couple of cafés, also rivals. Separated by perhaps some seventy yards, they played against one another with gay indifference. Tables and chairs were set out about the orchestras, and the café clientele drank and gossiped and listened to the music in a semicircle, backs turned to the rival orchestra whose beat and rhythm made discord to the ear. I happened to be closest to the orchestra in mid-piazza. I found an empty table and sat down. A burst of applause from the second audience nearer the church gave warning that the rival orchestra had come to a breathing space in its repertoire. This was the signal for ours to play louder still. It was Puccini, of course. As the evening progressed there came the songs of the day, the hit tunes of the moment, but as I sat down and looked about for a waiter to bring me a liqueur, and accept—at a price—the rose offered to me by an ancient crone in a black shawl, the orchestra was playing *Madame Butterfly*. I felt relaxed, amused. And then I saw him.

I told you I was a classical scholar. Therefore you will understand—you should understand—that what happened in that second was transformation. The electricity that had charged me all evening focussed on a single point in my brain to the exclusion of all else; the rest of me was jelly. I could sense the man at my table raising his hand and summoning the lad in the white coat carrying a tray, but I myself was above him, did not exist in his time; and this self who was nonexistent knew with every nerve fibre, every brain cell, every blood corpuscle that he was indeed Zeus, the giver of life and death, the immortal one, the lover; and that the boy who came towards him was his own beloved, his cupbearer, his slave, his Ganymede. I was poised, not in the body, not in the world, and I summoned him. He knew me and he came.

Then it was all over. The tears were pouring down my face and I heard a voice saying, "Is anything wrong, signore?"

The lad was watching me with some concern. Nobody had noticed anything: they were all intent upon their drinks, or

their friends, or the orchestra, and I fumbled for my handkerchief and blew my nose and said, "Bring me a curaçao."

3

I remember sitting staring at the table in front of me, still
smoking my cigar, not daring to raise my head, and I heard
his quick footstep beside me. He put down the drink and
went away again, and the question uppermost in my mind
was, "Does he know?"

You see, the flash of recognition was so swift, so overwhelming, that it was like being jerked into consciousness
from a lifetime of sleep. The absolute certainty of who I was
and where I was, and the bond between us, possessed me just
as Paul was possessed on the Damascus road. Thank heaven I
was not blinded by my visions; no one would have to lead me
back to the hotel. No, I was just another tourist come to
Venice, listening to a little string band and smoking a cigar.

I let five minutes or so go by, and then I lifted my head
and casually, very casually, looked over the heads of the
people towards the café. He was standing alone, his hands
behind his back, watching the orchestra. He seemed to me
about fifteen, not more, and he was small for his age, and
slight, and his white mess jacket and dark trousers reminded
me of an officer's kit in Her Majesty's Mediterranean fleet.
He did not look Italian. His forehead was high, and he wore
his light brown hair *en brosse*. His eyes were not brown but
blue, and his complexion was fair, not olive. There were two
other waiters hovering between the tables, one of them about
eighteen or nineteen and both of them obvious Italians, the
eighteen-year-old swarthy and fat. You could tell at a glance
they were born to be waiters, they would never rise to anything else, but my boy, my Ganymede, the very set of his
proud head, the expression on his face, the air of grave tolerance with which he regarded the orchestra, showed him to
be a different stamp . . . my stamp, the stamp of the im-
mortals.

I watched him covertly, the small clasped hands, the small
foot in its black shoe tapping time to the music. If he recognised me, I said to myself, he will look at me. This evasion,

this play of watching the orchestra, is only a pretext, because what we have felt together, in that moment out of time, has been too strong for both of us. Suddenly—and with an exquisite feeling of delight and apprehension in one—I knew what was going to happen. He made a decision. He looked away from the orchestra and directly across to my table and, still grave, still thoughtful, walked up to me and said:

"Do you wish for anything more, signore?"

It was foolish of me, but, do you know, I could not speak. I could only shake my head. Then he took away the ash tray and put a clean one in its place. The very gesture was somehow thoughtful, loving, and my throat tightened and I was reminded of a biblical expression surely used by Joseph about Benjamin. I forget the context, but it says somewhere in the Old Testament, "for his bowels did yearn upon his brother." I felt that, exactly.

I went on sitting there until midnight, when the great bells sounded and filled the air, and the orchestras—both of them —put away their instruments, and the straggling listeners melted away. I looked down at the scrap of paper, the bill, which he had brought me and put beside the ash tray, and, as I glanced at the scribbled figures and paid, it seemed to me that the smile he gave me, and the little bow of deference, were the answer I had been seeking. He knew. Ganymede knew.

I went off alone across the now deserted piazza and passed under the colonnade by the Doge's palace where an old hunched man was sleeping. The lights were no longer bright but dim, the damp wind troubled the water and rocked the rows of gondolas on the black lagoon, but my boy's spirit was with me, and his shadow too.

I awoke to brilliance. The long day to be filled, and what a day! So much to experience and to see, from the obvious interiors of San Marco and the Doge's palace to a visit to the Accademia and an excursion up and down the Grand Canal. I did everything the tourist does except feed the pigeons; too fat, too sleek as they were, I picked my way amongst them with distaste. I had an ice at Florian's. I bought picture postcards for my nieces. I leant over the Rialto bridge. And the happy day, of which I enjoyed every moment, was only a preliminary to the evening. Deliberately I had avoided the café on the righthand side of the piazza. I had walked only on the opposite side.

I remember I got back to my hotel about six, and lay down on my bed and read Chaucer for an hour—the *Canterbury Tales* in a Penguin edition. Then I had a bath and changed. I went to the same restaurant to dine where I had dined the night before. The dinner was equally good and equally cheap. I lit my cigar and strolled to the piazza. The orchestras were playing. I chose a table on the fringe of the crowd, and as I put down my cigar for a moment I noticed that my hand was trembling. The excitement, the suspense were unbearable. It seemed to me impossible that the family group at the table beside me should not perceive my emotion. Luckily I had an evening paper with me. I opened it and pretended to read. Someone flicked a cloth on my table, and it was the swarthy waiter, the ungainly youth, asking for my order. I motioned him away. "Presently," I said, and went on reading, or rather going through the motions of reading. The orchestra began to play a little jigging tune, and looking up, I saw that Ganymede was watching me. He was standing by the orchestra, his hands clasped behind his back. I did nothing, I did not even move my head, but in a moment he was at my side.

"A curaçao, signore?" he said.

Tonight recognition went beyond the first instantaneous flash. I could feel the chair of gold, and the clouds above my head, and the boy was kneeling beside me, and the cup he offered me was gold as well. His humility was not the shamed humility of a slave but the reverence of a loved one to his master, to his god. Then the flash was gone and, thank heaven, I was in control of emotion. I nodded my head and said, "Yes, please," and ordered half a bottle of Evian water to be brought to me with the curaçao.

As I watched him slip past the tables towards the café, I saw a large man in a white raincoat and a broad-brimmed trilby hat step out from the shadows beneath the colonnade and tap him on the shoulder. My boy raised his head and smiled. In that brief moment I experienced evil. A premonition of disaster. The man, like a great white slug, smiled back at Ganymede and gave him an order. The boy smiled again and disappeared.

The orchestra swung out of the jigging tune and ceased, with a flourish, to a burst of applause. The violinist wiped the perspiration from his forehead and laughed at the pianist. The swarthy waiter brought them drinks. The old woman in the shawl came to my table as she had done the night before and offered me a rose. This time I was wiser, I refused. And I became aware that the man in the white mackintosh was watching me from behind a column . . .

Do you know anything of Greek mythology? I only mention the fact because Poseidon, the brother of Zeus, was also his rival. He was especially associated with the horse; and a horse—unless it is winged—symbolises corruption. The man in the white mackintosh was corrupt. I knew it instinctively. Intuition bade me beware. When Ganymede returned with my curaçao and my Evian I did not even look up, but continued reading the newspaper. The orchestra, refreshed, took the air once more. The strains of "Softly Awakes My Heart" strove for supremacy with the "Colonel Bogey" march from its rival near the church. The woman with the shawl, her roses all unsold, came back to my table in desperation. Brutally I shook my head, and in doing so saw that the man in the white mackintosh and the trilby hat had moved from the column and was now standing beside my chair.

The aroma of evil is a deadly thing. It penetrates, and stifles, and somehow challenges at the same time. I was afraid. Most definitely I was afraid, but determined to give battle to prove that I was the stronger. I relaxed in my chair, and, inhaling the last breath of my cigar before laying it in the ash tray, puffed the smoke full in his face. An extraordinary thing happened. I don't know whether the final inhalation turned me giddy, but for an instant my head swam, and the smoke made rings before my eyes, and I saw his hideous, grinning face subside into what seemed to be a trough of sea and foam. I could even feel the spray. When I had recovered from the attack of coughing brought on by my cigar the air cleared: the man in the white mackintosh had disappeared, and I found that I had knocked over and smashed my half bottle of Evian water. It was Ganymede himself who picked up the broken pieces, it was Ganymede who wiped the table with his cloth, it was Ganymede who suggested, without my ordering it, a fresh half bottle.

"The signore has not cut himself?" he said.

"No."

"The signore will have another curaçao. There may be some pieces of glass in this. There will be no extra charge."

He spoke with authority, with quiet confidence, this child of fifteen who had the grace of a prince, and then, with exquisite hauteur, he turned to the swarthy youth who was his companion-at-arms and handed him my debris with a flow of Italian. Then he brought me the second half bottle of Evian, and the second glass of curaçao.

"*Un sedativo*," he said, and smiled.

He was not cocky. He was not familiar. He knew, because he had always known, that my hands were trembling and my heart was beating, and I wanted to be calm, to be still.

"*Piove*," he said, lifting his face and holding up his hand, and indeed it was beginning to rain, suddenly, for no reason, out of a star-studded sky. But a black straggling cloud like a gigantic hand blotted out the stars as he spoke, and down came the rain on to the piazza. Umbrellas went up like mushrooms, and those without them spread across the piazza and away home like beetles to their lair.

Desolation was instant. The tables were bare, the chairs upturned against them. The piano was covered with a tarpaulin, the music stands were folded, the lights inside the café became dim. Everyone melted away. It was as though there had never been an orchestra, never been an audience of clapping people. The whole thing was a dream.

I was not dreaming, though. I had come out, like a fool, without my umbrella. I waited under the colonnade beside the now deserted café, with the rain from a nearby spout spattering the ground in front of me. I could hardly believe it possible that five minutes ago all had been gay and crowded, and now this wintered gloom.

I turned up the collar of my coat, trying to make up my mind whether to venture forth across the streaming piazza, and then I heard a quick brisk footstep leave the café and trot away under the colonnade. It was Ganymede, his small upright figure still clad in his white mess jacket, his large umbrella held above him like a pennant.

My way was to the left, towards the church. He was walking to the right. In a moment or two he might turn away altogether and disappear. It was a moment of decision. You will say I made the wrong one. I turned to the right, I followed him.

It was a strange and mad pursuit. I had never done such a thing in my life before. I could not help myself. He trotted ahead, his footsteps loud and clear, along the tortuous narrow passages winding in and out beside silent, dark canals, and there was no other sound at all except his footsteps and the rain, and he never once looked back to see who followed him. Once or twice I slipped: he must have heard me. On, on he went, over bridges, into the shadows, his umbrella bobbing up and down above his head, and a glimpse of his white mess jacket showing now and then as he lifted the umbrella higher. And the rain still sluiced from the roofs of the silent houses, down to the cobbles and the pavings below, down to the Styx-like canals.

Then I missed him. He had turned a corner sharply. I began to run. I ran into a narrow passage, where the tall houses almost touched their neighbours opposite, and he was standing in front of a great door with an iron grille before it, pulling a bell. The door opened, he folded his umbrella and went inside. The door clanged behind him. He must have heard me running, he must have seen me brought up short when I turned the corner into the passage. I stood for a moment staring at the iron grille above the heavy oak door. I looked at my watch: it wanted five minutes to midnight. The folly of my pursuit struck me in all its force. Nothing had been achieved but to get very wet, to have caught a chill in all probability, and to have lost my way.

I turned to go, and a figure stepped out of a doorway opposite the house with the grille and came towards me. It was the man in the white mackintosh and the broad-brimmed trilby hat.

He said, with a bastard American accent, "Are you looking for somebody, signore?"

4

I ask you, what would you have done in my position? I was a stranger in Venice, a tourist. The alleyway was deserted. One had read stories of Italians and vendettas, of knives, of stabs in the back. One false move and this might happen to me.

"I was taking a walk," I replied, "but I seem to have missed my way."

He was standing very close to me, much too close for comfort. "Ah! you missa your way," he repeated, the American accent blending with music-hall Italian. "In Venice, that happens all the time. I see you home."

The lantern light above his head turned his face yellow under the broad-brimmed hat. He smiled as he spoke, showing teeth full of gold stoppings. The smile was sinister.

"Thank you," I said, "but I can manage very well."

I turned and began to walk back to the corner. He fell into step beside me.

"No trouble," he said, "no trouble at all-a."

He kept his hands in the pockets of his white mackintosh, and his shoulder brushed mine as we walked side by side. We moved out of the alleyway into the narrow street by the side canal. It was dark. Drips of water fell from the roof-gutters into the canal.

"You like Venice?" he asked.

"Very much," I answered, and then—foolishly, perhaps—"It's my first visit."

I felt like a prisoner under escort. The tramp-tramp of our feet echoed in hollow fashion. And there was no one to hear us. The whole of Venice slept. He gave a grunt of satisfaction.

"Venice very dear," he said. "In the hotels, they robba you always. Where are you staying?"

I hesitated. I did not want to give my address, but if he insisted on coming with me what could I do?

"The Hotel Byron," I said.

He laughed in scorn. "They putta twenty per cent on the bill," he said. "You ask for a cup of coffee, twenty per cent. It's always the same. They robba the tourist."

"My terms are reasonable," I said. "I can't complain."

"Whatta you pay them?" he asked.

The cheek of the man staggered me. But the path by the canal was very narrow, and his shoulder still touched mine as we walked. I told him the price of my room at the hotel and the pension terms. He whistled.

"They take the skin off your back," he said. "Tomorrow you senda them to hell. I find you little apartment. Very cheap, very O.K."

I did not want a little apartment. All I wanted was to be rid of the man, and back in the comparative civilisation of the Piazza San Marco. "Thank you," I replied, "but I'm quite comfortable at the Hotel Byron."

He edged even closer to me, and I found myself nearer still to the black waters of the canal. "In little apartment," he said, "you do as you like-a. You see your friends. Nobody worry you."

"I'm not worried at the Hotel Byron," I said.

I began to walk faster, but he kept pace with me, and suddenly he withdrew his right hand from his pocket and my heart missed a beat. I thought he had a knife. But it was to offer me a tattered packet of Lucky Strikes. I shook my head. He lit one for himself.

"I finda you little apartment," he persisted.

We passed over a bridge and plunged into yet another street, silent, ill-lit, and as we walked he told me the names of people for whom he had found apartments.

"You English?" he asked. "I thought-a so. I found apartment last year for Sir Johnson. You know Sir Johnson? Very nice man, very discreet. I find apartment too for film-star Bertie Poole. You know Bertie Poole? I save him five hundred thousand lire."

I had never heard of Sir Johnson or Bertie Poole. I became more and more angry, but there was nothing I could do. We crossed a second bridge, and to my relief I recognised the corner near the restaurant where I had dined. The canal here formed, as it were, a bay, and there were gondolas moored side by side.

"Don't bother to come any further," I said. "I know my way now."

The unbelievable happened. We had turned the corner together, marching as one man, and then, because the narrow path could not hold us two abreast, he dropped a pace behind, and, in doing so, slipped. I heard him gasp, and a second later he was in the canal, the white mackintosh splaying about him like a canopy, the splash of his great body rocking the gondolas. I stared for a moment, too surprised to take action. And then I did a terrible thing. I ran away. I ran into the passage that I knew would lead me finally into the Piazza San Marco, and, when I came to it, walked across it briskly, and so past the Doge's palace and back to my hotel. I encountered no one. As I said before, the whole of Venice slept. At the Hotel Byron, Prince Hal was yawning behind the desk. Rubbing the sleep from his eyes, he took me up in the lift. As soon as I entered my room I went straight to the washbasin and took the small bottle of medicinal brandy with which I invariably travelled. I swallowed the contents at a single draught.

5

I slept badly and had appalling dreams, which did not surprise me. I saw Poseidon, the god Poseidon, rising from an angry sea, and he shook his trident at me, and the sea became the canal, and then Poseidon himself mounted a bronze horse, the bronze horse of Colleoni, and rode away, with the limp body of Ganymede on the saddle before him.

I swallowed a couple of aspirin with my coffee and rose late. I don't know what I expected to see when I went out. Knots of people reading newspapers, or the police—some intimation of what had happened. Instead, it was a bright October day, and the life of Venice continued.

I took a steamer to the Lido and lunched there. I deliberately idled away the day at the Lido in case of trouble. What was worrying me was that, should the man in the white mackintosh have survived his ducking of the night before and bear malice towards me for leaving him to his plight, he might have informed the police—perhaps hinting, even, that I had pushed him in. And the police would be waiting for me at the hotel when I returned.

I gave myself until six o'clock. Then, a little before sunset, I took the steamer back. No cloudbursts tonight. The sky was a gentle gold, and Venice basked in the soft light, painfully beautiful.

I entered the hotel and asked for my key. It was handed to me by the clerk with a cheerful, *"Buona sera, signore,"* together with a letter from my sister. Nobody had enquired for me. I went upstairs and changed, came down again, and had dinner in the hotel restaurant. The dinner was not in the same class as the dinner in the restaurant the two preceding nights, but I did not mind. I was not very hungry. Nor did I fancy my usual cigar. I lit a cigarette instead. I stood for about ten minutes outside the hotel, smoking and watching the lights on the lagoon. The night was balmy. I wondered if the orchestra was playing in the piazza, and if Ganymede was serving drinks. The thought of him worried me. If he was in any way connected with the man in the white mackintosh, he might suffer for what had happened. The dream could have been a warning—I was a great believer in dreams. Poseidon carrying Ganymede astride his horse . . . I began to walk towards the Piazza San Marco. I told myself I would just stand near the church and see if both orchestras were playing.

When I came to the piazza I saw that all was as usual. There were the same crowds, the same rival orchestras, the same repertoires played against each other. I moved slowly across the piazza towards the second orchestra, and I put on my dark glasses as a form of protection. Yes, there he was. There was Ganymede. I spotted his brush of light hair and his white mess jacket almost immediately. He and his swarthy companion were very busy. The crowd round the orchestra was thicker than usual because of the warm night. I scanned the audience and the shadows behind the colonnade. There was no sign of the man in the white mackintosh. The wisest thing, I knew, was to leave, return to the hotel, go to bed, and read my Chaucer. Yet I lingered. The old woman selling roses was making her rounds. I drew nearer. The orchestra was playing the theme-song from a Chaplin film. Was it *Limelight?* I did not remember. But the song was haunting, and the violinist drew every ounce of sentiment from it. I decided to wait until the end of the song and then return to the hotel.

Someone snapped his fingers to give an order, and Ganymede turned to take it. As he did so he looked over the heads of the seated crowd straight at me. I was wearing the dark glasses and I had a hat. Yet he knew me. He gave me a radiant smile of welcome, and ignoring the client's order darted forward, seized a chair, and placed it beside an empty table.

"No rain tonight," he said. "Tonight everybody is happy. A curaçao, signore?"

How could I refuse him, the smile, the almost pleading gesture? If anything had been wrong, if he had been anxious about the man in the white mackintosh, surely, I thought, there would have been some sort of hint, some warning glance? I sat down. A moment later he was back again with my curaçao.

Perhaps it was more potent than the night before, or perhaps, in my disturbed mood, it had a greater effect on me. Whatever it was, the curaçao went to my head. My nervousness vanished. The man in the white mackintosh and his evil influence no longer troubled me. Perhaps he was dead. What of it? Ganymede remained unharmed. And to show his favour he stood only a few feet away from my table, hands clasped behind his back, on the alert to serve my instant whim.

"Do you never get tired?" I said boldly.

He whisked away my ash tray and flicked the table.

"No, signore," he answered, "for my work is a pleasure. This sort of work." He gave me a little bow.

"Don't you go to school?"

"School?" He jerked his thumb in a gesture of dismissal. "*Finito,* school. I am a man. I work for my living. To keep my mother and my sister."

I was touched. He believed himself a man. And I had an

instant vision of his mother, a sad, complaining woman, and of a little sister. They all of them lived behind the door with the grille.

"Do they pay you well here in the café?" I asked.

He shrugged his shoulders.

"In the season, not so bad," he said, "but the season is over. Two more weeks and it is finished. Everyone goes away."

"What will you do?"

He shrugged again.

"I have to find work somewhere else," he said. "Perhaps I go to Rome. I have friends in Rome."

I did not like to think of him in Rome—such a child in such a city. Besides, who were his friends?

"What would you like to do?" I enquired.

He bit his lips. For a moment he looked sad. "I should like to go to London," he said. "I should like to go to one of your big hotels. But that is impossible. I have no friends in London."

I thought of my own immediate superior, who happened to be a director, amongst his other activities, of the Majestic in Park Lane.

"It might be arranged," I said, "with a little pulling of strings."

He smiled and made an amusing gesture of manipulating with both hands. "It is easy, if you know how," he said, "but if you don't know how, better to . . ." and he smacked his lips and raised his eyes. The expression implied defeat. Forget about it.

"We'll see," I said. "I have influential friends."

He made no attempt to seize advantage.

"You are kind to me, signore," he murmured, "very kind indeed."

At that moment the orchestra stopped, and as the crowd applauded he clapped with them, his condescension perfect.

"Bravo . . . bravo . . ." he said. I almost wept.

When later I paid my bill, I hesitated to overtip in case he was offended. Besides, I did not want him to look upon me merely as a tourist client. Our relationship went deeper.

"For your mother and your little sister," I said, pressing five hundred lire into his hand, seeing, in my mind's eye, the three of them tiptoeing to Mass in St. Mark's, the mother voluminous, Ganymede in his Sunday black, and the little sister veiled for her first Communion.

"Thank you, thank you, signore," he said, and added, "*A domani.*"

"*A domani*," I echoed, touched that he should already be looking forward to our next encounter. As for the wretch in the white mackintosh, he was already feeding the fishes in the Adriatic.

The following morning I had a shock. The reception clerk telephoned my room to ask whether I would mind leaving it vacant by midday. I did not know what he meant. The room had been booked for a fortnight. He was full of excuses. There had been a misunderstanding, he said: this particular room had been engaged for many weeks, he thought the travel agent had explained the fact. Very well, I said, huffed, put me somewhere else. He expressed a thousand regrets. The hotel was full. But he could recommend a very comfortable little flat that the management used from time to time as an annex. And there would be no extra charge. My breakfast would be brought to me just the same, and I should even have a private bath.

"It's very upsetting," I fumed. "I have all my things unpacked."

Again a thousand regrets. The porter would move my luggage. He would even pack for me. I need not stir hand or foot myself. Finally I consented to the new arrangement, though I certainly would not permit anyone but myself to touch my things. Then I went downstairs and found Prince Hal, with a barrow for my luggage, awaiting me below. I was in a bad humour, with my arrangements upset, and quite determined to refuse the room in the annex on sight, and demand another.

We skirted the lagoon, Prince Hal trundling the baggage, and I felt something of a fool stalking along behind him, bumping into the promenaders, and cursed the travel agent who had presumably made the muddle about the room in the hotel.

When we arrived at our destination, though, I was obliged to change my tune. Prince Hal entered a house with a fine, even beautiful façade, whose spacious staircase was spotlessly clean. There was no lift, and he carried my luggage on his shoulder. He stopped on the first floor, took out a key, fitted it to the left-hand door, and threw it open. "Please to enter," he said.

It was a charming apartment, and must have been at some time or other the salon of a private *palazzo*. The windows, instead of being closed and shuttered like the windows in the Hotel Byron, were wide open to a balcony, and to my delight the balcony looked out upon the Grand Canal. I could not be better placed.

"Are you sure," I enquired, "that this room is the same price as the room in the hotel?"

Prince Hal stared. He obviously did not understand my question.

"Please?" he said.

I left it. After all, the reception clerk had said so. I looked about me. A bathroom led out of the apartment. There were even flowers by the bed.

"What do I do about breakfast?" I asked.

Prince Hal pointed to the telephone. "You ring," he said, "they answer below. They bring it." Then he handed over the key.

When he had gone I went once more to the balcony and looked out. The canal was full of bustle and life. All Venice was below me. The speedboats and the *vaporetti* did not worry me, the changing animated scene was one of which I felt I could never grow tired. Here I could sit and laze all day if I so desired. My luck was incredible. Instead of cursing the travel agent I blessed him. I unpacked my things for the second time in three days, but this time, instead of being a number on the third floor of the Hotel Byron, I was lord and master of my own minute *palazzo*. I felt like a king. The great Campanile bell sounded midday, and, since I had breakfasted early, I was in the mood for more coffee. I lifted the telephone. I heard a buzz in answer, and then a click. A voice said, "Yes?"

"*Café complet*," I ordered.

"At once," replied the voice. Was it . . . could it be
. . . that too-familiar American accent?

I went into the bathroom to wash my hands, and when I
returned there was a knock at the door. I called out, "*Avanti!*"
The man who bore in the tray was not wearing a white mackintosh or a trilby hat. The light-grey suit was carefully
pressed. The terrible suède shoes were yellow. And he had
a piece of sticking plaster on his forehead. "What did I tell
you?" he said. "I arrange-a everything. Very nice. Very O.K."

6

He put the tray down on the table near the window and
waved his hand at the balcony and the sounds from the
Grand Canal.

"Sir Johnson spend-a the day here," he said. "All day he lie
on the balcony with his, how-do-you-call-them?"

He raised his hands in the gesture of field glasses, and
swerved from side to side. His gold-filled teeth showed as he
smiled.

"Mr. Bertie Poole, different altogether," he added. "A
speedboat to the Lido, and back here after dark. Little din-
ners, little parties, with his friends. He made-a de whoopee."

The knowing wink filled me with disgust. Officiously he began to pour out the coffee for me. It was too much.

"Look here," I said, "I don't know your name and I don't
know how this business has come about. If you have come to
an understanding with the clerk at the Hotel Byron it's nothing
to do with me."

He opened his eyes in astonishment.

"You don't like-a the apartment?" he said.

"Of course I like it," I replied. "That's not the point. The
point is, I made my own arrangements and now . . ."

But he cut me short. "Don't worry, don't worry," he said,
waving his hand. "You pay here less than you pay at Hotel
Byron. I see to it. And nobody come to disturb you. Nobody
at all-a." He winked again, and moved heavily towards the
door. "If there is anything you want," he said, "just ring-a
the bell. O.K.?"

He left the room. I poured the coffee into the Grand Canal. For all I knew it might be poisoned. Then I sat down to think out the situation.

I had been in Venice for three days. I had booked, as I thought, my room at the Hotel Byron for a fortnight. I had, therefore, ten days left of my holiday. Was I prepared to spend the ten days in this delicious apartment, at what I had been assured was no extra expense, under the aegis of this tout? He apparently bore no malice towards me for his tumble in the canal. The sticking plaster bore evidence to his fall, but the subject had not been mentioned. He looked less sinister in his light-grey suit than he had done in the white mackintosh. Perhaps I had let my imagination run away with me. And yet. . . . I dipped my finger in the coffeepot and raised it to my lips. It tasted all right. I glanced at the telephone. If I lifted it his odious American voice would answer. I had better telephone the Hotel Byron from outside, or, better still, make my enquiry in person.

I locked the cupboards and the chest of drawers, and my suitcases too, and pocketed the keys. I left the room, locking the door of the apartment. No doubt he would have a pass-key, but it could not be helped. Then I went downstairs, walking stick at the ready in case of attack, and so out into the street. No sign of the enemy anywhere below. The building appeared uninhabited. I went back to the Hotel Byron and tried to get some information from the staff, but my luck was out. The clerk at the reception desk was not the one who had telephoned me in the morning about the change of room. Some new arrival was waiting to check in, and the clerk was impatient. Because I was no longer under the roof I did not interest him. "Yes, yes," he said, "it's all right, when we are full here we make arrangements to board our guests outside. We have had no complaints." The couple waiting to check in sighed heavily. I was holding them up.

Frustrated, I left the desk and walked away. There seemed nothing to be done. The sun was shining, a light breeze rippled the water of the lagoon, and the promenaders, without coats and hats, strolled peacefully, taking the air. I supposed I could do the same. After all, nothing very grave had happened. I was the temporary owner of an apartment over-looking the Grand Canal, a matter to strike envy into the breasts of all these tourists. Why should I worry? I boarded a *vaporetto*, and went and sat in the church by the Accademia to gaze at the Bellini Madonna and Child. It calmed my nerves.

I spent the afternoon sleeping and reading upon my balcony without benefit of field glasses—unlike Sir Johnson, whoever he might be—and nobody came near me. As far as I could see none of my things had been touched. The little trap I had set—a hundred-lire note between two ties—was still in place. I breathed a sigh of relief. Possibly, after all, things would work out well.

Before going out to dinner I wrote a letter to my superior. He was always inclined to patronise me, and it was something of a coup to tell him that I had found myself a delightful apartment with quite the finest view in Venice. "By the way," I said, "what chance is there at the Majestic for young waiters to train? There is a very good lad here, of excellent appearance and manners, just the right type for the Majestic. Can I give him any hope? He is the sole support of a widowed mother and orphan sister."

I dined in my favourite restaurant—I was *persona grata* by now, in spite of the lapse of the night before—and strolled on to the Piazza San Marco without a qualm. The tout might appear, white mackintosh and all, but I had dined too well to care. The orchestra was surrounded by sailors from a de-stroyer which had anchored in the lagoon. There was much changing of hats, and laughter, and demanding of popular tunes, and the audience entered into the fun, clapping the sailor who pretended to seize the fiddle. I laughed uproari-ously with the rest of them, Ganymede by my side. How right my sister had been to encourage me to go to Venice in-stead of to Devon. How I blessed the vagaries of her cook!

It was in mid-laughter that I was carried out of myself. There were clouds above my head and below me, and my right arm, outstretched on the empty chair beside me, was a wing. Both arms were wings, and I was soaring above the earth. Yet I had claws too. The claws held the lifeless body of the boy. His eyes were closed. The wind currents bore me upward through the clouds, and my triumph was such that the still body of the boy only seemed to me more precious and more mine. Then I heard the sound of the orchestra again, and with it laughter and clapping, and I saw that I had put out my hand and gripped Ganymede's, and he had not withdrawn it but had let it remain there.

I was filled with embarrassment. I snatched mine away and joined in the applause. Then I picked up my glass of curaçao.

"Fortune," I said, raising my glass to the crowd, to the orchestra, to the world at large. It would not do to single out the child.

Ganymede smiled. "The signore enjoys himself," he said.

Just that and no more. But I felt he shared my mood. An impulse made me lean forward. "I have written to a friend in London," I said, "a friend who is a director of a big hotel. I hope to have an answer from him in a few days' time."

He showed no surprise. He bowed, then clasped his hands behind his back and looked over the heads of the crowd.

"It is very kind of the signore," he said.

I wondered how much faith he had in me, and whether it exceeded that which he put in his friends in Rome.

"You will have to give me your name and all particulars," I told him, "and I suppose a reference from the proprietor here."

A brief nod of the head showed that he understood. "I have my papers," he said proudly, and I could not help smiling, thinking of the dossier that probably contained a report from his school and a recommendation to whoever might employ him. "My uncle too will speak for me," he added. "The signore has only to ask my uncle."

"And who is your uncle?" I enquired.

He turned to me, looking for the first time a little modest, a little shy. "The signore has moved to his apartment in the Via Goldoni, I believe," he said. "My uncle is a great man of business in Venice."

His uncle . . . the appalling tout was his uncle. All was explained. It was a family relationship. I need never have worried. Instantly I placed the man as the brother of the nagging mother, both of them, no doubt, playing on the feelings of my Ganymede, who wished to show his independence and get away from them. Still, it had been a narrow escape. I might have offended the man mortally when he took his tumble into the canal.

"Of course, of course," I said, pretending I had known all the time, for he seemed to take it for granted that this was the case and I had no desire to seem a fool. Then I went on, "A very comfortable apartment. Do you know it?"

"Naturally I know it, signore," he said, smiling. "It is I who will bring you your breakfast every morning."

I nearly fainted. Ganymede bring my breakfast . . . It was too much to absorb in one moment. I concealed my emotion by ordering another curaçao, and he darted off to obey me. I was, as the French say, *bouleversé*. To be tenant of the delicious apartment was one thing—and at no extra cost—but to have Ganymede thrown in, as it were, with my breakfast was almost more than flesh and blood could stand. I made an effort to compose myself before he returned, but his announcement had thrown me into such a flutter that I could hardly sit in my seat. He was back with the glass of curaçao.

"Pleasant dreams, signore," he said.

Pleasant dreams, indeed. . . . I had not the courage to look at him. And when I had swallowed my curaçao I took advantage of his temporary summons by another client to slip away, although it was long before midnight. I got back to the apartment by instinct rather than by conscious thought —I had not seen where I was going—and then noticed, on the table, the still unposted letter to London. I could have sworn I had taken it with me when I went out to dinner. However, the morning would do. I was too agitated to go out again tonight.

I stood on the balcony and smoked another cigar, an unheard-of excess, and then went through my small store of books with the idea of presenting one to Ganymede when he brought me my breakfast. His English was so good that it needed a tribute, and the idea of a tip was somehow distasteful. Trollope was not right for him, nor Chaucer either.

And the volume of Edwardian memoirs would be quite beyond his understanding. Could I bear to part with my well-worn Shakespeare sonnets? Impossible to come to a decision. I would sleep on it—if I could sleep, which seemed very doubtful. I took two Seconal tablets and passed out.

When I awoke it was past nine o'clock. The traffic on the canal might have indicated high noon. The day was brilliantly fine. I rushed from my bed to the bathroom and shaved, a thing I usually did after breakfast, and then, putting on my dressing gown and slippers, moved the table and the chair on to the balcony. Then, in trepidation, I went to the telephone and lifted the receiver. There came the buzz and the click, and with a rush of blood to the heart I recognised his voice.

"*Buon giorno, signore.* You slept well?"

"Very well," I answered. "Will you bring me a *café complet?*"

"*Café complet,*" he repeated.

I hung up and went and sat on the balcony. Then I remembered I had not unlocked the door. I did this, and returned to the balcony. My excitement was intense and irrational. I even felt a trifle sick. Then, after five minutes that seemed eternity, came the knock on the door. He entered, tray poised high at shoulder level, and his bearing was so regal, his carriage so proud that he might have been bringing me ambrosia or a swan instead of coffee and a roll and butter. He was wearing a morning coat with thin black stripes, the type of jacket worn by valets at a club.

"A good appetite, signore," he said.

"Thank you," I replied.

I had my small present ready on my knee. The Shakespeare sonnets must be sacrificed. They were irreplaceable in that particular edition, but no matter. Nothing else would do. First, though, before the presentation, I would sound him.

"I want to make you a little present," I told him.

He bowed in courtesy. "The signore is too good," he murmured.

"You speak English so well," I continued, "that you need

to hear only the best. Now, tell me, who do you think has been the greatest Englishman?"

He considered the matter gravely. And he stood, as he did on the Piazza San Marco, with his hands clasped behind his back.

"Winston Churchill," he said.

I might have known it. Naturally the boy lived in the present, or it would be more correct to say, in this instance, the immediate past.

"A good answer," I said, smiling, "but I want you to think again. No, I'll put my question another way. If you had some money to spend, and you could spend it on anything you wanted connected with the English language, what would be the first thing you would buy?"

This time there was no hesitation. "I would buy a long-playing gramophone record," he said, "a long-playing gramophone record of Elvis Presley or Johnnie Ray."

I was disappointed. It was not the answer I had hoped for. Who were these creatures? Crooners? Ganymede must be educated to better things. On second thought, I would not part with the sonnets.

"Very well," I said, hoping I did not sound offhand, and I put my hand in my pocket and took out a thousand-lire note, "but I suggest you buy Mozart instead."

The note disappeared, crumpled out of sight in his hand. It was discreetly done, and I wondered if he had been able to glimpse the figure. After all, a thousand lire is a thousand lire. I asked him how he managed to evade his duties at the café to bring me my breakfast, and he explained that his work did not begin there until just before midday. And, anyway, there was an understanding between the proprietor of the café and his uncle.

"Your uncle," I said, "seems to have an understanding with many people." I was thinking of the reception clerk at the Hotel Byron.

Ganymede smiled. "In Venice," he said, "everybody knows everybody."

I noticed that he glanced with admiration at my dressing gown, which, when I had bought it for travelling, I had thought a shade too bright. Remembering the gramophone records, I reminded myself that he was, after all, nothing but a child, and one should not expect too much.

"Do you ever have a day off?" I asked him.

"On Sundays," he said. "I take it in turn with Beppo."

Beppo must be the unsuitable name of the swarthy youth at the café.

"And what do you do on your day off?" I enquired.

"I go out with my friends," he replied.

I poured myself more coffee and wondered if I dared. A rebuff would be so hurtful.

"If you have nothing better to do," I said, "and should be free next Sunday, I will take you for a trip to the Lido." I felt myself blush, and bent over the coffeepot to hide it.

"In a speedboat?" he asked quickly.

I was rather nonplussed. I had visualised the usual *vaporetto*. A speedboat would be very expensive.

"That would depend," I hedged. "Surely on a Sunday they would all be booked?"

He shook his head firmly. "My uncle knows a man who has speedboats for hire," he said. "They can be hired for the whole day."

Heavens above, it would cost a fortune! It would not do to commit myself. "We'll see," I said. "It would depend upon the weather."

"The weather will be fine," he said, smiling. "It will stay fine now for the rest of the week."

His enthusiasm was infectious. Poor child, he must have few treats. On his feet all day and half the night serving tourists. A breath of air in a speedboat would seem like paradise.

"Very well, then," I said. "If it's fine, we'll go."

I stood up, brushing the crumbs off my dressing gown. He took my gesture as one of dismissal and seized the tray.

"Can I do anything else for the signore?" he asked.

"You can post my letter," I said. "It's the one I told you about, to the friend who is a director of a hotel."

He lowered his eyes modestly and waited for me to hand him the letter.

"Shall I see you this evening?" I asked.

"Of course, signore," he said. "I will keep a table for you at the usual time."

I let him go and went to run my bath, and it was only when I lay soaking in the hot water that an unpleasant thought occurred to me. Was it possible that Ganymede had also brought breakfast for Sir Johnson, and had gone to the Lido in a speedboat with Bertie Poole? I dismissed the thought. It was far too offensive . . .

The week remained fine, as he had foretold, and each day I became more entranced with my surroundings. No sign of anyone in the apartment. My bed was made as if by magic. The uncle remained *perdu*. And in the morning, as soon as I touched the telephone, Ganymede replied and brought my breakfast. Every evening the table at the café awaited me, the chair upturned, the glass of curaçao and the half bottle of Evian in their place. If I had no more strange visions and no more dreams, at least I found myself in happy holiday mood, without a care in the world, and with what I can only call a telepathic understanding, an extraordinary sympathy, between Ganymede and myself. No other client existed but me. He did his duty, but remained at my beck and call. And the morning breakfasts on the balcony were the high peak of the day.

Sunday dawned fine. The high wind that might have meant a *vaporetto* was not forthcoming, and when he bore in my coffee and roll the smile on his face betrayed his excitement.

"The signore will come to the Lido?" he asked.

I waved my hand. "Of course," I said. "I never break a promise."

"I will make arrangements," he said, "if the signore will be at the first landing stage to the apartment by half-past eleven."

And for the first time since bringing my breakfast he vanished without further conversation, such was his haste. It was a little alarming. I had not even enquired about the price.

I attended Mass in St. Mark's, a moving experience, and one that put me in a lofty mood. The setting was magnificent, and the singing could not have been bettered. I looked around for Ganymede, half expecting to see him enter leading a little sister by the hand, but there was no sign of him in the vast crowd. Oh well, the excitement of the speedboat had proved too much for him.

I came out of the church into the dazzling sunshine and put on my dark glasses. There was scarcely a ripple on the lagoon. I wished he had chosen a gondola. In a gondola I could have lain full-length, stretched at my ease, and we could have gone to Torcello. I might even have brought the Shakespeare sonnets with me and read one or two of them aloud to him. Instead, I must indulge his youthful whim and enter the age of speed. Blow the expense! It would never happen again.

I saw him standing by the water's edge, changed into brief shorts and a blue shirt. He looked very much younger, a complete child. I waved my walking stick and smiled.

"All aboard?" I called gaily.

"All aboard, signore," he replied.

I made for the landing stage and saw, drawn up to it, a magnificent varnished speedboat complete with cabin, a small pennant at the prow, a large ensign at the stern. And standing by the controls, in a flaming orange shirt open at the neck, betraying his hairy chest, was a great ungainly figure I recognised with dismay. At sight of me he touched the klaxon and revved up the engine so that it roared.

"We go places," he said, with a revolting smile. "We hit-a the headlines. We have fun."

7

I stepped aboard, my heart like lead, and was instantly thrown off balance as our horrible mechanic thrust the engine into gear. I clutched at his ape-like arm to save myself from falling, and he steadied me into the seat beside him, at the same time opening the throttle to such an extent that I feared for my eardrums. We bounced across the lagoon at a fearful speed, hitting the surface every moment with a crash that nearly split the craft in two, and nothing could be seen of the grace and colour of Venice because of the wall of water that rose on either side of us.

"Must we go so fast?" I screamed, endeavouring to make myself heard above the deafening roar of the engine. The tout grinned at me, showing his gold-filled teeth, and shouted back, "We break-a the records. This most powerful boat in Venice."

I resigned myself to doom. I was not only ill-prepared for the ordeal, but ill-dressed. My dark blue coat was already spattered with salt water, and there was a smear of oil on my trouser leg. The hat I had brought to protect me against the sun was useless. I needed a flying helmet and a pair of goggles. To leave my exposed seat and crawl to the cabin would be risking certain injury to my limbs. Besides, I should get claustrophobia, and the noise inside a confined space would be even worse. On, on we sped, rocking every craft in sight, heading for the Adriatic, and to show off his skill as a helmsman the monster beside me began to perform acrobatics, making great circles and heading into our own wash.

"You watch-a her rise," he bellowed in my ear, and rise we did, to such an extent that my stomach turned over with the inevitable thud of our descent, and the spray that we had not left behind us trickled over my collar and down my back. Standing in the prow, revelling in every moment, his light hair tossed about in the breeze we were making, stood Ganymede, a sea sprite, joyous and free. He was my only consolation, and the sight of him there, turning now and again to smile, prevented me from ordering an instant return to Venice.

When we reached the Lido, a pleasant enough trip by *vaporetto*, I was not only wet but deaf into the bargain, the spray and the roar of the engine combined having successfully blocked my right ear. I stepped ashore shaken and silent, and it was odious when the tout took my arm in a familiar gesture and shepherded me into a waiting taxi, while Ganymede leapt in front beside the driver. Where to now, I asked myself? How fatal to make a picture of one's day in fantasy. In the church, during the singing of Mass, I had seen myself landing with Ganymede from some smooth craft

119

piloted by a discreet nonentity, and then the two of us strolling to a little restaurant I had marked down on my previous visit. How delightful, I had thought, to sit at a corner table with him, choosing the menu, watching his happy face, seeing it colour, perhaps, with the wine, and getting him to talk about himself, about his life, about the complaining mother and little sister. Then, with the liqueurs, we would make plans for the future, should my letter to my London superior prove successful.

None of this happened. The taxi drew up with a swerve before a modern hotel facing the Lido bathing beach. The place was crammed, despite the lateness of the season, and the tout, known apparently to the maître d'hôtel, thrust his way through the chattering crowd into the airless restaurant. To follow in his wake was bad enough, the flaming orange shirt making him conspicuous, but worse was to come. The table in the centre was already filled with hilarious Italians, talking at the tops of their voices, who at sight of us rose in unison, pushing back their chairs to make room. A dyed blonde with enormous earrings and reeking of scent swooped upon me with a flow of Italian.

"My sister, signore," said the tout, "she make-a you welcome. She no speak-a the English."

Was this Ganymede's mother? And the full-bosomed young woman beside her with scarlet fingernails and jangling bangles, was this the little sister? My head whirled.

"It is a great honour, signore," Ganymede murmured, "that you invite my family to lunch."

I sat down, defeated. I had invited nobody. But the matter was out of my hands. The uncle—if uncle indeed he was, the monster, the tout—was handing round to everyone menus the size of placards. The maître d'hôtel was bending himself in two in his effort to please. And Ganymede . . . Ganymede was smiling into the eyes of some loathsome cousin who, with clipped moustache and crew cut, was making the motions of a speedboat going through the water with a pudgy, olive hand.

I turned to the tout in desperation. "I had not expected a

120

party," I said. "I'm afraid I may not have brought enough money."

He broke off his discussion with the maître d'hôtel.

"Don't worry . . . don't worry . . ." he said, waving the air. "You leave-a the bill to me. We settle later."

Settle later. . . . It was all very well. By the time the day was over I should not be in a position to settle anything. An enormous plate of noodles was set before me, topped with a rich meat sauce, and I saw that my glass was being filled with a particular barolo that, taken in the middle of the day, means certain death.

"You 'avin' fun?" said Ganymede's sister, pressing my foot with hers.

Hours later I found myself on the beach, still seated between her and her mother, both of them changed into bikinis, lying on either side of me like porpoises, while the cousins, the uncles, the aunts splashed into the sea and back again, shrieking and laughing, and Ganymede, beautiful as an angel from heaven, presided at the gramophone that had suddenly materialised from outer space, repeating again and again the long-playing record that he had bought with my thousand lire.

"My mother wants so much to thank you," said Ganymede, "for writing to London. If I go, she will come too, and my sister."

"We all go," said his uncle. "We make one big party. We all go to London and set-a the Thames on fire."

It was over at last. The final splashing in the sea, the final poke from the scarlet toe of the sister, the final bottle of wine. I had a splitting head, and my insides had turned on me. One by one the relations came to shake me by the hand. The mother, voluble with thanks, embraced me. That none of them were to accompany us back to Venice in the speedboat and continue the party there was the one measure of solace left to me at the end of the disastrous day.

We climbed aboard. The engine started. We were away. And this should have been the return journey I had already made in fantasy—the smooth, rather idling return over limpid water, Ganymede at my side, a new intimacy having grown up between us because of the hours spent in each other's company, the sun, low on the horizon, turning the island that was Venice into a rose façade.

Halfway across, I saw that Ganymede was struggling with a rope that lay coiled across the stern of our craft, and the uncle, easing the throttle so that our progress was suddenly slowed, left the controls to help him. We began to rock from side to side in a sickly fashion.

"What is going to happen now?" I called.

Ganymede shook the hair out of his eyes and smiled. "I water-ski," he said. "I follow you home to Venice on my skis."

He dived into the cabin and came out again with the skis. Together the uncle and nephew fixed the rope and the skis, and then Ganymede flung off his shirt and his shorts and stood upright, a small bronzed figure in bathing slip.

The uncle beckoned me. "You sit-a here," he said. "You pay out the rope so."

He secured the rope to a bollard in the stern and put the end into my hands, then rushed forward to the driving seat and started to roar the engine.

"What do you mean?" I cried. "What do I have to do?"

Ganymede was already over the side and in the water, fixing his bare feet into the slots of the skis, and then, unbelievably, pulling himself up into a standing position while the craft began to race ahead. The uncle sounded the klaxon with an ear-splitting screech, and the craft, gathering momentum, sped over the water at top speed. The rope, made fast to the bollard, held, though I still clung to the end, while in our wake, steady as a rock on his dancing skis, the small figure of Ganymede was silhouetted against the already vanishing Lido.

I seated myself in the stern of the boat and watched him. He might have been a charioteer, and the two skis his racing steeds. His hands were stretched before him, holding the guide rope as a charioteer would gather his reins, and as we circled once, twice, and he swung out in an arc on his corresponding course, he raised his hand to me in salutation, a smile of triumph on his face.

The sea was the sky, the ripple on the water wisps of cloud, and heaven knows what meteors we drove and scattered, the boy and I, soaring towards the sun. I know that at times I bore him on my shoulders, and at others he slipped away, and once it was as though both of us plunged headlong into a molten mist which was neither sea nor sky but the luminous rings encircling a star.

As the craft swung into the straight again and bounced away on its course, he signalled to me with one hand, pointing to the rope on the bollard. I did not know whether he meant me to loosen it or make it more secure, and I did the wrong thing, jerked it, for he overbalanced instantly and was flung into the water. He must have hurt himself, for I saw that he made no attempt to swim.

Flustered, I shouted to the uncle, "Stop the engine! Go astern!"

Surely the right thing to do was to bring the boat to a standstill? The uncle, startled, seeing nothing but my agitated face, put the engine hard into reverse. His action threw me off my feet, and by the time I had scrambled up again we were almost on top of the boy. There was a mass of churning water, of tangled rope, of sudden, splintering wood, and leaning over the side of the boat, I saw the slim body of Ganymede drawn into the suction of the propeller, his legs enmeshed, and I bent down to lift him clear. I put out my hands to grip his shoulders.

"Watch the rope," yelled the uncle. "Pull it clear."

But he did not know that the boy was beside us, was beneath us, and that already he had slipped from my hands which struggled to hold him, to bear him aloft, that already . . . God, already . . . the water was beginning to colour crimson with his blood.

8

Yes, yes, I told the uncle. Yes, I would pay compensation, I would pay anything they asked. It had been my fault, an error of judgment. I had not understood. Yes, I would pay any and every item he liked to put down on his list. I would telegraph to my bank in London, and perhaps the British

Consul would help me, would give advice. If I could not raise the money immediately I would pay so much a week, so much a month, so much a year. Indeed, the rest of my life I would continue to pay, I would continue to support the bereaved, because it was my fault, I agreed that it was all my fault.

An error of judgment on my part had been the cause of the accident. The British Consul sat by my side, and he listened to the explanations of the uncle, who produced his notebook and his sheaf of bills.

"This gentleman take-a my apartment for two weeks, and my nephew he bring-a him his breakfast every day. He bring-a flowers. He bring-a coffee and rolls. He insists my nephew look after him and no one else. This gentleman take great fancy to the boy."

"Is that true?"

"Yes, it's true."

The lighting of the apartment was extra, it seemed. And the heating for the bath. The bath had to be heated from below in a special way. There was a man's time for coming in to repair a shutter. The boy's time, he told the consul, for bringing my breakfast, for not going to the café before midday. And the time for taking a Sunday off that was not the regular Sunday. He did not know if the gentleman was prepared to pay for these items.

"I have already said that I will pay for everything."

The notebook was consulted again, and there was the damage to the engines of the speedboat, the cost of the waterskis that were smashed beyond repair, the charge for the craft that had been hailed to tow us back to Venice, to tow the speedboat back to Venice with Ganymede unconscious in my arms, and the telephone call from the quayside for the ambulance. One by one he read out the items from the notebook. The hospital charges, the doctor's fees, the surgeon's fees.

"This gentleman, he insist he pay for everything."

"Is that true?"

"Yes, it's true."

The yellow face against the dark suit seemed fatter than

before, and the eyes, puffy with weeping, looked sideways at the consul.

"This gentleman, he write to his friend in London about my nephew. Perhaps already there is a job waiting for the boy, a job he can no longer take. I have a son, Beppo, my son also a very good boy, known to the gentleman here. Beppo and my nephew they both work at the café every night, and serve the gentleman. The gentleman so fond of these boys, he follow them home. Yes, I see it with my own eyes, he follow them home. Beppo would like to go to London in place of his poor cousin. This gentleman arrange it, perhaps? He write again to his friend in London?"

The consul coughed discreetly. "Is that true? Did you follow them home?"

"Yes, it's true."

The uncle took out a large handkerchief and blew his nose.

"My nephew very well brought-up boy. My son the same. Never give any trouble. All the money they earn they give to their family. My nephew he had very great trust in this gentleman, and he tell me, he tell all the family, his mother, his sister, that this gentleman will take him back to London. His mother, she buy a new dress, and his sister too, she buy new clothes for the boy to go to London. Now, she ask-a herself, what happens to the clothes, they cannot be worn, they are no use."

I said to the consul that I would pay for everything.

"His poor mother, she break-a her heart," the voice continued, "and his sister too, she lose-a all interest in her work, she become nervous, ill. Who is to pay for the funeral of my nephew? Then this gentleman, he kindly say, no expense to be spared."

No expense to be spared, and let that go, too, for the mourning, and the veils, and the wreaths, and the music, and the weeping, and the procession, the endless long procession. And I would pay, too, for the tourists clicking cameras and feeding pigeons who knew nothing of what had happened, and for those lovers lying in each other's arms in gondolas, and for the echo of the Angelus sounding from the Campanile, and the lapping water from the lagoon, and the chug-chug of the *vaporetto* leaving the landing stage which turns into the chug-chug of a coal barge in the Paddington canal.

It passes, of course—not the coal barge over there, I mean, but the horror. The horror of accident, of sudden death. You see, as I told myself afterwards, if it had not been an accident it would have been a war. Or he would have come to London and grown up, grown fat, turned into a tout like the uncle, grown ugly, old. I don't want to make excuses for anything. I don't want to make excuses for anything at all. But—because of what happened—my life has become rather different. As I said before, I've moved my quarters in London to this district. I've given up my job, I've dropped my friends, in a word . . . I've changed. I still see my sister and my nieces from time to time. No, I don't possess any other family. There was a younger brother who died when I was five, but I don't remember him at all: I've never given him a thought. My sister has been my only living relative for years.

Now, if you will excuse me, I see by my watch it is nearly seven o'clock. The restaurant down the road will be open. And I like to be there on time. The fact is, the boy who is training there as a waiter celebrates his fifteenth birthday this evening, and I have a little present for him. Nothing very much, you understand—I don't believe in spoiling these lads—but it seems there is a singer called Perry Como much in favour amongst the young. I have the latest record here. He likes bright colours, too—I rather thought this blue and gold cravat might catch his eye . . .

The Pool

THE CHILDREN RAN out on to the lawn. There was space all around them, and light, and air, with the trees indeterminate beyond. The gardener had cut the grass. The lawn was crisp and firm now, because of the hot sun through the day; but near the summerhouse where the tall grass stood there were dewdrops like frost clinging to the narrow stems.

The children said nothing. The first moment always took them by surprise. The fact that it waited, thought Deborah, all the time they were away; that day after day while they were at school, or in the Easter holidays with the aunts at Hunstanton being blown to bits, or in the Christmas holidays with their father in London riding on buses and going to theatres—the fact that the garden waited for them was a miracle known only to herself. A year was so long. How did the garden endure the snows clamping down upon it, or the chilly rain that fell in November? Surely sometimes it must mock the slow steps of Grandpapa pacing up and down the terrace in front of the windows, or Grandmama calling to Patch? The garden had to endure month after month of silence while the children were gone. Even the spring and the days of May and June were wasted, all those mornings of butterflies and darting birds, with no one to watch but Patch gasping for breath on a cool stone slab. So wasted was the garden, so lost.

"You must never think we forget," said Deborah in the silent voice she used to her own possessions. "I remember, even at school, in the middle of French"—but the ache then was unbearable that it should be the hard grain of a desk under her hands and not the grass she bent to touch now.

The children had had an argument once about whether there was more grass in the world or more sand, and Roger said that of course there must be more sand, because of under the sea; in every ocean all over the world there would be sand, if you looked deep down. But there could be grass too, argued Deborah, a waving grass, a grass that nobody had ever seen, and the colour of that ocean grass would be darker than any grass on the surface of the world, in fields or prairies or people's gardens in America. It would be taller than trees and it would move like corn in a wind.

They had run in to ask somebody adult, "What is there most of in the world, grass or sand?"—both children hot and passionate from the argument. But Grandpapa stood there in his old panama hat looking for clippers to trim the hedge— he was rummaging in the drawer full of screws—and he said, "What? What?" impatiently.

The boy turned red—perhaps it was a stupid question— but the girl thought, he doesn't know, they never know, and she made a face at her brother to show that she was on his side. Later they asked their grandmother, and she, being practical, said briskly, "I should think sand. Think of all the grains," and Roger turned in triumph. "I told you so!" The grains. Deborah had not considered the grains. The magic of millions and millions of grains clinging together in the world and under the oceans made her sick. Let Roger win, it did not matter. It was better to be in the minority of the waving grass.

Now, on this first evening of summer holiday, she knelt and then lay full-length on the lawn, and stretched her hands out on either side like Jesus on the Cross, only face downwards, and murmured over and over again the words she had memorised from Confirmation preparation. "A full, perfect, and sufficient sacrifice . . . a full, perfect, and sufficient sacrifice . . . satisfaction, and oblation, for the sins of the whole world." To offer herself to the earth, to the garden, the garden that had waited patiently all these months since last summer, surely this must be her first gesture.

"Come on," said Roger, rousing himself from his appreciation of how Willis the gardener had mown the lawn to just the right closeness for cricket, and without waiting for his sister's answer he ran to the summerhouse and made a dive at the long box in the corner where the stumps were kept. He smiled as he lifted the lid. The familiarity of the smell was satisfying. Old varnish and chipped paint, and surely that must be the same spider and the same cobweb? He drew out the stumps one by one, and the bails, and there was the ball—it had not been lost after all as he had feared. It was worn, though, a greyish red—he smelt it and bit it to taste the shabby leather. Then he gathered the things in his arms and went out to set up the stumps.

"Come and help me measure the pitch," he called to his sister, and looking at her, squatting in the grass with her face hidden, he felt his heart sink, because it meant that she was in one of her absent moods and would not concentrate on the cricket.

"Deb?" he called anxiously. "You are going to play?"

Deborah heard his voice through the multitude of earth sounds, the heartbeat, and the pulse. If she listened with her ear to the ground there was a humming much deeper than anything that bees did, or the sea at Hunstanton. The nearest to it was the wind, but the wind was reckless. The humming of the earth was patient. Deborah sat up, and her heart sank just as her brother's had done, for the same reason in reverse. The monotony of the game ahead would be like a great chunk torn out of privacy.

"How long shall we have to be?" she called.

The lack of enthusiasm damped the boy. It was not going to be any fun at all if she made a favour of it. He must be firm, though. Any concession on his part she snatched and turned to her advantage.

"Half an hour," he said, and then, for encouragement's sake, "you can bat first."

Deborah smelt her knees. They had not yet got the country smell, but if she rubbed them in the grass, and in the earth too, the white London look would go.

"All right," she said, "but no longer than half an hour."

He nodded quickly, and so as not to lose time measured out the pitch and then began ramming the stumps in the ground. Deborah went into the summerhouse to get the bats. The familiarity of the little wooden hut pleased her as it had her brother. It was a long time now, many years, since they had played in the summerhouse, making yet another house inside this one with the help of broken deck chairs; but just as the garden waited for them a whole year, so did the summerhouse, the windows on either side, cobweb-wrapped and stained, gazing out like eyes. Deborah did her ritual of bowing twice. If she should forget this, on her first entrance, it spelt ill luck.

She picked out the two bats from the corner, where they were stacked with old croquet hoops, and she knew at once that Roger would choose the one with the rubber handle, even though they could not bat at the same time, and for the whole of the holidays she must make do with the smaller one that had half the whipping off. There was a croquet clip lying on the floor. She picked it up and put it on her nose and stood a moment, wondering how it would be if forever more she had to live thus, nostrils pinched, making her voice like Punch. Would people pity her?

"Hurry," shouted Roger, and she threw the clip into the corner, then quickly returned when she was halfway to the pitch, because she knew the clip was lying apart from its fellows and she might wake in the night and remember it. The clip would turn malevolent and haunt her. She replaced him on the floor with two others, and now she was absolved and the summerhouse at peace.

"Don't get out too soon," warned Roger as she stood in the crease he had marked for her, and with a tremendous effort of concentration Deborah forced her eyes to his retreating figure and watched him roll up his sleeves and pace the required length for his run-up. Down came the ball and she lunged out, smacking it in the air in an easy catch. The impact of ball on bat stung her hands. Roger missed the catch on purpose. Neither of them said anything.

"Who shall I be?" called Deborah.

The game could only be endured, and concentration kept, if Roger gave her a part to play. Not an individual, but a country.

"You're India," he said, and Deborah felt herself grow dark and lean. Part of her was tiger, part of her was sacred cow, the long grass fringing the lawn was jungle, the roof of the summerhouse a minaret.

Even so, the half hour dragged, and, when her turn came to bowl, the ball she threw fell wider every time, so that Roger, flushed and self-conscious because their grandfather had come out on to the terrace and was watching them, called angrily, "Do try."

Once again the effort at concentration, the figure of their grandfather—a source of apprehension to the boy, for he might criticise them—acting as a spur to his sister. Grand-papa was an Indian god, and tribute must be paid to him, a golden apple. The apple must be flung to slay his enemies. Deborah muttered a prayer, and the ball she bowled came fast and true and hit Roger's off-stump. In the moment of delivery their grandfather had turned away and pottered back again through the french windows of the drawing-room.

Roger looked round swiftly. His disgrace had not been seen. "Jolly good ball," he said. "It's your turn to bat again."

But his time was up. The stable clock chimed six. Solemnly Roger drew stumps.

"What shall we do now?" he asked.

Deborah wanted to be alone, but if she said so, on this first evening of the holiday, he would be offended.

"Go to the orchard and see how the apples are coming on," she suggested, "and then round by the kitchen-garden in case the raspberries haven't all been picked. But you have to do it all without meeting anyone. If you see Willis or anyone, even the cat, you lose a mark."

It was these sudden inventions that saved her. She knew her brother would be stimulated at the thought of outwitting the gardener. The aimless wander round the orchard would turn into a stalking exercise.

"Will you come too?" he asked.

"No," she said, "you have to test your skill."

He seemed satisfied with this and ran off towards the or-chard, stopping on the way to cut himself a switch from the bamboo.

As soon as he had disappeared Deborah made for the trees fringing the lawn and once in the shrouded wood felt herself safe. She walked softly along the alleyway to the pool. The late sun sent shafts of light between the trees and on to the alleyway, and myriad insects webbed their way in the beams, ascending and descending like angels on Jacob's ladder. But were they insects, wondered Deborah, or particles of dust, or even split fragments of light itself, beaten out and scattered by the sun?

It was very quiet. The woods were made for secrecy. They did not recognise her as the garden did. They did not care that for a whole year she could be at school, or at Hunstanton, or in London. The woods would never miss her: they had their own dark, passionate life.

Deborah came to the opening where the pool lay, with the five alleyways branching from it, and she stood a moment before advancing to the brink, because this was holy ground and required atonement. She crossed her hands on her breast and shut her eyes. Then she kicked off her shoes. "Mother of all things wild, do with me what you will," she said aloud. The sound of her own voice gave her a slight shock. Then she went down on her knees and touched the ground three times with her forehead.

The first part of her atonement was accomplished, but the pool demanded sacrifice and Deborah had come prepared. There was a stub of pencil she had carried in her pocket throughout the school term which she called her luck. It had teeth marks on it and a chewed piece of rubber at one end. The treasure must be given to the pool just as other treasures had been given in the past, a miniature jug, a crested button, a china pig. Deborah felt for the stub of pencil and kissed it. She had carried and caressed it for so many lonely months, and now the moment of parting had come. The pool must not be denied. She flung out her right hand, her eyes still shut, and heard the faint plop as the stub of pencil struck the water. Then she opened her eyes and saw in mid-pool a ripple. The pencil had gone but the ripple moved, gently shaking the water lilies. The movement symbolised acceptance.

Deborah, still on her knees and crossing her hands once

more, edged her way to the brink of the pool and then, crouching there beside it, looked down into the water. Her reflection wavered up at her, and it was not the face she knew, not even the looking-glass face which anyway was false, but a disturbed image, dark-skinned and ghostly. The crossed hands were like the petals of the water lilies themselves, and the colour was not waxen white but phantom green. The hair, too, was not the live clump she brushed every day and tied back with ribbon, but a canopy, a shroud. When the image smiled it became more distorted still. Uncrossing her hands, Deborah leant forward, took a twig, and drew a circle three times on the smooth surface. The water shook in ever-widening ripples, and her reflection, broken into fragments, heaved and danced, a sort of monster, and the eyes were there no longer, nor the mouth.

Presently the water became still. Insects, long-legged flies and beetles with spread wings hummed upon it. A dragonfly had all the magnificence of a lily leaf to himself. He hovered there, rejoicing. But when Deborah took her eyes off him for a moment he was gone. At the far end of the pool, beyond the clustering lilies, green scum had formed, and beneath the scum were rooted, tangled weeds. They were so thick, and had lain in the pool so long, that if a man walked into them from the bank he would be held and choked. A fly, though, or a beetle, could sit upon the surface, and to him the pale green scum would not be treacherous at all, but a resting place, a haven. And if someone threw a stone, so that the ripples formed, eventually they came to the scum and rocked it, and the whole of the mossy surface moved in rhythm, a dancing floor for those who played upon it.

There was a dead tree standing by the far end of the pool. He could have been fir or pine, or even larch, for time had stripped him of identity. He had no distinguishing mark upon his person but with grotesque limbs straddled the sky. A cap of ivy crowned his naked head. Last winter a dangling branch had broken loose, and this now lay in the pool half submerged, the green scum dripping from the withered twigs. The soggy branch made a vantage point for birds, and, as Deborah watched, a nestling suddenly flew from the undergrowth enveloping the dead tree and perched for an instant on the mossy filigree. He was lost in terror. The parent bird cried warningly from some dark safety, and the nestling, pricking to the cry, took off from the branch that had offered him temporary salvation. He swerved across the pool, his flight mistimed, yet reached security. The chitter from the undergrowth told of his scolding. When he had gone, silence returned to the pool.

It was, so Deborah thought, the time for prayer. The water lilies were folding upon themselves. The ripples ceased. And that dark hollow in the centre of the pool, that black stillness where the water was deepest, was surely a funnel to the kingdom that lay below. Down that funnel had travelled the discarded treasures. The stub of pencil had lately plunged the depths. He had now been received as an equal among his fellows. This was the single law of the pool, for there were no other commandments. Once it was over, that first cold headlong flight, Deborah knew that the softness of the welcoming water took away all fear. It lapped the face and cleansed the eyes, and the plunge was not into darkness at all but into light. It did not become blacker as the pool was penetrated, but paler, more golden green, and the mud that people told themselves was there was only a defence against strangers. Those who belonged, who knew, went to the source at once, and there were caverns and fountains and rainbow-coloured seas. There were shores of the whitest sand. There was soundless music.

Once again Deborah closed her eyes and bent lower to the pool. Her lips nearly touched the water. This was the great silence, when she had no thoughts and was accepted by the pool. Waves of quiet ringed themselves about her, and slowly she lost all feeling, and had no knowledge of her legs, or of her kneeling body, or of her cold, clasped hands. There was nothing but the intensity of peace. It was a deeper acceptance than listening to the earth, because the earth was of the world, the earth was a throbbing pulse, but the acceptance of the pool meant another kind of hearing, a closing in of the waters, and just as the lilies folded so did the soul submerge.

"Deborah . . . ? Deborah . . . ?" Oh no! Not now, don't let them call me back now! It was as though someone had hit her on the back, or jumped out at her from behind a corner, the sharp and sudden clamour of another life destroying the silence, the secrecy. And then came the tinkle of the cowbells. It was the signal from their grandmother that the time had come to go in. Not imperious and ugly with authority, like the clanging bell at school summoning those at play to lessons or chapel, but a reminder, nevertheless, that Time was all-important, that life was ruled to order, that even here, in the holiday home the children loved, the adult reigned supreme.

"All right, all right," muttered Deborah, standing up and thrusting her numbed feet into her shoes. This time the rather raised tone of "Deborah?" and the more hurried clanging of the cowbells, brought long ago from Switzerland, suggested a more imperious Grandmama than the tolerant one who seldom questioned. It must mean their supper was already laid, soup perhaps getting cold, and the farce of washing hands, of tidying, of combing hair must first be gone through.

"Come on, Deb," and now the shout was close, was right at hand, privacy lost forever, for her brother came running down the alleyway, swishing his bamboo stick in the air.

"What *have* you been doing?" The question was an intrusion and a threat. She would never have asked him what he had been doing, had he wandered away wanting to be alone, but Roger, alas, did not claim privacy. He liked companionship, and his question now, asked half in irritation, half in resentment, came really from the fear that he might lose her.

"Nothing," said Deborah.

Roger eyed her suspiciously. She was in that mooning mood. And it meant, when they went to bed, that she would not talk. One of the best things, in the holidays, was having the two adjoining rooms and calling through to Deb, making her talk.

"Come on," he said, "they've rung," and the making of their grandmother into "they," turning a loved individual into something impersonal, showed Deborah that even if he did not understand he was on her side. He had been called from play, just as she had.

They ran from the woods to the lawn and on to the terrace. Their grandmother had gone inside, but the cowbells hanging by the french window were still jangling.

The custom was for the children to have their supper first, at seven, and it was laid for them in the dining-room on a hot plate. They served themselves. At a quarter to eight their grandparents had dinner. It was called dinner, but this was a concession to their status. They ate the same as the children, though Grandpapa had a savoury which was not served to the children. If the children were late for supper then it put out Time, as well as Agnes, who cooked for both generations, and it might mean five minutes' delay before Grandpapa had his soup. This shook routine.

The children ran up to the bathroom to wash, then downstairs to the dining-room. Their grandfather was standing in the hall. Deborah sometimes thought that he would have enjoyed sitting with them while they ate their supper, but he never suggested it. Grandmama had warned them, too, never to be a nuisance, or indeed to shout, if Grandpapa was near. This was not because he was nervous, but because he liked to shout himself.

"There's going to be a heat wave," he said. He had been listening to the news.

"That will mean lunch outside tomorrow," said Roger swiftly. Lunch was the meal they took in common with the grandparents, and it was the moment of the day he disliked. He was nervous that his grandfather would ask him how he was getting on at school.

"Not for me, thank you," said Grandpapa. "Too many wasps."

Roger was at once relieved. This meant that he and Deborah would have the little round garden table to themselves. But Deborah felt sorry for her grandfather as he went back into the drawing-room. Lunch on the terrace could be gay and would liven him up. When people grew old they had so few treats.

"What do you look forward to most in the day?" she once asked her grandmother.

"Going to bed," was the reply, "and filling my two hot-water bottles." Why work through being young, thought Deborah, to this?

Back in the dining-room the children discussed what they should do during the heat wave. It would be too hot, Deborah said, for cricket. But they might make a house, suggested Roger, in the trees by the paddock. If he got a few old boards from Willis, and nailed them together like a platform, and borrowed the orchard ladder, then they could take fruit and bottles of orange squash and keep them up there, and it would be a camp from which they could spy on Willis afterwards.

Deborah's first instinct was to say she did not want to play, but she checked herself in time. Finding the boards and fixing them would take Roger a whole morning. It would keep him employed. "Yes, it's a good idea," she said, and to foster his spirit of adventure she looked at his notebook, as they were drinking their soup, and approved of items necessary for the camp while he jotted them down. It was all part of the day-long deceit she practised to express understanding of his way of life.

When they had finished supper they took their trays to the kitchen and watched Agnes, for a moment, as she prepared the second meal for the grandparents. The soup was the same, but garnished. Little croutons of toasted bread were added to it. And the butter was made into pats, not cut in a slab. The savoury tonight was to be cheese straws. The children finished the ones that Agnes had burnt. Then they went through to the drawing-room to say good night. The older people had both changed. Grandpapa was in a smoking jacket and wore soft slippers. Grandmama had on a dress that she had worn several years ago in London. She had a cardigan round her shoulders like a cape.

"Go carefully with the bath water," she said. "We'll be short if there's no rain."

They kissed her smooth, soft skin. It smelt of rose leaves. Grandpapa's chin was sharp and bony. He did not kiss Roger.

"Be quiet overhead," whispered their grandmother. The children nodded. The dining-room was underneath their rooms, and any jumping about or laughter would make a disturbance.

Deborah felt a wave of affection for the two old people. Their lives must be empty and sad. "We *are* glad to be here," she said. Grandmama smiled. This was how she lived, thought Deborah, on little crumbs of comfort.

Once out of the room their spirits soared, and to show relief Roger chased Deborah upstairs, both laughing for no reason. Undressing, they forgot the instructions about the bath, and when they went into the bathroom—Deborah was to have first go—the water was gurgling into the overflow. They tore out the plug in a panic and listened to the waste roaring down the pipe to the drain below. If Agnes did not have the wireless on she would hear it.

The children were too old now for boats or play, but the bathroom was a place for confidences, for a sharing of those few tastes they agreed upon, or, after quarrelling, for moody silence. The one who broke silence first would then lose face.

"Willis has a new bicycle," said Roger. "I saw it propped against the shed. I couldn't try it because he was there. But I shall tomorrow. It's a Raleigh."

He liked all practical things, and the trying of the gardener's bicycle would give an added interest to the morning of next day. Willis had a bag of tools in a leather pouch behind the saddle. These could all be felt and the spanners, smelling of oil, tested for shape and usefulness.

"If Willis died," said Deborah, "I wonder what age he would be."

It was the kind of remark that Roger resented always. What had death to do with bicycles? "He's sixty-five," he said, "so he'd be sixty-five."

"No," said Deborah, "what age when he got *there*."

Roger did not want to discuss it. "I bet I can ride it round the stables if I lower the seat," he said. "I bet I don't fall off."

But if Roger would not rise to death, Deborah would not rise to the wager. "Who cares?" she said.

The sudden streak of cruelty stung the brother. Who cared

indeed. . . . The horror of an empty world encompassed him, and to give himself confidence he seized the wet sponge and flung it out of the window. They heard it splosh on the terrace below.

"Grandpapa will step on it and slip," said Deborah, aghast. The image seized them and, choking back laughter, they covered their faces. Hysteria doubled them up. Roger rolled over and over on the bathroom floor. Deborah, the first to recover, wondered why laughter was so near to pain, why Roger's face, twisted now in merriment, was yet the same crumpled thing when his heart was breaking.

"Hurry up," she said briefly, "let's dry the floor," and as they wiped the linoleum with their towels the action sobered them both.

Back in their bedrooms, the door open between them, they watched the light slowly fading. But the air was warm like day. Their grandfather and the people who said what the weather was going to be were right. The heat wave was on its way. Deborah, leaning out of the open window, fancied she could see it in the sky, a dull haze where the sun had been before; and the trees beyond the lawn, day-coloured when they were having their supper in the dining-room, had turned into night birds with outstretched wings. The garden knew about the promised heat wave and rejoiced: the lack of rain was of no consequence yet, for the warm air was a trap, lulling it into a drowsy contentment.

The dull murmur of their grandparents' voices came from the dining-room below. What did they discuss, wondered Deborah. Did they make those sounds to reassure the children, or were their voices part of their unreal world? Presently the voices ceased, and then there was a scraping of chairs, and voices from a different quarter, the drawing-room now, and a faint smell of their grandfather's cigarette.

Deborah called softly to her brother but he did not answer. She went through to his room and he was asleep. He must have fallen asleep suddenly, in the midst of talking. She was relieved. Now she could be alone again and not have to keep up the pretence of sharing conversation. Dusk was everywhere, the sky a deepening black. "When they've gone up to bed," thought Deborah, "then I'll be truly alone." She knew what she was going to do. She waited there by the open window, and the deepening sky lost the veil that covered it, the haze disintegrated, and the stars broke through. Where there had been nothing was life, dusky and bright, and the waiting earth gave off a scent of knowledge. Dew rose from the pores. The lawn was white.

Patch, the old dog, who slept at the end of Grandpapa's bed on a plaid rug, came out on to the terrace and barked hoarsely. Deborah leant out and threw a piece of creeper on to him. He shook his back. Then he waddled slowly to the flower tub above the steps and cocked his leg. It was his nightly routine. He barked once more, staring blindly at the hostile trees, and went back into the drawing-room. Soon afterwards, someone came to close the windows—Grandmama, thought Deborah, for the touch was light. "They are shutting out the best," said the child to herself, "all the meaning and all the point." Patch, being an animal, should know better. He ought to be in a kennel where he could watch, but instead, grown fat and soft, he preferred the bumpiness of her grandfather's bed. He had forgotten the secrets. So had they, the old people.

Deborah heard her grandparents come upstairs. First her grandmother, the quicker of the two, and then her grandfather, more laboured, saying a word or two to Patch as the little dog wheezed his way up. There was a general clicking of lights and shutting of doors. Then silence. How remote, the world of the grandparents, undressing with curtains closed. A pattern of life unchanged for so many years. What went on without would never be known. " 'He that has ears to hear, let him hear,' " said Deborah, and she thought of the callousness of Jesus which no priest could explain. Let the dead bury their dead. All the people in the world, undressing now, or sleeping, not just in the village but in cities and capitals, they were shutting out the truth, they were burying their dead. They wasted silence.

The stable clock struck eleven. Deborah pulled on her clothes. Not the cotton frock of the day, but her old jeans that Grandmama disliked, rolled up above her knees. And a jersey. Sand shoes with a hole that did not matter. She was cunning enough to go down by the back stairs. Patch would bark if she tried the front stairs, close to the grandparents' rooms. The back stairs led past Agnes' room, which smelt of apples though she never ate fruit. Deborah could hear her snoring. She would not even wake on Judgment Day. And this led her to wonder on the truth of that fable, too, for there might be so many millions by then who liked their graves—Grandpapa, for instance, fond of his routine, and irritated at the sudden riot of trumpets.

Deborah crept past the pantry and the servants' hall—it was only a tiny sitting-room for Agnes, but long usage had given it the dignity of the name—and unlatched and unbolted the heavy back door. Then she stepped outside, on to the gravel, and took the long way round by the front of the house so as not to tread on the terrace fronting the lawns and the garden.

The warm night claimed her. In a moment it was part of her. She walked on the grass, and her shoes were instantly soaked. She flung up her arms to the sky. Power ran to her fingertips. Excitement was communicated from the waiting trees, and the orchard, and the paddock; the intensity of their secret life caught at her and made her run. It was nothing like the excitement of ordinary looking forward, of birthday presents, of Christmas stockings, but the pull of a magnet—her grandfather had shown her once how it worked, little needles springing to the jaws—and now night and the sky above were a vast magnet, and the things that waited below were needles caught up in the great demand.

Deborah went to the summerhouse, and it was not sleeping like the house fronting the terrace but open to understanding, sharing complicity. Even the dusty windows caught the light, and the cobwebs shone. She rummaged for the old lilo and the moth-eaten car rug that Grandmama had thrown out two summers ago, and, bearing them over her shoulder, she made her way to the pool. The alleyway was ghostly, and Deborah knew, for all her mounting tension, that the test was hard. Part of her was still body-bound and afraid of shadows. If anything stirred she would jump and know true terror. She must show defiance, though. The woods expected it. Like old wise lamas they expected courage.

She sensed approval as she ran the gauntlet, the tall trees watching. Any sign of turning back, of panic, and they would crowd upon her in a choking mass, smothering protest. Branches would become arms, gnarled and knotty, ready to strangle, and the leaves of the higher trees fold in and close like the sudden furling of giant umbrellas. The smaller undergrowth, obedient to the will, would become a briary of a million thorns where animals of no known world crouched, snarling, their eyes on fire. To show fear was to show misunderstanding. The woods were merciless.

Deborah walked the alleyway to the pool, her left hand holding the lilo and the rug on her shoulder, her right hand raised in salutation. This was a gesture of respect. Then she paused before the pool and laid down her burden beside it. The lilo was to be her bed, the rug her cover. She took off her shoes, also in respect, and lay down upon the lilo. Then, drawing the rug to her chin, she lay flat, her eyes upon the sky. The gauntlet of the alleyway over, she had no more fear. The woods had accepted her, and the pool was the final resting place, the doorway, the key.

"I shan't sleep," thought Deborah. "I shall just lie awake here all the night and wait for morning, but it will be a kind of introduction to life, like being confirmed."

The stars were thicker now than they had been before. No space in the sky without a prick of light, each star a sun. Some, she thought, were newly born, white-hot, and others wise and colder, nearing completion. The law encompassed them, fixing the riotous path, but how they fell and tumbled depended upon themselves. Such peace, such stillness, such sudden quietude, excitement gone. The trees were no longer menacing but guardians, and the pool was primeval water, the first, the last.

Then Deborah stood at the wicket gate, the boundary, and there was a woman with outstretched hand, demanding tickets. "Pass through," she said when Deborah reached her. "We saw you coming." The wicket gate became a turnstile.

Deborah pushed against it and there was no resistance; she was through.

"What is it?" she asked. "Am I really here at last? Is this the bottom of the pool?"

"It could be," smiled the woman. "There are so many ways. You just happened to choose this one."

Other people were pressing to come through. They had no faces, they were only shadows. Deborah stood aside to let them by, and in a moment they had gone, all phantoms.

"Why only now, tonight?" asked Deborah. "Why not in the afternoon, when I came to the pool?"

"It's a trick," said the woman. "You seize on the moment in time. We were here this afternoon. We're always here. Our life goes on around you, but nobody knows it. The trick's easier by night, that's all."

"Am I dreaming, then?" asked Deborah.

"No," said the woman, "this isn't a dream. And it isn't death, either. It's the secret world."

The secret world . . . It was something Deborah had always known, and now the pattern was complete. The memory of it and the relief were so tremendous that something seemed to burst inside her heart.

"Of course . . ." she said, "of course . . ." and everything that had ever been fell into place. There was no disharmony. The joy was indescribable, and the surge of feeling, like wings about her in the air, lifted her away from the turnstile and the woman, and she had all knowledge. That was it—the invasion of knowledge.

"I'm not myself, then, after all," she thought. "I knew I wasn't. It was only the task given," and, looking down, she saw a little child who was blind trying to find her way. Pity seized her. She bent down and put her hands on the child's eyes, and they opened, and the child was herself at two years old. The incident came back. It was when her mother died and Roger was born.

"It doesn't matter after all," she told the child. "You are not lost. You don't have to go on crying." Then the child that had been herself melted and became absorbed in the water and the sky, and the joy of the invading flood intensified so

145

that there was no body at all but only being. No words, only movements. And the beating of wings. This above all, the beating of wings.

"Don't let me go!" It was a pulse in her ear, and a cry, and she saw the woman at the turnstile put up her hands to hold her. Then there was such darkness, such dragging, terrible darkness, and the beginning of pain all over again, the leaden heart, the tears, the misunderstanding. The voice saying "No!" was her own harsh, worldly voice, and she was staring at the restless trees, black and ominous against the sky. One hand trailed in the water of the pool.

Deborah sat up, sobbing. The hand that had been in the pool was wet and cold. She dried it on the rug. And suddenly she was seized with such fear that her body took possession, and throwing aside the rug she began to run along the alleyway, the dark trees mocking and the welcome of the woman at the turnstile turned to treachery. Safety lay in the house behind the closed curtains, security was with the grandparents sleeping in their beds, and like a leaf driven before a whirlwind Deborah was out of the woods and across the silver soaking lawn, up the steps beyond the terrace and through the garden gate to the back door.

The slumbering solid house received her. It was like an old staid person who, surviving many trials, had learnt experience. "Don't take any notice of them," it seemed to say, jerking its head—did a house have a head?—towards the woods beyond. "They've made no contribution to civilisation. I'm man-made and different. This is where you belong, dear child. Now settle down."

Deborah went back again upstairs and into her bedroom. Nothing had changed. It was still the same. Going to the open window, she saw that the woods and the lawn seemed unaltered from the moment, how long back she did not know, when she had stood there, deciding upon the visit to the pool. The only difference now was in herself. The excitement had gone, the tension too. Even the terror of those last moments, when her flying feet had brought her to the house, seemed unreal.

She drew the curtains, just as her grandmother might have

done, and climbed into bed. Her mind was now preoccupied with practical difficulties, like explaining the presence of the lilo and the rug beside the pool. Willis might find them and tell her grandfather. The feel of her own pillow and of her own blankets reassured her. Both were familiar. And being tired was familiar too—it was a solid bodily ache, like the tiredness after too much jumping or cricket. The thing was, though—and the last remaining conscious thread of thought decided to postpone conclusion until the morning—which was real? This safety of the house or the secret world?

2

When Deborah woke next morning she knew at once that her mood was bad. It would last her for the day. Her eyes ached, and her neck was stiff, and there was a taste in her mouth like magnesia. Immediately Roger came running into her room, his face refreshed and smiling from some dreamless sleep, and jumped on her bed.

"It's come," he said, "the heat wave's come. It's going to be ninety in the shade."

Deborah considered how best she could damp his day. "It can go to a hundred for all I care," she said. "I'm going to read all morning."

His face fell. A look of bewilderment came into his eyes. "But the house?" he said. "We'd decided to have a house in the trees, don't you remember? I was going to get some planks from Willis."

Deborah turned over in bed and humped her knees. "You can if you like," she said. "I think it's a silly game."

She shut her eyes, feigning sleep, and presently she heard his feet patter slowly back to his own room, and then the thud of a ball against the wall. If he goes on doing that, she thought maliciously, Grandpapa will ring his bell and Agnes will come panting up the stairs. She hoped for destruction, for grumbling and snapping, and everyone falling out, not speaking. That was the way of the world.

The kitchen, where the children breakfasted, faced west, so it did not get the morning sun. Agnes had hung up fly-papers to catch wasps. The cereal, Puffed Wheat, was soggy. Deborah complained, mashing the mess with her spoon.

"It's a new packet," said Agnes. "You're mighty particular all of a sudden."

"Deb's got out of bed the wrong side," said Roger.

The two remarks fused to make a challenge. Deborah seized the nearest weapon, a knife, and threw it at her brother. It narrowly missed his eye but cut his cheek. Surprised, he put his hand to his face and felt the blood. Hurt, not by the knife but by his sister's action, his face turned red and his lower lip quivered. Deborah ran out of the kitchen and slammed the door. Her own violence distressed her, but the power of the mood was too strong. Going on to the terrace, she saw that the worst had happened. Willis had found the lilo and the rug, and had put them to dry in the sun. He was talking to her grandmother. Deborah tried to slip back into the house, but it was too late.

"Deborah, how very thoughtless of you," said Grandmama. "I tell you children every summer that I don't mind your taking the things from the hut into the garden if only you'll put them back."

Deborah knew she should apologise, but the mood forbade it. "That old rug is full of moths," she said contemptuously, "and the lilo has a rainproof back. It doesn't hurt them."

They both stared at her, and her grandmother flushed, just as Roger had done when she had thrown the knife at him. Then her grandmother turned her back and continued giving some instructions to the gardener.

Deborah stalked along the terrace, pretending that nothing had happened, and, skirting the lawn, she made her way towards the orchard and so to the fields beyond. She picked up a windfall, but as soon as her teeth bit into it the taste was green. She threw it away. She went and sat on a gate and stared in front of her, looking at nothing. Such deception everywhere. Such sour sadness. It was like Adam and Eve being locked out of paradise. The Garden of Eden was no more. Somewhere, very close, the woman at the turnstile waited to let her in, the secret world was all about her, but the key was gone. Why had she ever come back? What had brought her?

People were going about their business. The old man who came three days a week to help Willis was sharpening his scythe behind the tool shed. Beyond the field where the lane ran towards the main road she could see the top of the postman's head. He was pedalling his bicycle towards the village. She heard Roger calling, "Deb? Deb . . . ?" which meant that he had forgiven her, but still the mood held sway and she did not answer. Her own dullness made her own punishment. Presently a knocking sound told her that he had got the planks from Willis and had embarked on the building of his house. He was like his grandfather; he kept to the routine set for himself.

Deborah was consumed with pity. Not for the sullen self humped upon the gate, but for all of them going about their business in the world who did not hold the key. The key was hers and she had lost it. Perhaps if she worked her way through the long day the magic would return with evening and she would find it once again. Or even now. Even now, by the pool, there might be a clue, a vision.

Deborah slid off the gate and went the long way round. By skirting the fields, parched under the sun, she could reach the other side of the wood and meet no one. The husky wheat was stiff. She had to keep close to the hedge to avoid brushing it, and the hedge was tangled. Foxgloves had grown too tall and were bending with empty sockets, their flowers gone. There were nettles everywhere. There was no gate into the wood, and she had to climb the pricking hedge with the barbed wire, tearing her knickers. Once in the wood some measure of peace returned, but the alleyways this side had not been scythed and the grass was long. She had to wade through it like a sea, brushing it aside with her hands.

She came upon the pool from behind the monster tree, the hybrid whose naked arms were like a dead man's stumps, projecting at all angles. This side, on the lip of the pool, the scum was carpet-thick, and all the lilies, coaxed by the risen sun, had opened wide. They basked as lizards bask on hot stone walls. But here, with stems in water, they swung in grace, cluster upon cluster, pink and waxen white. "They're asleep," thought Deborah. "So is the wood. The morning is not their time," and it seemed to her beyond possibility that the turnstile was at hand and the woman waiting, smiling. "She said they were always there, even in the day, but the truth is that, being a child, I'm blinded in the day. I don't know how to see."

She dipped her hands in the pool, and the water was tepid brown. She tasted her fingers and the taste was rank. Brackish water, stagnant from long stillness. Yet beneath . . . beneath, she knew, by night the woman waited, and not only the woman but the whole secret world. Deborah began to pray. "Let it happen again," she whispered. "Let it happen again. Tonight. I won't be afraid."

The sluggish pool made no acknowledgment, but the very silence seemed a testimony of faith, of acceptance. Beside the pool, where the imprint of the lilo had marked the moss, Deborah found a Kirbigrip, fallen from her hair during the night. It was proof of visitation. She threw it into the pool as part of the treasury. Then she walked back into the ordinary day and the heat wave, and her black mood was softened. She went to find Roger in the orchard. He was busy with the platform. Three of the boards were fixed, and the noisy hammering was something that had to be borne. He saw her coming, and as always, after trouble, sensed that her mood had changed and mention must never be made of it. Had he called, "Feeling better?" it would have revived the antagonism, and she might not play with him all the day. Instead, he took no notice. She must be the first to speak.

Deborah waited at the foot of the tree, then bent, and handed him up an apple. It was green, but the offering meant peace. He ate it manfully. "Thanks," he said. She climbed into the tree beside him and reached for the box of nails. Contact had been renewed. All was well between them.

3

The hot day spun itself out like a web. The heat haze stretched across the sky, dun-coloured and opaque. Crouching on the burning boards of the apple tree, the children drank ginger beer and fanned themselves with dock leaves. They grew hotter still. When the cowbells summoned them for lunch they found that their grandmother had drawn the curtains of all the rooms downstairs, and the drawing-room was a vault and strangely cool. They flung themselves into chairs. No one was hungry. Patch lay under the piano, his soft mouth dripping saliva. Grandmama had changed into a sleeveless linen dress never before seen, and Grandpapa, in a dented panama, carried a fly whisk used years ago in Egypt.

"Ninety-one," he said grimly, "on the Air Ministry roof. It was on the one o'clock news."

Deborah thought of the men who must measure heat, toiling up and down on this Ministry roof with rods and tapes and odd-shaped instruments. Did anyone care but Grandpapa?

"Can we take our lunch outside?" asked Roger.

His grandmother nodded. Speech was too much effort, and she sank languidly into her chair at the foot of the dining-room table. The roses she had picked last night had wilted.

The children carried chicken drumsticks to the summer-house. It was too hot to sit inside, but they sprawled in the shadow it cast, their heads on faded cushions shedding kapok. Somewhere, far above their heads, an aeroplane climbed like a small silver fish, and was lost in space.

"A Meteor," said Roger. "Grandpapa says they're obsolete."

Deborah thought of Icarus, soaring towards the sun. Did he know when his wings began to melt? How did he feel? She stretched out her arms and thought of them as wings. The fingertips would be the first to curl, and then turn cloggy soft and useless. What terror in the sudden loss of height, the drooping power. . . .

Roger, watching her, hoped it was some game. He threw his picked drumstick into a flower bed and jumped to his feet.

"Look," he said, "I'm a Javelin," and he too stretched his arms and ran in circles, banking. Jet noises came from his clenched teeth. Deborah dropped her arms and looked at the drumstick. What had been clean and white from Roger's teeth was now earth-brown. Was it offended to be chucked away? Years later, when everyone was dead, it would be found, moulded like a fossil. Nobody would care.

"Come on," said Roger.

"Where to?" she asked.

"To fetch the raspberries," he said.

"You go," she told him.

Roger did not like going into the dining-room alone. He was self-conscious. Deborah made a shield from the adult eyes. In the end he consented to fetch the raspberries without her on condition that she played cricket after tea. After tea was a long way off.

She watched him return, walking very slowly, bearing the plates of raspberries and clotted cream. She was seized with sudden pity, that same pity which, earlier, she had felt for all people other than herself. How absorbed he was, how intent on the moment that held him. But tomorrow he would be some old man far away, the garden forgotten and this day long past.

"Grandmama says it can't go on," he announced. "There'll have to be a storm."

But why? Why not forever? Why not breathe a spell so that all of them could stay locked and dreaming like the courtiers in the *Sleeping Beauty*, never knowing, never waking, cobwebs in their hair and on their hands, tendrils imprisoning the house itself?

"Race me," said Roger, and to please him she plunged her spoon into the mush of raspberries but finished last, to his delight.

No one moved during the long afternoon. Grandmama went upstairs to her room. The children saw her at her window in her petticoat drawing the curtains close. Grandpapa put his feet up in the drawing-room, a handkerchief over his face. Patch did not stir from his place under the piano. Roger, undefeated, found employment still. He first helped Agnes to shell peas for supper, squatting on the back-door step while she relaxed on a lopsided basket chair dragged from the servants' hall. This task finished, he discovered a tin bath, put away in the cellar, in which Patch had been washed in younger days. He carried it to the lawn and filled it with water. Then he stripped to bathing trunks and sat in it solemnly, an umbrella over his head to keep off the sun.

Deborah lay on her back behind the summerhouse, wondering what would happen if Jesus and Buddha met. Would there be discussion, courtesy, an exchange of views like politicians at summit talks? Or were they after all the same person, born at separate times? The queer thing was that this topic, interesting now, meant nothing in the secret world. Last night, through the turnstile, all problems disappeared. They were nonexistent. There was only the knowledge and the joy.

She must have slept, because when she opened her eyes she saw to her dismay that Roger was no longer in the bath but was hammering the cricket stumps into the lawn. It was a quarter to five.

"Hurry up," he called, when he saw her move. "I've had tea."

She got up and dragged herself into the house, sleepy still, and giddy. The grandparents were in the drawing-room, refreshed from the long repose of the afternoon. Grandpapa smelt of eau de cologne. Even Patch had come to and was lapping his saucer of cold tea.

"You look tired," said Grandmama critically. "Are you feeling all right?"

Deborah was not sure. Her head was heavy. It must have been sleeping in the afternoon, a thing she never did.

"I think so," she answered, "but if anyone gave me roast pork I know I'd be sick."

"No one suggested you should eat roast pork," said her grandmother, surprised. "Have a cucumber sandwich, they're cool enough."

Grandpapa was lying in wait for a wasp. He watched it hover over his tea, grim, expectant. Suddenly he slammed at the air with his whisk. "Got the brute," he said in triumph. He ground it into the carpet with his heel. It made Deborah think of Jehovah.

"Don't rush around in the heat," said Grandmama. "It isn't wise. Can't you and Roger play some nice, quiet game?"

"What sort of game?" asked Deborah.

But her grandmother was without invention. The croquet mallets were all broken. "We might pretend to be dwarfs and use the heads," said Deborah, and she toyed for a moment with the idea of squatting to croquet. Their knees would stiffen, though, it would be too difficult.

"I'll read aloud to you, if you like," said Grandmama.

Deborah seized upon the suggestion. It delayed cricket. She ran out on to the lawn and padded the idea to make it acceptable to Roger.

"I'll play afterwards," she said, "and that ice cream that Agnes has in the fridge, you can eat all of it. I'll talk tonight in bed."

Roger hesitated. Everything must be weighed. Three goods to balance evil.

"You know that stick of sealing wax Daddy gave you?" he said.

"Yes."

"Can I have it?"

The balance for Deborah too. The quiet of the moment in opposition to the loss of the long thick stick so brightly red.

"All right," she grudged.

Roger left the cricket stumps and they went into the drawing-room. Grandpapa, at the first suggestion of reading aloud, had disappeared, taking Patch with him. Grandmama had cleared away the tea. She found her spectacles and the book. It was *Black Beauty*. Grandmama kept no modern children's books, and this made common ground for the three of them. She read the terrible chapter where the stable lad lets Beauty get overheated and gives him a cold drink and does not put on his blanket. The story was suited to the day. Even Roger listened entranced. And Deborah, watching her grandmother's calm face and hearing her careful voice reading the sentences, thought how strange it was that Grandmama could turn herself into Beauty with such ease. She *was* a horse, suffering there with pneumonia in the stable, being saved by the wise coachman.

After the reading, cricket was anticlimax, but Deborah must keep her bargain. She kept thinking of Black Beauty writing the book. It showed how good the story was, Grandmama said, because no child had ever yet questioned the practical side of it, or posed the picture of a horse with a pen in its hoof.

"A modern horse would have a typewriter," thought Deborah, and she began to bowl to Roger, smiling to herself as she did so because of the twentieth-century Beauty clacking with both hoofs at a machine.

This evening, because of the heat wave, the routine was changed. They had their baths first, before their supper, for they were hot and exhausted from the cricket. Then, putting on pyjamas and cardigans, they ate their supper on the terrace. For once Grandmama was indulgent. It was still so hot that they could not take chill, and the dew had not yet risen. It made a small excitement, being in pyjamas on the terrace. Like people abroad, said Roger. Or natives in the South Seas, said Deborah. Or beachcombers who had lost caste. Grandpapa, changed into a white tropical jacket, had not lost caste.

"He's a white trader," whispered Deborah. "He's made a fortune out of pearls."

Roger choked. Any joke about his grandfather, whom he feared, had all the sweet agony of danger.

"What's the thermometer say?" asked Deborah.

Her grandfather, pleased at her interest, went to inspect it.

"Still above eighty," he said with relish.

Deborah, when she cleaned her teeth later, thought how pale her face looked in the mirror above the washbasin. It was not brown, like Roger's, from the day in the sun, but wan and yellow. She tied back her hair with a ribbon, and the nose and chin were peaky sharp. She yawned largely, as Agnes did in the kitchen on Sunday afternoons.

"Don't forget you promised to talk," said Roger quickly.

Talk . . . that was the burden. She was so tired she longed for the white smoothness of her pillow, all blankets thrown aside, bearing only a single sheet. But Roger, wakeful on his bed, the door between them wide, would not relent. Laughter was the one solution, and to make him hysterical, and so exhaust him sooner, she fabricated a day in the life of Willis, from his first morning kipper to his final glass of beer at the village inn. The adventures in between would have tried Gulliver. Roger's delight drew protests from the adult world below. There was the sound of a bell, and then Agnes came up the stairs and put her head round the corner of Deborah's door.

"Your granny says you're not to make so much noise," she said.

Deborah, spent with invention, lay back and closed her eyes. She could go no further. The children called good night to each other, both speaking at the same time, from age-long custom, beginning with their names and addresses and ending with the world, the universe, and space. Then the final main "Good night," after which neither must ever speak, on pain of unknown calamity.

"I must try and keep awake," thought Deborah, but the power was not in her. Sleep was too compelling, and it was hours later that she opened her eyes and saw her curtains blowing and the forked flash light the ceiling, and heard the trees tossing and sobbing against the sky. She was out of bed in an instant. Chaos had come. There were no stars, and the night was sulphurous. A great crack split the heavens and tore them in two. The garden groaned. If the rain would only fall there might be mercy, and the trees, imploring, bowed themselves this way and that, while the vivid lawn, bright in expectation, lay like a sheet of metal exposed to flame. Let the waters break. Bring down the rain.

Suddenly the lightning forked again, and standing there, alive yet immobile, was the woman by the turnstile. She stared up at the windows of the house, and Deborah recognised her. The turnstile was there, inviting entry, and already the phantom figures, passing through it, crowded towards the trees beyond the lawn. The secret world was waiting. Through the long day, while the storm was brewing, it had hovered there unseen beyond her reach, but now that night had come, and the thunder with it, the barriers were down. Another crack, mighty in its summons, the turnstile yawned, and the woman with her hand upon it smiled and beckoned.

Deborah ran out of the room and down the stairs. Somewhere somebody called—Roger, perhaps, it did not matter—and Patch was barking; but, caring nothing for concealment, she went through the dark drawing-room and opened the french window on to the terrace. The lightning searched the terrace and lit the paving, and Deborah ran down the steps on to the lawn where the turnstile gleamed.

Haste was imperative. If she did not run, the turnstile might be closed, the woman vanish, and all the wonder of the sacred world be taken from her. She was in time. The woman was still waiting. She held out her hand for tickets, but Deborah shook her head. "I have none." The woman, laughing, brushed her through into the secret world where there were no laws, no rules, and all the faceless phantoms ran before her to the woods, blown by the rising wind. Then the rain came. The sky, deep brown as the lightning pierced it, opened, and the water hissed to the ground, rebounding from the earth in bubbles. There was no order now in the alleyway. The ferns had turned to trees, the trees to Titans. All moved in ecstasy, with sweeping limbs, but the rhythm was broken up, tumultuous, so that some of them were bent backwards, torn by the sky, and others dashed their heads to the undergrowth where they were caught and beaten.

In the world behind, laughed Deborah as she ran, this would be punishment, but here in the secret world it was a tribute. The phantoms who ran beside her were like waves. They were linked one with another, and they were, each one of them, and Deborah too, part of the night force that made the sobbing and the laughter. The lightning forked where they willed it, and the thunder cracked as they looked upwards to the sky.

The pool had come alive. The water lilies had turned to hands, with palms upraised, and in the far corner, usually so still under the green scum, bubbles sucked at the surface, steaming and multiplying as the torrents fell. Everyone crowded to the pool. The phantoms bowed and crouched by the water's edge, and now the woman had set up her turnstile in the middle of the pool, beckoning them once more.

Some remnant of a sense of social order rose in Deborah and protested.

"But we've already paid," she shouted, and remembered a second later that she had passed through free. Must there be duplication? Was the secret world a rainbow, always repeating itself, alighting on another hill when you believed yourself beneath it? No time to think. The phantoms had gone through. The lightning, streaky white, lit the old dead monster tree with his crown of ivy, and because he had no spring now in his joints he could not sway in tribute with the trees and ferns, but had to remain there, rigid, like a crucifix.

"And now . . . and now . . . and now . . ." called Deborah.

The triumph was that she was not afraid, was filled with such wild acceptance. . . . She ran into the pool. Her living feet felt the mud and the broken sticks and all the tangle of old weeds, and the water was up to her armpits and her chin. The lilies held her. The rain blinded her. The woman and the turnstile were no more.

"Take me too," cried the child. "Don't leave me behind!" In her heart was a savage disenchantment. They had broken their promise, they had left her in the world. The pool that claimed her now was not the pool of secrecy, but dank, dark, brackish water choked with scum.

4

"Grandpapa says he's going to have it fenced round," said Roger. "It should have been done years ago. A proper fence, then nothing can ever happen. But barrowloads of shingle tipped in it first. Then it won't be a pool, but just a dew pond. Dew ponds aren't dangerous."

He was looking at her over the edge of her bed. He had risen in status, being the only one of them downstairs, the bearer of tidings good or ill, the go-between. Deborah had been ordered two days in bed.

"I should think by Wednesday," he went on, "you'd be able to play cricket. It's not as if you're hurt. People who walk in their sleep are just a bit potty."

"I did not walk in my sleep," said Deborah.

"Grandpapa said you must have done," said Roger. "It was a good thing that Patch woke him up and he saw you going across the lawn . . ." Then, to show his release from tension, he stood on his hands.

Deborah could see the sky from her bed. It was flat and dull. The day was a summer day that had worked through storm. Agnes came into the room with junket on a tray. She looked important.

"Now run off," she said to Roger. "Deborah doesn't want to talk to you. She's supposed to rest."

Surprisingly, Roger obeyed, and Agnes placed the junket on the table beside the bed. "You don't feel hungry, I expect," she said. "Never mind, you can eat this later when you fancy it. Have you got a pain? It's usual, the first time."

"No," said Deborah.

What had happened to her was personal. They had prepared her for it at school, but nevertheless it was a shock, not to be discussed with Agnes. The woman hovered a moment, in case the child asked questions; but, seeing that none came, she turned and left the room.

Deborah, her cheek on her hand, stared at the empty sky. The heaviness of knowledge lay upon her, a strange, deep sorrow.

"It won't come back," she thought. "I've lost the key."

The hidden world, like ripples on the pool so soon to be filled in and fenced, was out of her reach forever.

THE PRINCIPALITY of Ronda, in southern Europe, has been a republic now for many years. It was the last country to throw off the chains of the monarchical system, and its revolution, when it came, was a particularly bloody one. The *volte-face* from dependence on the rule of one leader, the Archduke, whose family had been in power for nearly seven hundred years, to the enlightened government of the Popular Front, or P.F. Ltd., as it came to be known—it was a combination of big business and communism—shook the rest of the Western world, which had long since recognised the red light and given way to expediency, packing off the remaining monarchs on an endless cruise in a giant ocean liner. Here they lived very happily together, enjoying perpetual intrigues, intermarrying, and never setting foot on land to bring strife again to the freed peoples of Europe.

The revolution came as a shock, because Ronda had been for so long not only the butt of the democratic states, but also a favourite playground for tourists. Its attraction was understandable. The very smallness of Ronda made it unlike any other country. Moreover, although it was so minute, it had everything the heart could desire. Its one mountain, Ronderhof, was twelve thousand feet high, the summit accessible from all four faces, and the skiing on the lower slopes was the best in Europe. Its one river, the Rondaquiver, was navigable to the capital, and the lower reaches, dotted with islets each boasting its own casino and bathing beach, drew thousands of tourists in the warm season. And then there were its waters.

The famous springs were in the hills behind the capital,

and it was really these which had constituted the greatest asset of the reigning family throughout the centuries, for they possessed extraordinary, even unique, properties. For one thing, used in conjunction with a certain formula they bestowed perpetual youth. This formula was the secret of the reigning Archduke, who, on his deathbed, handed it on to his heir. Even if it could not keep the last enemy at bay for ever—since even princes must die—the waters of Ronda did at least ensure that the Archdukes were laid in their graves without wrinkles and without grey hairs.

This formula, as I have said, was known only to the reigning prince, who alone benefited from it; but the natural waters could be drunk by any tourist who visited the principality, and had a marvellously revitalising effect. Certainly until the revolution they flocked to Ronda in their thousands, men and women from all over the world, who wished to take back with them, into their humdrum lives, something of the elixir that the waters contained.

It is hard to define, in so many words, what Ronda did to the tourists. They were easily recognisable, on their return, by the very special bronze of the skin, by the dreamy, almost faraway expression in the eyes, and by the curious attitude to life that nothing mattered. "He who has been in Ronda has seen God," was the well-known phrase, and indeed the shrug of the shoulder, the careless yawn, the half smile on the faces of those whose winter or summer vacation had been spent "across the border" suggested some sort of other-world intimacy, a knowledge of secret places denied to those who had remained at home.

The effect wore off, of course. The factory bench claimed the worker, the office desk the administrator, the laboratory the chemist; but sometimes, during the brief moments when they had time to reflect, these tourists who had been to Ronda thought of the ice-cold water they had borne away from the springs in the high mountain, of the islets in the Rondaquiver, of the cafés in the great square of the capital city, dominated as it was by the palace of the Archduke—now a museum hung with trophies of the revolution and dull as ditchwater.

In old days, when the palace was guarded by members of

the Imperial guard in their splendid uniforms of blue and gold, and the royal standard—an emblem of the water of Life against a white field—flew from its flagpole, and the Imperial band played the haunting Rondese folk songs that were half gypsy and half chant, then the tourists would sit in the square after dinner and wait for the Archduke to appear on the balcony. It was the great climax of the day. To anyone who had climbed the Ronderhof or swum in the Rondaquiver, and had also drunk the elixir from the spring, this appearance of the reigning monarch somehow epitomised all that the visitor felt about the duchy, whether he had come to scoff or to admire. A little intoxicated, because the wine made from the Ronda grape is potent and very dry, a little full, because the flesh of the fish from the Rondaquiver is rich, a little sad, because the gypsy-chant music touches forgotten memories, the visitor was therefore prepared, despite his more rational self, for some sort of picturesque denouement; yet even so he was always surprised, and later moved.

First there was silence. The lights in the square dimmed. Then, softly, the Imperial band began to play the national anthem, the first line of which, roughly translated, ran, "I am that which you seek, I am the water of Life." Then the windows of the palace opened, and a figure in a white uniform appeared on the balcony. Bats or airy mice, symbolising dreams, were at the same moment let loose from the royal belfry, and the effect was weird and oddly beautiful, the night creatures flying blindly in ever-widening circles round the shining head of the Archduke—the Archdukes of Ronda were always blond—and no sound but the beating of innumerable tiny wings. The Archduke would remain motionless on the balcony, lit by arc lights concealed in the stonework of the balustrade, the red ribbon of the Order of the Just the only patch of colour on the white uniform. Even at a distance the figure was appealing, giving the hardiest republican tourist a reactionary lump in the throat. As a well-known foreign journalist put it, the first glimpse of the Archduke of Ronda awoke the protective instinct in man lying dormant beneath the surface, that instinct which, he continued, for the safety of the human race is better extinguished.

According to those who were lucky enough to have seats near the palace, and were themselves bathed in the glow from the arc lights, the most extraordinary thing about these nightly appearances was the fact that they never varied. The precision and timing were perfect, and the Archduke really did have the miraculous beauty of eternal youth. There was a breath-catching quality about the radiant figure with his hands clasped on his sword, alone there on the balcony, and it was no use for the scoffers to remind their neighbours that the Archduke was now in his nineties and had been doing this for years, long before many of those present were born; nobody cared or even listened. Each appearance was, in a sense, an incarnation of that original prince who had appeared to the people of Ronda after the great flooding of the Rondaquiver in mediaeval times, when three quarters of the inhabitants lost their lives, and suddenly in their midst, as Rondese history has it, "The waters subsided, all but the springs from the mountain face, and a prince came forth bearing the chalice of immortality, and he ruled over them."

Modern historians, of course, say all this is nonsense, and claim that the original Archduke was not miraculous at all, but a goatherd who, after the disaster, rose up to lead and encourage the few exhausted and despairing survivors. Be that as it may, the legend dies hard, and even now, when the republic is of many years' standing, the older people treasure little ikons that, they whisper, were blessed by the hand of the late Archduke, before the revolutionaries hung him by the heels in the palace square. But I anticipate . . .

Ronda, as you have learnt, was a country given over to pleasure, to healing, to peace. There man found his heart's desire. Volumes have been written about Rondese women. They are, or were, shy as squirrels, beautiful as gazelles, and with the grace of Etruscan figurines. No man ever had the luck to bring back a bride from Ronda—marriage outside the country was forbidden—but love affairs were not unknown, and those fortunate tourists who hazarded rebuff, and were not killed by angry fathers, husbands, or brothers, used to swear, on returning to their own enlightened land, that never until the day they died would they forget what it had meant to lie in the arms of a Rondese woman, and experience the extraordinary intoxication of her caress.

Ronda had no religion, as such. By that I mean no dogma, no state church. The Rondese believed in the healing waters from the spring and in the secret formula of eternal youth known to the Archduke, but other than this they had no place of worship, no church dignitaries; and oddly enough the Rondese language—which sounds like a mixture of French and Greek—has no word for God.

It has altered a lot, though, that's the pity. Now Ronda is a republic all sorts of other Western words have crept into the common speech, words like weekend and Coca-Cola. The marriage barrier has broken down—you can see Rondese girls on Broadway and in Piccadilly, hardly distinguishable from their companions. And the customs that were so essentially Rondese in the days of the Archdukes, such as fish spearing, fountain leaping, and snow dancing, have all died out. The only thing about Ronda that cannot be spoilt is the contour of the land—the high mountain, the winding river. And of course the light, the clear radiance that is never overcast, never dull, and can only be compared to the reflection from purest aquamarine. The light of Ronda can be seen by a departing aircraft—for there is an airport now, built soon after the revolution—long after the take-off, when the aircraft is already many miles across the frontier.

Even now, when so much has been changed, the tourist leaves Ronda with regret and nostalgia. He sips his last Ritzo —the sweet insidious liqueur of the country—he smells his last Rovlvula flower, that heady blossom whose golden petals cover the streets in late summer, he waves his hand for the last time to a bronzed figure bathing in the Rondaquiver; and he is standing in the impersonal lounge of the airport, soon to be heading east or west, back to work, to the cause, to the bettering of the lives of his fellow creatures, away from the land of unfulfilled desire, away from Ronda.

Perhaps the most poignant thing about the capital today— apart from the palace, which, as I have said, is now a museum—is the one remaining member of the reigning family. They still call her the Archduchess. For a reason which will be later revealed, they did not butcher her with her brother. The Archduchess holds the secret of eternal youth—the only member of the archducal family, other than the reigning Archduke, ever to have done so. Her brother told her the formula before they came to kill him. She has never revealed it, and she will carry the secret with her to the grave. They tried everything, of course: imprisonment, torture, exile, truth-revealing drugs and brainwashing; but nothing would make her give to the world the secret of the elixir of youth.

The Archduchess must be over eighty, and she has not been well for some months. Doctors say that her ordeal can hardly last another winter. She comes of rare stock, though, and she may yet defeat the pessimists. She is still the most beautiful girl in the whole republic, and I use the word girl advisedly, because, in spite of her years, the Archduchess *is* still a girl in appearance and in ways. The golden hair, the liquid eyes, the grace of manner that fascinated so many of her contemporaries, now dead—murdered, most of them, on the Night of the Big Knives—have not altered. She still dances to the old folk tunes, if you throw her a rondip (which is a coin about the value of one dollar). But to those of us who remember her in her prime, who remember her popularity among the people—I would go so far as to say her adulation by them—her patronage of the arts, her great romance with her cousin Count Anton, which the growing revolutionary feeling in the country denied . . . to those of us who remember these things, the sight of the Archduchess Paula of Ronda dancing for her supper and for the amusement of the tourists brings a feeling of nausea, a constriction of the heart. It was not so once. We remember the days of the balcony, and the airy mice.

So . . . if it would not bore you too much—and remember, the details are not in the modern history books of the country that students are rewriting for the instruction of future generations—I will tell you, as briefly as I can, how the last principality in Europe fell, how Ronda became a republic, and how the first feelings of unrest stirred the people, partly through misunderstanding of this same Arch-duchess, whom, fallen from favour, you can now see dipping and bobbing in the palace square.

2

I propose to skip Rondese history. The original peoples came by sea from Crete and overland from Gaul, and later there was a mixture of Romany blood. Then, as you have heard, during the early part of the fourteenth century the flooding of the Rondaquiver killed off at least three quarters of the inhabitants. The first Archduke restored order, rebuilt the capital, saw to the planting of the crops and the tending of the vines—in short, gave back to the stricken people the desire to live.

In his self-imposed mission he was largely helped by the spring waters, which, even if the Archduke was the only one to hold the secret of how they could be made to give eternal youth, did in themselves contain valuable properties. They gave, to whosoever drank them, that sense of well-being on waking which a child has before puberty; or perhaps it would be more correct to say the renewal of wonder. A child who fears neither parent nor instructor has but one desire when he opens his eyes, and that is to leave his bed and run out with bare feet under the sun. Then alone his dream can be recaptured, for the day that has dawned has dawned for him. The waters of Ronda gave this renewal.

It was by no means an illusion, as sceptics have sometimes maintained. Modern scientists know that the chemical prop-erties release certain substances in the endocrine glands, which is why the bottling of the waters now constitutes the main industry of Ronda. The United States buys over eighty per cent of the total annual output. Originally, though, since the industry was in the hands of the Archduke, the waters were bottled privately and sold only to those visitors who crossed the borders into the country. The wastage must have been enormous, if you consider the source, flowing as it did from the cave nine thousand feet up on Ronderhof and cascading in falls down the mountainside. All that energy, which might have been tapped and pumped into the veins of tired Americans, merely tumbled over bare rocks into the air and down to the valleys below, where it nourished the already rich earth and produced the golden Rovlvula flower.

The people of Ronda, of course, drank the waters with their mother's milk: hence their beauty, and their *joie de vivre*, and the gaiety which made them incapable of ill-feeling or ambition. That, I have always understood from the historians, was the essence of the Rondese character—contentment, lack of ambition. Why, asked Oldo, Ronda's famous poet, why kill, when we are lovers? Why weep, when we are glad? And why indeed should the Rondese cross the Ronderhof to countries where there was sickness and plague, poverty and war, or sail down the Rondaquiver to lands where the people were herded together in slums and tenements, each man imbued with the determination to do better than his neighbour?

It did not make sense to the Rondese. They had had their flood. Their ancestors had perished. One day perhaps the Rondaquiver would rise and overwhelm them again, but until that day came let them live and dance and dream. Let them spear the leaping fish in the Rondaquiver, let them jump the waters of the Ronderhof, let them gather the golden Rovlvula flowers and tread the petals and the vines, harvest the grain, tend the cattle and the sheep, cherished and watched over by the prince of eternal youth, the prince who passed and was born again. This is roughly what Oldo said, but Rondese translates with difficulty, for the whole idiom is so different from that of any other European language.

Life in Ronda, therefore, changed little during the centuries after the flood. Archduke succeeded Archduke, and no one ever knew the age of the ruler or of his heir apparent. Rumour would go about that the monarch was ailing or had suffered some accident—there was never anything secret about it; the thing happened and was accepted—and then the proclamation was fastened to the palace gates and it would be learnt that the Archduke had died and that the Archduke lived again. It could be called religion. Theosophists argue that it *was* religion, that the Archduke symbolised spring. Whatever it was, religion or working tradition, it suited the Rondese. They liked to think of their monarch handing on the secret of eternal youth to his successor, and they liked his blond beauty, and his white uniform, and the shining scabbards of the palace guards.

The monarch did not interfere with their pleasures, or indeed with their lives at all. As long as the land was tilled, and the harvest gathered, and enough food grown to feed the people—after all, their wants were few, with fish and fowl and vegetables and fruit, and the wine and liqueur from the vines—no laws needed to be passed. The marriage law was so self-evident that no one ever dreamt of breaking it. Who would want to marry a woman who was not Rondese? And what woman would consent to hold a child in her arms that might be born with the pudgy limbs and flabby skin of some stranger over the border?

It will be argued that the Rondese intermarried, that a small country the size of Cornwall was populated by people who were all related. This cannot be denied. It was indeed obvious to those who knew Ronda well in old days that, though nothing was said, many brothers paired with many sisters. Physically, the result appeared beneficial, mentally it did no harm. There were very few idiot children born in Ronda. It was this intermarrying, though, which, according to historians, made for lack of ambition amongst the Rondese, their rather lazy contentment, and their disinclination for war.

Why fight, as Oldo said, when we want for nothing? Why steal, when my purse is full? Why ravish a stranger, when my sister is my bride? No doubt these sentiments could be described as shocking, and many tourists were shocked when they came to a country so flowing with sensuous charm, so empty of moral principle; but however carping, however outraged, in the end the tourist was won. He could not stand up to beauty. Argument fell away, and by the time his holiday was over the tourist who had partaken of the spring waters was himself a proselyte, having discovered in Ronda an attitude to living that was both selfless and hedonistic, with mind and body in perfect harmony.

Here lay the tragedy. Western man is so constituted that he

cannot abide contentment. It is the unforgivable sin. He must forever strive towards some unseen goal, whether it be material comfort, a greater and purer God, or some weapon that will make him master of the universe. As he becomes more conscious he becomes more restless, more grasping, forever finding fault with the warm dust from which he sprang and to which he must return, forever desirous of improving and so enslaving his fellow men. It was this poison of discontent that finally infiltrated to Ronda, bred, alas, by contact with the outside world, and nurtured to maturity by the two revolutionary leaders, Markoi and Grandos.

You ask what made them revolutionaries? Other Rondese had crossed the borders and returned again unharmed. What was so special about Markoi and Grandos that made them wish to destroy the Ronda which had remained virtually unchanged for seven centuries?

The explanation is simple. Markoi, like Oedipus, was born lame, with a twisted foot: therefore he had a grudge against his parents. They had brought into the world a maimed being, and he could not forgive them for not having made him beautiful. The child who cannot forgive his parents cannot forgive the country that cradled him, and Markoi grew up with the desire to lame his country, even as he himself was lame. Grandos was born greedy. It has been said that he was not of pure blood, and that his mother, in a moment best forgotten, had coupled with some stranger from beyond the seas, who afterwards boasted of his conquest. Whether true or not, Grandos inherited an acquisitive nature and a quick intelligence. At school—there were never any distinctions in education, all receiving the same tuition except the reigning family—Grandos was always first in his class. He often knew an answer before his teacher. This made him conceited. The boy who knows more than his master knows more than his prince, and so eventually feels himself superior to the society into which he has been born.

The two boys became friends. Together they crossed the border and travelled in Europe. They returned, after six months, with the seed of discontent, unconscious hitherto, ripened and ready to break surface. Grandos went into the fishing industry and, being intelligent, made the discovery that the fish of the Rondaquiver—the staple diet of the Rondese, and so delectable to the connoisseur—could be used in other ways. The backbone, when split, was so curved that it was the exact shape of a woman's breast supporter, and the oil of the fish, if smoothed into a paste and scented with the Rovlvula flower, made a beauty cream that would nourish the toughest and oldest of complexions.

Grandos started an export business, sending his products all over the Western world, and was soon the richest man in Ronda. His own countrywomen, who hitherto had never used a breast supporter or a beauty cream in their lives, found themselves beguiled by the advertisements that he inserted in the newspapers, and began to wonder whether they would not increase their happiness by making use of his products.

Markoi did not go into industry. Despising his parents' vineyard, he became a journalist, and was soon appointed editor of the *Ronda News*. This had originally been a news-sheet giving the events of the day and the particulars of Rondese agriculture or trade, with an art supplement three times a week. It was the custom to read the news during the midday siesta, whether in the countryside or in the cafés. Markoi changed all this. The news was still given, but with a subtle slant, a mockery at the old-established customs such as treading the vines (this was a hit at his parents, of course), and spearing the fish (this to help Grandos, because spearing injured the fish's backbone and so harmed the export business), and gathering the Rovlvula flower (another piece of indirect assistance to Grandos, whose beauty paste demanded the crushed heart of the flower, which meant tearing the golden Rovlvula to pieces). Markoi encouraged the tearing of the flower because he liked to see anything beautiful destroyed, and because it hurt the feelings of the older people of Ronda, whose favourite springtime custom had been the flower gathering and the decorating of home and capital and palace with the fragrant blossoms. This artless enjoyment was something that Markoi could not bear, and he was determined to put an end to it, together with the other customs he disliked. Grandos was his ally not because he himself felt any sort of hatred towards the customs or traditions of Ronda, but because in destroying them he furthered his export trade and therefore became richer and more powerful than his neighbours.

Little by little the young Rondese were indoctrinated with the new values which they read about every day. The appearance of the newspaper was cunningly timed as well. It was no longer issued at midday, to be browsed over and then forgotten during the siesta, but was sold on the palace square and in the villages at sundown, that moment before dusk when the Rondese sips his Ritzo and is therefore more susceptible, more easily seduced. The effect was marked. The youthful Rondese, who until now had thought of little else but enjoying the two most perfect seasons of the year, the winter snows and the spring verdure, and making love through both, began to question their upbringing.

"Have we endured," asked Markoi, "seven centuries of neglect? Has Ronda become a paradise for fools? Anyone who crosses the border knows that the real world lies outside our frontiers, the world of achievement, the world of progress. The Rondese have been nurtured too long on lies. We are unique only that we are idiots, despised by men and women of intelligence."

No man likes to be called a fool. A gibe brings shame and doubt. The more advanced of the young people felt themselves insecure. And, whatever their occupation, the worth of what they did became doubtful.

"He who treads the vine with his bare feet treads himself into the ground," said Markoi. "Whoever spades the earth digs his own grave."

He was, you will observe, a bit of a poet, and had a clever knack of twisting the philosophy of Oldo into derogatory phrases.

"Why," he asked, "are we, the young and the strong, deliberately kept under by a system of government that withholds from us our own possession? We could all be leaders. Instead, we are led. The immortality that could make us rule the world is vested in the sham personage of one man who, by a trick, holds a chemical secret."

When Markoi wrote this on the day of the spring festival, and saw that a copy of the newspaper reached every household in Ronda, there was no longer any doubt amongst the inhabitants that their little world must change.

"There's truth in it, you know," said one man to his neighbour. "We've been too easygoing. We've just sat down through the centuries and accepted what's been handed to us."

"Look what it says here," said a woman to her companion. "The spring waters could be shared out, and none of us need ever grow old. There's more than enough for every woman in Ronda."

No one had the discourtesy to attack the Archduke himself, but there was, nevertheless, an undercurrent of criticism, a growing belief that the people of Ronda had been hoodwinked, kept in subjection, and because of this were in reality the laughingstock of the world. The spring festival, for the first time in centuries, lacked its essential gaiety.

"These nonsensical blossoms," wrote Markoi, "gathered by the toiling masses of Rondese men and women merely to drug the senses of the older generation and appease the vanity of one man, might have been crushed and distilled for *our* use, for *our* enrichment. The natural resources of Ronda should be exploited and sold, to benefit ourselves and all mankind."

There was logic in his argument. The waste, people whispered, of all those golden blossoms, of all that flowing water, of all the untrapped fish surging down the Ronda-quiver to the open sea, fish whose backbones might have braced the bosoms and enlaced the hips of the ungirt Rondese women, who must surely, as the newspaper said, be despised and laughed at by the rest of the Western world.

That night, for the first time in history, there was silence when the Archduke appeared on the balcony.

"What right," whispered a boy, "has he to lord it over us? He's made of flesh and blood, isn't he, no better than ourselves? It's only the elixir that keeps him young."

"They say," whispered the girl beside him, "that he has other secrets too. The palace is full of them. Not only how to prolong youth, but how to prolong love as well."

So envy was born, fostered by Markoi and Grandos, and the tourists who crossed the border were aware of the new spirit amongst the Rondese, an irritability and shortness of temper ill-suited to their fine physique. Instead of showing off the national ways and customs with unaffected enjoyment, they began, for the first time in history, to apologise for their imperfections. Imported words like "enslaved," "backward," "unprogressive" were used with a shamefaced shrug, and the tourists, with lack of intuition, added fuel to the smouldering fires of discontent by calling the Rondese "picturesque" and "quaint."

"Give me a year," Markoi is supposed to have said, "give me a year, and I'll bring down the ruling house by ridicule alone."

This suited Grandos. In a year he would have an agreement with every fisherman of the Rondaquiver to supply him with the backbones and oil from the fish caught in their nets, and by the end of the same year all flower gatherers under seventeen would have contracted to hand over the pulped hearts of the Rovlvula flowers, whose essence Grandos would manufacture into scent and export to the United States. Together he and Markoi, industrialist and journalist combined, would control the destiny of the Rondese people.

"Remember," said Grandos, "that united we are unbreakable, divided we fall apart. If you attack me in your paper I sell out to the highest bidders across the border. They walk in, and Ronda merges with the rest of Europe. You lose your power."

"And don't forget," said Markoi, "that unless you support my policy, and share your fish oil and your beauty paste, I'll turn every youngster in the republic against you."

"Republic?" asked Grandos, raising his eyebrows.

"Republic," nodded Markoi.

"The principality has lasted for seven centuries," ventured Grandos.

"I can destroy it in seven days," said Markoi.

This conversation is not recorded in the documents relating to the revolution, but it was reported, nevertheless, by word of mouth.

"And the Archduke?" mused Grandos. "How do we dispose of the immortal one?"

"In the same way," said Markoi, "as I dispose of the Rovlvula flower. By tearing him apart."

"He may escape us," Grandos said, "flee the country, and join the other exiles on that ridiculous liner."

"Not the Archduke," said Markoi. "You forget your history. All princes who believe in eternal youth offer themselves as victims."

"That's only myth," observed Grandos.

"True," agreed Markoi, "but most myths have a sound factual basis."

"In that case," said Grandos, "not one member of the reigning family must remain alive. One member would encourage reaction."

"No," said Markoi, "one member must remain. Not, as you may fear, for purposes of adoration, but as a human scarecrow. The Rondese people must be taught rejection."

The next day Markoi started his campaign, designed to spread over the year until the spring festival should come again. His purpose was to decry the Archduke, in the columns of the *Ronda News,* in so subtle a fashion that the people of the country would absorb the poison unconsciously. The idol must become the target, the figurehead the cutty stool. The way of attack lay through his sister, the Archduchess. Loveliest of women, without an enemy in the country, she was known as the Flower of Ronda. Markoi's intention was to bring about her moral and physical degradation. Whether he succeeded or failed, you shall hear in due course, if the subject interests you.

This man was evil, you say? Nonsense, he was an ideologist.

3

The Archduke was several years older than his sister. How many years, no one could say. And anyway, all records were burnt during the Night of the Big Knives. But it might have been as much as thirty years. The archducal birth dates were kept only in the palace archives, and the people had no curiosity. All they knew was that the Archduke of Ronda was in essence immortal, and that his spirit passed to his successor. Each prince was virtually the same through the seven centuries, and the time factor was unimportant. Perhaps the Archduchess Paula was not the Archduke's sister. Perhaps she was his great-granddaughter. You have to realise that the relationship was really immaterial, but she was of the blood royal, and had from the beginning been known as his sister.

Tourists from across the border were always baffled by the reigning family of Ronda. How can they exist, they asked, century after century, behind those palace walls and in those grounds—admittedly beautiful, what could be glimpsed of them—and up in the Ronderhof chalet during the skiing season and at high summer, and on Quiver islet when the fish were in spawn? What do they do all day? Are they never bored? And surely the intermarriage is shocking besides being dull? What about protocol? Is it rigid? Are they hemmed about with ceremony? The Rondese, when questioned, used to smile and say, "Frankly, we don't know. We believe them to be happy, as we are ourselves. Indeed, why not?" Why not? Nations other than the Rondese—in which I include all Europeans and citizens of the United States, all the so-called "civilised" races—simply could not understand happiness. It was impossible for them to realise that a Rondese man or woman, whether he ran a café in the capital, tended a vineyard on the slopes of the Ronderhof, kept a fishing boat on the Rondaquiver, or lived as a minor princeling or princess behind palace walls, was content with his lot and loved life. That was the fundamental truth. They loved life. "It isn't natural," I have heard tourists say, "to live as the Rondese do. If they only realised what the rest of the world has to put up with, day in, day out . . ." an oddly grudging point of view, if you come to think of it. The Rondese did not realise and did not care. They were happy. If the rest of the world chose to herd in skyscrapers or prefabricated hovels and then blow themselves to pieces, it was their affair. *Tandos pisos*, which can be translated as so what?

To return to the royal family, of course they intermarried, just as the Rondese people did, cousin with cousin and closer than that; but they had brought emotional life to such delicacy of interpretation that the coarser methods of so-called love-making were rarely used, and then only to ensure the birth of a prince. There was no sort of congestion behind the palace walls, because there was no necessity to breed. As to boredom, that curious supposition of the tourist, it is impossible to be bored if you are happy.

The royal family of Ronda were all poets, painters, musicians, skiers, riders, divers, gardeners—whatever pleasure attracted them they sought and so enjoyed. There was no competition and therefore no jealousy. As for protocol, I have heard that it did not exist. The Archduke made his evening appearance on the balcony and that was all. He was, naturally, in charge of the elixir and, not only of his own formula, but of the spring waters. The cave whence the waters came was royal property, and managed entirely by the Archduke and his team of experts, bred in the mountains and trained by their fathers before them. The seizure of the cave was, of course, the ultimate aim of Grandos.

The royal family was in no way narrow or boorish. The palace library—and what a crime it was to burn the books, most of them irreplaceable—had been added to by every prince through the centuries. The standard of education among the young princes and princesses would have frightened even a French professor.

The Archduchess Paula was exceptionally gifted even for a Rondese princess. She spoke five languages, played the piano, and sang remarkably well; and a famous English collector who acquired one of the bronze heads that escaped destruction on the Night of the Big Knives gave it as his opinion that whoever sculptured the head was a genius. It was believed to be the work of the Archduchess. She skied, of course, as all the Rondese did, and swam and rode, but from her birth there was something about this princess of the royal blood which fired the imagination of the people and made her beloved. For one thing, her mother was said to have died at her birth, and her father soon afterwards. Secondly, the Archduke, her brother—if he was her brother —was unmarried, and so made a particular pet of the small girl whose birth coincided with his accession to the ducal throne. There were no very young children being brought up within the palace at that time, previous generations having grown up and married, and Paula—offspring of the former Archduke and one of his nieces—was the first baby to be born at the palace for nearly fifteen years.

The people gradually became aware of her existence. A nurse, carrying an infant, looked out of one of the high windows of the palace. A boy picking Rovlvula blossoms saw a perambulator in the royal gardens. Then story followed story, and a golden-haired child was seen skiing on the Ronderhof slopes, diving in the Rondaquiver, and, more intimate and delightful still, holding the hand of the Archduke before he made his nightly appearance on the palace balcony. It became known that this was indeed the last baby to be born in Ronda palace, the sister of the present Archduke, the little Archduchess Paula.

As the years passed and she grew to womanhood, the legends and the stories multiplied. Always good-natured, always amusing, the tales would be handed from one Rondese to another—how the Archduchess Paula had jumped the Ronderhof cascades at their highest and most dangerous point, the Ronda leap, attempted hitherto only by the finest athletes; how the Archduchess Paula had rounded up the sheep from the slopes above the capital and let them loose into the vineyards; how the Archduchess Paula had netted the upper reaches of the Rondaquiver so that the fish could not escape, and a multiple catch splayed over the meadows, to the astonishment of every farmer when he visited his crops the next morning; how the Archduchess had placed wreaths of Rovlvula blossoms on the heads of the sacred statues in the palace portrait gallery; how she had crept into the Archduke's bedroom and hidden his white uniform, and would not tell him where she had concealed it until he had given her a sip of the elixir.

There may not have been one word of truth in any of these tales, but they delighted the Rondese. A medal of her likeness hung in every home. "That," said the proud Rondese to the tourist enquiries, "that is our Archduchess." It was never "the" Archduchess, but always "our."

She became patron—corresponding to the Christian godmother—of almost every child born in Ronda. Special purifying water from the springs and a message of goodwill would be sent to her patron-children on their birthday and, at their marriage, crystals of potent dew. This custom was considered repugnant by Anglo-Saxon tourists, but southern Europeans were amused.

Since the Archduke and his sister were so close in sympathy, it was taken as a matter of course by the Rondese people that they would one day marry. This was considered so shocking by the tourists of the Western world that there was a movement among the European and American churches to ban further visits to Ronda, but nothing came of it. And anyway, if revolution had not taken place, it is certain that the Archduchess would have married her first cousin Anton, ski champion of Ronda, and a poet. One servant who managed to survive the Night of the Big Knives said they had been in love for years.

Markoi knew this. A journalist has spies everywhere, even within a palace. He knew very well that a wedding between the Archduchess and her cousin Anton, or a wedding between the Archduchess and the Archduke, would be enough to keep the ruling house in power for at least another generation. The Rondese people believed in romance. Nothing could be more romantic than the immortal one spending his eternal youth in courtship, but if he had no such desire it was not their business. He could then bless the nuptials of his sister with her heart's choice, and his subjects would make merry in consequence. Markoi, therefore, had to act with subtlety and to propagate his gospel among the younger people before any such wedding took place.

During the first weeks of his campaign, he placed a daily column about the activities of the Archduchess in the *Ronda News*. The column was harmless enough and there was never direct criticism of the Archduke, but always a vague implication that all was not well with the idol of the Rondese people. She looked thoughtful, pale. She was said to gaze wistfully out of the palace windows at the carefree crowds below. Could it be possible that there was an estrangement between the Archduke and his sister, that she was shrinking from the near alliance pressed upon her by palace protocol?

"The Flower of Ronda," dared Markoi, "belongs to the Rondese people. If she could have her way she would marry a commoner, but she is prevented from doing so by outworn tradition. The loveliest girl in the country can never be free."

In truth, the Archduchess was up at the Ronderhof chalet with her cousin Anton the very evening that particular statement appeared in the *Ronda News*. They were alone for a brief courtship holiday to discover for themselves how much they were in love. But this was not known outside the palace. Therefore the absence of the Archduchess from the capital—she usually waved from the window—was the more marked. Was she in disgrace? Or, worse, a prisoner? Markoi let the rumour spread that the Archduchess was indeed under guard in the mountains and would remain under guard until she submitted to the will of the Archduke and became his consort. The high-spirited darling of the Rondese people must be disciplined and broken. The rights and wrongs of the case were hotly disputed during the next few days, the arguments instigated invariably by the supporters of Markoi and Grandos.

"It has always been thus and it will continue," said the older, more conservative of the Rondese, generally hill or village folk. "The Archduchess will settle down and breed a fine immortal. No good comes of mixed marriages. Look at the Europeans and the Americans."

"But why deny her happiness?" argued the intelligentsia in the capital. "Why should she not be free to choose? Aren't most of us every jot as cultured and fit as her blood relatives? If the Archduchess wants one of us, why can't she take one of us?"

"Who says she wants one of you?" put in the hill folk.

"Everyone," declared the hotheads.

The evening Ritzo, tingling the blood, made possibility a proven fact. The young men of the capital, glancing at each other as the warm night fell, wondered which of them it could be who, glimpsed from a palace window, had caught the fancy of the Rondese Flower. Rumour seized upon one and then another. A handkerchief had been found in the high snow of the topmost crags of Ronderhof, and in it a message, "Save me." An earring had been discovered hidden in the heart of a Rovlvula blossom tossed over the palace wall. A medal of the Archduchess bearing the words, "I love you," had fallen into the midst of a party of young huntsmen returning from a chamois chase at dawn, and no one knew for whom the medal was intended or whence it fell. How can we save her? Which of us is beloved? It is easy enough to see how passions became enflamed and the seed was sown for revolution. Silence greeted the appearance of the Archduke upon his balcony. Even the older people kept away or withdrew.

Then Markoi changed his tactics. For a week the subject of the Archduchess was dropped. Instead, the properties of the spring waters were discussed. "Scientists from northern Europe," ran a leading article, "who have lately tested the water from the Rondese spring, declare that it contains minerals of a value hitherto unknown to the Rondese people. Whether they are in fact known to the Archduke we are not in a position to say. But evidence goes to show that they are. These minerals, according to the scientists, prolong not only life, but love as well, and confer immunity from sickness. The scientists professed themselves astonished that these valuable waters should remain the property of one man." The article went on to give technical details of the minerals and wound up by stating the benefit they might bring to the whole world.

Once again there was a division between the older and the younger people as they read the news over the evening Ritzo. "There's one thing about the spring waters," said the cautious middle-aged farmers and vineyard planters. "We can be sure they are safe in the hands of the Archduke. If they got into other hands, who knows what might happen? You can't play about with minerals, solid or liquid. Why, there might be some property in the Rondese spring which could blow us all to pieces!"

"Exactly!" said the hotheads in the capital. "All that power at the whim of one man. All that power for good or evil. The Archduke can keep young, can't he? And we live our usual little span and then wrinkle up and die. No immortality for us."

"The Archduke dies in the flesh like the rest of us," said the older folk. "When illness strikes him down, he goes."

"Eventually," said the young people, "after he has seized everything in life he wants, including his own sister, if she is his sister and not his great-niece. Why can't *we* live to a hundred years and look as we do now?"

"Because it would not be good for you," said the old folk calmly. "You wouldn't know how to use the gift of eternal youth."

"Why not?" cried the boys and girls. "Why not? Does he?"

They thrashed the matter out amongst themselves. When all was said and done, what was so remarkable about the Archduke? He appeared every evening on the balcony and that was all. What he did all day inside the palace no one knew. He could be a tyrant, forcing all his younger relatives to do his bidding. He could be a monster, murdering his older relatives so that they could never betray the facts about his age. Who had ever seen the burial grounds of the palace? What deeds were done in secret there, in the attics, in the cellars, in those mountain fastnesses on the Ronderhof, in that rock-bound islet on the Rondaquiver? What plots were hatched? What poison brewed?

Rumour can make cowards of the most courageous and sow panic amongst the most serene. Markoi watched the result of his propaganda, keeping aloof himself and merely replying, when questioned, that he was obliged to print public opinion. For himself, he had no views.

"It is disquieting," ran a second leader, "when we consider that these mineral properties of Ronda water might—we use the word 'might' advisedly, for we do not suggest that such an event may already have taken place—be sold to a foreign power above the heads of the people, and eventually used against them. What is to prevent the Archduke from leaving Ronda, if he so desired, taking the formula with him, or handing over the entire workings of the springs to some other power at whose mercy we should be? The people of Ronda have no say in their own destiny. We are all living on the edge of an abyss that may crack and engulf us at any moment. It is time the Rondese people possessed the springs. Tomorrow will be too late."

It was at this moment that Grandos entered the campaign. He wrote a letter to the *Ronda News* expressing alarm because one of his best foremen, in charge of the plant down on the Rondaquiver where the fishbones were prepared before being sent to the factory, had been found drowned. His body, weighted with a stone, had been washed up at the mouth of the river. A contented man with a family, he had no reason to take his life. Could it be foul play, and, if so, who was responsible? He had been seen talking with a servant from the palace the preceding day. That servant had since disappeared. Was it possible that the powers that be (the word Archduke was not used) wished to obtain the secrets of the new progressive fish industry, which benefited so many of the river people, and control it? What was Grandos to do? Was he expected to hand over his industry to the monarch without a word, or, if he failed to do so, have his workmen murdered? If the ruling powers controlled the spring waters, that was one thing. It might be unfair and even dangerous, but it was not the affair of Grandos. What was his affair was his own fish trade, created and built by himself, owing nothing to any tradition, and he wanted the advice of the Rondese people as to how he should act if one of his foremen was threatened again.

This outburst could not have been better timed. The spring waters . . . well, that was a big subject and would continue to be discussed. But a man found drowned, probably murdered, and the fishbone industry threatened, that was another matter. Letters poured into the *Ronda News* from throughout the country. If the fish industry was threatened, what about the vineyards? What about the wine trade? What about the cafés? Was there to be no security any more for any man?

Grandos replied to the letters, thanking all correspondents for their warmhearted support for freedom of action, and added that he had posted guards outside his plant on the Rondaquiver.

Guards outside the fishbone factory. . . . Nothing had ever been guarded in Ronda except the palace. The older people were much disturbed, but the young Rondese were jubilant. "That'll show them," they said. "They can't take our rights away from us. Hurrah for Grandos and the right of every man to work for himself!"

"They," of course, meant the Archduke. The fact that he had never threatened anyone, drowned any man, or taken the slightest interest in the fishbone industry except to make jokes to the Archduchess about women who needed to have their breasts supported, was not realised by the people, now thoroughly upset by what they read in the *Ronda News*.

The moment was ripe for a deputation to the palace, and with some manoeuvring by Grandos and Markoi, who themselves did not take a part in it, a body of young people formed up outside the palace gates and handed in a protest, signed by the sons and daughters of leading Ronda citizens, asking for a statement of policy from the Archduke.

"Will the Archduke give his solemn word," ran part of the protest, "that the rights and liberties of the Rondese people will not be attacked, and that there will be no attempt to control the new industries which are making progressive Ronda the most forward of European countries?"

The following day a notice was attached to the gates of the palace. "If any attempt is made to control the industries of Ronda, or to attack the centuries-old rights and liberties of the Rondese people, this attempt will not be made by the Archduke."

The young Rondese were nonplussed. The reply was so terse, so noncommittal that it amounted almost to an affront. Besides, what did it mean? Who, other than the Archduke, would seek to control the industries and the rights of the people? A reply of some two dozen or more words to a protest of half a dozen pages. The *Ronda News* hinted that the Rondese youth had been slapped in the face.

"The overprivileged cling to outworn symbols as a means of protecting themselves," said an article on the front page. "Hence the mystique of the uniform, of the solitary public appearance, of the ritual of intermarriage. The young people of Ronda can no longer be deceived. The power of action lies in their hands. Those who wish to preserve their own youth and pass on the secret to future generations know that the answer lies in the cave on Ronderhof, and the key to the cave in the laboratories of Ronda palace."

This was the most direct attack yet made on the Archduke. The next day the subject was dropped, and prominence was given to a botanical article on the Rovlvula flower, which, so the botanist said, was in danger of losing its sheen and scent because of contamination from certain radioactive particles caused by the high snows of Ronderhof avalanching into the valleys. These avalanches were all on the western side of Ronderhof, never on the eastern face; and the reason for this was that the eastern face was kept clear for the ski jumping and water leaping of members of the royal family.

"The natural fall of snow," said the botanist, "is to the east, but, because the fall would interfere with the pleasures of the privileged, it is learnt that orders have been given to the mountain guards to divert to the west all avalanches that threaten the skiing grounds. That these avalanches may be detrimental to the flower industry on the western slopes apparently does not matter, nor that the contamination from radioactive snow may affect the Rondese market gardeners."

This article brought a quick response from one of the leading flower gatherers in the country to say that he had always understood the snow to be the cause of the very rare texture of the Rovlvula buds, and the avalanches had been appreciated by his forefathers for that very reason. Had they all been mistaken?

"We are afraid," said the Ronda News, "that our correspondent has been misinformed and his forebears brought up in a false tradition. Recent tests prove that snow is harmful to the bud, and a number of the workers in the Grandos factory employed in pulping the Rovlvula into paste for export have had the palms of their hands affected by some itching substance that is feared to contain particles of radio-active dust."

The newspaper gave an alarming photograph of the skin of a man's hand covered with eczema. This eczema had appeared after the man had crushed a bud gathered from the slopes of the Ronderhof. The man had lost the use of his hand and was said to be seriously ill.

Grandos announced forthwith that he was fitting every workman in his employment with gloves so that they should run no risk of contamination if the Rovlvula flower were in fact radioactive.

"The people of Ronda can be proud," said the newspaper, "that at least one citizen of this country has the welfare of the common man at heart. We take the opportunity of saluting Grandos."

And what of the Archduchess all this time? Had she been forgotten? One of the chalet attendants who escaped on the Night of the Big Knives and took refuge in eastern Europe told those who gave him shelter that he had had the good fortune to wait upon the Archduchess and her cousin Anton during their brief courtship.

"No two people have ever been so happy," he is supposed to have said, "no two people more artlessly in love. They used to ski on the high slopes and swim in the summit pools, and in the evenings I and my fellow attendant, later murdered, would serve them the young fish from the high reaches of the Rondaquiver, braised in Rovlvula leaves, and the fermented juice of the white grapes grown on Ronderhof. The Archduke had placed at their disposal his own suite of rooms, which had windows and balconies facing east and west. They could watch the sunrise and the dawn, but in point of fact the Archduchess told me herself that they watched neither."

This story found its way into the American press after the revolution, and was supposed to be a tissue of lies. Many old people believed it.

In early March the Archduchess and her cousin Anton returned from the mountain chalet and took up their quarters in the palace in preparation for their wedding. And this, of course, was where she made her mistake. They should both of them have stayed in the mountain chalet. But the Archduchess, so full of happiness herself, wished to share her good fortune with the Rondese people. She did not realise that in such a short time their attitude could change. Later, rumour had it that the Archduke warned her, and that she did not listen. "I have always loved the people, and the people have loved me." Certainly she is known to have said this; and on an impulse, because she was happy and in love, she took her cousin Anton by the hand and appeared at an upper window of the palace, waving and smiling, on the night of her return. The people and the tourists were gathered there, as usual, and suddenly they raised their heads and saw the Archduchess Paula, who they had been told was in disgrace or even imprisoned, with Anton by her side. Quickly she withdrew, beckoned into the shadows by the Archduke himself, perhaps, and everyone began to talk and to ask questions.

"Then she is not a prisoner?" said some. "She's there, and she was smiling, and that chap beside her is Anton, the ski champion and poet. What does it mean? Are they in love, then, after all?"

The moment might have been disastrous for Markoi, who happened to be sitting himself in the square that very evening with some of his friends. He sipped his Riivi tea—he never touched Ritzo or any alcohol, and Riivi was an herb concoction good for the bile—but he was intelligent enough to smile and to say little.

"It's all part of a plan," he said. "Tomorrow there will be an announcement from the palace. Wait and see."

In the morning the placard on the palace gates said briefly that a marriage had been arranged and would take place shortly between the Archduchess Paula, beloved sister of the Archduke, and her cousin Anton. And Markoi brought out a midday edition of the *Ronda News*.

"What this newspaper has foretold has happened," said gigantic letters on the front page. "The Rondese Flower, against her own wishes, has submitted to a marriage of convenience with a blood relative. Weeks of solitary confinement have finally broken the spirit of this beautiful and courageous young woman. Her expressed desire to marry a commoner and give herself to the Rondese people has been ruthlessly, brutally set aside. Who can tell what methods were used, within the palace, to force the Archduchess Paula to obedience? These methods have been used perhaps for years, for centuries, to subdue their young relatives, by fanatics clinging to power. Anton, the prospective bridegroom, and favourite of the Archduke since boyhood, no doubt came to a private arrangement with the monarch months ago to share his bride and therefore ensure the succession. The Rondese people have lost their Archduchess. The Archduchess has been stolen from the people."

That night the first riots broke out in the capital. Buildings were set on fire, café windows broken, older people, begging for calm and order, beaten up. There was no attack upon the palace. The Imperial guard remained at their posts, but the Imperial band did not play the national anthem and for the first time the Archduke did not appear on the balcony.

In the morning the crowd, gathered sullenly before the palace gates, read the notice fixed there by the guard. It was in the Archduchess' own handwriting and said, "I want the people of Ronda to know that I am in love with my cousin Anton, that we have had our prenuptial honeymoon, which was exceedingly happy, and that this marriage, soon to be solemnized, is of my own choosing."

The crowd stared at the notice. They did not know what to believe. But agitators, placed here and there by Markoi and Grandos, soon set the murmurs going. "They made her write it. They stood over her and threatened her. Prenuptial honeymoon my foot. An unwilling prisoner of the ski champion Anton. That mountain chalet ought to be burnt to the ground."

There was no issue of the *Ronda News* at midday. The evening edition made no reference to the notice written by the Archduchess. A brief paragraph, tucked away in small type, said, "The Archduchess Paula has signified her acceptance of the hand of Anton, close friend to the Archduke. The marriage will take place immediately, if it has not already done so. The Rondese people will draw their own conclusions."

The centre page was given up almost entirely to an account of fresh outbreaks of eczema on the palms of Grandos's petal pulpers. Eczema was also breaking out, according to the *Ronda News,* among the workers in the fishbone industry. The management was seriously concerned and had ordered an immediate close-down of both industries while the matter was being investigated. There was a photograph of Grandos patting the head of a flower pulper's child, and giving him a pair of minute gloves.

Tourists began to leave the country the following day, and the island hotels in the Rondaquiver emptied.

"We don't want to catch this eczema," complained many of the tourists. "We've been told it may spread. And one of the fishermen had it from an authority that the fish caught in the river is polluted. Something to do with the snow from the mountains."

"Too bad about your little Archduchess," said the more romantic-minded of the visitors, "forced into marriage with a man she hates. Is it true she's terribly in love with a café proprietor? In the States she'd be allowed to marry him."

Friends of Markoi and Grandos mixed with the crowds at the airport and frontier posts.

"Just as well you're leaving Ronda," they hinted. "We understand there may be trouble. The Archduke is in an ugly mood. If the people show they dislike this forced marriage, there's no knowing what he may do."

But what can he do?" objected the more complacent of the tourists. "He hasn't any armed forces to speak of, only that Imperial guard dressed up for show."

The agitators looked grave. "You forget," they said, "he owns the spring waters. If he cared to release them he could flood the entire country. Ronda could be under water tomorrow."

The various European airlines had to make changes in their normal running schedules and send extra aircraft to Ronda, so great was the demand to get away. A United States liner anchored off the mouth of the Rondaquiver to take on board all American citizens who could not bribe their way on to the aeroplanes. The Rondese people themselves remained calm, but they were bewildered and anxious, and the rumours of flood soon spread from one end of the small principality to the other.

"Would he do it?" asked one Rondese of another. "Would the Archduke ever unleash the waters?"

The people of the plains gazed up at the Ronderhof, remote and still, so many thousands of feet above their heads, and the people of the hills came out of their chalets and listened to the falls as they cascaded down from the great caves.

"If it should happen . . . where could we go? Who would be safe?"

Ronda, the paradise for fools, knew fear for the first time.

4

What you have to realise is that no one faction brought about the revolution. The leaders behind the scenes were undoubtedly Markoi and Grandos, but the people themselves were split into groups according to their way of life and their interests.

The young romantics—and these were mostly in the capital itself—believed that the Archduchess Paula, the Flower of Ronda, had been forced into a hated marriage because of tradition, and that she had in reality given her heart to one of them. No one knew the secret lover, mark you, but he was said to be the son of a prominent citizen, and none of the young men in the capital was going to give away the fact that he was not the chosen one. It became the fashion to look mysterious and melancholy in turn, to sport a Rovlvula flower in the buttonhole, to sit in the palace square of an evening sipping Ritzo and staring moodily at the palace windows.

The more practical—and these were generally in industry—were disturbed by the original drowning of the foreman at the fishbone plant, and by the eczema discovered on the palms of their fellow workers. It was perfectly true, as a matter of fact, that the eczema did break out amongst the fishbone workers and flower pulpers, and the reason for this was very simple. The fishbones were sharp, and contained a substance which could irritate a sensitive skin; while the heart of the Rovlvula flower, if crushed, emitted a poisonous juice. Grandos had chosen to industrialize just the two natural resources that of their very nature were unsuited for manufacturing purposes. Had the Rondese realised this, they would have shrugged *Tandos pisos* and left the industries. Grandos suspected the truth, if he did not know it for a certainty. But industrialists have a knack of ignoring potential trouble if the trouble is likely to affect their finances.

The progressive Rondese were angry because they had read in the *Ronda News* that the new industries would be likely to fail through the selfishness of the Archduke, who wished to control them himself; and the independent-minded Rondese understood, from the same newspaper, that their liberties were threatened. As for the more simple-minded, the very thought of floods, of havoc to crops and vines, of disaster to livestock and indeed to human life, was enough to make them rally to any faction which might offer them some promise of security.

The dread of the spring waters flooding, and the fear that these spring waters could be unleashed by the Archduke in anger, were the great factors that turned the older Rondese people into revolutionaries. The knowledge that the spring waters contained properties which could give them eternal youth and that these waters were held by a single prince for his own use was the first reason for making rebels of the young. The Archduchess was a figurehead, a symbol. She was beauty kept in subjection by the beast. She was the cry, the rallying point. It was not really difficult to see how the different threads converged into a single aim . . . the overthrow and destruction of the Archduke.

The spring festival drew near. Every man knew in his heart that something would happen. The winter snows on Ronderhof must break, as they always did in early March, but this year would something else break with them? Would the Archduke, who gave no sign from within the palace that anything was changed, suddenly take the Rondese people unawares and release catastrophe?

There were meetings and gatherings throughout the whole of Ronda. Up on the hills, in the plains, by the banks of the Rondaquiver, on the slopes of Ronderhof, in the capital city of Ronda itself, bands of men and women murmured, whispered. The old people, fearful, anguished, locked themselves behind doors. "If it has to be done," they said amongst themselves, "let it be done quickly. Let us close our eyes and shut our ears."

The day of the spring festival was a national holiday, and as a rule it was warm and fine. The country people were able to gather the early Rovlvula flowers, which they would bring to the capital to decorate the city and the palace, and in the afternoon the Ronda Games were held in the stadium a few miles from the capital.

It is a curious thing how the elements often combine with earthly unrest to produce crisis. The last few days before the festival were unusually cold, and on the evening before the festival itself snow began to fall and in the morning was still falling. The Rondese awoke to find their whole world white. There was no sun, but only the great wet blanket of sky, and giant flakes the size of a man's hand which drifted upon the upturned faces of the people. It was almost as if the snow had some evil purpose and had been sent to Ronda as a cloak to hide ill intent.

"In all the years," said the old people, "we cannot remember weather like this for the spring festival."

Was it possible, they asked themselves, that what the young folks hinted was true, and that the Archduke could control the weather just as he controlled the spring waters? Did this unnatural fall of snow herald their doom?

No gathering of flowers . . . no games . . . no dancing on the slopes or in the palace square. Then the first shepherd, high on Ronderhof in search of his lost sheep, came stumbling through the drifts to the nearest village. "It's come," he said, "the avalanche! I heard it as I stood blinded by snow in the high forest. There's no time to lose."

Now there had been avalanches before on Ronderhof, time without number, winter after winter through the centuries, but this one was different. This avalanche had all the weight of propaganda behind it. The villagers fled through the driving snow to the safety of the capital, and as they fled the rumours fled with them, and met them, and encircled them, encircled all the Rondese who were standing despondent, watching the wet sky, watching the failure of the national holiday. "The Archduke has let loose the waters, the Archduke has made the mountain move!" The primitive fear of the villagers infected the people of the city. "The Archduke has escaped. He's caused the snow to fall and blind all of us so that he and the royal family can flee across the frontier Then, when they are safe, the floods will destroy Ronda."

The most fearful of all were the workmen from the Grandos factories. "Don't touch the snow, it's contaminated, poisoned, don't touch the snow. . . ." They came running from the villages, running from the plains, men and women, boys and girls, running to the capital of Ronda. "Help us, save us, the snow is poisoned!"

In Markoi's headquarters, the offices of the *Ronda News*, Markoi was handing out to his followers the big knives used in the Rondese vineyards to prune the vines. He had handled these knives as a boy and he knew their cutting powers. For weeks now he had been collecting them from every vineyard in the country.

"There will be no issue of the *Ronda News* today," he said. "Go out into the streets."

Then, with great self-denial, he shut himself up in his small room at the back of the building and took no part in the proceedings that followed. He had no food that day. He disconnected the telephone. He sat watching the falling snow. Markoi was a purist.

Grandos also kept himself aloof. But he opened his doors to the refugees who fled from the hills. He fed them with broth and wine and he gave them warm clothing—it was extraordinary, refugees said afterwards, how he seemed to be prepared for calamity—and he was unfailingly thoughtful, full of assurances of help, ready with medicines and bandages, going from one to the other panic-stricken individual. "Keep calm. You have been fearfully treated, terribly misled. But I promise you everything will soon be under control." He did not mention the palace or the Archduke. He put one single telephone call through to Markoi before Markoi disconnected the telephone, and the message was this: "Let the people be told that a pipeline, connecting the palace with the spring on Ronderhof, has been filled with radioactive water, and that at a signal from the Archduke this pipe water is to be turned on to the Rondese in the palace square. The first jet will scald and blind and maim." Then he hung up and distributed more food and clothing to the weeping refugees.

So there it was. No one can say the revolution was the fault of one particular man, although Markoi and Grandos played so large a part in bringing it to a head. It was the awakening of a seed, a seed that must have lain dormant in the hearts of the Rondese for centuries. Fear of the snows, fear of the flood, fear of annihilation, and, because of fear, resentment of the Archduke, said to control these powers, and envy, too, envy of eternal youth.

Wicked? No, of course they were not wicked. What the Rondese felt was very natural. Why should one being control the elements? Why should one spirit possess the gift of eternal youth? Should not these things be shared by humanity at large? And if one being alone is trusted, is it not placing in that being the most tremendous faith, a faith that might not be justified? After all, the Archduke did control the spring waters. I don't say the avalanches had anything to do with him. It was true that the royal skiing grounds were on the east face of Ronderhof and the avalanches always fell on the western face, but that merely showed his wisdom in choosing the best playground. There was never any proof that the snows were deliberately diverted. But it was not beyond the bounds of possibility.

The point is, when a people begins to doubt there is no end to it. The doubt splits up into so many altered moods, and nothing is safe any more, no man is true. He who loses faith loses his own soul. Yes . . . yes . . . yes . . . I know what you are trying to say. So many tourists from across the border have said it since the revolution. The Rondese had no moral standards by which to live, no dogma, no system of ethics. Therefore, as soon as doubt and fear seized them they were wholly possessed. I say, with due respect, that the tourists and yourself are talking nonsense. The reason why the Rondese had lived in such perfect harmony for centuries was surely their freedom from standards, their freedom from dogma, their ignorance of ethics. All they asked for was life, and life was given them, and happiness, which springs from within. It was unfortunate that one of their number, Markoi, should have been born lame, and another, Grandos, greedy; but there it was. It happened. These handicaps—for handicaps they surely are, greed being an excess of hunger, and lameness the faulty balance of a human structure—infected two persons, and those two persons infected others; but you have to remember that excess of hunger and faulty balance are one and the same thing, creating a driving force that sweeps everything before it. Like the original flooding of the Rondaquiver. So . . .

In the meantime, while the snow was falling and the short day was turning to darkness and the Rondese people were converging upon the capital, what was happening inside the palace itself?

Opinions will always differ. No one will ever be sure. The hotheads of the revolution declare to this day that the Archduke was in the laboratory making the final adjustment to the machinery which would loosen the springs from Ronderhof upon the plains, and fixing too the powerful jet of radioactive water which would contaminate and maim the Rondese people. They also declare that he and Anton were engaged in some refinement of torture upon the Archduchess, who, imprisoned in the cellars, begged for the life of the people. Then there are others who say that nothing of the sort was going on at all. That the Archduke was playing the violin— he was a fine musician—and the Archduchess and her betrothed were making love. Others again insist that panic had seized the palace and hurried preparations for departure were being made.

All these things could be true. When the palace was sacked, a pipeline *was* discovered in the laboratory leading up underground to the caves of Ronderhof, from which flowed the spring water. The music room *was* shown to have been lately used, as were the royal sleeping apartments. And there *was* evidence of packing, though this could have been the usual preparation before leaving for the chalet. Certainly there was no evidence of torture, though when the Archduchess was found it was seen that her eyes were wan as though from fatigue, and from weeping too. But this could mean anything.

All I can tell you is this—and it is the sworn evidence of the servant spy who at midnight admitted the revolutionaries inside the palace. (How did he get there? I have no idea. There are always servant spies in all revolutions.) His statement is as follows:

"There seemed to be nothing unusual going on during the morning of the spring festival. The heavy fall of snow during the night made it seem likely that the festival plans would be cancelled. And indeed, shortly after ten we had word— that is to say, the door servants—that the gathering of the Rovlvula flowers and the holding of the Games was cancelled. I have no idea if there had been any preparations for going to the chalet, not being a servant of the royal apartments.

"At eleven o'clock the Archduke held a council with members of the royal family. I don't know how many were present. I never found out in all the three months I served at the palace what the numbers were of princes and princesses of the blood. I knew Anton by sight. He was present, and the Archduchess Paula. And three or four others I knew by sight but not by name. I saw them come down the stairs from the royal apartments and pass into the white room. We servants called the room with the balcony, overlooking the palace square, the white room. I was stationed at the foot of the stairs at the time and I saw them go in. Anton was joking and laughing. I did not hear what he said, and anyway they spoke a special patois, the royal family, a kind of old-fashioned Rondese. The Archduchess looked pale. Then the door was shut, and they remained in there for a full hour.

"At twelve o'clock the doors opened again and everyone came out, except the Archduke and the Archduchess. I had been relieved, so I did not see them come out. But one of the other servants told me, and I have no reason to doubt his word. Shortly after one, something happened of curious significance. We servants were all told to go up to the white room, one by one, because the Archduke wished to see us. I thought it was a trap and was alarmed, but I could not escape from the palace because at that time I was still off duty and could not go near the doors. Besides, I had my orders from the revolutionary leaders to remain within the palace until the hour came for me to admit those chosen to enter. However, I tried not to show my uneasiness, and waited for my turn to enter the white room.

"The first thing I noticed was that the Archduke was wearing his white uniform, with the red ribbon of the Order of the Just, and he never wore this uniform except when he made the evening appearances and on days such as this, the spring festival. So I concluded at once that he was going on to the balcony, in spite of the cancelled festivities and the falling snow and the antagonism of the crowd. I thought to myself that he must have the jets prepared, that there was probably a tap and everything ready, concealed somewhere in the room. I had no time to glance about me. I could just see the Archduchess sitting on a chair, away from the windows. She was reading something and took no notice of me. As far as I could tell she showed no signs of ill-treatment, but she looked very pale. There was no one else in the room.

"The Archduke came forward and held out his hand. 'Good-bye,' he said. 'I wish you happiness.'

"Ah! I thought to myself. Now this means one of two things. Either he has planned escape and is going to leave the palace before midnight, or this is a supreme piece of cruelty because he knows he is going to flood the city and destroy us all. In other words, and whichever way I took it, his words were bluff.

" 'Is anything wrong, sir?' I asked. I put on the proper face of astonishment.

" 'That depends on you,' he answered. And he had the nerve to smile. 'After all, our future is in your hands. I am saying good-bye because it is unlikely that we shall meet again.'

"I thought very hard. It would do no harm to put a question.

" 'Are you going away, sir?' I asked, feeling rather frightened, nevertheless, as I spoke, for he might have turned the jet on me there and then.

" 'No, I shan't be going away,' he said. 'But we are unlikely to meet again.'

"He had our death planned all right. There was no mistaking the note in his voice. It did something to my spine. I did not know how I was going to get out of the room.

" 'The Archduchess, too,' he continued, 'wishes to say good-bye.' And then he turned—and you could not imagine anyone more cool and deliberate—and said, 'Paula, I present your servant.' I stood where I was, not knowing what to do, and the Archduchess left her chair and whatever it was she was reading, and came up to me and put her hand in mine.

" 'I wish you happiness,' she said. She did not speak the palace patois but the Rondese we use in the capital.

" 'Thank you, madam,' I replied.

"Now it is my belief she had been hypnotized or drugged, or in some way interfered with by that archdevil, her brother. Because her eyes had all the grief in the world. And in old days it was not so. I remember the Flower of Ronda riding through the forests of Ronderhof, and she was a patron, too, of my own sister. She was gay and lighthearted then—this was long before the plans of the forced marriage to Anton. But standing there in the white room, holding out her hand, I could not look into her eyes. I took the hand and mumbled something, and I wanted to say, 'It's all right. Don't you worry. We are going to save you,' but of course I did not dare.

" 'That's all,' said the Archduke. And, glancing up, I saw that he was looking at me, and the expression was strange. Frankly, I did not care for it. It was as though he read my thoughts and sensed my uneasiness. It proved one thing to me. He was a devil, and no mistake. . . . Then I turned my back on both of them and went out of the white room.

"He was perfectly right, of course. I never did meet him again, alive. . . . Like a true revolutionary, I paid my tribute to him when he was hanging by the heels in the palace square.

"The rest of the day passed without incident. I took my turn on the doors with the other servants. None of us mentioned the falling snow or the crowds gathering outside the palace. At one time there was a sound of music from the royal apartments, but who was playing I could not say. Lunch and dinner were served at the usual time. I kept myself to myself for fear of anything going wrong with the plan. I expected to be arrested any moment. I could not believe that the Archduke did not suspect my intentions. But nothing happened and nothing was said.

"At ten minutes to midnight I stationed myself in my usual position beside the door leading to the main courtyard. I had been told by my leaders to open the door when I heard someone strike it three blows. Who was to strike it, and how they were to pass the Imperial guard, it was not my business to know. I felt uneasy as the minutes ran out, and fearful that something would go wrong with the plan. The music from the royal apartments had ceased, and there was a sudden silence throughout the palace. So far as I knew the Archduke was still in the white room, but he might have been anywhere; he might have been in the laboratory or the cellars, or he might have escaped to the heights of Ronderhof. My job was not to ask questions or think out solutions. My job was to open that side door.

"At three minutes to midnight, without preliminary warning, I heard the three blows upon the door. And at that same moment the servant who was standing at the top of the stairs flung open the door of the white room and called down to me, 'The Archduke is going out on to the balcony.'

"He has the jet, I thought, he's going to turn it on to the people. I opened the side door and they brushed past me, those of the Big Knives. I had no further part in the business. I had done what I had been told to do."

Here the report ended. It can be seen today in the museum, where it is kept under glass in the muniment room. Some of the Big Knives hang there, too, on the wall. The muniment room is the same as the white room mentioned in the report, but it looks very different now.

You ask how did the revolutionaries get past the Imperial

guard? The Imperial guard had no orders from the Archduke to stop anyone. There never had been any such orders, through seven centuries. It was not a case of being taken by surprise or overrun. They allowed themselves to be cut down, to be slaughtered without defence of any kind. The massacre was complete. Every servant, every person, every animal found within the palace walls was cut down and slaughtered. All except the Archduchess, and I'll tell you about that in a minute.

The revolutionaries entered that side door, and there must have been seven hundred of them—it was always said there were seven hundred, Markoi having a fancy that the number should be the same as the seven centuries—and it was the easiest thing in the world, so they declared afterwards, to cut down the inhabitants of the palace, simply because there was no resistance. It was easier than pruning the vines. In a sense, you might say they offered themselves as victims. And—it's rather unpleasant, but it's a fact, for the young people discussed it afterwards amongst themselves—the first blow with the knife brought the same sort of intoxication that you get with Ritzo, the contact with the flesh and the sight of the blood. The young people said they just couldn't stop, and could think of nothing else but cutting down the waiting victims whoever they were: servants, guards, princes, pet dogs, canaries, little lizards; whatever had life inside the palace had to go.

As for the Archduke . . . Yes, he came out on to the balcony. He had no jet. There was no sign of the spring waters that made him immortal. He just stood there, in his white uniform with the red Order of the Just, and he waited. He waited for the people to storm forward over the heads of their fellows and climb the balcony, and he waited for them to join forces with those of the Big Knives who had already entered the palace. The older Rondese who had shut themselves away from it all within doors said afterwards that the cry of rage and hatred and envy—yes, above all, of envy—that went up from the throats of the Rondese revolutionaries as they flung themselves upon the Archduke could be heard right up on the high slopes of Ronderhof and away down to the banks of the Rondaquiver. And the snow was falling all the time. Yes, the snow was falling.

When there was no more life anywhere, and the staircase and the corridors ran with blood, the young men of the revolution sent a report to Markoi, who was still sitting in his office building, and the report said, "Justice has been done."

Markoi came out of his office, and out of the building of the *Ronda News*, and walked through the falling snow to the palace. He made his way to the room of the Archduchess, with his followers falling into step behind him, and it is said that he knocked on the door and she told him to come in. She was standing there by the open window. She was quite alone. Markoi went straight up to her and said, "There is nothing more to fear, madam. We have liberated you. You are free."

Now . . . I can't tell you what he expected, or what the revolutionary Rondese expected, whether tears of gratitude or grief or some expression of horror or fear or goodwill: no one knew, for no one had any idea of the feelings or the emotions of the Archduchess. The only thing was this. She had changed from the kilted skirt she usually dressed in, which she had been wearing earlier in the day (this was corroborated by the servant spy afterwards), and she was wearing a white uniform with the Order of the Just upon it. She carried a sword as well. And she said to Markoi and the revolutionaries, "I wish you happiness. I am your Archduchess. The spring waters are my inheritance, and I hold the secret of eternal youth. Do with me what you will."

Then they took her out on to the balcony and showed her to the people. And the body of the Archduke was displayed for her to see. Some people may say this was cruel. It depends upon the point of view. The Rondese will continue to argue the question, and so will the tourists. The point is, which was massacred that night of the spring festival, that Night of the Big Knives? Innocence or guilt?

Well, there it is. Some say that Ronda is spoilt beyond recognition, and that apart from natural scenic advantages— the heights of Ronderhof, the islets on the Rondaquiver, the charm of the capital, and of course the climate—it could be any small European state decked out to catch the tourist's eye, with the people falling over themselves to make money. Others disagree. Ronda is progressive, the new industries thrive, the towns springing up on the banks of the Ronda-quiver are filled with energetic youngsters determined to make their voices heard in world councils. They even have a slogan about it—"Ronda speaks, the world echoes"—and in a sense it's true, for you see Rondese youth everywhere these days, in all the European capitals and in the United States; they are compensating for what they call centuries of apathy by a determined endeavour to lead the world.

Psychologically they make an interesting study. You see, for all the nationalistic spirit, the progressive movement, the slogan of Ronda for the Rondese, and the what-we-say-today-you-say-tomorrow attitude, they still haven't succeeded in winning for themselves the secret of eternal youth. And this was really what the revolution was all about. They bottle the waters, yes, Grandos saw to that. You can buy them in any country in the world—at a price. But they are not the waters of the formula. The formula is still the secret of the Arch-duchess. As I told you before, they have tried everything, beginning with flattery and progressing to rape, torture, imprisonment, starvation, and disease. They can't break her. She must be nearly eighty, as I've said, and after all she has endured you would think it would show somewhere, some-how, but her face is a girl's face, the face of the Flower of Ronda, and no degradation can mar the perfect beauty. The only thing is that if you go close to her, when she is dancing in the palace, or rather in the museum, square, and should see her eyes, should have the fortune—or perhaps it is mis-fortune—to look into her eyes, they say that you can read there the agony of the whole world, and compassion too.

Nobody knows what will happen when she dies. It can't be long now. There is no one left of the blood royal to whom she could pass on the formula. And one can't help wondering if it is worth possessing. I mean, it has not brought her any-thing except a legacy of pain. The men who wished so much to possess her secret are both dead, ironically enough. Grandos died of some stomach trouble on a visit to the

United States—he had done himself too well for years—and Markoi was attacked by a wasting disease: he visibly shrank before his friends and in the end was hardly more than a shadow. The older Rondese, who had never cared for him, said he was eaten up with envy of the Archduchess, and because his plan of mockery and ridicule had not succeeded. But that was probably just old people's talk.

No, when the Archduchess dies, the secret of eternal youth dies too. There will no longer be an immortal one in Ronda or the world. So it's worth visiting the country—you can buy a ticket at any tourist agency—because, as the tough young Rondese say, you never know. She might break tomorrow, or next week, or next season, and if she does it would be worth watching. And if she never breaks, but just dies, dancing there night after night in the square, then something will have gone from the world that no one, now or in the future, will ever see again. Even today it may be too late. . . .

The Menace

Barry Jeans—when his fans did not call him Barry and wanted a bigger word for him—was known as the Menace. The Menace, in movie language, and especially among women, means a heart throb, a lover, someone with wide shoulders and no hips. A Menace does not have long lashes or a profile; he is always ugly, generally with a crooked nose and if possible a scar; his voice is deep; and he does not say much. When he does speak, the script-writers give him short, terse snaps of dialogue, phrases like "Lady, take care!" or "Break it up!" or even just "Maybe." The expression on the ugly face has to be deadpan and give nothing away, so that sudden death or a woman's passion leaves it unmoved. Only the muscle at the side of the lean jaw tautens, and then the fans know that Barry is either going to hit someone, and hit him hard, or stagger in a torn shirt through a jungle carrying on his back a man who hates him, or lie in an open boat after shipwreck with the woman he loves but is far too honorable to touch.

Barry Jeans the Menace must have made more money for the movie world than anyone living. He was English by birth; his father was a clergyman, and vicar of Herne Bay for many years. Old people say they remember Barry as a boy singing in the choir, but it is not true. His mother was half Irish, and that is why they called their son Barry. He went to grammar school and was just too young to join up for World War I, which puts him in the mid-fifties age group. Everyone knows this and nobody minds. It's a good age for Menaces. The fans don't want to see a youngster stagger through the jungle or lie in an open boat—it would not look right.

Barry's father was broad-minded and let his son go on the stage. He was in repertory for a while, and then got a job as understudy in a London production. From understudy he graduated to small parts in drawing-room comedies, which were fashionable in those immediate postwar years, but he never did much good. Producers found him too stiff, and he got the name for being, in theatrical jargon, a "stick." Nowadays producers who have long retired, and others still active but in their dotage, say they always foretold a big future for Barry. But in fact the only person who ever believed in him was his wife May, and perhaps because of that belief they have never parted but are still together after thirty years. Everyone knows May. She is not one of those wives who remains hidden and then appear shy and rather sweet at gala performances. May is there—in the dressing-room and very often on the set. Barry says he would be lost without her.

It was May who pushed Barry into having an audition for the Lonsdale play that was going into production in New York at the end of the twenties. It was a small part, and the chap the producer and Lonsdale wanted had appendicitis at the last moment, so they were obliged to take Barry. After that he never looked back. It's a curious thing how actors who fail to make the grade in London go over big in New York. Like ne'er-do-wells in Australia. A fellow slips away below decks, and the next thing you hear is that he has a million sheep on a ranch the size of Cornwall.

It was the women who went for Barry. They adored the way he stood there on the stage, in his English clothes, with his hands clenched. It was strange it had meant so little to the women in England.

When the Lonsdale comedy came off, Barry was offered a part in an American play, and although it folded quickly he hit the headlines. He hadn't a great deal to do, but he had to bring the curtain down in the second act with the words "Scram, baby, scram!" and the way he said it did something to the American Women. Barry's future was assured, and he had an offer from Hollywood the opening night. May told him to accept, and three weeks later they were on the Coast. Barry Jeans the Menace.

In a matter of months his face was more familiar to women all over the world than that of their own husbands. And the husbands did not mind. In a sense, it was a sort of compliment if a girl married a chap at all. It must mean that the chap she married was a super-Barry. His hat—a trilby with a dent in it—his cigarette, never hanging from his lips but always held between his fingers, the little scar on the side of the temple that suggested a brush with a rhino or a knife thrown in a Shanghai joint (in fact he had slipped on the breakwater at Herne Bay when he was not looking)—it all exercised a subtle and indefinable magic which left every other movie star standing at the post. But above all it was the mouth, firm and decisive above that square jaw with the cleft in the chin, which maddened millions. It never relaxed, it never smiled, it never, in fact, did anything. That was what got them. Women were weary of close-ups of their favourite stars lip to lip in a passionate embrace, and Barry did not give them that. Instead, he turned away. Or stared over the girl's shoulder. Or just murmured the word "You!" and nothing else. Then there would be a fade-out into the next scene, and the fans would be left writhing.

Barry Jeans the Menace really started the fashion that became so prevalent between the two wars on both sides of the Atlantic of men and women not making love at all. What was vulgarly called "making a pass" was no longer done. If a fellow took a girl home in his car, and drew up in front of her house, there was no question of parking and staying put for half an hour. Barry Jeans never did that. He pulled the trilby hat still further over his eyes, his mouth became more stern, and he said something like "Quit . . ." The next thing you saw was the girl on the front doorstep, fitting a key in the lock and crying, and Barry Jeans banking the corner in his Cadillac. It was the same on mountains or in the desert. If Barry Jeans got himself on the edge of a crevasse in the Andes or Alps, or lay beside a mud-pool oasis with three palm trees five hundred miles from the nearest Legion outpost, the woman of course by his side, he never touched her. He did not even have a rope to help her out of the crevasse, or a tin mug to scoop up the dirty water from the pool. He just said "This is it," and either walked away or died.

It was his manner that made the Menace popular with men as well as with women. You did not have to take trouble any more. You did not have to kiss your girl. You did not have to make love. And all that tedious business of booking a table at a restaurant, and seeing the headwaiter, and ordering the wine, became completely *vieux jeu*. Barry Jeans never did it. He walked into any place with his woman, and he just held up one finger, and everyone seemed to know what he meant. Waiters fell over themselves, guests already seated were told there wasn't a table, and the Menace sat down with his woman watching him, waved the menu aside, and uttered the one word "Clams."

Barry Jeans began the vogue of eating your steaks so rare that it was hard to tell whether they had been cooked at all, of wearing no topcoat in a blizzard, of sleeping nude (this the fans supposed, because no one in any movie saw him put on pyjamas), of having a tenderness for objects rather than human beings. Thus, in his most famous movies, the ones that went over the biggest, the last shot would be of the Menace stroking his old Ford car, or holding the tiller of a sailboat, or even looking up at a giant oak tree with an axe in his hand and saying, "You've got to go." People came out with a lump in the throat. It made ordinary romance seem so trivial. The only bad picture Barry Jeans ever made was when he took the part of Adam in the great biblical version of Genesis, and they had a shot of him patting a dinosaur on the back and saying, "I've lost my rib." It did not ring true. But that was the fault of the script-writer.

When World War II came along the Menace wanted to join up, but the Pentagon rated his entertainment value so high, in helping to keep up the morale of the troops, that they wouldn't let him, and he went right on making films. But he compensated for the lack of active service by sending more food parcels to Europe than all the rest of the British contingent in the United States put together. Barry's Spam kept many homes going, and thousands of housewives would have fallen for Goebbels' propaganda about starving Britain if they had not been able to use Barry's cooking fat.

When the war was over, and the Menace paid his first visit to Europe in ten years, with the idea of looking up his father —who had retired by now but was still living in Herne Bay —the crowds were so thick at Waterloo that they stretched right away to the river. Mounted police had to be called in, and people who did not know thought it was a Communist revolution at last.

Barry was embarrassed by the demonstration, but May enjoyed it. She had picked up an American accent during her years in the States, which Barry had not, and used a lot of phrases like "gotten" and "I know it" and "you're welcome." She did most of the talking into the microphone when they arrived, and told Barry to sit low in the car with his hat over his eyes. It made him more inaccessible than ever, and the crowd loved it. The publicity was so tremendous that they gave up the idea of getting to Herne Bay, and sent for Barry's father to join them in their hide-out at Cape Wrath, where pictures were taken of Barry and his father looking out to sea, and Barry saying, "It's good to be home." Rumour had it that they were invited to Balmoral, but this was never proved.

New names, pop singers, and the teen-age craze made no difference to the Menace. His fame was too deeply graven into the hearts of all men and women over thirty-five. They had been born and bred in the faith of Barry Jeans, and they would die in the faith of Barry Jeans. Besides, the kids liked him too. The greying hair—only at the temples, mind—and the slightest suspicion of a bag under the eye, and that line on the jaw, it did the same thing to the daughters that it had done to the mothers twenty years before; it made them dream. Who wanted to be kissed by the boy next door or the young man round the block when you could sit alone in perfect darkness and have Barry Jeans say "Someday" out of a wide screen, and turn his back on you, and go? The inflection of his voice, the meaning he put into it, and never a glint in the eye, never a smile. Just the word "Someday." Phew!

The Menace never touched Shakespeare. May said it would be a mistake. Anyone can put on a beard and mouth a lot of words, she told him. God gave you a personality and you ought to keep to it. Barry was disappointed. He would have liked to have a shot at Lear. Hamlet and Richard the Third had been pinched already. "May's right," said the entourage. "You don't want to touch that stuff. And it doesn't go over in Tokyo. No, you stick to the parts that made you big, and you'll stay big."

The entourage, otherwise "the boys," consisted of Barry's personal manager, his agent, his press agent, his secretary, his make-up man, and his stand-in. May would not have a woman secretary because if she was of a certain age she would try to boss Barry, and if she was young she would try something else. "The boys" were safe. They were all hand-picked, with wives who did not matter.

Barry did not move without the boys and May, and even at home in Beverly Hills, in the lovely old reproduction of a Kent oasthouse which had been built for him, the boys stayed around at weekends just in case. A new script might come along, or a millionaire with money to burn, or an accountant with a new tax dodge, and if this should happen May wanted the boys to handle it. Barry himself must not be worried.

The Menace had no family. Only May. In early days this had been a disappointment. Publicity could have used photographs of Barry holding a youngster on his shoulder, or teaching a kid to swim in the pool or fly a kite. But as the years went by May and the boys agreed it was just as well as things were. A lanky son or a great gaggling daughter would have spoilt the Menace legend. Barry Jeans could remain the unknown, the untouchable, the guy who was every woman's lover and no girl's father. When a star begins to play fathers it is the thin edge of the wedge, and a grandfather, of course, is his finish.

"Sweetie pie," May would say, "the world wants you just the way you are. Your hands in your pockets, your hat over your eyes. Don't alter a thing. And stay that way when you come off the set."

Barry did. He hardly ever spoke, even at home. The people

who knew him, all of them in Hollywood or elsewhere in the movie world, would gaze at the long spare figure drinking orange juice through a straw—he never touched hard liquor —and wonder how the devil he did it. His contemporaries had most of them got thick necks and paunches. Not Barry Jeans. Not the Menace. May had him up at six every morning, when he was not in the studio, doing Swedish exercises. And if there was not a party he was in bed by nine.

In all the years that the Menace had held the world, his name had never been connected with any scandal. He had broken up no homes. The beautiful women who had played opposite him could not even get a still of him sitting near them in the studio to take home. May did not allow it. The still might get publicized and printed in the papers, and then everyone would begin to talk. Passionate Italians, languorous French *vedettes*, belles from the deep South, dusky Puerto Ricans, whatever star of the moment was signed on to play opposite the Menace, they never got a word alone with him off the set. May or the boys were always there. And if a reporter, more enterprising than his fellows, caught Barry off guard in the break for lunch when the boys were in the washroom and May was powdering her nose, and asked him, "What do you think of Mitsi Sulva?" or whatever the name was of the beautiful girl billed beneath him, he only answered just the one word "Great." It was noncommittal and absolutely safe. It could not give offence to the lady, and it could not offend May. Not even the most treacherous reporter could twist the word into anything else. A headline saying "Barry Jeans thinks Mitsi Sulva's great" did not mean a thing. And by the time the reporter was bringing up another question the boys were out of the washroom.

It was during the making of the first "feelie" that the boys began to wonder whether the methods they had used to date would work any longer. As everybody knows, the "feelies" came in during the late fall of '59 and revolutionized the film business. The result was chaos until the technicians got the thing under control and the big combines had all their houses wired for "feel," but the real panic was in the studios. How would the stars get by? How would the big names, and the

215

biggest name of all—Barry Jeans the Menace—hold their own in the new medium? The point being that it was not just the wiring of the houses that fixed the "feelie"; the star had to be wired during shooting—the gadget was concealed in his clothing—and the power was transmitted back to the "barker," the name of the mechanism that in its turn fed the power machine which was hired out to the movie houses. Unless the current was Force A the barker could not do its stuff. And the terrible thing was that a star's motivation, or Force, was an unknown quantity until it was put to the test.

It was not until Barry Jeans was on the floor rehearsing with Vanda Gray that the technicians signalled to the director that Barry's Force was only ticking over at G. It was the lowest number on the dial, and not strong enough to feed the barker. The director ordered a break and went into a consultation with the team.

It was a delicate situation. Not even the director, who knew Barry well, had the courage to tell him he was only sending out Force G. The expert in charge of the mechanism was tough, though. He was in a strong position, because nobody else on the floor knew how it worked.

"Let's be realistic," he said. "This guy's no damn good. I know he's a star, I know he's world-famous. So what? We've entered a new era. The 'feelies' are going to put Jeans out of business."

The production manager swallowed two tranquillizers.

"This is serious," he said. "Not a word of all this must leave these four walls. If gossip got around the studios that Barry Jeans couldn't make a higher grade than Force G, there would be such a scandal that Gigantic Enterprise Ltd. would never recover. Speaking personally, I could never hold up my head again, and I'm not joking when I warn you that it would strike a serious blow at the entire film industry."

The "feelie" expert chewed gum and shrugged his shoulders.

"Your move," he said. "I've done all I can. I've stepped up the kicking rate until the feeder's darn near busted, but nothing happens. If I play about with the mechanism it may

216

pack up altogether, and that'll cost Gigantic Enterprises a million dollars."

The director was saying something about getting in a psychiatrist to talk to Barry, and the production manager nodded thoughtfully.

"There's a Swede over at International," he said. "I believe he did wonders for Leila Montana when her voice went bass."

"That's right," said the director. "Leila got back her confidence fine, but they still had to dub the voice in *Golden Girl*. Wait a minute . . ." He turned to the expert, and asked if there was not some method similar to dubbing that could be worked with the feelie gadget. "Can't we fake it?" he said. "Try somebody else's Force, and feed it to the barker?"

The expert shook his head. "No go," he said. "You've got to have direct transmission," and he launched into technical details far above any of their heads. The director listened carefully. It was vital for him and the team to understand the jargon. Unless a director knew exactly what happened on the floor he was no use. He was out of date. The feelies were here to stay.

"We ought to have tested," he said. "We were crazy not to test. I had a hunch at the time that we were slipping somewhere."

"And what if we had tested?" asked the production manager. "Do you mean to say that I should have gone to Barry Jeans and told him the result? He'd have blown his brains out."

"Not Barry," said the director. "He's a grand fellow. Barry's all right. It's just that . . ." He looked about him desperately. "Do you mean there's no way of combining the Forces?" he asked the expert as a final gesture. "No way of using some of Vanda's Force in their scenes together? I mean, she's Force A, isn't she?"

"She's Force A all right," said the expert, still chewing.

"Then how about it?" said the production manager eagerly.

"The ratio's different for a female," said the expert, "and you can't mix 'em. Not right now, anyway. Maybe in ten years when they've worked on it awhile."

The director spread out his hands in a movement of defeat.

"I've had it," he said. "I'm through. I can't make this picture."

The production manager, white to the lips, went to all the team in turn, swearing each of them to secrecy.

"There must be no leakage," he said, "absolutely none at all. If I hear there's been a leak everyone is fired."

Then he called up Barry's boys and asked for a consultation in absolute secrecy. He did not even want May. May must be kept out of it for the moment.

The boys turned up, and they locked the doors of the production manager's office and posted a guard outside.

"What's wrong?" said Alf Burnell, Barry's manager.

The production manager for Gigantic Enterprises put on his horn-rimmed spectacles. He wanted the full weight of the news to sink in.

"A very serious situation has arisen," he said. "A discovery was made on the floor this morning. Barry is Force G."

The boys sat in stunned silence. Then Bob Elder wiped his forehead. "Jesus," he said. He was Barry's press agent.

"I need hardly tell you," said the production manager, "that I have sworn everyone to secrecy. And of course Barry himself does not know. We said there was a technical hitch."

Ken Dory, Barry's dramatic agent, asked the question the director had asked about combining it with that of someone else on the set. The production manager put him wise.

"Nothing technical can be done," he said. "We've got to work on a different level. I suggest psychiatry. Call in the Swede from International."

The boys whistled in unison. "May wouldn't stand for it," said Alf Burnell. "She wouldn't let a psychiatrist within a hundred miles of Barry."

"Then what are we going to do?" asked the production manager. "You must realise that I'm responsible to Gigantic Enterprises for any holdup, and a report will have to go through tonight."

Slip Jewett, Barry's make-up man, leant forward.

"We can say Barry's sick," he suggested. "I can work on him. I can produce a grand jaundice for you if you'll give the word."

"How does that help us in the long run?" said Ken, who was a realist. "Jaundice would tide Barry over a few days, or maybe a few weeks, but after that?"

"Yep, after that?" said Bob Elder. "What am I to tell the press? That the Menace is Force G? Do we all have to go in the poorhouse?"

The production manager took off his spectacles and polished them.

"I'm afraid," he said, "sympathetic as I am to the long-term policy of you and Barry Jeans, that I am not concerned in it. Gigantic Enterprises have engaged his services for this picture on the full understanding that he rated Force A or B, or at the worst C. I doubt if Gigantic Enterprises would employ anyone of a lower category. I very much doubt it."

The stand-in, Bim Spooner, gave a gentle cough.

"I was fooling around the floor the other day," he said. "I got talking to the feelie expert. I got him to test me. I was Force A."

Nobody paid any attention to Bim. He was a good guy, but naïve. The secretary, Pat Price, stumped out his cigarette.

"We won't get anywhere in this without May," he said. "She's got to be in on it. It's tough, but there it is."

Bob Elder stumped out his cigarette likewise.

"I agree with Pat," he said. "May's closer to Barry than anyone else. Let's throw the ball to May."

The conference was ended. The production manager took two more tranquillizers and went to lunch. The boys walked round in a bunch to the dressing-room. May was having sandwiches and Barry was asleep.

"What's cooking?" asked May. "Barry told me the feelie gadget wasn't working. I don't know how they have the face to get Barry made up and on the set and then find out the wires don't click."

"It wasn't the wires," said Alf, and he jerked his head towards the sleeping Barry. "Come outside."

He and Bob and Ken had agreed that they would explain the situation to May while the rest stayed in the dressing-room with Barry. They led her out of the building and walked up and down the garden behind the studios. They did not mince matters. They let her have it straight. She took it well. And being a woman, she went right to the heart of the matter.

"It's Vanda's fault," she said at once. "Barry never did think much of Vanda. Of course his Force is G when he's on the set with her. She makes him shy."

"O.K., O.K.," said Ken, "but he's got to act with her, hasn't he? That was all agreed when we decided to make this picture. It don't matter a damn to Gigantic Enterprises if Barry hates the sight of Vanda. They want results. Barry's got to rate Force A or they'll fire him."

"They wouldn't dare," cried May. "Fire Barry? Fire the Menace?"

"They'd fire the Almighty," said Ken, "if he didn't do his stuff. The feelies are new, May. They're going to kill everything that's gone before. If Barry misses out on this he's finished."

"We're all finished," said Bob.

They looked at May, who had aged about ten years while they were speaking. She knew they were right. She was a realist too.

"We've got to get the rating up," she said, as though speaking to herself. "We've just got to make the grade."

"Do you think you can do it, May?" asked Ken. "I mean . . ." He broke off. After all, it was rather a delicate situation.

"I'm going to try," said May. "If I fail . . ." and she also did not finish her sentence.

"Good girl," said Alf, patting her shoulder. "Don't rush your fences. One thing at a time."

"How long have we got?" put in Ken, as a reminder, while they were walking back to the dressing-room. "May's never going to get the ratio up in time for work tomorrow morning."

"I'll ask for a twenty-four-hour postponement," said Alf. "G.E. can blame the barker. I'll make it square with the chaps."

They found that Barry had wakened up from his sleep and was eating porridge. The rare steaks were just a publicity stunt that had been worked in the distant past by Bob Elder.

Barry practically lived on porridge. May signalled to the boys to leave them alone.

"Well, honey," she said, "how would you like a little vacation?"

Barry did not answer immediately. It always took time for any remark to sink in. "H'm . . . h'm . . ." he said. Then he frowned and wiped the porridge off his chin.

"I thought we'd had our vacation," he said. "I thought we were starting work again."

"We are, sweetie pie," said May, "but there's been a postponement for twenty-four hours. A technical hitch with the new gadget. I thought we might go out and have dinner someplace tonight."

Barry stared. "Go out?" he said.

"Yes, honey," smiled May. "The boys and I don't think you relax enough. You're worrying about the picture."

"I'm not worrying," said Barry. "I never worry."

He helped himself to more porridge. May frowned. It could be that with these new feelies diet and routine would have to undergo a drastic change.

"That's enough now," she said, removing the plate. "Too much porridge isn't good for you. I tell you what. We'll try out that place they're all raving about in town, the Silver Slipper. We'll treat ourselves to a really good dinner and get a little high, just the two of us. What do you say, honey?"

Barry watched his plate of porridge go into the serving lift. May pulled back the shutter and it disappeared.

"I don't know, dear," he said. "I'd rather stay at home."

"Whatever you say," smiled May, kissing the top of his head, "whatever you say."

Next morning Alf Burnell was awakened from sleep at six-thirty by the telephone ringing beside his bed.

"Yes?" he said.

"It's May," answered the voice. "Bad news, I'm afraid."

"Nothing doing?" asked Alf.

"Nothing at all. He played patience all evening and was sound asleep by ten. He's still sleeping."

"I'll wake the boys," said Alf. "Don't worry. We'll be around."

He called a consultation for eight o'clock. After they had met and found they shared identical views on the next step to be taken, they jumped in the car and drove the five hundred yards to Barry's place. May was waiting for them on the terrace.

"I tried everything I knew," she said. She looked tired.

She led them indoors to the living-room, and they all sat down. Alf cleared his throat. He was senior, and therefore spokesman.

"Listen, May," he said, "you're a grand girl, and we all respect you. We know how hard this is for you. But we can't let sentiment ruin Barry's life. I think we're agreed about that."

"Yes, sure we're agreed," said May.

"Well, then, the boys and I think you'd best run off to the country club for a couple of nights and leave us to fix Barry."

The boys kept their eyes on the floor. They could not be sure how May would take it. She had guts though.

"Alf," she said, "I decided that myself at half-past three this morning. But I don't think you'll get anywhere."

"We can try," said Ken.

"After all," said Bob, "there are some things a guy can't tell his wife. Old Barry might come clean with us."

May handed round the cigarettes and poured coffee.

"There's nothing that Barry could tell you I don't know," she said. "I've looked after him day and night for thirty years."

"Maybe that's it," said Bob.

There was silence. The situation was tough all right. The question was, what next? Before any of them knew anything, Gigantic Enterprises would be on the line asking for news.

"O.K.," snapped May suddenly. "I'll disappear for a couple of nights. He's all yours. Whatever you do, don't hurt him."

"Atta girl," said Alf. The boys relaxed.

When Barry awoke about ten o'clock and asked for his orange juice, Pat, his secretary, and Slip, his make-up man, were sitting on chairs by the window. The rest of the boys were below, talking on the telephone and keeping G.E. quiet for twenty-four hours.

"Where's May?" asked Barry.

"May's tired," said Pat. "She woke up with a migraine head, and we called the doctor and he advised her to run over to the club for a night or two and have a massage."

Barry sipped his orange juice. "I never knew May to have migraine heads before," he said. He lay back on his pillow to think it out.

"It's her age," said Slip. "It gets women that way."

He came over to the bedside, propped Barry up with pillows and bolster, and began snipping at his hair with his scissors.

Barry looked at the clock. "It's after ten," he said.

"That's right," said Pat. "We let you sleep. No work today. They still can't fix the barker."

"Uhuh," said Barry.

They ran his bath and gave him his breakfast, got him into his clothes, and then took him downstairs to the car. The car was drawn up outside the house, with the rest of the boys packed inside it. "Hullo, Barry," they called.

Ken was at the wheel. "Hop inside," he said. "We're going down to Poncho beach."

They all watched for Barry's reaction. Poncho beach was ten miles down the coast, and there was nothing like it in the whole American continent between Los Angeles and Peru. It was that hot. If a star or employee of Gigantic Enterprises or any of the other big companies was seen there, he was fired. Alf Burnell had fixed this trip with the head of G.E. himself.

"Poncho beach?" said Barry. "That's great. Can I swim?"

"Of course you can swim," said Alf. "This is your day."

They got down to the beach about half-past eleven, which was about right for time, because it was then that the coloured boys and girls did the midday nude parade before taking to the water. Ken parked the car right on the beach near the huts, and Pat and Slip and Bim got the crate of lunch and liquor out of the car and dumped it beside the cushions and the lilos.

"Have a drink, Barry?" said Ken.

He had been rattling the shaker, and he poured what was in it into a glass. "Try this, old son," he said. "It's good."

Barry sniffed the glass suspiciously. "What is it?" he said. "It smells funny."

The boys all looked the other way. It was somehow hard having to deceive the Menace this way. But it was for his good.

"It's vitamin juice," said Don. "Just on the market."

Barry swallowed some and pulled a face. "Tastes sour," he said. "Do I have to take it?"

"And another," said Ken. "Just put it down."

The girls and boys were coming down the beach as he spoke, and they were really something. None of them was above seventeen, and they were all hand-picked by the syndicate which ran Poncho beach from Rockefeller Center in New York. They were trained to walk that way, of course —the training was very stiff, and took six months—but the syndicate had taken advice from a ring of experts in Tangier and Port Said, and these kids made anything else look silly.

They did the first dance right in front of Barry. It was only a warm-up, but it was quite enough for Bim. He got up and disappeared. The others stuck it and observed Barry's face. He looked puzzled. "Do we have to watch these niggers?" he said. "I'd like to swim." Alf motioned him to be quiet, and Don poured some more vitamin juice out of the shaker.

"Wait for the feather dance," murmured Alf.

The feather dance was really the works. Done with great delicacy and skill, but of course performed under the sun at eleven-thirty in the morning by these capable youngsters, it was a test of endurance for the spectators. Halfway through it Bob Elder and Pat Price and even Slip had to get up and disappear as Bim had done.

"Where are they going?" asked Barry. "Are they sick?"

"No, no," said Ken impatiently. "Watch these kids."

The feather dance came to an end, and the performers who had survived it clapped their hands delightedly and made for the water. The spectators who found themselves overcome were edging with their chosen companions towards the bathing huts. Alf and Ken looked at Barry. He was lifting the lid of the picnic box and peering inside.

"Those fools at home have forgotten my porridge," he said.

Alf and Ken saw it was no good. If the kids on Poncho beach did not stir Barry, nothing would. Maybe they would have to try the Swedish psychiatrist after all. They hung around on the beach waiting for Barry to have his swim—he would not go into the water until all the kids came out of it —and then he swam round and round in circles, doing the breast stroke. It was enough to break your heart.

"Enjoy yourself, Barry?" asked Alf.

"Great," said Barry, "just great."

Ken went along to the restaurant to order steaks and champagne, and the rest of the boys flocked round him, looking shamefaced and foolish.

"I tell you what it is," said Bob. "Barry's hard-boiled."

"Nuts," said Ken. "We're on the wrong track."

In the afternoon, after Barry had had his sleep, they went along to see the floor show that was only shown to ticket holders, and you had to get the tickets direct from Rockefeller Center. Alf produced tickets for all of them, and they sat jammed together in a private box. The boys agreed afterwards that the show was not a patch on the one put up by the kids on the beach, for all the sophistication, but Alf said it was a matter of taste.

"It depends what you go for," he said. "This gets me."

After the show Barry went for another swim. Round and round in circles he went, his arms spread stiffly in front of him, while the boys threw pebbles in the water and discussed the situation.

"Alf promised to call G.E. tonight," said Bob. "If we don't call there's going to be a row. Barry is due on the floor at 8 A.M. tomorrow morning."

"There's still sixteen hours in hand," said Ken.

Barry came out of the sea. He looked wonderful. You'd never have guessed he'd been a household name for over thirty years.

"What's so great about the sea, Barry?" asked Ken sourly.

Barry sat down and began to dry his toes.

"It takes me back," he said. "It's like Herne Bay."

The boys packed up the lunch crate, and the cushions, and the lilos. What the hell was the use of coming to Poncho beach when all Barry cared about was Herne Bay? May was right. They knew nothing.

"We've wasted about a thousand dollars," said Ken as he took the wheel of the car once more.

"Not our dollars," said Alf. "G.E. paid for this outing."

They drove Barry back home, got him changed and into evening clothes, and took him along to the Silver Slipper to dine. Alf had arranged for the three loveliest girls on tap to G.E. to come and join them at the table. Bim had a grand time, and so did Pat, and Ken and Bob made good weather with the little Japanese beauty who had only arrived in Hollywood that morning, but it was no go. Barry kept complaining that they did not give him porridge to eat, and he was going to call up May and see if she could fix something.

"O.K. Go ahead and call her up," said Alf.

He was fed to the teeth. It was nearly midnight. The girls had done no good. The Jamaican wrestlers had done no good. The acrobats from Korea who had raised a sparkle in the dim, dead eyes of poor old wasted Harry Fitch, after he had tried every mortal thing under the sun and had dragged round the world for years, had done no good. It was zero hour. The boys had reached their limit.

"Tomorrow," said Alf, when Barry had gone to call up May, "all of us sitting round this table are going to be out of a job."

Meanwhile Barry had got one of the waiters to show him a call box and lend him a dollar, and he waited in the box for the call to come through. The call box was just opposite the ladies' powder room, and the attendant was standing in the doorway knitting. The clients were all in the restaurant and it was not her busy time. She gave a sort of half smile when she saw Barry, and went on with her knitting. She was plump and middle-aged, and her hair was grey in the old-fashioned manner except for a purple streak down the middle. Barry did not notice her. His call came through and he spoke to May.

"That you, dear?" he said. "I can't hear you very well."

"I've got my chin strapped," she said. "I'm having treatment. How are you, honey?"

"I'm great," he said, "just great."

"Where are you speaking from? Are the boys with you?" she asked.

"We're in some night club," he told her. "We're quite a crowd."

"How do you mean, quite a crowd? Who's there?" she asked.

"I don't know their names, dear," he said. "There's a Japanese girl just off the plane, and an acrobat and his sister, and two darkies from Jamaica . . ." and then the line went funny and he could not make himself heard, though he could hear May's voice clearly enough. She kept saying, "What are you all doing?" in a strange, agitated sort of way. He reckoned it must be the strap on her chin that prevented her from speaking properly. Then the line cleared.

"We're doing fine," he said. "There's just one thing wrong. They will keep feeding me steaks, and I want porridge."

Silence from May. Perhaps she was thinking out some way to help.

"Do you go to work tomorrow?" she said at last.

"I think so, dear. I don't know."

"What did you do all day?"

"We spent all day on Poncho beach."

"On Poncho beach . . . ?" May's voice sounded as if someone was trying to strangle her.

"Take that strap off your chin, dear," he told her. "I can't hear a damn thing."

He must have irritated May in some way, because it sounded as if she was telling him to go back and eat his bloody steak, which was rather unkind of her. And she was saying something also about the best years of her life, and how much she loved him, and did the whole thing have to smash because of his career, and what happened on Poncho beach?

"Don't fuss, dear," he said. "I didn't go out of my depth. The boys got stomach trouble, but I was fine. Just fine."

Then the line went completely dead, and the operator told him the other party had hung up. It was too bad. The treatment at the club could not be suiting May. Barry came out of the call box.

He saw the attendant in front of the powder room smiling at him and her lips open as if to speak. He felt in his top pocket for his pen. The boys made him keep a pen handy for autographs. When anyone smiled at him it always meant she wanted his autograph. He slipped the cap off the pen and waited. But the woman did not produce a book or the back of a menu card. Barry waited.

"Where do you want me to write it?" he said at last.

"Write what?" asked the woman.

"My autograph," said Barry.

"I haven't asked you for your autograph," replied the woman.

"Oh," said Barry, "I beg your pardon."

He put the cap back on the pen and replaced it in his pocket.

"You haven't changed much," said the woman.

Barry scratched the back of his head. It was a reflex gesture taught him by the boys long ago as the stock answer to a fan's compliment. The compliment never required an answer.

"Remember Windy Gap?" pursued the woman.

Barry stared. Windy Gap . . . Funny thing, he had thought about Windy Gap only that afternoon. It was when he was coming in from his second swim and was splashing in the shallows and trod on a small shell, and the feeling of the shell under his foot took him back to the beach at Herne Bay and the spot near the breakwater where he used to dump his clothes. There was a hole in the breakwater where the wind from the east caught him undressing, and he used to hurry on with his bathing drawers so as not to catch a chill. There could not be anyone in the world who remembered the name Windy Gap except himself and . . . and . . . Barry stared a little harder at the woman, and then everything seemed to fall away and he was seventeen again, and thin and long, shivering in a pair of navy blue bathing shorts, and Pinkie

228

Brown was giggling beside him in a cotton frock and jabbing at his bare toes with a shrimping net.

"Go on," said Pinkie, "go on, dive."

"I don't like getting my head under water," said Barry.

Then she pushed him over the breakwater, and he had never forgotten the awful feeling of the swirling water, and the singing in his ears, and the choking, spluttering gasp for breath. He had thrashed out wildly with both arms and struggled ashore, and there was Pinkie running up the breakwater to get out of his way. He started in pursuit, and tripped and fell, knocking his forehead on an old stump full of barnacles, and his forehead began to bleed. He shouted, "Pinkie . . . hi, Pinkie, come back!"

She looked over her shoulder and saw him standing there, shivering, trying to staunch the blood with his clumsy fingers, and she came running back, pulling her own handkerchief out of her knickers.

"Here, take this," she said scornfully, and then, because it would not stop bleeding, bound the handkerchief round his head and stood there holding it. When it was safe to take the handkerchief away they climbed down to the beach and sat on Barry's clothes by Windy Gap, and Barry put his vest over his shoulders to keep out the draught, and then he kissed Pinkie until she got fed up and pushed him away, after which they both sat eating Herne Bay rock. Even now he could feel the crunch of it.

The powder-room attendant was smiling at him, and for the first time in over thirty years Barry Jeans was aware of a tremor in his cheek, some sort of slackening of the muscle line of his jaw.

"Yes," said the woman, "it's Pinkie Brown all right."

If the press had been around at that moment they would have seen an expression on the Menace's face that none of the fans had ever seen. It might be called emotion. Or, in modern speech, a double take.

"Gosh!" said Barry. "Gosh! I'm glad to see you, Pinkie."

He put out his hand, and the woman tucked her knitting under her arm and shook it.

"I'm glad to see you too, Barry," she said.

He looked about him, trying to take it all in, and then he said to her, "You must come and join us. We have a table here."

The woman shook her head.

"I can't do that," she answered. "I can't leave here until closing time. That won't be until about 3 A.M."

Barry stared at the notice above the door—Powder Room —and saw the dressing tables inside the room and the long mirrors.

"You work here, Pinkie?" he said.

"Yes," she told him. "I've had this job ever since it opened. It suits me a treat. Now my kids are grown-up and married it gets dull at home."

She had started knitting again. Something white and loose. He put out his hand and touched it.

"You did a scarf for me once," he said, "that time I got the flu. It was white, too, and had little dancing dogs in crimson in the front."

"That's right," she said. "What a memory you've got. This is going to be a shawl for my next grandchild. I've got two already."

Barry thought a moment, then looked at his watch.

"I wish you didn't have to work," he said. "I wish we could just sit and talk."

The powder-room attendant looked doubtful.

"Haven't you a party on in there?" she asked, nodding her head towards the restaurant.

"Yes," said Barry, "but nothing important. Just the boys and some of their friends. We don't have to worry about them."

The woman gave a quick look up and down. Then she beckoned Barry inside the powder room.

"There's a little place in here behind the cloaks," she said, and drew him swiftly into a recess that led from the hanging space where the women left their wraps while they were in the restaurant. "It's only a cubbyhole," she went on, "but there's a stool to sit on and no one can see you. Look . . ." and she drew a curtain so that it hid the recess. It was a bit stuffy with the curtain drawn, but Barry did not mind that, and he saw she had an electric kettle fixed to a point in the wall. There was a cup and saucer there.

"Like some tea?" she asked.

"I'd rather have hot milk," said Barry.

"That's all right," she said. "I've got some milk in the cupboard. I'll heat it for you in the kettle."

She peeped out of the recess to see if the coast was still clear.

"They won't be in yet," she said. "It's generally around one when they begin to come along. I'll have to pop in and out then, but we can talk in-between times. Sit down and make yourself at home."

Barry sat down on the stool and leant his head against the wall. His long legs were rather cramped, but he could not stretch them out because they would reach under the curtain, and then the girls would see them when they came into the powder room.

"You been out here long, Pinkie?" he asked.

"Twenty years," she said. "I won a beauty prize home at Herne Bay, and the prize was a film test in Hollywood. I had the test but it wasn't any good, so I got married instead, and I've been out here ever since. My poor husband died of ulcers two years ago, but I've three lovely daughters, and a boy in Canada."

"You're lucky, Pinkie," said Barry. "May and I have no family."

"No, I'm sorry about that," she said. "I always think having a family keeps you young."

She had heated the milk by now and was pouring it into the cup.

"Remember the prawns at Herne Bay, Pinkie?" he said.

"I should think I do," she said, "and the way they wriggled in the net. I was better at catching them than you were. You wouldn't go in the deeper pools because of the crabs."

"I got caught by a crab once," he said. "The horrid brute tweaked my toe. Got any sugar, Pinkie? I like my milk sweet."

"Here you are," she said, and she dropped in three lumps.

"I'll say one thing for this country," she went on. "You can eat well. But the cost of living is awful high."

"I know," he said. "It's the taxes. The taxes kill me. Do you have to pay a lot in tax too?"

"Not too bad," she said. "I seem to get by. I have quite a nice apartment. Everything laboursaving."

"Our house is laboursaving too," he told her, "and the view's good from the terrace. That was a nice place you had at Herne Bay, Pinkie. Leonard Terrace, wasn't it, the last house?"

"That's right," she said. "Poor old Dad, he's been gone a long time. He didn't half tell you off that time you came to supper and spilt the soup. 'Don't parsons' sons learn manners?' he said. He was surprised when you did well. But I don't think he ever saw one of your pictures. Pity, really."

"Do you see my pictures?" he asked.

"I used to," she said. "Not lately, though. They seem to have gone off. The last one was such a silly story. But the girl was good."

She poked her head through the curtains and motioned him to silence.

"Someone coming," she said. "I'll have to go through. Finish up your milk. It hasn't turned, has it? There's no ice-box here."

"No, it's great," he said, "just great."

She went into the powder room, and the girl who came in asked for safety pins to fix her slip. Barry hoped the girl would not stay long. He wanted to go on talking to Pinkie. He remembered the time they had gone walking along the cliff and it had come on to thunder, and they had had an argument as to whether to shelter under a bush or run for it. He had warned Pinkie it was dangerous to go near trees in a thunderstorm because of the likelihood of being struck by lightning. She said that if they did not shelter he must give her his coat to put over her head.

"But I'm only wearing an aertex shirt," he pointed out. "I'll get soaked to the skin."

Finally they had compromised and shared the coat, and Pinkie kept telling him as they stumbled along the cliff that he was pulling it all his side.

Barry peeped through a slit in the curtain to see if the girl had left the powder room, but she had been joined by another, who was making up in front of the mirror. She had spilt her compact in the washbasin, and Pinkie was wiping the basin with a cloth. Presently the girls went off, leaving twenty-five cents in the tray on the dressing table.

Pinkie left it lying there, and Barry wondered why she did not put it for safety in her bag. She said it looked better that way. It showed clients they were meant to tip. If the tray was empty nobody bothered to put anything in.

"How much do you pick up of an evening, Pinkie?" he asked.

"It all depends," she said. "Saturdays are good. I sometimes clear twenty-five dollars on Saturdays."

"I wish I had twenty-five dollars," said Barry. "The boys never give me anything."

"Well, you're clothed and fed, aren't you?" she said. "After all, that's the main thing."

He gave her the cup and saucer, and she put them back on the ledge by the kettle. Then she took up her knitting again.

"I wish you could see my grandsons," she continued. "They're lovely boys. I've got snapshots of the whole family at home. The girls all married—well, I'm glad to say—and my son David has a big gas station up in Winnipeg."

"They none of them went into movies, then?" asked Barry.

"Oh no," she said. "No, they've done really well."

Back in the restaurant the boys were getting restive. The Japanese girl kept looking at the clock and yawning, and the Korean acrobats had finished all the champagne.

"Barry's a hell of a time making that call to May," said Alf. "Go and dig him out of it, Pat."

Pat pushed aside the blonde, who had fallen asleep on his shoulder, and went through the swing door to the call box. In a few moments he was back again, his face serious.

"Barry's not there," he said. "The chap on the switchboard said he finished making the call all of fifteen minutes ago. He's not in the men's room either."

"Maybe he's gone to the car park," said Ken. "Bet you anything you like he's curled up asleep in the back of the car."

Pat went to see, and Slip went with him. It did not do for Barry to get his hair mussed up or his clothes rumpled, unless Slip was there beside him to put things straight. In less than five minutes they were back in the restaurant again, both looking haggard.

"Barry's not there," said Pat. "He's not in the car, or any other car. The car-park attendant hasn't seen him. And the chap on the door hasn't seen him either."

The Japanese girl looked interested at last. She accepted a cigarette from one of the Jamaican wrestlers.

"You know what it is, Mr. Burnell," she said to Alf. "Barry Jeans has given you the slip."

"That's right," said the wrestler. "The telephone call was a blind. How say we all go after him and beat up the town?"

Alf rose from the table and the boys rose with him. The maître d'hôtel hurried forward, but Alf waved him away.

"No, we don't want any more champagne," he said. "We're going. And Gigantic Enterprises is taking care of the check. Thank you, yes, Mr. Jeans had a wonderful time. Come on, fellows."

They went to the car and climbed in, leaving the girls with the wrestlers and the acrobats on the steps of the Silver Slipper. Gigantic Enterprises could take care of their evening, too, or what was left of it. The boys were going to hit the road for home, which was where Ken said they would surely find the Menace.

"I tell you what," said Bob. "May's ratted on us. May told him over the phone to get home to bed."

"How would he get home?" asked Alf. "He hadn't money for a taxi."

"Maybe he walked," said Bob. "That's it, he walked."

"Barry's never walked five yards in his whole life," said Slip. "If he walked five yards he'd get a stitch."

"What if he's been kidnapped?" said Ken. "My God, what if some bunch of chaps have kidnapped the Menace?"

"There's one thing," said Bim, "it would let him out of going on the floor tomorrow morning. I could take his place."

Ken told Bim to put a sock in it. The thing was too darn serious. If Barry Jeans had been kidnapped the whole of

Hollywood would go up in smoke. They'd have to call the State Department, they'd have to call Washington, the FBI. Chaps would have to ground all aircraft taking off east or west.

"Wait awhile, wait awhile," said Alf. "Let's see if Barry's tucked up safe and sound in bed."

They roared up the driveway to the house and woke the frightened butler. They searched the rooms, but there was no sign of the Menace. Then Pat put through a call to May at the country club. He was careful not to alarm her. He just said they were all back home, and Barry seemed a bit quiet, and he and the rest of the boys wondered if May had said anything to upset him.

May's voice was muffled and strange, and she sounded as if she had been crying.

"I trusted you," she said. "I trusted you to look after him. And then you went and took him to Poncho beach."

"See here, May . . ." said Pat, but May had rung off and he could not get the connection through again.

"Any news?" asked the boys as he slammed down the receiver.

"May's sore," said Pat. "That's all the news."

"What's she got to be sore about?" asked Ken.

"She's sore because we took Barry to Poncho beach."

They all went out to the car again, each with a different suggestion. Bob thought they ought to call the FBI right away, but Alf said once the dope was spilt to the FBI then it would be all down the Coast about what had gone wrong and how Barry's rating was Force G.

"Those fellows can't keep a secret," he said. "We only go to the FBI if we can't produce Barry in the studio by eight o'clock tomorrow morning."

"Tomorrow morning?" said Slip. "It's half-past one now. There's only seven hours to go."

They all climbed into the car again and started driving back to town.

"I've a hunch," said Bob, "I've a hunch he's got a lift somehow and gone back to Poncho beach. That pose of his about not showing interest was all my eye. Bet you he's gone to see the kids do their stuff again."

"Bob's right," said Pat. "They have the beach floodlit at 2 A.M. The kids do the feather dance under the arc lights. It would be dangerous to leave Barry down there without us."

Ken turned the car down the road that led out of town to Poncho beach.

"I don't know," said Alf. "I can't believe those kids meant a darn thing to Barry. But when we were watching the floor show I had the impression he was restless. I felt him move, I was next him in the box. If Barry's anywhere he's down at Poncho casino watching the floor show."

"We'd better do both," said Ken. "We'd better do the beach first and then the floor show. How long will it take?"

"I guess they close at five," said Slip. "They couldn't get through with all they do before five."

Ken stepped on the accelerator, and the car sped along the road to Poncho beach.

The departure of Barry Jeans's party from the Silver Slipper killed the evening. There was no fun in dancing or sitting around when the big names had gone. Those who still felt energetic went home to bed, and the people who were always tired decided to go on to Poncho beach. At two-thirty the band packed up, the tables were cleared, and the lights were dimmed. The chap on the switchboard had fallen asleep. No one noticed that the light was still on in the ladies' powder room. The curtains were pulled back now that everyone had gone home, and Barry had come out of the cubbyhole. He was sitting in a chair by one of the dressing tables, and he had put his feet up on the table itself. He was drinking hot milk. Pinkie was going round the powder room with the basin cloth, seeing that everything was neat and clean for the following night.

"I don't remember that bit about the Bath buns," she was saying. "I know you always pinched the currants out of mine, but I had forgotten I made a bet you couldn't eat ten at a sitting."

"I ate twelve," he said, "and then I was sick."

"Shame it didn't put some weight on you," she said, "but you were always scrawny. You're scrawny now."

She wrung out her basin cloth, and tidied the brushes and combs, and then went to the row of hooks by the curtain and lifted down her coat and her head scarf.

"What's the time?" asked Barry.

"It's nearly four," she said. "I'm going to be dead on my feet in the morning after gossiping here all this time."

"I'm sorry," said Barry. "I've kept you. I'm sorry, Pinkie."

He dragged his feet down from the dressing table and stood up.

"I'll see you home," he said. "It will be like old times."

Pinkie was adjusting the head scarf in front of the mirror, and she tied it under her chin and put her handbag over her arm.

"I don't know about that," she said. "It wouldn't do for me to be seen coming out of the powder room with you. I might lose my job."

"You go first," he said. "You go first and I'll wait, and then I'll slip out after you."

She seemed dubious, and kept muttering something about losing her reputation.

"I don't want to get into trouble," she said. "They think a lot of me here."

She looked through the door into the empty passage, and at the far end of the passage she could see the chap at the switchboard fast asleep.

"All right," she said, "I'll risk it. I'll go through the door on the right there, and wait on the street. Give me three minutes and then come after me."

Barry gave her three minutes, and then, when he judged it safe, he slipped out after her and joined her on the street as she had told him. It could have been the draught from the open door that awoke the chap on the switchboard, but he came to feeling a breeze on his face just after Pinkie had passed him, and as he sat up yawning and rubbing his eyes he caught a glimpse of a male figure creeping stealthily out of the ladies' powder room and sneaking on tiptoe down the passage towards the door. He was too startled at first to press the alarm which would have brought the watchman from the front of the building, and it was only after the man had passed him and gone through the door that he decided after all not to give the alarm. He was a married man and had been on switchboard duty at the Silver Slipper for many years, but in all his time there, and at other restaurants and night clubs, he had never seen a man come out of the ladies' powder room before. The sight was shocking enough in itself, but that was not all. What made it doubly shocking was that he had recognized Barry Jeans.

Pinkie was already walking down the street, and when she reached the corner she stood and waited for her companion to join her.

"I suppose you haven't a car?" he asked. "Mine seems to have gone. The boys must have got tired and slipped off home."

"I generally get a trolley," she said, "but I've never been so late. We might pick up a taxi if we're lucky."

They were lucky some five minutes later. Pinkie hailed the taxi, and she and Barry both climbed in.

"I haven't any money," said Barry. "I'm awfully sorry."

"That's all right," said Pinkie. "I always did pay."

When they came to Pinkie's block she got out first and paid the taxi, and then she said to Barry, "I'd better tell him to drive you straight home."

Barry had been thinking during the drive that he would get hell from the boys for being out late, and Slip might call up the masseur to get to work on him as soon as he put foot inside the house. They would turn the shower on him, too, the one with high pressure, and Slip would use the electric ray on his scalp to stimulate the hair, and they might even insist on that pinching and kneading of his arms and legs so as to ginger the muscle tone. The funny thing was he was not tired. He did not feel tired at all. He just did not want to go home.

"Pinkie," he asked, "Pinkie, couldn't I come up with you and see your place?"

Pinkie considered. "It's a bit late," she said.

"Not late, Pinkie," he urged, "it's early. It's not last night, it's tomorrow morning. I have to be in the studio soon after seven. I'll come to breakfast."

"All right," she said, "as long as no one sees you. I don't want my neighbours to think I give fellows breakfast."

They went inside the building and up to the fifth floor. It was a new apartment house, and Pinkie had a nice little three-room home. She showed Barry round, and introduced him to the canary, and then made him lie down on the settee in the living-room and take his ease. She put a piece of newspaper under his feet so that he did not spoil the new covers, and then she went into the kitchen to get him some breakfast.

"You can't make porridge, can you, Pinkie?" he asked.

"Not without Quaker Oats," she told him, "but I've got some rice here. I could make you a rice pudding."

"I'd like that," he said. "I'd like that more than anything."

He must remember to tell May to ring the changes sometimes with his breakfast, and to serve rice pudding instead of porridge. He lay stretched out on the settee and watched the canary hop about in its cage, and he listened to Pinkie bustling in the kitchen getting the crockery and setting the milk to boil. He wondered what the boys had done when he had not returned to the table. They must have been anxious. The best thing to do would be to have Pinkie put him in a taxi just before seven, and go straight to the studio and not back home at all. Then Slip could only make him up and get him on the set in time for shooting. There would not be time to give him hell or insist on massage. He settled himself more comfortably on the cushions and glanced at his watch. He had about two and a half hours to go.

"Pinkie?" he called.

"Yes?" She came through from the kitchen. She had taken off her coat and dress and was wearing a flowered overall. It had a beige background and great big roses on it, and it buttoned all down the front.

"There's something I'd like to do," he said.

"What is it?"

"I'd like to look at all those snapshots you were telling me about. The ones of you and your family, the children and the grandchildren. I'd just love to lie here looking at the snapshots while you get on with making the rice pudding."

Down at Poncho beach the line of cars was queueing up to drive back the ten miles into town. It was after five-thirty when Ken got all the boys together. Bob and Pat and Slip had held them up. They had stayed down on the beach after the feather dance while the others went to see the floor show, and when the floor show was over Alf had gone round the back of the stage to talk to some of the girls. He said he wanted to ask them if they had seen Barry. Then Bob, Pat, and Slip came up from the beach and they said the coloured kids had not even heard of Barry. It was really astonishing. They had not heard of the Menace. It had taken them nearly an hour to convince the kids that the Menace existed and had been down on Poncho beach that very day to watch them dance. It had been pretty exhausting work looking for Barry up and down Poncho beach, and the boys could hardly stand up. They all had to go to the bar and have stiff drinks to get them steady. Alf had to have a stiff drink too. Ken and Bim seemed to be the only ones who were in any shape at all.

"There has to be someone in this outfit in a state to take the wheel and get us back to town," said Ken, "and, when we get there, go to the studio and deal with Gigantic Enterprises."

"That's right," said Bim, "that's why I stayed sober. If Barry don't turn up I can go on the floor for him."

Ken took the ten miles back to town slowly. It would give the boys time to pull themselves together. First they would have to check at the house to see if Barry had come home, and after that they must all of them shower and shave and dress to be down at the studio by seven. They must come to some decision as to what was to be said. Alf was of the opinion that, if there was no news at all, then they must call up the FBI. It meant Barry had been kidnapped, and the matter was out of their hands. The news would break, of course, but it could not be helped. Ken agreed with Alf, and one by one as the car slid slowly along the road the boys came round to the same belief. It would have to be the FBI.

They pulled up in front of the house and, as they had

feared, there was no word of Barry. The boys went round to their own place, and showered and changed, and then they all met once more in the living-room of Barry's house, and Pat called up May and told her to come right back.

"I can't speak over the wire," he said. "It's serious."

None of them had any stomach for breakfast. The butler served them coffee and that was all. They sat there watching the clock, and they saw the hands creep up to a quarter of seven.

"Well?" said Alf. "Do I call the FBI?"

The boys looked at one another. It was a fateful decision to have to make. Once done, the Menace would no longer be their property, but the property of the United States Government.

"Hang on," said Pat. "How about checking with the Silver Slipper just once more, in case the doorman or someone saw Barry get away?"

"We tried them before," said Ken impatiently. "It's a waste of time."

"I don't know," said Bob. "It's worth trying again."

Although it was always Pat's job to put through calls, Alf was on the buzzer because it had been agreed that he was the one to speak to the FBI, so he carried on and asked for the Silver Slipper. The boys sat waiting, and watched his face for any change in expression. When they answered him from the Silver Slipper and he asked if anything had been seen of Mr. Barry Jeans, the effect was instantaneous. Alf said, "What?" excitedly, and nodded to the boys, and then he listened to what the operator had to say. The boys saw his jaw drop and a look, first of disbelief, then of dismay, then of shocked resignation and despair, pass over his features.

"O.K.," he said grimly. "Sit on it. We'll call you back."

He clamped the receiver down and sagged in his chair.

"Dead?" asked Ken.

"Worse."

Alf pulled out his handkerchief and blew his nose. Then he took a swig of coffee and pushed back his chair.

"Barry's sick," he said briefly. "We'll have to call the psychiatrist after all. Get that Swede's number, Pat, but don't get it through International. If International has this story we're through."

"But Jesus, Alf," said Bob, "what's happened?"

Alf stared at the floor. Then he straightened his shoulders and looked at the boys.

"Barry never left the Silver Slipper all evening," he said. "The operator on the switchboard saw him sneaking out of the ladies' powder room just after 4 A.M."

In Pinkie's living-room the Menace had finished his second plate of rice pudding and was licking the spoon. With his left hand he turned over the pages of Pinkie's photograph album.

"This one's great," he said, "just great."

He was pointing to a snapshot of Pinkie's second grandson in paddling drawers bending down and patting a sand castle with a wooden spade.

"How old is the little chap in this one?" he asked.

Pinkie bent over his shoulder and put on her spectacles.

"That's Ronnie," she said, "that's Ronnie on his second birthday. He doesn't take after our side of the family, though, he's a real McCaw. Turn back and you'll see Mr. and Mrs. McCaw, that's to say my Vivian's in-laws, sitting on their verandah. There they are. You see Mr. McCaw's big ears? Ronnie has them too. That little girl on Mrs. McCaw's knee is another grandchild, Sue, she's the child of Tom McCaw, who had the bad motor accident I was telling you about."

"Oh, yes," said Barry, "I remember. And who's this?"

"They're just friends we used to know, the Harrisons. Such a nice couple. They lost a son in Korea. That girl there is the married daughter. Now, I don't want to hurry you, but time's getting on. If you want to be at the studio by seven you'll have to think of getting into that taxi."

"Damn," said Barry.

He shut the album and glanced at his watch. Pinkie was right. There was just time to straighten up and get a taxi and arrive at the studio. He swung his long legs over the settee and on to the floor.

"I can't tell you, Pinkie," he said, "what this has meant to me."

"I'm so glad," she said. "It's nice to see old friends."

He washed his hands, and brushed his hair, and touched his jaw where the beard was beginning to show. Slip must deal with that when he got to the studio. Then he bent down and kissed Pinkie.

"It's been great," he said, "just great."

She opened the door of the apartment and looked up and down.

"Just one thing," she said. "Don't tell anyone where you've been, or who you've been with. A woman living alone has to be so careful, and I couldn't hold up my head if I thought there might be talk."

"I won't say a word, Pinkie," he assured her.

"It never seemed worth telling the children about how we knew each other at Herne Bay," she went on. "I thought about it once or twice, and then it seemed silly. They would have thought I was making it up. So I left it. But of course if you like to come again some time I shall always be glad to see you."

"Thank you, Pinkie," he said.

"No one saw us at the Silver Slipper," she said. "The operator on the switchboard was fast asleep. It's a good job and I should hate to lose it."

"Of course you won't lose it," he told her. "What an idea. Could you let me have some money for the taxi?"

"I'll give you five bucks," she said. "It shouldn't be more than that. If there's any over keep the change."

Pinkie had called up a taxi from the stand at the end of her block, and it was waiting for Barry when he got downstairs. The driver smiled when he recognized the Menace, and he opened the door for him to hop inside.

"I haven't had the luck to drive you before, Mr. Jeans," he said.

"No," said Barry, "I don't often ride in a taxi."

The driver passed an autograph book through the window to the back.

"To please the wife," he said.

Barry took out his pen and wrote his name in the book.

"Don't say where you picked me up," he said. "I've been out all night."

The driver winked and reached back for his book.

"Good job you picked on me," he said. "Some of the lads sell all the dope they get to *Confidential*."

Barry paid off the driver before they reached the studio, and then walked through the gates and along to his dressing-room just as the big clock was striking seven. The boys had beaten him to it and were already waiting there. He could hear them talking inside as he opened the door, and it sounded as if Pat was on the telephone. Anyway, there would not be time for a massage.

"Morning," he said. "How's tricks?"

It was not an expression he had ever used before, but it was one he dimly remembered hearing one of the technicians say to the continuity girl. The boys stared at him. They might have seen a ghost. Then Pat put down the telephone. Alf threw him a warning glance and rose slowly to his feet.

"Morning, Barry," he said.

The rest of the boys sat very tight and still. They none of them smiled. It reminded Barry of when his father, the parson, called him into the study of the old home in Herne Bay and asked him why he had missed the bus from Ramsgate. It was too late for hair drill, too late for massage, too late for a pressure shower. There was only time for a shave and for Slip to get him ready for the floor.

"You fellows enjoy yourself last night?" Barry asked, and he strolled over to the mirror and examined his own blue jaw.

The boys said nothing. Barry was either very sick indeed, and they would have to watch out for violence, or he had been fooling the lot of them for years.

"How are you, Barry?" said Ken gently.

Barry began taking off his coat and undoing his collar and tie.

"I'm great," he said, "just great."

It was true, too. He still did not feel tired. And that rice pudding Pinkie had made him was a much better breakfast than porridge. It was more substantial, somehow. More packed.

244

"Get any sleep?" said Bob.

Barry threw down his tie and unbuttoned his shirt. The little tremor that had come into his face when he first recognised Pinkie broke at the corner of his mouth once more. The boys saw it and gasped. The Menace was smiling. He was actually smiling.

"No, sir," said Barry. "I had better things to do last night than sleep."

It was grim. The boys felt sick at heart. To think they had known Barry for the best part of a quarter of a century, known him and respected him and served him, and it was all to end in this way. He looked well, that was the worst thing about it. Had he come into the dressing-room with dragging feet and green about the gills, they would have called an ambulance right away and warned the hospital to be ready for him, and then got the Swede and other experts along for consultation. But Barry had not dragged into the room. He had even whistled outside the door. It was terrible.

"May shown up yet?" asked Barry. "What news of her migraine?"

It was so cold-blooded. Bim could not stand it. Tears came into his eyes and he had to go and look out of the window. The rest were not softhearted. They were shocked and disgusted, but they were not softhearted. It was obvious now that Barry was not sick. The man they had nursed to fame was vicious, and hard as steel. He had been deceiving them all for thirty years.

"Look here, Barry," said Alf, and there was a threat in his voice and his face was ugly. "You can't get away with it like this. We happen to know where you were last night."

"So what?" said Barry.

He went and sat in the chair and waited for Slip to come and shave him. Slip looked at Alf for orders, and Alf motioned him to go ahead. The telephone rang, and Pat reached for it. It was the production manager wanting to know the form. He said he had been up all night trying to keep Gigantic Enterprises quiet for the twenty-four-hour break, and now the time limit had expired and he had to tell them something. The unit was waiting. The technicians were ready. Were the boys going to get Barry Jeans on the set by eight o'clock to have a test? Pat explained the situation to Alf in low tones.

"We'll have to play for time," said Alf. "We'll have to ask for a postponement."

Slip's hand was shaking so that he got the shaving soap into Barry's eyes. Barry reached for the towel and heard the word postponement.

"What's going on?" he said. "Haven't they got that gadget working yet?"

Pat threw eyes to heaven and looked at Bob. The sound of the production manager's voice kept coming down the receiver. At that moment the door opened and May came into the room. She looked round wildly for Barry, and when she saw him in the chair with the last of the lather on his face she burst into tears.

"My poor honey," she said, "what have they done to you?"

Barry looked at her, and he looked at the boys, and it came to him slowly that something was going on that he did not understand. May disappearing to the club with a migraine head, and the boys not letting him stay at home and play patience but dragging him off to that beach in the sun, and then taking him off to dinner with a crowd of wrestlers and Japanese girls and acrobats. And now everyone was trying to pin something on him because he had spent the night drinking hot milk in the powder room with Pinkie and going back with her to the apartment to look at snapshots of her grandchildren. If the boys got Pinkie into trouble he would never forgive them.

Barry stood up, and he looked terrific standing there, a head and shoulders taller than any of them in the room. He was bronzed, too, from his day on Poncho beach, and he felt fine and relaxed after his talk with Pinkie and the rice pudding he had had for breakfast. If any of the fans had seen him at that moment they would have said he had another ten years before he dropped to second place on the popularity list, and that if he went on looking as he did right now the youngsters coming up would never lick him. Even the boys were amazed. Barry had never looked so good.

"Now listen, all of you," said Barry. "I'm boss here. And that goes for you too, May. Nobody's going to ask me questions about last night. I had a good time. That's all there is to it. I never had such a time since I've been on the Coast. I feel great, just great. And if those damn fools on the floor haven't got their feelie gadget fixed by eight o'clock I'll tear up my contract with G.E. and quit business. And the first one of you who opens his mouth is fired."

Then he threw off his braces and told Slip to reach for his trousers.

It was a minute to eight o'clock when Barry Jeans walked on to the studio floor followed by May and the boys. No one had spoken in the dressing-room, and May's eyes were still red from crying. The director came forward and glanced first at Alf and then at Ken, but they both avoided his eyes. The production manager was standing by the set. He did not say anything either. He fumbled in his pocket for his box of tranquillizers.

"Everyone O.K.?" asked the director.

"I'm O.K.," said Barry. "The boys are a bit tired. And May has migraine."

He went straight over to the feelie expert and held out his wrists.

"Get a jerk on it," he said. "We've wasted enough working time already on this damn-fool gadget of yours."

The expert spat out his gum and fixed the wires. His assistant wheeled up the barker into position. Then the expert turned on a switch and watched the dial. Vanda Gray was looking on from her chair. She did not believe it, of course, but someone had called her up from International to say Barry Jeans had been seen the day before on Poncho beach. There had never been any rumours before. He looked wonderful, though. It might be true. If it was, there might be some fun in three weeks' time when they went on location to Arizona.

The expert switched off the connection and murmured

something to his assistant. The assistant scribbled some figures on a pad. The expert took the pad, and handed it to the director. The director glanced at it, and then walked over to the production manager, and May, and the boys.

"We'll go ahead," he said.

The Menace had clocked Force A.

The Chamois

WE WERE TOLD there were chamois in the Pindus. The report came to us in a roundabout way. A member of the British school of archaeology in Athens, writing to Stephen about the season's "dig," reported that he had dined with a friend, John Evans, who had been staying in one of the monasteries at Meteora. During his three-day visit, a man from Kalabaka with supplies for the monastery told one of the monks that a bus driver, bringing passengers over the pass from Malakasi, had stopped for his usual five minutes at the store, and picked up a rumour from the storekeeper that woodcutters had seen a doe and kid flit past the young beech growth about five hundred yards away. The story was as vague as that. Yet it was enough to make Stephen cancel our Austrian plans and book seats on the Athens plane for the following week.

This is what it means to be a fanatic—but a fanatic, that is to say, in a very special sense. It has little in common with the obsession of the politician or the artist, for instance, for both of these understand in a greater or lesser degree the impulse which drives them. But the sportsman-fanatic—that is another matter entirely. His thoughts fixed solely on a vision of that mounted trophy against the wall, the eyes now dead that were once living, the tremulous nostrils stilled, the sensitive pricked ears closed to sound at the instant when the rifleshot echoed from the naked rocks, this man hunts his quarry through some instinct unknown even to himself.

Stephen was a sportsman of this kind. It was not the skill needed that drove him, nor the delight and excitement of the

251

stalk itself, but a desire, so I told myself, to destroy something beautiful and rare. Hence his obsession with chamois.

Chamois, as all sportsmen know, have become scarce through the years. They are hardly seen today in Switzerland and Austria. Stephen tried to explain the reasons once. The breakup of the big estates, two world wars, promiscuous shooting by peasants which would have been forbidden in the old days, and the growing popularity of the Alps, and indeed of every region of mountains amongst climbers and tourists—all this has led to a general trampling and desecration of land once sacred to the chamois.

He is the shyest of all creatures. He shuns human beings and does not mix with other deer. Always on the alert for anything that may threaten his safety, his note of warning is a curious shrill whistle; and the first hint of danger will send him headlong to the highest and most inaccessible crags. The buck lives alone at all times of the year, except in the late fall, in the brief rutting season, when the chemical change in his blood drives him to the doe. This, according to Stephen, is the moment to catch him; this is when he falls a prey. Watchfulness, intuition of danger, that sixth sense which normally keeps him safe, all these lie in abeyance because of the urge for a mate. He deserts the narrow ledges and the steep cliff faces, and follows the little herd of does and yearlings, the secretive shy mothers who have no need of him until now; and then blood answers blood, the chase begins, the wild scamper over rock and precipice, the little kids surprised at the sudden fever of their mothers, so quickly stirred and put to flight by the black stranger. For he is black in winter, the adult chamois buck: the reddish-yellow summer coat has gone, and the thick protecting fur covers him, the wave of long hair rising on his back like a crest.

When Stephen talked about stalking chamois his whole expression changed. The features became more aquiline, the nose sharpened, the chin narrowed, and his eyes—steel blue —somehow took on the cold brilliance of a northern sky. I am being very frank about my husband. He attracted me at those times, and he repelled me too. This man, I told myself when I first met him, is a perfectionist. And he has no compassion. Gratified like all women who find themselves sought after and desired—a mutual love for Sibelius had been our common ground at our first encounter—after a few weeks in his company I shut my eyes to further judgment, because being with him gave me pleasure. It flattered my self-esteem. The perfectionist, admired by other women, now sought me. Marriage was in every sense a coup. It was only afterwards that I knew myself deceived.

Some men are born adult, without the redeeming and endearing faults of childhood; Stephen was one of them. Born and bred in the hard home of a Scots father and an Italian mother—none of your beautiful opera singers, but the daughter of a Milan industrialist—he shook off all family ties at fifteen and began earning his living in a shipping office in Glasgow. Those early days would make a book, and it may get written one day, but not now. Now I want to tell how we sought the chamois.

Stephen handed me the letter across the breakfast table, and said briefly, "I shall telegraph Bruno right away and say we have changed our plans." Bruno was the Austrian friend who, at great trouble to himself and with much forethought and care, had arranged the shoot in his own Alpine district, solely to please Stephen. Chamois had been the bait. Deer in plenty would not have tempted him: it must be chamois.

"What's the difference," I asked, "between chamois in Austria and chamois in northern Greece?"

The sport meant nothing to me. I went for adventure, for mountain air. Stephen was welcome to go off by himself all day, either alone or with other friends armed with rifles. My holiday worked in, a breathing space, stocktaking for a woman who had not borne children.

"The difference," said Stephen, his blue eyes colder than ever, "lies in the rarity of the prey. I have never heard of anyone who has shot chamois in the Pindus, or anywhere else in Greece."

"Then probably the story is not true," I suggested. "The woodcutters saw a wild goat and mistook it for a chamois."

"Probably," said Stephen, but he got up from the breakfast

table, and a few minutes afterwards I heard him give out the telegram on the phone to his friend in Austria.

I watched his back and the powerful shoulders. He looked taller than his six feet two inches because of his build, and his voice became impatient as he spelt out the Austrian address, which the telephone operator did not immediately understand. It held the same impatience with a mentality less quick and incisive than his own that had been apparent to me ten years previously, when we had become engaged. He had taken me to see that austere house of his near Portland Place—a far cry from the shipping office in Glasgow, for he was head of the London office by then—and the trophies on the wall. I wondered straight away how he could sit at peace there, of an evening, with the row of heads staring down at him. There were no pictures, no flowers: only the heads of chamois. The concession to melody was the radiogram and the stack of records of classical music.

Foolishly I had asked, "Why only chamois?"

He answered at once, "They fear man."

This might have led to an argument about animals in general, domestic, wild, and those which adapt themselves to the whims and vagaries of the human race; but instead he changed the subject abruptly, put on a Sibelius record, and presently made love to me, intently but without emotion. I was surprised but pleased. I thought, "We are suited to one another. There will be no demands. Each of us will be self-contained and not beholden to the other."

All this came true, but something was amiss. There was a flaw—not only the nonappearance of children, but a division of the spirit. The communion of flesh which brought us together was in reality a chasm, and I despised the bridge we made. Perhaps he did as well. I had been endeavouring for ten years to build for myself a ledge of safety.

"So we are going to Greece?" I said to Stephen that evening, when he came home rather later than usual and threw down the air tickets and a brochure and a map. "You've definitely made up your mind, although you haven't confirmed the rumour about the chamois seen near a mountain pass?"

"I have confirmed the rumour," said Stephen. "I traced

the fellow Evans to a bank in Athens and put through a call to him. He says the story is true. The monk at Meteora had spoken since to the bus driver himself. The driver is a brother-in-law of the man who owns the store and saw the wood-cutters. There are no wild goats in the area. It was chamois all right."

A smile should be a means of communication. It is not always, though, and it was not with Stephen when he spoke of chamois. The smile was secretive, an answer to a question which he put to himself, but without pleasure. Then he left the living-room and went to the music-room—we called it that because of the radio, and the television, and my piano, an odd juxtaposition of objects that bore a relation to one another—and I knew he was standing there, looking up at the chamois trophies on the wall. There were twenty altogether, including three does and two kids shot in error. They were all exquisitely cured and mounted, a silver plate beneath each head giving the date and place of the kill. As I said before, chamois are scarce these days. They retreat more and more to the inaccessible crags. There are no longer the big chamois drives in Switzerland, and for stalking you must know your territory, and your host too, for these matters are not easily arranged.

When Stephen returned from the music-room he was wiping his hands on a rag, and I knew from his same smile that he had been cleaning his rifle. It was not the comforted smile of one pottering with a favourite hobby—the photographic expert, the Sunday painter, the carpenter—or even the country well-being of the sportsman before an annual partridge drive (I had brothers once who shot). This was a killer's smile, obeying an impulse deep within himself.

"Snap out of it," I said suddenly.

He looked across at me, startled, as I was myself, by the curious note of urgency in my voice.

"Snap out of what?" he asked.

"This obsession with chamois," I said. "It isn't balanced."

I thought for a moment that he would hit me. The look of terror—and it was terror, swiftly and indecently unmasked

—came and went at the speed of thought, to be replaced by anger, the cold anger of a man caught off guard.

"You don't have to come with me," he said. "Make your own plans. I'm going. Do as you please."

He did not reply to my attack, though. The answer was evasion.

"Oh, I'll come, right enough," I said. "I may be in search of something myself, for all you know."

I did the irritating, wifely thing of tidying, snapping off the dead head of a flower, straightening a cushion, but I felt his eyes on my back. It was not a comfortable sensation. However, the tension passed, and at dinner we were on our usual easy footing of mutual tolerance, and this continued through the days that followed before our departure.

A certain date in mid-October found us on the plane for Athens. The letter of regret and disappointment from our friend in Austria had been thrown, almost unskimmed, into the wastepaper basket. Instead, new contacts, arranged through Stephen's own shipping firm, had fixed our itinerary in Greece. Use people, whenever you can, as a means to an end. This was one of Stephen's maxims. Drop them when they no longer serve your purpose.

I do not give the year of this particular October in case there should be any recognition of individuals. It is enough to say that it was in the early fifties, there was as yet no Cyprus question, the summer had been hot, and there had been two earthquakes.

It might have been midsummer still when we landed to drop and pick up passengers in Rome. As we stood on the hot tarmac the sun was merciless, and the ugly high buildings fringing the airport, alternating with wasteland, gave off a yellow glare. How different was Athens. A cool serenity seemed to come to us even in the aircraft, as we stared down on Corinth bathed in the afterglow of sunset; and the airport —at the time I speak of—was like a casual provincial station, with attendants in shirt sleeves smiling, handling passports and baggage checks as though all time were theirs and would endure forever.

A rattling bus took us into Athens. I liked my husband's

company when travelling. He never fussed, tickets were not mislaid, and he left me to sort impressions for myself. There was no elbow jerking, no sudden exclamations at new things perceived. But later, over a drink or at dinner, we would find we had usually noticed the same points of beauty or interest. This thread of appreciation was one of our few links.

That evening we were met at the airport terminus by a Greek from the shipping firm contacted by Stephen—his name was inevitably George—and taken to our hotel. Once bathed and changed, we were joined by Stephen's archaeologist friend, whom I will call Burns, and the John Evans who had stayed at Meteora and first passed on the rumour of the chamois. They had come to take us out to dinner. These arrangements were all part of Stephen's clocklike mind, his talent for seizing upon the essential.

There was to be no ambling in Athens for us, no strolling on the Acropolis. Later, when we returned from the Pindus, if we had the time, said Stephen, but meanwhile one certainty alone lay ahead of us, the knowledge that tickets had already been taken on the train leaving Athens for the north the following morning. I can remember still the look of bewilderment on the face of young John Evans, an expert on Byzantine churches; and even Burns, who knew something of Stephen's vagaries, was shocked at what must have seemed excess of passion.

"You surely could afford one day," he said, "or even half a day. I could call for you early, with my car . . ." but Stephen brushed him aside.

"How's the weather in the north?" he asked. "You've checked that the road over the pass is open?"

I left them to it, the pointing of fingers on maps, the tracing of mountain villages, the tracks and contours on maps of larger scale, and basked for the one evening allowed to me in the casual, happy atmosphere of the *taverna* where we dined. I enjoyed poking my finger in a pan and choosing my own piece of lamb. I liked the chatter and the laughter from neighbouring tables. The gay intensity of talk—none of which I could understand, naturally—reminded me of left-bank

Paris. A man from one table would suddenly rise to his feet and stroll over to another, discussion would follow, argument at heat perhaps swiftly dissolving into laughter. This, I thought to myself, has been happening through the centuries under this same sky, in the warm air with a bite to it, the sap drink pungent as the sap running through the veins of these Greeks, witty and cynical as Aristophanes himself, in the shadow, unmoved, inviolate, of Athene's Parthenon.

"The cabin store will be open then?" pursued Stephen. "They don't shut down when the weather breaks? And the bus runs from Kalabaka until the pass is closed by snow?"

I felt it time to intervene. Our hosts were drained and had no more to give.

"Listen, Stephen," I said, "if the pass is closed, and the store is burnt to the ground, I'm still willing to take a ground sheet and sleep in the open, so long as you find your chamois. Let's give it a miss until tomorrow. I want to see the Parthenon by moonlight."

I had my way. They floodlight it now, to great advantage I am told, but it was not so then, and since it was late in the year there were few tourists. My companions were all intelligent men, including my own husband, and they had the sense to stay mute. I suppose, being a woman, I confuse beauty with sentiment, but, as I looked on the Parthenon for the first time in my life, I found myself crying. It had never happened to me before. Your sunset weepers I despise. It was not full moon, or anywhere near it. The half circle put me in mind of the labrys, the Cretan double axe, and the pillars were the more ghostly in consequence. What a shock for the modern aesthete, I thought when my crying was done, if he could see the ruddy glow of colour, the painted eyes, the garish lips, the orange reds and blues that were there once, and Athene herself a giantess on her pedestal touched by the rising sun. Even in those distant times the exigencies of a state religion had brought their own traffic, the buying and selling of doves, of trinkets: to find himself, a man had to go to the woods, to the hills.

"Come on," said Stephen. "It's beautiful and stark, if you

like, but so is St. Pancras station at 4 A.M. It depends on your association of ideas."

We crammed into Burns's small car and went back to our hotel.

We left Athens early the next morning, seen off at the station by our still bewildered friends. Stephen, of course, had no regrets. As to myself, it was like being dragged from Paris at seventeen, having glimpsed the Champs-Elysées overnight. Athens had that same surge of life, that same bright air, the crowded morning streets at once urgent and indolent.

We rattled our way north, Stephen at his maps again, myself at the window. The plains of Thessaly to me spelt armies of the past, to my husband the narrowing of distance between us and the chamois.

We changed trains at one point. Where it was I cannot remember. There were signs of a recent earthquake, houses in half, buildings in rubble, unmoving to our eyes who had seen all this in war. The bright light faded. It began to rain. The earth turned yellow-brown, and dispirited women, their faces veiled from the hidden sun like Moslems, scratched at the lean ground. As we passed through empty stations donkeys brayed. A rising wind drove the rain slantways. In the far distance I saw mountains, and, touching Stephen on the knee, I pointed to them. Once again he consulted his map. Somewhere, amongst that misty range, snow-capped and hidden from us, would be Olympus, stronghold of the gods. Not for us, alas, that ultimate discovery. Our trek was westward, to the chamois.

Kalabaka, crouching muddied and wet at the foot of rock-bound Meteora, offered no temptation as a refuge. Nevertheless, it was our station of descent. Rapid enquiries—and Stephen's smattering of Greek seemed to me well-laced with Italian—soon showed that we had, in the full sense of the phrase, missed our bus. There was only one a day, at this time of the year, which climbed the winding road to the pass: and it left in the early morning. Stephen was not to be deterred. Means of transport other than a bus must be found, and we sat down in the ticket collector's office—ourselves, the ticket collector, a bearded patriarch, a young boy, the ticket collector's brother-in-law, who happened to be passing by—all gesturing, arguing in high excitement the possibility of our reaching the top of the pass before nightfall.

The ticket collector's brother-in-law brought light out of darkness. His nephew had a car. A good car. A car that not only held the road and the twists in the road, but whose lights worked. The three of us went to a café to celebrate, and while we pledged each other in coffee dregs and ouzo the nephew's car was driven to a nearby garage to be filled with petrol. The nephew had a walleye. I could not help wondering if the walleye would affect his driving. As we started off, taking the road out of Kalabaka like a speedway, it occurred to me that the walleye gave him confidence, making him unconscious of danger. It was his left eye, and as we started to climb it was this side of his face that was turned to the precipices.

Climbing a mountain road by car is always a doubtful pleasure. As a test of skill for experts it is endurable. In northern Greece, however, after autumn rains, when the road is heavy with loose stones and falls of earth, and it is late afternoon, and the car's chassis shakes in protest, and its engine groans as it approaches each fresh bend, and the walleyed chauffeur suddenly seizes the crucifix hanging on the dashboard and kisses it with fervour, in these circumstances climbing a mountain road brings destruction of thought. Stephen, on the right side of the car, had only bank to daunt him, but I, glancing leftwards through the window to the tumbling gorge below, was less happily placed. The grunts of the chauffeur, harmonising with each change of gear as we came to the bends in the road, were not conducive to a sense of security, nor, as I peered ahead through the rain, was the long sight of the distant bridge spanning a ravine over which we must in some five minutes cross. The bridge looked broken. Planks from it appeared tossed amongst the boulders far below. I was not altogether surprised that our walleyed driver kissed his crucifix, but his action did not increase my confidence.

The dusk crept upon us. Our chauffeur switched on his

lights. This, more than the kissing of the crucifix, seemed a measure of defeat, for they hardly broke the growing dark. The road wound its way ever upward, and at no place was there a possibility of turning and going back to Kalabaka. Like Roland in *Childe Harold*, we must go on, naught else remained to do. I shut my eyes. And it was only then, after a moment or two, that I heard Stephen say beside me, "What's the matter? Feeling sick?" I could only conclude that, as always, my husband lacked perception.

The final roar of the engine and a furious grinding of gears warned me that death was imminent, and, not to miss the experience, I opened my eyes. We had come to our journey's end.

I do not know what buildings stand at Malakasi today. For all I know there may be a motel. In the year of which I speak there was a log cabin at the top of the pass, standing a little apart from the road, with room enough for a bus or lorry to park beside it. Forests of beech surrounded the cabin. The rain had ceased. The crisp cold air had all the stark invigoration that comes with a height of some seven thousand feet. A single light shone from the window of the cabin. Our driver sounded his horn, and as he did so the door of the cabin opened and a man stood on the threshold.

"Come on," said Stephen, "help me unload. We'll leave them to the explanations."

My trepidation had vanished the moment the car stopped. One sniff of that mountain air was like a whiff of alcohol to an addict. I got out and stamped and stretched my legs, and if Stephen had said to me that we were to start climbing now, on foot, striking off through the trees in darkness in search of chamois, I would have followed him. Instead, we carried our traps through to the log cabin.

While Stephen interposed his odd mixture of Greek and Italian in the torrent of discussion taking place between the walleyed driver and the tenant of the cabin, I had time to look around me. The room was half café, half store, shaped like a short L, the floor earth-covered, a ladder rising from it to the lofts above, and a small kitchen at one end. I could smell food, something cooking in a pan. There were rows of goods, cigarettes, chocolate, coils of rope, toothpaste, cloths —all the things you find in a well-stocked village shop— and the owner, a cheerful-looking man of middle age, received us without surprise, shaking our hands in true Greek courtesy. Indeed, it might have been every day that a fanatical Englishman in search of the mythical chamois arrived at his store after dark demanding supper and a bed.

I made gestures of smoking, and pointed to his store of cartons behind the counter, but he brushed the idea aside and with a bow offered me one from his own packet. Then, bowing still, he led me up the ladder to the communicating rooms above, and I saw that we must all of us, proprietor, walleyed driver, Stephen, and myself, share the pile of blankets for the night, heaped carelessly upon the wooden floor—unless I removed myself, in modesty, to a cupboard. I smiled and nodded, hoping to express appreciation, and followed my host down the ladder to the store below.

The first person I saw was Stephen. He had taken his rifle from its cover and was showing it to a small, rat-faced man who had appeared in shirt sleeves from the kitchen. The rat-faced man was nodding in great excitement, and then, in fine pantomime, made a pretence of crouching, animal fashion, after which he leapt in the air, to the applause of our walleyed driver.

"It's all right," called Stephen at sight of me, "there's no mistake. These are the chaps who know the woodcutters who saw the chamois."

His voice was triumphant. Foolishly I was reminded of the House that Jack built. This was the bull, that worried the dog, that killed the cat, that ate the malt . . . Had we come all this way to the top of the Pindus Mountains only to destroy?

"Fine," I said, shrugging my shoulders, and, making a concession to femininity, I took out my lipstick. There was a little cracked mirror hanging behind the counter. The men watched in admiration. My status was established. I knew that, without a word from me, those blankets in the room above would be redistributed before the night was older, and the best folded for me in the cupboard apart. The Greeks paid tribute to Gaia before the birth of Zeus.

"That small chap understands Italian," said Stephen, as we sat down to eggs fried in oil and a tinned sardine. "He was in some prison camp during the war. He says the wood-cutters have gone down for the winter, but there's some fellow still grazing goats a couple of hundred feet higher up, above the tree line, who knows all about chamois. He sometimes calls in here during the evening. He may look in tonight."

I glanced across at our three companions. The rat-faced cook had returned to his pots and pans, and our walleyed driver was being shaved by the proprietor of the store. He leant back at ease, a towel round his shoulders, his face in lather, the walleye staring up in confidence at the broad-shouldered, smiling proprietor, who leant over him, razor in hand. Somewhere a cracked loud-speaker gave forth a South American song. We were at the top of a Pindus pass. Nothing was really out of place.

I finished spooning sheep's cream from a saucer—our dessert —and Stephen began drawing a chamois head on the bare boards of our table. The proprietor of the store came to watch, and with him our walleyed driver, newly shaved. Somewhere outside I thought I heard a dog barking, but no one paid any attention, the men too intent upon the chamois head. I got up and went to the door. Observation before supper had warned me that, if I desired to wash, a stream ran beside the road and lost itself in the gorge below. I went out into the night and crunched across the gravel clearing to the stream. Last evening the quarter moon upon the Parthenon, and now the nearby naked Pindus beeches seven thousand feet closer to the stars. No wind to stir the leaves that yet remained. The sky looked wider than it did at home.

I washed in the gully by the road and once more heard the barking of a dog. I raised my head, and looked beyond the log cabin to a narrow plateau stretching to the very lip of the gorge. Something moved there in the darkness. I dried my hands on my woollen jersey and crossed back over the road, past the clearing by the cabin, towards the plateau.

Someone whistled. The sound was uncanny, heard there on the mountain pass, remote from town and village. It was the hissing whistle blown between tooth and lip heard on the sidewalk of a garish city, and the woman who hears it quickens her step instinctively. I paused. Then I saw the herd of goats, crowded together, bedded for the night, the narrow plateau their pillow. Two dogs stood guardian, one at either end. And motionless, in the midst of his herd, hooded, leaning on his crook, stood their master, staring not at me but at the hills above. It must have been he who whistled.

I watched them a moment, the man, and the bedded goats, and the sentinel dogs, and they seemed to me remote from the little world of the log cabin and the men within. To look upon them was intrusion. They belonged elsewhere. Their very stillness put them apart and gave me a strange feeling of disquiet. Yet why the whistle? Why the lewd, low hiss of warning? I turned away, went back to the cabin, and opened the door.

The store with its earth floor, its canned food, its coils of rope, and the chattering voices of the men—all three of them now bending over Stephen, absorbed in his drawing— was somehow welcoming. Even the cracked loud-speaker and the confused babble of radio Athens seemed at that moment reassuring, part of a life that was familiar. I went and sat down at the table beside Stephen, and helped myself to another of the proprietor's cigarettes.

"They're here," said Stephen, not bothering to look at me, and sketching in a stunted bush beside his chamois head.

"Who's here?" I asked.

"Chamois," he answered. "They were seen again two days ago."

I don't know why—perhaps I was tired, for our journey had been long that day: we had left Athens in the early morning, and the drive up to the pass had told on nerve and muscle—but a wave of depression came upon me with his words. I wanted to say, "Oh, be damned to chamois. Can't we forget them until tomorrow?" but to do so would have brought tension between us, happily stilled since leaving London. So I said nothing and watched him draw, the smoke from the cigarette making my eyes smart, and presently, yawning, I let my head rest on the wall behind me and dozed, like a nodding passenger in a railway carriage.

The change of music woke me. Radio Athens had become an accordion. I opened my eyes, and the rat-faced cook had turned into entertainer and was now sitting cross-legged on his chair, instrument in hand, applauded by the proprietor and the walleyed driver, and by Stephen too. His song was melancholy, wild, Slav, bred in heaven knows what bald Macedonian vale by a long-forgotten forebear, but there was rhythm somewhere, and ferocity as well, and his thin voice like a reed was also the pipe of Pan.

It was only when he had finished and laid his accordion down that I noticed we were no longer five, but six. The goatherd from the night had come to join us. He sat on a bench apart, still wrapped in his hooded burnous, leaning upon his crook, but the swinging lamp from the beam shone upon his face and into his eyes. They were the strangest eyes I had ever looked upon. Golden brown in colour, large and widely set, they stared from his narrow face as though suddenly startled into life. I thought, at first glance, that the abrupt cessation of the music had surprised him; but when the expression did not change, but remained constant, with all the alert watchfulness of one poised for flight or for attack, I knew myself mistaken, that he was perhaps blind, that his wide stare was in reality the sightless gaze of a man without vision. Then he shifted his posture and said something to the proprietor of the store; and from the way he moved, catching a packet of cigarettes thrown to him, I saw that he was not blind but on the contrary had a sight keener than most men—for the cigarettes were poorly thrown and the catch was quick—and the eyes, shifting now to the rest of us round the table, and finally resting upon Stephen, were now larger, if possible, than before, and the searching stare impossible to hold.

I said to Stephen in a low voice, "Do you think he's mad?"

"No," said my husband. "He lives a lot alone. He's the fellow they've been talking about. We're going with him in the morning."

My spirits ebbed. The doze against the wall had rested me and I was no longer tired. But apprehension filled me.

"Go with him where?" I asked. The man was watching us.

"He has a hut in the forest," said Stephen impatiently. "It's all settled. An hour's climb from here. He'll put us up."

From the way Stephen spoke he might have been arranging a weekend with some obliging golfing friend. I looked at the goatherd again. The honey-coloured eyes never moved from Stephen's face, and his whole body was taut, as though he waited for us to spring and must seize advantage first.

"I don't think he likes us," I said.

"Rubbish," said Stephen, and, rising to his feet, he picked up his rifle.

The goatherd moved. It was strange, he was by the door. I had not seen him shift from chair to door, so swift had been his passage. Yet he was standing there, his hand on the latch, and the door was open. No one noticed anything unusual in the quickness of the flight—if flight it was. Stephen's back was turned. The rat-faced cook was strumming his accordion. The proprietor and the walleyed driver were sitting down to dominoes.

"Come to bed," said Stephen. "You're dead on your feet."

The door closed. The goatherd had gone. I had shifted my eyes for the passing of a second, and I had not seen him go. I followed Stephen up the ladder to the lofts above.

"You're for the cupboard," said my husband. "I'll turn in with the chaps." Already he was choosing his particular heap of blankets.

"What about the man?" I asked.

"What man?"

"The goatherd. The one we're to go with in the morning."

"Oh, he'll wrap himself in his hood out there with the goats."

Stephen took off his coat, and I groped my way to the cupboard. Below, the rat-faced cook had started once more upon the accordion, and the reedy voice floated up through the floorboards. A crack in the planking of my cupboard gave me a view upon a narrow strand of plateau beyond the cabin. I could see a single beech tree and a star. Beneath

266

the tree stood the hooded figure leaning upon a crook. I lay down on my blankets. The cold air from the crack in the planking blew upon my face. Presently the sound of the accordion stopped. The voices too. I heard the men come up the ladder to the loft and go into the room with Stephen. Later their varying snores told me of their sleep, and of Stephen's too. I listened, every sense alert, for a sound I somehow knew must come. I heard it, finally, more distant than before. Not a bird's cry, nor a shepherd's call to his dogs, but more penetrating, more intense; the low whistle of one who sees a woman on a street.

2

Something in me grudges sleep to others when my own night has been poor. The sight of Stephen, tackling fried eggs again at seven and drinking the muddied grains of coffee, fresh-shaved, too, from water boiled by the cook, was unbearably irritating as I climbed down the ladder to the store below.

He hailed me cheerfully. "Slept like a top," he said. "How was the cupboard?"

"The Little Ease," I told him, remembering Harrison Ainsworth's *Tower of London* and the torture chamber, and I glanced with a queasy stomach at the egg yolk on his oily plate.

"Better get something inside you," he said. "We've a steep climb ahead of us. If you don't want to face it, you can always drive back to Kalabaka with our walleyed friend."

I felt myself a drag upon his day. The bread, brought yesterday, I supposed, in the bus from north or west, was moderately fresh, and I spread it with honey. I would have given much for French coffee instead of the Breek-Turkish brew that never satisfied a void.

"What exactly do you mean to do?" I asked.

Stephen had the inevitable large-scale map on the table in front of him. "We're here," he said, pointing to the cross he had marked on the map, "and we have to walk to this." A speck in the nick of a fold showed our destination. "That is where the goatherd—his name is Jesus, by the way, but he answers to Zus—has his lair. It's primitive, I gather, but clean. We'll carry stores with us from here. That extra rucksack will prove a godsend."

It was all very well for Stephen. He had slept. The smell of brewing eggs was nauseous. I hastily swallowed my coffee dregs and went outside. The bright clear day helped to pull me together. There was no sign of the goatherd with his unlikely name, nor of his goats. Our driver from Kalabaka was washing his car. He greeted me with enthusiasm, and then made great play of gesturing to the woods above us, bending himself as if under a rucksack and shaking his head. Laughing, he pointed downwards where the road twisted like a snake to the depths beneath, and from the road to his car. His meaning was plain. I would do better to return with him. The thought of the descent was worse than the climb to the unknown. And somehow, now that morning had come, now that I could breathe the sharp air and glimpse the great sky, cloudless and blue above the yet golden beech trees, the unknown did not seem to hold much danger.

I washed in the stream—the saucepanned water in the kitchen amongst the oil did not tempt me—and while Stephen and I were packing our rucksacks the first bus of the day arrived, travelling from the west. It halted for five minutes, while the driver and the few passengers stretched their legs. Inevitably our walleyed chauffeur had a cousin among the passengers, inevitably the purpose of our journey became known, and we were surrounded at once by eager questioners, poking our rucksacks, peeping at Stephen's rifle, overwhelming the pair of us with advice we could not understand. The cousin had a sister in America. This supposed bond between us made him spokesman of the group.

"No good," he said, pointing to the trees, "too late, no good." And then, feigning the posture of one holding a gun, he said, "Bang . . . bang . . . bang . . ." rapidly. A chorus of approval came from his fellow passengers.

Stephen continued to strap his rucksack. The proprietor of the store came out carrying more goods for us to pack away. Perched on the top, incongruous, was a great packet of soap flakes and a bottle of bull's-eyes. Everybody suddenly started shaking hands.

When the bus pulled away down the road to Kalabaka, followed by our walleyed driver and his cousin in the car, it was as though our last link with sanity had snapped. I looked up and saw the goatherd emerging from the trees. I stood my ground and waited. He was smaller than I had thought, barely my own height, and the hooded burnous dwarfed him further. He came and took my rucksack without a word, seizing at the same time the extra pack with the stores. He had the two slung over his shoulder in an instant.

"He can't very well take both," I murmured to Stephen.

"Rot," said my husband. "He won't notice them, any more than one of his own goats."

The proprietor and the cook stood waving at the door of the store. It seemed suddenly a home, a long-known refuge, in the full sunlight. I forgot the cupboard where I had spent the night, and the oily eggs. The little store was friendly and the red earth comforting, the smiling proprietor and the rat-faced cook with his accordion men of goodwill. Then I turned my back on them and followed Stephen and Jesus the goatherd through the trees.

We must have made a queer procession, no one speaking, the three of us in single file. The goats and the dogs had vanished. Perhaps this was the goatherd's second journey of the day. Our way lay through forest at first, mostly beech but pine as well, then clearings of tufty grass and box and shrub. As we climbed, the trees thinned, the air became purer, sweeter, the range of mountains opened up on either side and above and beyond us, some of them already capped with snow. Now and again Stephen halted, not for breath— I believe he could have climbed without pause all day—but to swing his field glasses on the nearer ridge above the tree line to the left of us. I knew better than to talk. So did our guide. He was always just ahead, and when Stephen lifted the binoculars the goatherd followed their direction, his face impassive, but those honey-coloured eyes staring wild and startled from beneath the gaping hood. It could be some disease, I told myself, like goitre; yet the eyes were not full, they did not protrude. It was the expression that was so unusual, so compelling, yet not compelling in an hypnotic, penetrating sense—these eyes did not only see, but appeared to listen as well. And not to us. That was the curious thing. Stephen and I were of no account. The goatherd, although our beast of burden, did not listen or watch for us.

Now it was all sun, all sky, and the trees were beneath us, except for one lone blasted pine, lording it over a crisp sheet of recent snow, and above our heads, dark and formidable, circled our first eagle. A dog came bounding over the ridge towards us, and as we topped the rise I saw the goats, spread out and snuffing at the ground. Hard against an overhanging rock was a cabin, a quarter the size of our store below on the pass. Shelter from the elements it might have been— I was no judge of that—but a hermit saint or an aesthete could not have picked upon a spot more apt for contemplation or for beauty.

"H'm," said Stephen, "it looks central enough, if that's our shakedown." Central. He might have been talking about the Underground at Piccadilly. "Hi, Zus!" he called, and jerked his head towards the hut. "Is this the spot? Do we unload?" He was still talking in Italian, believing, by some process of thought peculiar to him, that the language meant more to the goatherd than English could.

The man replied in Greek. It was the first time I had heard him speak. Once again it was disconcerting. The voice was not harsh, as I had expected, but oddly soft, and pitched a little high, like the voice of a child. Had I, in fact, not guessed his age as forty or thereabouts, I would have said that a child was speaking to us.

"Don't know what that was about," said Stephen to me, "but I'm sure it's the place all right. Let's have a look at it."

The dogs, for the second one had now appeared, watched us gravely. Their master led us to his refuge. Blinking because of the strong sunlight without, we lowered our heads from the beam and stepped inside. It was just a plain wood shelter, with a partition down the centre. There was no furniture, except for a bench at one end on which stood

270

a small Primus stove. The earth floor had more sand on it than the floor of our overnight cabin store. It must have been built to serve as a shelter only in the case of sudden storm.

"Nothing wrong with this," said Stephen, looking about him. "We can spread our ground sheets on the floor and the sleeping bags on top."

The goatherd, our host, had stood aside as we explored his premises. Even the space behind the partition was unfurnished like the rest. There was not even a blanket. Now, silently, he unloaded our things for us and left us to arrange them as we pleased.

"Funny sort of bloke," said Stephen. "Hardly the type to make us crack our ribs with laughter."

"It's his eyes," I said. "Have you noticed his eyes?"

"Yes," said Stephen, "they look a bit frozen. So would you be, if you lived up here for long."

Frozen, though, was a new thought. Frozen, petrified. A petrified forest was surely the life-sap of a substance turned to stone. Were the goatherd's emotions petrified? Had he no blood in his veins, no warmth, no sap? Perhaps he was blasted, like the lone pine outside his hut. I helped my husband to unpack, and soon we had some semblance of comfort within the four blank walls.

It was only ten o'clock, but I was hungry. The proprietor of the store had put a tin opener amongst our rations, and I was soon eating Spam, canned in the United States, and dates thrown in for good measure. I sat cross-legged in the sun outside the hut, and the eagle still soared above me in the sky.

"I'm off," said Stephen.

Glancing up, I saw that he had his cartridge bag at his belt, his field glasses round his neck, and his rifle slung over his shoulder. The easy camaraderie had gone, his manner was terse, abrupt. I scrambled to my feet. "You'll never keep up," he said. "You'll only hold us back."

"Us?" I asked.

"Friend Jesus has to set me on the way," replied my husband.

The goatherd, silent as ever, waited by a cairn of stones. He was unarmed, save for his shepherd's crook.

"Can you understand a word he says?" I spoke in doubt.

"Sign language is enough," said Stephen. "Enjoy yourself."

The goatherd had already turned, and Stephen followed. In a moment they were lost in scrub. I had never felt more alone. I went into the hut to fetch my camera—the panorama was too good to miss, though it would be dull enough, no doubt, when it was printed—and the sight of the ground sheets, the rucksacks, the stores, and my thicker jersey restored confidence. The height, the solitude, the bright sun, and the scent of the air, these were things I loved; why, then, my seed of melancholy? The sense, hard to describe, of mutability?

I went outside and found a hollow, and, with a piece of rock at my back, made myself a resting place near the browsing goats. The forest was below and somewhere—in the depths—our lodging of last night. Away to the northeast, hidden from me by a range of mountains, were the plains of the civilised world. I smoked my first cigarette of the day and watched the eagle. The hot sun made me drowsy, and I was short of sleep.

When I opened my eyes the sun had shifted, and it was half-past one by my watch. I had slept for over three hours. I got up and stretched, and as I did so the dog, watching me a few hundred yards away, growled. So did his companion. I called to them and moved towards the hut, and at this the pair of them advanced, snarling. I remained where I was. They crouched once more, and as long as I did not move they remained silent. One step, however, brought an instant snarl and a stealthy lowering of the head, a forward padding movement as if to spring. I did not fancy being torn to pieces. I sat down again and waited, but, knowing my husband, I was aware that it might be nightfall before he returned. Meanwhile I must remain, marked by the dogs, the full force of the sun already spent. I could not even get to the hut for another jersey.

Somewhere, from what direction I could not tell, I heard a shot, and the sound echoed from the gorges far below.

The dogs heard it too. They cocked their heads and stared. The goats rustled in the scrub, surprised, and one old patriarch, bearded to his breast, bleated his disapproval like some professor roused from sleep.

I waited for a second shot but none came. I wondered if Stephen had found his mark or missed. At any rate, he had sighted chamois. He would not have wasted his bullet on other game. If he had hit and killed, it would not be long before he returned, bearing his prey upon his shoulder. If he had hit and wounded only—but that would be unlike Stephen—he would go after the poor beast and shoot again.

I went on sitting above my hollow, close to the blasted pine. Then one of the dogs whined. I saw nothing. But the next moment the goatherd was behind me.

"Any luck?" I asked. I spoke in English, having no Greek, but the tone of my voice should tell him what I meant. His strange eyes stared down at me. Slowly he shook his head. He raised his hand, pointing over his shoulder. He continued to shake his head gently from side to side, and suddenly—fool that I was—I remembered that the Greek "yes," the affirmation, is always given with this same shake of the head, suggesting its opposite, denial. The child's voice coming from the impassive face said "*nei*," and this was repeated, the head still moving slowly.

"He has found them, then?" I said. "There are chamois?" and he reaffirmed his *nei*, which looked so much like contradiction, and went on staring at me with his great honey-coloured eyes, the frozen petrified eyes, until I was seized with a kind of horror, for they did not go with the gentle childish voice. I moved away through the scrub to put some distance between us, calling over my shoulder uselessly—for he could not understand me—"I'll go and find out what's happened." This time the dogs did not snarl but stayed where they were, watching their master, and he remained motionless, leaning on his crook and staring after me.

I crawled through the scrub and up a track which I judged to be the one taken by Stephen and the goatherd earlier. Soon the scrub gave place to rock, a track of a sort beneath the overhanging face, and as I went I shouted

"Stephen!" for the sound of my voice must carry even as the sound of the rifleshot had done. I had no answer.

The world in which I found myself was sparse and bare, and I could see no footprints in the snow in front of me. Had Stephen come this way there must be footprints. Now from my vantage point it was as though the whole of Greece was spread beneath me, infinitely far, belonging to another age, another time, and I was indeed at the summit of my world and quite alone. I could see the forests and the foothills and the plains and a river like a little silken thread, but my husband was not with me, nor anyone at all, not even the eagle that had soared above at midday.

"Stephen," I shouted, my voice flat and feeble against the rock.

I stood and listened. It might be that I should hear a rifleshot again. Any sound would be welcome in such barren solitude. Yet when one came I was shocked out of immobility, for it was no rifleshot, but a whistle. That same lewd whistle to attract attention, coming from fifty feet above my head, from the jutting ledge, the overhanging rock. I saw his horns, his questing eyes, his satyr's face staring down at me, suspicious, curious, and he whistled again, a hiss, a mockery, and stamped his hoofs, releasing a crumbling stone. Then he was gone—the chamois was gone, my first live chamois—he was away and lost, but crouching below me, on a narrow lip over a precipice, clinging to the rock face, his rifle vanished, was a white-faced man who could not speak from fear, my husband, Stephen.

He could not move. I could not reach him. That was the horror. I could not reach him. He must have edged his way on to the lip of rock and found that he could go no further. In some extremity he had dropped his rifle. The thing that appalled me most was the terror on his face. Stephen, who rode roughshod over the feelings of his friends, Stephen the cold, the calculating. I threw myself down full length on the ground and stretched out my hands. There was a gap between us of a few feet, no more.

"Keep your eyes turned to the rock," I said softly—instinct warned me not to speak too loudly—"edge your way

274

inch by inch. If you got yourself there you must be able to return."

He did not answer. He moistened his lips with his tongue. He was deadly pale.

"Stephen," I said, "you've got to try."

He tried to speak but nothing came, and as though to mock us both the lewd warning whistle of the chamois sounded once again. It was more distant now, and the chamois itself was out of sight on some unattainable fastness of his own, secure from human penetration.

It seemed to me that if Stephen had had his rifle with him he would not have been afraid. The loss of the rifle had unmanned him. All power, all confidence had gone, and with it, in some sickening way, his personality. The man clinging to the rock face was a puppet. Then I saw the goatherd, staring down at us from a rock above our heads.

"Please come," I called gently, "my husband's in danger."

He disappeared. A loose stone crumbled and fell past Stephen's head. I saw my husband's knuckles turn white under the strain. A moment's horror suggested that the crumbling of the stone had been intentional, that the goatherd had vanished on purpose, leaving Stephen to his fate. A movement behind me told me I had misjudged him. He was by my side.

I crawled away to let him have my place. He did not look at me, only at Stephen. He threw off his burnous, and I was aware of something lithe and compact, with a shock of black hair. He leapt on to the narrow lip beside Stephen and seized hold of him as an adult would seize a child, and all the six feet two of my husband's body was thrown like a sack across the goatherd's shoulder. I put my hand over my mouth to stifle the cry that must surely come. He was going to throw Stephen into the depths below. I shrank away, my legs turned to jelly, and the next moment the goatherd was back on the track beside me, and Stephen too; Stephen was sitting hunched on the ground, his face in his hands, rocking from side to side. When I looked back from him I saw that the goatherd was dressed in his burnous again and was standing some little distance away from us, his head averted.

I was quietly sick into a hole I scooped out of the snow. Then I shut my eyes and waited. It seemed a very long time before I heard Stephen rise to his feet. I opened my eyes and looked up at him. The colour had returned to his face. The goatherd had gone.

"Now do you understand?" asked Stephen.

"Understand what?" I asked weakly.

"Why I must shoot chamois."

He stood there, defenceless without his rifle; and although he was no longer pale he was somehow shrunken in stature. One of his bootlaces was undone. I found myself staring at that rather than at his face.

"It's fear, isn't it?" I said. "Have you always had it?"

"Always," he answered, "from the very first. It's something I have to conquer. The chamois gives the greatest chance because he climbs the highest. The more I kill, the more I destroy fear." Then absently, as if thinking of something else, he pointed downward. "I dropped my rifle," he said. "I fired when I saw the brute, but it whistled at me instead of taking to its heels, and then the giddiness came, the giddiness that's part of fear."

I was still much shaken but I got up and took his arm.

"Let's go back," I said. "I want a drink. Thank God for the brandy flasks."

His confidence was returning; nevertheless, he allowed me to lead him like a child. We made short work of the descent. When we came to the hut the two dogs were waiting on guard by the entrance and the goatherd was gathering chips of wood to make kindling for a fire. He took no notice of us, and the dogs ignored us too. We went into the hut and took a good swig at our flasks. Then we lighted cigarettes and smoked for a while in silence, watching the goatherd with his armfuls of wood and scattered cones.

"You'll never tell anyone, will you?" Stephen said suddenly.

I looked at him, startled by the harsh note in his voice betraying the strain he would not otherwise show. "You mean about the fear?"

"Yes," he replied. "I don't mind you knowing—you were

276

bound to find out one day. And that fellow there—well, he's not the kind to talk. But I won't have anyone else knowing."

"Of course I won't say anything," I replied quickly to reassure him, and after a moment I turned away and began wrestling with the Primus stove. First things first. We should both of us feel more normal if we had hot food inside us.

Baked beans have never tasted more delicious. And the retsina wine on top of brandy helped to dull speculation. The short day faded quickly. We had scarcely eaten and put on warmer jerseys when the temperature fell at least twenty degrees, the sky deepened, and the sun had gone. The fire at the threshold of the hut threw leaping flames into the air.

"Tomorrow," said Stephen, "I'll go and find my rifle."

I looked at him across the flames. His face was set, the face of the man I knew, the old Stephen.

"You'll never find it," I said. "It might be anywhere."

"I know the place," he replied impatiently, "amongst a heap of boulders and some dwarf pines. I marked it down."

I wondered how he proposed to get himself down there, knowing his limitations as I did now. He must have read my thoughts, for he added, "I can get round to it from here. There shouldn't be any difficulty."

I threw my cigarette into the heart of the fire. It was a mistake to smoke it. Somehow I had not much stomach for cigarettes tonight.

"If you do find it," I said, "what then?"

"A last crack at the chamois," he said.

His fanaticism, instead of cooling, had intensified. He was staring intently into the darkness over my shoulder. I turned and saw Jesus, the goatherd and his saviour, come towards us to drop more chips into the fire.

"*Kalinykta,*" said Stephen.

It was the Greek for good night. And a sign of dismissal. The goatherd paused, and with a little gesture bowed to each of us in turn. "*Kalinykta,*" he said.

The voice was as shrouded as he himself in his burnous, the childish timbre of it muted in some strange fashion because of darkness. The hood was thrown further back than it had been, so that the sharp outline of his face was

277

more revealed, and the firelight turned his skin ruddy, the staring eyes bright like live coals.

He withdrew and left us together. Presently the sharp air, for all the leaping flames, drove us to our sleeping bags inside the hut. We lit candles and read our Penguins for a time. Then Stephen fell asleep, and I blew out the candles and did likewise, worn with the emotion I'd been unable to express. What shocked me were my dreams. The goatherd had stripped off his burnous, and it was not Stephen that he carried in his arms but myself. I put out my hands to feel the shock of hair. It rose from his head like a black crest.

I woke and lit the candle. Stephen was sleeping still. I went to the door of the hut and saw that the fire had died; not even the ashes glowed. The moon, past its quarter mark and swelling, was hanging like a half cheese in the sky. The dogs, the goats, the goatherd had all gone. Silhouetted on the skyline beyond the blasted pine stood a chamois buck, his sharp horns curving backward, his listening head uptilted to the moon, and grazing beneath him, silently, delicately, were the does and the yearling kids.

3

It was a curious thing, I considered, as I brewed our break-fast tea on the Primus and spread cheese over slices of Spam, but danger shared had brought Stephen and myself together. Or else I had turned compassionate. He was human after all, weak like the rest of us. He must have sensed my sym-pathy, because he talked at breakfast, telling me of adven-tures in the past, of near escapes.

"I remember once," he said, "falling some fifteen feet, but I only sprained an ankle."

He laughed in high good humour, and I thought that if he could joke at fear his battle was half won.

"I'll come with you today," I told him, "when you look for your rifle."

"Will you?" he said. "Splendid. It's going to be fine, after that sharp frost. No mist about, the bugbear of all stalkers."

The zest, the keenness had returned. And what was more, I shared it. I wanted to stalk with him. This was a new emotion, something I could not explain. We ate our breakfast and straightened our sleeping bags, and, going out into the sunlight, I kicked at the ashes of last night's fire. There was no sign of the goatherd or his dogs, or of his flock either. He must have taken them to graze elsewhere. I hardly thought of him: I was anxious to be off. Stephen led the way down the forested mountainside, for he knew by instinct where he wished to go, and we scrambled over scrub and slag and stunted bushes, part box, part thorn, away from the overhanging crags above.

High in the blue sky soared the eagle of yesterday, or perhaps his fellow, and, as the sun rose and warmed us so that we took off our jerseys and tied them round our waists, life seemed suddenly very good, very full. There was none of the strain that had been with us yesterday. I put it down to sleeping well, to the new bond shared, and to the absence of the goatherd Jesus.

When we had scrambled thus for half an hour or more Stephen said, "There it is—look, the sun's caught the barrel."

He smiled and ran ahead, and indeed I could see the shining metal, caught sideways between a thorn and a lump of rock. He seized his gun and waved it above his head in triumph.

"I could never have gone home if I'd lost this," he said.

He handled the rifle with care, still smiling—it was almost a caress the way he stroked it. I watched him, indulgent for the first time in my life. He took a cloth from his pouch and began to polish it. I let my eyes roam above him to the rugged heights above, to the lips and ledges where we had climbed yesterday. It was sparse and naked, bare of vegetation. A black speck like a humped rock caught my eye that I had not remembered the previous day. The black speck moved. I touched Stephen's elbow. "There . . ." I murmured, and put my pocket spyglass into his hand. Cautiously he lifted it to his eye.

"He's there," he whispered, "he's there, my buck of yesterday."

I had not thought Stephen could move so stealthily or so fast. He was away from me in a moment, crawling upward through the scrub, and seized with a curious enchantment, I crawled after him. He motioned me back, and I lay still and looked through my glass again. Now the picture was indistinct: one second it looked like the chamois, and the next like our goatherd, yes, our goatherd. I called to Stephen.

"It isn't chamois," I said, "it's your saviour, Zus."

He glanced back at me over his shoulder, impatient, angry.

"What the hell are you shouting for?" he said. "He'll get away from us."

Once again I thrust my glass into his hand, crawling close to him to do so. "Look there," I said, "it isn't chamois."

He seized the glass and after adjusting it to his eye gave it back with an exclamation of disgust.

"Are you mad?" he said. "Of course it's chamois. I can see the horns."

Then, shrill, unmistakable, came the whistle of warning, the mocking chamois call.

"Do you still think it isn't chamois?" said Stephen, and he put his rifle to his shoulder and fired. The explosion was like an echo to the whistle. It ricocheted away from the rocks above us and carried to the depths below. The black speck leapt and vanished. Loose stones fell upon our heads.

"You've missed him," I said.

"No," said Stephen, "I'm going after him."

There was a gully immediately above us. He climbed to the left of it, I to the right, and as we made towards the jutting ledge where we had seen the black speck leap, neck and neck on opposite sides of the gully, I knew, with sudden certainty, that we were after different quarry. Stephen was after chamois. I was after man. Both were symbolic of something abhorrent to our natures, and so held fascination and great fear. We wanted to destroy the thing that shamed us most.

My heart was singing as I climbed, and pounding too. It was worth having been born, having lived my span of years for this alone. There had been no other experience. Nothing else compared with the stalk, and I had my goatherd on the run. It was he who fled from me, not I from him.

I could see him now, jumping from rock to rock. How Stephen could mistake him for a chamois, God alone could tell. He had thrown off his burnous, and his shaggy head was like a wave crest, thick and black. It was glorious. I had no fear of the jutting rocks, and climbed them steadily and surely, with never a slip and never a moment's pause. Silence no longer mattered, for he knew I was after him.

"I'll get you," I called, "you can't escape. You know very well I've hunted you all my life."

Such savagery and power—I, who hated violence; intoxication, too, and wild delight. Once more the hiss, the whistle. Fear and warning and mockery in one. The rattle of stones, the scampering of hoofs.

"Lie down," shouted Stephen, "lie down. I'm going to shoot."

I remember laughing as the shot rang out. This time Stephen did not miss. The black form crumpled to its knees and fell. As I hauled myself to the ledge I saw the honey-coloured eyes glaze in death. They would never stare at me again. My husband had destroyed the thing that frightened me.

4

"He's smaller than I thought," said Stephen, turning the dead buck over with his feet, "and younger too. Not more than five years old."

He lit a cigarette. I took it from him. Sweat was pouring from both of us. The eagle was still soaring against the sun.

"I shan't carry him back," said my husband. "I don't even want his head. That's my last chamois. Don't ask me why—I just know it, that's all. We'll leave him out here in grandeur, where he belongs. Nature has her own way of disposing of the dead." He glanced up at the eagle.

We left the chamois on the ledge of rock under the sky and climbed down again, through the scrub and stones, back to the hut and our belongings. The rucksacks and the sleeping bags seemed part of another life.

"No sign of our host," said Stephen, "and we've finished all the rations. Let's pack and spend tonight down at the store. We can catch the morning bus in the other direction. Go to Metsovon, and Ioannina, and down the west coast to Missolonghi and across to Delphi. You'd like that, wouldn't you?"

I did not answer, but I put out my hand to him for no reason. It was very peaceful, very still on the quiet mountain. Suddenly Stephen kissed me. Then he put his hand in his pocket, and, bending down, placed two small metal objects in the white ash of the fire.

"We'll leave the empty cartridges for Jesus," Stephen said.

The Lordly Ones

BEN WAS THOUGHT to be backward. He could not speak. When he tried to form words sounds came, harsh and ugly, and he did not know what to do with his tongue. He pointed when he wanted something, or fetched it for himself. They said he was tongue-tied, and that in a few years' time he would be taken to hospital and something could be done. His mother said he was sharp enough, he took in what you told him all right and knew good from bad, but he was stubborn, he did not take kindly to "no." Because of his silence they forgot to explain things to him, arrivals and departures and changes of plan, and his world was made up of whims, the whims of older people. He would be told to dress for no reason, or to go out into the street to play; or some toy was denied him that had been given him an hour before.

When the stress became too great to bear he opened his mouth, and the sound that came out of it alarmed him even more than it alarmed his parents. Why did it rise? How did it come? Then someone, usually his mother, picked him up and shut him away in the cupboard under the stairs, amongst the mackintoshes and the shopping baskets, and he could hear her calling through the keyhole, "You'll stop there until you're quiet!" The noise would not be quelled. It did not belong to him. The anger was a force that had to have its way.

Later, crouched beside the keyhole, spent and tired, he would hear the noise die away, and peace would come to the cupboard. The fear would then be that his mother would go away and forget to let him out, and he would rattle the handle of the door to remind her. A flash of her skirt through the keyhole meant reassurance, and he would sit down and wait until the grinding of the key in the lock spelt release. Then he would step out into the daylight, blinking, and glance up at his mother to gauge her mood. If she was dusting or sweeping she ignored him. All would be well until the next moment of anger or frustration, when the performance would be repeated—either the cupboard again, or his bedroom with no tea, his toys taken from him. The way to ensure against their anger was to please his parents, but this could not always be done, for the strain was too great. In the middle of play, absorbed, he forgot their commands.

One day suitcases were packed and he was dressed in his warmest clothes, although it was early spring, and they left the house in Exeter, where he had been born, and went to the moors. There had been talk about the moors for some weeks past.

"It's different up there from what it is down here," his parents would say. Somehow cajolery and threats were combined: one day he was to be lucky, another he had better not get out of sight once they moved. The very words "the moors" sounded dark and ominous, a sort of threat.

The bustle of departure added to fear. The rooms of his home, suddenly bare, were unfamiliar, and his mother, impatient, scolded him ceaselessly. She, too, wore different clothes and an ugly hat. It clung round her ears, changing the shape of her face. As they left home she seized his hand, dragging it, and, bewildered, he watched his parents as they sat, anxious themselves, among the boxes and the packing cases. Could it be that they were uncertain too? That none of them knew where they were going?

The train bore them away, but he could not see out of the windows. He was in the middle seat between his parents, and only the tops of trees told him of country. His mother gave him an orange he did not want. Forgetting caution, he threw it on the floor. She smacked him hard. The smack coincided with a sudden jolt of the train and the darkness of a tunnel, the two combined suggesting the cupboard under the stairs and punishment. He opened his mouth and the cry came from it.

As always, the sound brought panic. His mother shook

him and he bit his tongue. The carriage was full of strangers. An old man behind a newspaper frowned. A woman, showing her teeth, offered him a green sweet. No one could be trusted. His cries became louder still, and his mother, her face red, picked him up and took him into the rattling corridor. "Will you be quiet?" she shouted. All was confusion. Fatigue seized him and he crumpled. Rage and fear made him stamp his feet, clad in new brown-laced shoes, adding to the clatter. The sound, coming from his belly, ceased; only the gasp for breath, the stifling sobs, told him that the pain was with him, but for what reason he could not tell.

"He's tired," somebody said.

They were back again in the carriage, and room was made for him by the window. The world outside went past. Houses clustered. He saw a road with cars upon it, and fields, then high banks swaying up and down. With the gradual slowing of the train his parents stood up and began to reach for their belongings. The fluster of departure was with them once again. The train ground to a standstill. Doors opened and clanged, and a porter shouted. They tumbled out on to the platform.

His mother clutched him by the hand and he peered up at her face and at his father's, too, to try and discover from their expressions whether what was happening was customary, expected by them, and if they knew what was to happen now. They climbed into a car, the luggage piled about them, and through the gathering dusk he understood that they were not back again in the town from which they had come but in open country. The air bit sharp, cool-smelling, and his father turned with a laugh to him and said, "Can you smell the moors?"

The moors . . . He tried to see from the window of the car, but a suitcase balked his view. His mother and father were talking amongst themselves. "She'll surely have put on a kettle for us, and give us a hand," said his mother, and, "We'll not unpack everything tonight. It will take days to get straight."

"I don't know," said his father. "It's surprising how different it will seem in a small house."

The road twisted, the car swaying at the corners. Ben felt sick. This would be the final disgrace. The sourness was coming and he shut his mouth. But the urge was too strong, and it came from him in a burst, splaying out over the car.

"Oh no, that's too much," cried his mother, and she pushed him from her knee against the sharp end of the suitcase, bruising his cheek. His father tapped the window. "Stop . . . the boy's been sick." The shame, the inevitable confusion of sickness, and with it the sudden cold so that he shivered. Everywhere lay the evidence of his shame, and an old cloth, evil-smelling, was produced by the driver to wipe his mouth.

On again, but slower now, standing between his father's knees, and at last the rutty, bumpy road came to an end and a light was in front of them.

"It's not raining, that's one blessing," said his mother. "Don't ask me what we'll do here when it does."

The small house stood alone, light in the windows. Ben, blinking and shivering still, climbed down from the car. He stood looking about him as the luggage was lifted out. For the moment he was ignored. The small house faced a green, smooth as a carpet in the dark, and behind the house, which was thatched, were humped black hills. The sharp sweet smell he had noticed on leaving the station was stronger still. He lifted his face to sniff the air. Where were the moors? He saw them as a band of brothers, powerful and friendly.

"Come on in, my handsome," said a woman from the house, and he did not draw back when she bore down upon him, welcoming and large, and led him into the paved kitchen. A stool was drawn up to the table and a glass of milk put in front of him. He sipped it slowly, his eyes sizing up the flagged kitchen, the scullery pump, the small latticed windows.

"Is he shy?" asked the woman, and the whispers began, the grown-up talk, something about his tongue. His father and his mother looked embarrassed and awkward. The woman glanced back again in pity, and Ben dipped his face in his glass of milk. Then they forgot him, the dull talk passed him by, and, unwatched, he was able to eat bread and butter without hindrance, help himself to biscuits, his sickness gone and appetite returned.

"Oh yes, watch out for them," the woman said. "They're terrible thieves. They'll come by night and raid your larder if you leave it open. Especially if it continues cold like this. Watch out for snow."

So the moors were robbers. A band of robbers wandering by night. Ben remembered the comic paper that his father had bought him, with the ogre's face upon the cover. Yet they could not be like that, for the woman was saying something about their fine looks.

"They won't hurt you," she said, "they're friendly enough." This to Ben, who watched her, puzzled. Then she laughed, and everyone got up to clear the tea, to unpack, to settle.

"Now then, don't wander off," said his mother. "If you don't behave you'll go straight to bed."

"He can't come to harm," the woman said. "I've latched the gate."

When they were not looking Ben slipped out of the open door and stood outside. The car that had brought them had disappeared. The silence, so different from the noise of the street at home, was like the silence that came when his parents were not angry. It wrapped itself about him. The little lights winking from the other cottages, away down the green, were distant as stars. He went and rested his chin on the gate and stared into the peaceful darkness. He felt himself at rest. He had no wish to go indoors, to unpack his toys.

There must be a farm somewhere close, for the smell of manure mixed with the cold air and a cow lowed from a stall. These discoveries were pleasing to him. Mostly he thought about the moors, the thieves of the night, but somehow they did not frighten him: the reassurance of the woman's smile and the way his parents had laughed showed that the moors were not to be feared. Anyway, it was to come to the moors that they had packed their things and left home. It was this that had been discussed now for so many weeks. "The boy will like the moors," people had said back at home. "He'll grow strong, up there. There's nothing like the moors for giving appetite."

It was true. Ben had eaten five pieces of bread and butter and three biscuits. Already the band of brothers had shown power. He wondered how close they were to the house, if they lurked, smiling encouragement, beyond those dark humped hills.

A sudden thought occurred to him. If food was put out for the thieves, they would not steal. They would eat it and be thankful. He went back inside the kitchen, and voices from upstairs told him that his parents and their helper were unpacking and out of the way. The table had been cleared, but the tea things, unwashed, were piled in the scullery. There was a loaf of bread, a cake still uncut, and the remaining biscuits. Ben filled his pockets with the biscuits, and carried the loaf of bread and the cake. He went to the door, and so down the path to the gate. He set the food on the ground and concentrated upon the task of unfastening the gate. It was easier than he had expected. He lifted the latch and the gate swung back. Then he picked up the loaf and the cake and went out on to the green. The thieves made for the green first, the woman had said. They prowled there, looking for odds and ends, and if nothing tempted them and no one shouted and drove them away, they would come to the cottages.

Ben walked a few yards on to the green and set out the food. The thieves could not miss it if they came. They would be grateful and go back to their lair in the black hills well satisfied. Looking back, he could see the figures of his parents moving backwards and forwards in the bedrooms upstairs. He jumped to try the feel of the grass under his feet, more pleasing than a pavement, and lifted his face once more to feel the air. It came, cold and clean, from the hills. It was as though the moors knew, the thieves knew, that a feast was prepared for them. Ben was happy.

He ran back to the house, and as he did so his mother came downstairs.

"Come on, bed," she said.

Bed? So soon? His face protested, but she was not to be moved.

"There's enough to do without you round my heels," she complained.

She pulled him up the steep little stairway after her, and he saw his own bed, miraculously brought from home, standing in a corner of the small room lit by candlelight. It was close to the window, and his first thought was that he would be able to look out from his bed and watch when the thieves came. This interest kept him quiet while his mother helped him to undress, but she was rougher than usual. Her nails got caught in a button and scratched his skin, and when he whimpered she said sharply, "Oh, be quiet, do." The candle, stuck in a saucer, threw a monster shadow on the ceiling. It flounced his mother's figure to a grotesque shape.

"I'm too tired to wash you tonight," she said. "You'll have to stay dirty."

His father's voice called up the stairs. "What did you do with the bread and the cake?" he called. "I can't find them."

"They're on the scullery table," she answered. "I'll be down in a minute."

Ben realised that his parents would search for the food to put it away. Instinct warned him to make no sound. She finished undressing him, and he went straight to his bed without delay.

"Now I don't want to hear any more from you tonight," she said. "If you make a sound I'll send your father to you."

She went downstairs, taking the candle with her.

Ben was used to darkness, but, even so, the room was unfamiliar. He had not yet had time to learn the shape. Was there a chair? A table? Was it long or square? He lay back in bed biting at the blanket. He heard footsteps underneath his window. Sitting up, he looked between the curtains and saw the woman who had welcomed them walk down the path, through the gate, and away down the road. She was carrying a lantern. She did not cross the green. The lantern danced as she moved, and soon she was swallowed up in darkness. Only the bobbing light betrayed her passage.

Ben lay back again in bed, disturbed by the flickering

lantern and voices raised in argument below. He heard his mother come upstairs. She threw open the door and stood there, holding the candle, the monstrous shadow behind her.

"Did you touch the tea things?" she said.

Ben made the sound his parents understood as a denial, but his mother was not satisfied. She came to the bed and, shielding her eyes, stared down at him.

"The bread and cake have gone," she said. "The biscuits too. You took them, didn't you? Where did you hide them?"

As always, the rising voice brought out antagonism. Ben shrank against his pillow and shut his eyes. It was not the way to question him. If she had smiled and made a joke of it, it would have been different.

"Very well," she said. "I'll settle you, young man."

She called for his father. Despair seized Ben. It would mean a whipping. He began to cry. Explanation was beyond him. He heard his father stump up the stairs and come into the room, his shadow monstrous too. The pair of them filled the small, unfamiliar room.

"Do you want a hiding?" his father asked. "Now then, what did you do with the bread?"

His father's face was ugly, worn with fatigue. The packing and unpacking, all the hustle of removal, of starting the new life, had meant strain. Ben sensed this, but he could not give way. He opened his mouth and yelled. The cry roused the full fatigue and anger of the father. Resentment, too. Why must his son be dumb?

"That's enough of that," he said.

He jerked Ben out of bed and stripped the pyjama legs. Then he laid the wriggling child across his knee. The hand found the flesh and hit hard, with all its force. Ben screamed louder still. The relentless hand, so large and powerful, smote and smote again.

"That's learned him, that's enough," said his mother. "There's neighbours across the green. We don't want trouble."

"He must know who's master," said his father, and it was not until his own hand ached with the force of the blows that he gave up and pushed Ben from his knee.

"Now holler if you dare," he said, rising abruptly, and Ben, face downwards on the bed, his sobs long ceased, heard them withdraw, felt the candle go, knew that the room was empty. Everything was pain. He tried to move his legs, but the movement sent a warning message to his brain. The pain travelled from his buttocks up his spine to the top of his head. No sound came from his lips now, only a trickle of tears from his eyes. Perhaps if he lay quite still the pain would go. He could not cover himself with the blanket, and the cold air found him, bringing its own dull ache.

Little by little the pain numbed. The tears dried on his cheeks. He had no thoughts at all, lying there on his face. He had forgotten the cause of his beating. He had forgotten the band of brothers, the thieves, the moors. If in a little while there could be nothing, let nothing come.

2

He awoke suddenly, every sense alert. The moon shone through the gap in the curtains. At first he thought that everything was still, and then the movement from the green outside told him they were there. They had come. He knew. Slowly, painfully, he dragged himself across his bed and so to the window. He pulled at the curtains. The white night showed him the wonder. The thieves were there, the lordly ones. Not as the woman had described them, but more beautiful. A little group, intent upon his offering. There was the mother, with two children, and another mother just behind, with a taller child, playing by himself. Two others ran round in circles, delighting in the snow, for with them the snow had come, turning the green white. That must be the father, watching. But he was not angry, like Ben's father: he was beautiful like the mothers and the children, beautiful and wise. He was staring at the window. He had already seen Ben, and then, to show his appreciation of the cake placed ready for him, he touched it gently and moved away, letting the son play with it instead.

It was the time of night when no one moves. Ben knew nothing of time, but instinct told him that his parents had long been in bed and that morning would not come for many hours. He watched them, the moors, the lordly ones. They were not thieves at all, they were far too proud. They ate with delicacy what Ben had given them, and they did not attempt to come near to the house, or prowl, as the woman had said. Like Ben, they did not speak. They talked by signal. The father, in command, moved his head, and, leaving the food, the mothers summoned their children, and the whole company settled themselves on the green, in the snow, to wait for morning. Their supreme disdain of the sleeping houses showed itself to Ben as contempt of authority. They made their own laws.

Ben lowered himself from his bed. His buttocks and back were still very sore, and the cold night had stiffened him, lying as he had done without a cover. Nevertheless, he began to put on his clothes. He dressed slowly, not yet accustomed to doing it quite alone, but finally he satisfied himself that he was ready, although his jersey was back to front. Luckily his Wellington boots were in the scullery. They had been among the first things to be unpacked.

He could see his room clearly now, for the moonlight turned it to day. There were no strange bulges or shapes. It was just a room, small and plain. The door latch was high above his head, so he dragged a chair beneath it and stood on it to lift the latch.

Cunningly he crept down the narrow stair. Below in the kitchen it was still dark, but instinct led him to the scullery and to the corner where his boots waited. He put them on. The larder was only a cupboard, part of the scullery, and the door was ajar. His mother, in her anger, must have forgotten to close it. Deliberately he took the last loaf, intended for breakfast, and then repeated his performance with the chair beneath the latch of the front door. There were bolts here, too, to be withdrawn. If his parents heard him he was lost. He climbed down from the chair. The door lay open. The white night was before him, the great moon benign, and the lordly ones were waiting on the green. It was green no longer, but glistening white.

Softly, his boots lightly crunching the snow, Ben tiptoed down the path and lifted the latch of the gate. The sound roused the watchers on the green. One of the mothers looked up, and although she said nothing her movement warned the father, and he, too, turned his head. They waited to see what Ben would do. Perhaps, thought Ben, they hoped for further gifts: they had not brought food with them and were hungry still.

He walked slowly towards them, holding out the loaf. The mother rose to her feet, and the children too. The action roused the others, and in a moment the little company, who had settled themselves for sleep, seemed ready to march once more. They did not try to take the bread from Ben. Some sense of delicacy, perhaps, forbade it. He wanted to show generosity to them and to flaunt his parents at the same time, so, tearing the loaf in two, he went to the smallest child, not much taller than himself, and offered him part of it. This surely would be understood.

The little moor came forward and took the bread, watching Ben when he had eaten it, and then he shook his hair out of his eyes, for he was wild and unkempt, and glanced at his mother. She did not do anything, she did not speak to him, and Ben, encouraged, offered her the other half of the loaf. She took it from him. Their silence pleased Ben, for it was something he understood and shared with them.

The mother had gold hair, like her ragged son, but the older boy was dark. Relationships were confusing, because there was another mother—or could it be an aunt?—who was standing quite close to the father, and a little apart, not taking much notice of anyone, was surely the gran, so grey and thin, who looked as if she did not care for the snow but would have been more at her ease before a good warm fire. Ben wondered at their roaming ways. What made them wander, rather than stay at home? They were not thieves, he was sure they were not thieves.

Then the father gave a signal. He turned and slowly, majestically led the way down the green. The others followed, the children dancing, glad to be on the move again, and the old gran, hobbling, brought up the rear. Ben watched them, then glanced back at the sleeping house. Decision came to him. He was not going to stay with the parents who did not love him. He was going to follow the moors, the lordly ones.

Ben ran across the crunching snow in the wake of his chosen companions. The old gran looked over her shoulder as she heard him coming, but she did not mind. She seemed to accept him. Ben ran until he caught up with the mother he liked best, the one with the golden hair and the ragged son, and when he was beside her she gave him a friendly nod of the head to show that he was now of the company. Ben trudged beside her in the snow. The father, still in front, was making for the hills, but he had a fine instinct for avoiding the deeper snow. He picked his way along a track, drifts on either side, and came at last to a high ridge where the world stretched wide and far on either side. The green was a long way below. Soon it was lost to sight. There were no houses in this wild country, lit by moonlight. Ben was warm from his climb, and so were his companions. Their breath went from them all like smoke in the frosted air.

What now? They looked to the father for instructions. He seemed to debate the move within himself. He glanced to right and to left. Then he decided to continue along the ridge, and once more led the way, with the family following.

The children dragged a little, for they were getting tired, and Ben, to encourage them, jumped and skipped, forgetting his bruised, stiff back. The pain made him cry out, and the cry startled the golden mother, who, staring at him, spoke to him. Was she asking a question? Ben did not understand her language. He thought that the noises in his throat must have told the mother that his back was stiff, for she seemed reassured and slowed her walk to his. Ben was relieved. He did not want to have to hobble in the rear with the old gran.

Presently the ridge sloped to an old trackway, banked high on either side with snow, and the father stopped here, making as though to camp. He stared across the wastes to the line of distant hills and did not move. He must be thinking very deeply, decided Ben; he did not want to talk to the others. The mothers wandered around in circles and then found a resting place for the children on firm ground against a bank of frozen snow. The old gran, discontented, could not settle. She found the night air cold. Ben wondered what he should do. His legs were aching and he was as tired as the gran. He watched the children curl up in a patch of snow. If they can do that, he thought to himself, I suppose I can too. But they are used to sleeping on the ground, and I am not.

Then the mother, the one he liked, decided to settle by her son. Her broad, comfortable body reminded Ben of the woman who had welcomed him and his parents the night before at the thatched house on the green. She had been kindly too. But this mother was beautiful, more beautiful by far than his own mother. He hesitated a moment, then he crept forward and crouched against her. Would she be angry? Would she push him away?

She did not look at him. She did not speak. She let him understand that he could lie there against her and receive her warmth. Her good body smell was comforting. He snuggled close, his head against her shoulder, and put up his hand to touch her hair. She shook her head gently, and sighed. Ben closed his eyes, eased by the warmth, the comfort, the tender understanding of the mother and the reassurance of the father, still watching the far hills. He was the guardian of his sons, he would never beat them. They were all of one company, these moors, not the band of brothers he had imagined, but a family, a tribe, belonging one to the other. He would never leave them, the lordly ones.

3

The sun came over the hills in splendour, and Ben opened his eyes. In a moment it was broad day. Already the old gran was on the move, hobbling about on her stiff legs. Her example put the others to shame, and they rose in turn, the children reluctantly, for they could have done with an hour or two more of sleep. No one had breakfast, and Ben was hungry. What was to be done about food? The bread he had brought with him had all been finished on the green. Uneasily, he remembered that the woman had called them thieves. Perhaps, after all, it was true. They were going to wait until night and then descend to a village and either beg for bread or steal it. What about the children? Would they last through the day?

Ben stood up and stamped his feet for warmth. Then he stared. The little ragged son, who must surely be of an age with himself, was feeding from his mother. Only babies did that. Was it because the lordly ones were wanderers that they had such wild ways? The mother did not hide herself with her son to do this, as a friend of his own mother's had once done in their back kitchen, but she let it happen now, in the open, with the others looking on. Then abruptly she pushed the small son away, showing him that he had had enough. She began to walk after the father. The long trail started, and Ben stumped along by the mother's side. After all, if it was their custom . . .

He began to wish the mother had fed him too. The ragged son, filled and happy, danced up to him, suggesting play, and Ben, forgetting his hunger, ran after him, laughing, pulling at his hair. They ran in circles, calling to one another. And the ragged son, as he might have done himself, pranced back to tease the gran. He skipped in front of her, mocking the hobbling gait, and nobody minded, thought Ben, nobody told him it was rude.

The sun was high now, the warmth of it melting the snow beneath, and with it came the gnawing pain of hunger in Ben's stomach, and there was nothing to eat, for the lordly ones gave him nothing. Quelling his shyness, he went to the mother and pointed, showing by the sound in his throat that he wanted to feed. She moved away, though, she would not let him. He understood that she kept her food for the son.

They went on walking, they followed the father. He was some way ahead when he suddenly stopped and, looking back, called to the mothers. They halted, and the mothers returned his cry. Then they waited. Instructions had been given not to move. There was a sound of running in the far distance, and over the hill came another moor, a stranger. He stopped when he saw the father, and the pair of them stared at each other. The mother beside Ben murmured something to her companion, and the company formed a little circle, wondering what the father was going to do.

Ben watched, apprehensive; he did not like the look of the threatening stranger. The newcomer advanced again, and then, without warning, hurled himself upon the father, and the pair of them wrestled there together in the snow, fiercely, without weapons, the watchful father turning of a sudden to a savage. There was a time of anger and stamping feet and strangled sobs, and the mothers, watching, huddled together for comfort, Ben in the midst of them. Their fear bred fear in Ben, and he began to cry again, remembering his own angry father. Would the battle never be done? Suddenly it was over. But the result was terror. For the father, the kind leader who had watched over them all night, began to run. Not towards his own family, the mothers and the children, but away across the snow to the distant hills. He was afraid of the stranger. The stranger had defeated him. As Ben watched he saw the trail of blood on the snow.

Ben put out his hand and touched the mother. He tried to tell her that they must follow the wounded father, follow their leader, but she shook herself away impatiently. She was looking at the conqueror. Slowly he advanced towards them. Ben shrank back against the ragged son, as frightened, surely, as he. The old gran turned away in disgust. She would have nothing to do with it. Then the mother, the golden mother beside whom Ben had slept, walked slowly towards the stranger, and Ben realised, by the way she touched him, that she acknowledged him as leader. He would be the father from now on. What if it happened in his own home? What if a neighbour came to fight with his father and, beating him, drove him away from home? Would his mother mind, would she go to the neighbour?

Ben waited and watched, and then the stranger, who was brown-haired and broad, less graceful than the defeated father but younger, jerked his head in signal to the mothers to follow him, and meekly, without a word, they obeyed, the children with them. Only the old gran looked backwards across the snow, where, in the distance, stood the smudged figure of the defeated leader, lost and alone.

The battle was over. The day went on as before. As Ben trudged beside his companions through the snow he became accustomed to the new father, the new leader. By afternoon he might have led them always. Perhaps after all he was a relation, an uncle—there was no way of telling what customs they had, the moors.

The sun travelled across the sky and began to sink on the other side of the hills. The company paused once more, and the new father, not so watchful as the first, walked round about the other mother, the aunt—he seemed to like her best. He did not stay on guard as the first father had done. They murmured together, sharing some secret, and when one of the children ran to join them the new father drove him away. He was not going to be so easy of temper as the first.

Ben was faint from hunger now. He went to the mother, the one he knew, the mother of the ragged son, and this time she was patient while he tried to feed and did not push him away, but suffered him to stay. Ben managed to feed a little, but it was hard. He was not certain of himself and he was clumsy. After a moment or two the mother moved, and then, as she had done the night before, she settled herself in the snow with her son, and Ben lay down beside her. The others waited around, but Ben had already closed his eyes, his head once more against the shoulder of the mother, his hand in her hair, and whether or not they settled he did not know. Nor did he bother about it, for all that mattered was to be warm and sheltered, protected and cherished by the one he loved.

The angry shouts brought the company to their feet. Bewildered, Ben rubbed his eyes. The moon was full. There, running across the snow, was a crowd of men with sticks, his own father among them, and they were shouting and yelling, waving their sticks at the lordly ones.

This time there was no battle. The leader ran. And with him galloped the mothers, the children, the old gran. They galloped quickly under the moonlight across the frozen snow, and Ben, deserted by his mother, the chestnut mare, deserted by his brothers the moors, the lordly ones, uttered a great cry. He heard the cry tear his chest and he shouted, "No . . . no . . . no . . ." for the first and the last time, and he fell face downwards in the snow.

The Limpet

No one can call me an insensitive woman. That has been my trouble. If I could harden myself to other people's feelings, life would be very different. As it is, here I am today a positive wreck, and through no fault of my own, but just because I can't bear to hurt the people I love.

What is the future to be? I ask myself the question a hundred times a day. I'm nearly forty, my looks are going, and if my health goes too—which wouldn't surprise me, after all I've been through—then I shall have to give up this job and live on the ridiculous alimony that I get from Kenneth. A fine outlook.

Well, there's one thing. I keep my sense of humour. My friends, the few I have, give me credit for that at least. And they say I'm plucky. They ought to see me sometimes. When I come back from work at the end of the day (and often it's after seven before I get home—my boss has no tender feelings, I can tell you that much), I have my little bit of supper to get. Then there's the flat to dust and put straight—the woman who comes in twice a week always leaves something in the wrong place. Coming on top of a heavy day, by this time I'm so exhausted that I just feel like throwing myself on my bed and ending it all.

Then perhaps the telephone rings, and I make the most tremendous effort to be bright. Sometimes I catch a glimpse of myself in the looking glass—sixty-five if I'm a day, with those dreary lines, and my hair's lost its colour too. As often as not it's some woman friend cancelling lunch on Sunday because she has something better to do, or my mother-in-law complaining of her bronchitis or the letter she's had from

Kenneth—as if that's my concern these days. The point is that none of them consider my feelings in the way I consider theirs.

I'm the one to get what Father used to call "the thick end of the stick," and it's been like that for as long as I can remember, way back in the days when he and Mother used to squabble like cat and dog and I had to play the part of go-between. I don't pretend to have brains—I never have had. Plenty of common sense when dealing with everyday matters, and I've never been sacked from a job yet—I've always been the one to hand in the notice. But when it comes to asking for anything for myself, or sticking up for my own rights, as I should have done with Kenneth, then I'm quite hopeless. I just give in and say nothing. I suppose I've been more put upon in life, more used, more hurt, than anyone would credit could be possible for one lone woman. Call it fate or misfortune, call it what you will, it's true.

And it comes from being unselfish, though I say it myself. Take what happened recently. I could have married Edward any time during the past three years, but I always refused to do anything drastic, for his sake. You have a wife and a career, I used to say to him, and your duty is to put them first. Silly, I dare say. I can't think of any other woman who would have behaved in that way. But then I have my ideals, and certain things are right and certain things are wrong. I inherited that from Father.

When Kenneth left me—and I'd been through hell for six years—I didn't go round complaining to all his friends. I just said we were incompatible, and his restless temperament clashed with my own more stay-at-home nature, and all that whisky drinking was not the happiest way to start a family. For a woman whose health has always been tricky he asked a lot, what with keeping him going while he had the drinking bouts, and cooking for him, and cleaning the flat, hardly able to stand myself—well, I said to his friends it seemed really wiser to let him go. I collapsed afterwards of course. Flesh and blood could bear no more. But blame him . . . no. It's far more dignified to keep silent when one is lacerated.

The first time I realised how much people were going to depend on me in life was when Father and Mother came to me in turn about their own troubles. I was only fourteen at the time. We were living in Eastbourne. My father was in a solicitor's office, not exactly a partner in the firm, but in an important position above the head clerk, and my mother looked after the house. It was quite a nice house, standing in its own garden, not semidetached or anything of that sort, and we kept a general maid.

Being an only child, I suppose I got into the habit of listening too much to grown-up conversation. I remember so well coming back from school wearing my little gym dress with the white-flannel shirt, and carrying the ugly school hat slung on my back. I stood in the hall, pulling off my shoes outside the dining-room—we used the dining-room as a living-room in winter, because the drawing-room faced north— and I heard Father say, "What *are* we going to say to Dilly?" Dilys is such a pretty name, too, but they always called me Dilly.

I knew at once that something was wrong, from the very tone of Father's voice and the emphasis on the "are," as if they were in some sort of quandary. Well, any other child would either have taken no notice and forgotten about it, or walked straight in and said there and then, "What's wrong?" I was far too sensitive for that. I stood outside the dining-room, trying to hear what my mother answered, but all I could catch was something about, "She'll soon settle down." Then I heard movement as if she was getting up from her chair, so I quickly ran upstairs. Something was afoot, some change, which was going to make a difference to all our lives, and from the way Mother said, "She'll soon settle down," it sounded as if they were doubtful how I should take it.

Now, I've never been strong, and as a child I used to catch the most appalling colds. I was at the tail end of one on that particular evening, and somehow hearing the whispered voices seemed to bring the cold back again. I had to keep blowing and blowing my nose up in that cold little bedroom of mine, so that when I went downstairs my poor eyes and nose were red and swollen, and I must have looked a miserable sight.

"Oh, Dilly," said my mother, "whatever's the matter? Is your cold worse?" And Father stared at me, too, in great concern.

"It's nothing," I told them. "I just haven't felt very well all day, and I've been working rather hard on the exams for the end of term."

Then suddenly—I couldn't stop myself—I burst into tears. There was silence from Father and Mother, but they both looked very uncomfortable and worried, and I saw them exchange glances.

"You ought to be in bed, dear," said Mother. "Why not go up, and I'll bring you your supper on a tray?"

Then—it just shows how sensitive I was—I jumped up and ran round to her and put my arms about her, and I said, "If anything ever happened to you and Father, I should die!"

That was all. Nothing more. Then I smiled, and wiped my eyes, and said, "I'm going to wait on you for a change. I'll get the supper." And I wouldn't hear of Mother helping me; I was determined to show how useful I could be.

That night my father came and sat on my bed and told me about the job he had been offered in Australia, and how if he went it would mean leaving me behind for the first year, while he and Mother got settled in and found a home for the three of us. I didn't attempt to cry or make any sort of fuss. I just nodded my head and said, "You've got to do what you think is best. You mustn't consider me."

"That's all very well," he answered, "but we can't go off and leave you at boarding school unless we are quite satisfied you're going to be happy, and that you'll make the best of it with your Aunt Madge." This was his sister, who lived in London.

"Of course I'll make the best of it," I said. "And I'll soon get used to being on my own. It may be a bit hard at first, because Aunt Madge has never cared twopence for me, and I know she has heaps of friends and likes going out in the evenings, which will mean I shall be left in that draughty old house by myself. Still, I can write to you and Mother every day during the holidays, and then I shan't feel so cut off, and at school I shall be working so hard there won't be time to think."

I remember he looked a bit upset—poor old Father, he was sensitive like me—and he said, "What makes you say that about your aunt?"

"Nothing definite," I told him. "It's just her manner and the way she's always been down on me. But don't let it worry you. I suppose I can take my own little possessions and have them in my bedroom there? It would mean a link with all the things I love."

He got up and walked about the room. Then he said, "It's not absolutely settled, you know. I've promised the firm I'll think it over."

I wasn't going to show him I minded, so I lay back in bed and hid my face in the blanket and said, "If you really and truly think you and Mother will be happy in Australia, you've got to go."

I was peeping over the blanket and I can see his expression now. His face was all puckered up and distressed, which made me quite certain that, if he did go to Australia, it would be a big mistake.

The next morning my cold was worse, and Mother tried to make me stay in bed, but I insisted on getting up and going off to school as usual.

"I can't go on making a fuss about a silly cold," I told her. "I've got to harden up, in future, and try to forget how you and Father have spoilt me. Aunt Madge will think me an awful nuisance if I expect to stay in bed whenever I have a cold. What with London fogs, and so on, I shall probably have a cold the whole winter, so I may as well become used to it." And I laughed cheerfully, so as not to worry her, and teased her too, and said how lovely it would be for her in the warm sunshine of Australia, while I was sitting alone in the bedroom of Aunt Madge's London house.

"You know we'd take you with us if we could," said Mother. "But it's the fare, for one thing, and not being quite certain what we shall find when we get there."

"I know," I said. "That's what's worrying Father, isn't it, the uncertainty of it, going to a life he doesn't know, and cutting himself off from all his old ties here."

"Did he tell you that?" Mother asked me.

"No, but I could feel it," I said. "It's a wrench, and he won't admit it."

Father had already left for the office, so we were alone, Mother and I. The maid was busy with the bedrooms upstairs, and I was stuffing my school things into my satchel.

"I thought he seemed so happy about it all," said Mother. "He was really excited when we first discussed the plan."

"Well, you know best," I said, "but Father's always been like that, hasn't he? Wild over something at first, and then he cools off when it's too late, like the time he bought that motor mower and you had to go without a winter coat. It would be terrible if you got out there and he found he didn't settle happily after all."

"Yes," said Mother, "yes, I know. . . . I admit I wasn't enthusiastic myself at first, but he talked me round."

It was time for me to catch the bus to school, so I didn't discuss it any more, but to show how much I sympathised I hugged her very hard, and said, "I do hope so much you're going to be happy and that you'll enjoy the business of hunting for a house and running it all yourself. You'll miss Florence at first"—Florence was our maid, she'd been with us a long time—"and I know it's hard to find help in Australia. One of the mistresses at school is an Australian, and it's a great place for young people but not for the middle-aged, according to her. But then, that will be part of the excitement, won't it, being a pioneer, and living rough."

I blew my nose again, because of the wretched cold, and left her to finish her breakfast, but I could see she wasn't all that happy about Australia, not deep down.

Well, the long and the short of it was, they never went in the end. I don't know to this day why it was, but I think it must have been because they both depended on me so much that they couldn't bear to part with me, even for a year.

It's a funny thing, but after that time, after the Australia plan was shelved, I mean, Father and Mother seemed to drift apart, and Father began to lose interest in life, and in his work, too. He used to nag at Mother, and Mother would nag at him, and I found myself acting the part of peacemaker. Father took to staying out in the evenings, at his club, so he said, and often I remember Mother would say to me with a sigh, "Your father's late again. I wonder what's kept him tonight?"

I would look up from my homework and say—just to tease, you know—"You shouldn't have married a man younger than yourself. He likes young company, that's what it is, and he finds it with those girls in the office, not all that older than I am myself."

Mother didn't make the best of herself, it was true. She was such a home bird, always in and out of the kitchen, making pastry and cakes, which she did so much better than Florence. I've inherited that from her, I'm glad to say —no one can teach me anything about cooking. But, of course, it meant she was apt to neglect her appearance. Then, when Father finally did come in, I would creep out into the hall to meet him, and make a face, and put my finger to my lips.

"You're in disgrace," I would whisper. "Mother's been on about it half the evening. Just come in and read the paper and don't say anything."

Poor Father, he immediately looked guilty, and there would be a fine evening in front of us, with Mother tight-lipped at her end of the table, and he sulky at his, and me between the pair of them trying to do the best for both.

When I left school the question arose, what was I to do? I've told you I had no brains, but I was quick, and fairly bright in the ordinary things, so I took a typing and short-hand course, and thank heaven I did, as events turned out. At the time I didn't think it would lead to anything. I was eighteen then, and, like most girls of my age, stage-struck. I had taken a leading part in *The School for Scandal* at school, played Lady Teazle, as a matter of fact, and could think of nothing else—the reporter was a friend of the head-mistress, and I got a mention in the local paper—but when

I suggested going on the stage both Father and Mother put their foot down.

"You don't know the first way to set about it," said Father, "apart from the cost of the training."

"Besides," said Mother, "it would mean living up in London and being on your own. It would never do!"

I took the secretarial course just to have it up my sleeve, but I hadn't given up all thoughts of the stage. The way I saw things, there was no future for any of us living in Eastbourne. There was Father still dug in at the solicitor's office, and Mother pottering about at home; it was so narrowing to their outlook that they seemed to get nothing out of life. Whereas if they went up to London to live, there would be a mass of new interests for them. Father would enjoy the football matches in winter, and cricket in the summer, and Mother could go to concerts and picture galleries. Now my Aunt Madge was getting on in life she must be lonely living in that house in Victoria all by herself. We could join forces with her, as paying guests, of course, and it would help her out.

"You know what it is," I said to Mother one evening. "Father will have to think of retiring soon, and what bothers me is how you're going to keep up this house when he does. Florence will have to go, and I shall be out all day at some job typing my poor old fingers to the bone, and here the pair of you will be stuck without anything to do except take Prince for a walk."

Prince was the dog, and he was getting old like Father.

"Well, I don't know," said Mother. "Your father's not due for retirement yet. There's time enough to plan in a year or two."

"I only hope somebody else doesn't plan for him," I told her. "I wouldn't trust that Betty Something-or-other at the office—she has far too much say in things, if you ask me."

Actually, Father had been looking tired the last few months, and I was not very happy about his health. I taxed him with it the very next day. "Are you feeling all right, Father?" I asked.

"Yes," he said. "Why?"

"You look as if you've lost weight this winter," I said, "and you've gone such a bad colour, too."

I remember he went and looked at himself in the mirror. "Yes," he said, "I am thinner. It hadn't struck me."

"It's worried me for some time," I told him. "I think you ought to see a doctor. You get a pain sometimes, don't you, just under the heart?"

"I thought that was indigestion," he said.

"Could be," I said doubtfully, "but when a man's getting on you never know."

Anyway, Father went and had a checkup, and although there was nothing radically wrong there was a suspicion of ulcer, the doctor said, and his blood pressure was high. If he hadn't gone for the checkup it might never have been discovered. It upset Father quite a bit, and Mother too, and I explained to Father that it really wasn't fair on Mother to continue working as he did, or on himself. One of these days he would get really ill and have a heart attack in the office, and heaven knew where it would end. Also, cancer doesn't show in the early stages, I told him, and there was no guarantee that he mightn't be suffering from that too.

Meanwhile, I went up to London to see Aunt Madge, and there she was still living all by herself in that house near Westminster Cathedral.

"Aren't you afraid of burglars?" I asked.

She told me she had never given them a thought. I looked astonished.

"Then it's time you did," I said. "The things one reads in the papers every day scare me stiff. It's always elderly women living on their own in big old-fashioned houses who get attacked. I hope you keep the chain on the door and never answer the bell after dark."

She admitted there had been a burglary in a neighbouring street.

"There you are," I said. "The brutes are going to start on this district. If you took paying guests, and had a man in the house, nothing would happen. Besides, living alone like this, you might fall and break a leg. Nobody would find you for days."

I suppose it took me about three months to make the poor dears realise—Father, Mother, and Aunt Madge—how much happier they would be if they pooled their resources and all lived together in the house in Victoria. It was much the best thing for Father, because it meant that he was near to the best hospitals if his health cracked up. It did, too, the following year, but not before I had found myself a job as understudy in a West End theatre.

Oh yes, I was stage-struck, I admit it. You remember Vernon Miles, the matinee idol before the war? He was the heart throb of my generation, like the pop singers for the teen-agers today, and I was mad about him like everyone else. The family were settling in with my Aunt Madge in Victoria—I had the two top rooms as a flat—and I used to go and wait outside the stage door every evening. In the end he had to notice me. My hair was blonde and fluffy in those days, not touched up as it is today, and I was really pretty, though I say it myself. Wet or fine, every evening I was there, and gradually it became a sort of joke with him. He started off by signing my autograph book, then he used to say good night and wave, and finally he asked me into the dressing-room for a drink with the rest of the company.

"Meet Old Faithful," he said—he had a great sense of humour—and they all laughed and shook hands with me, and I told him there and then that I wanted a job.

"You mean you want to act?" he asked.

"I don't mind what I do," I said, "as long as I'm inside a theatre. I'll help pull the curtain up and down, if you like."

I think the audacity of this really did the trick, and the way I wouldn't take no for an answer, because Vernon Miles did make a job for me as assistant to the assistant stage manager. Actually, I was a sort of glorified messenger girl, but it was a foot on the ladder all the same. And what it was to be able to go back to the house in Victoria and tell them I'd got a job on the stage with Vernon Miles!

Besides the stage directing part of my work, I understudied the understudies. Happy, carefree days they were. The best part, though, was seeing Vernon Miles every day. I was always one of the last out of the theatre and managed to leave at the same time as he did.

He stopped calling me "Old Faithful" and nicknamed me "Fidelity" instead, which was more complimentary, and I made it my business to keep away from the stage door all the fans who wanted to pester him. I did the same for other members of the company, and some of them got very jealous. There can be quite a lot of ill-feeling backstage one way or another, which the stars themselves don't see.

"I wouldn't like to be you," I said to Vernon Miles one night.

"Why not?" he asked.

"You'd be surprised," I told him, "the things some of them say behind your back. They flatter you to your face, but it's a different thing when you're looking the other way."

It seemed only fair to put him on his guard. He was such a kind, generous man, I hated to think of him being put upon in any way. He was a bit in love with me, too, though nothing serious. He kissed me under the mistletoe at a Christmas party, and he must have been a bit ashamed of himself the next day, because I remember he slipped out of the theatre without saying good night.

I waited in the passage every evening for a week, but he always managed to have someone with him—until the Saturday, when I knew there was no one in the dressing-room, and I knocked on the door. He looked quite scared when he saw me.

"Hullo, Fido," he said—it had got to Fido by now—"I thought you'd gone home."

"No," I said, "I wondered if you wanted anything."

"That's very sweet of you," he said. "No, I don't think I do."

I just stood there, waiting. If he really felt like kissing me again I didn't mind. It wouldn't be out of his way to drop me in Victoria, either. He lived in Chelsea himself. After waiting a moment or two, I suggested this, and he smiled, in a strained sort of way, and said he was terribly sorry but he was going out to supper at the Savoy, in the opposite direction.

And then he began to cough quite badly, putting his hand to his heart, and said he was afraid he was going to have one of his attacks—he suffered from asthma, you remember—and would I call his dresser, he would know what to do. I was really very alarmed and I called the dresser, who came at once and put me outside the room and said Mr. Miles would have to rest about twenty minutes before going to his supper engagement at the Savoy. I think the dresser was jealous of my friendship with Vernon Miles, because after that night he was always on guard by the dressing-room door and was almost offensive when I tried to hang about outside. It was all very petty and silly, and the atmosphere in the theatre became quite different, with people whispering in corners, and not speaking, and looking the other way whenever I appeared.

Anyway, my stage career was cut short, what with Father's death (he had an exploratory operation for stomach pain, and although they found nothing organically wrong he died under the anaesthetic), and Mother of course was very distressed. She was fond of Father, in spite of all that nagging, and I had to go home for a time to try and keep the peace between her and Aunt Madge.

The authorities ought to do something for elderly people. It's really terrible, I kept telling them both, how there is no sort of provision for those with failing health. Any day, I said, either of them might get the same sort of pain that Father had, and be whisked off to hospital, and perhaps kept there week after week with nothing wrong. There ought to be hostels, with hot and cold in every room, and a restaurant, and a staff of nurses, so that elderly people could relax and not be worrying about themselves all the time. Naturally I didn't grudge giving up my stage career to look after them, but where would the money come from to keep Mother when Aunt Madge had gone?

Well, that was 1939, and the pair of them were nervous enough then, so you can imagine what it was like when war broke out and the bomb scare started. "They'll go for Victoria first," I said, "because of the station," and in next to no time I had both of them packed off to Devonshire. But the terrible thing was that the boardinghouse they were staying in at Exeter received a direct hit. They were killed instantly, and the house in Victoria was never so much as scratched. That's life, isn't it? Or perhaps death, to put it correctly.

I was so shocked by the tragedy of poor Mother and Aunt Madge being wiped out by a single bomb that I had a nervous breakdown, and that was really how I came to miss being called up when they started putting girls and young women in the Services. I wasn't fit for nursing, either. I took a job as secretary to a dear old blind millionaire, to try and get my strength back. He had a huge house in Shropshire, and you'd hardly believe it, but, although he became devoted to me, he died without leaving me a penny.

His son came into the place, and his wife didn't like me, or rather I didn't like her, so, as the war in Europe was over, I decided to go back to London, and I got another secretarial job with a journalist in Fleet Street.

It was while I was working for him that I made contact with various reporters and other newspaper people. If you're mixed up in that world you can't help hearing a lot of gossip, and so on, however discreet you are—and no one can call me indiscreet. Scrupulous as you may be, there are limits to what one person can do to quash scandal, and it wasn't my business, even if I'd had the time, to track down every story to its source and find out whether it was true or not. The best I could do, with all the rumours that I heard, was to insist that they *were* rumours and mustn't on any account be passed on.

It was when I was working for the journalist that I met Kenneth. He was the other half of Rosanke. Everyone knows Rosanke, the dress designer and *haut couturier*—whatever you care to call it. I suppose they rank about third in the top ten. People think to this day that it's run by one person, a sort of recluse, shut away in an ivory tower, but the truth is that Rosanke is, or was, Rose and Kenneth Sawbones. The way they put the names together was rather clever, don't you think?

Rose and Kenneth Sawbones were brother and sister, and I married Kenneth. I admit that Rose was the artistic one of

the pair. She did the designing, and in fact all the creativ
work, and Kenneth ran the financial side of the business. M
journalist boss had a small interest in Rosanke, just a fe
shares, but still it paid him to get Rosanke into the gossi
columns, which he did very effectively. People were sick o
the uniform fashions of wartime, and Rose was clever th
way she laid such stress on femininity, hips and bosoms, an
so on, and clinging lines. Rosanke went to the top in ne
to no time, but there is no doubt that it was helped by th
push it got from the press.

I met Kenneth at one of their dress shows—I was using
press ticket, of course. He was pointed out to me by
journalist friend.

"There's the ke in Rosanke," said my friend, "and he hold
the tail end, and no mistake. Rose is the brains. Kenny ju
tots up the figures, then hands in the cheques to his sister

Kenneth was good-looking. The Jack Buchanan type,
perhaps you'd call it Rex Harrison. Tall and fair, with bag
of charm. The first thing I asked was whether he was ma
ried, but my journalist friend told me he hadn't been caugl
yet. He introduced me to Kenneth, and to Rose too—the
were not a scrap alike, although they were brother and siste
—and I told Rose what my boss planned to say about the
in his paper. Naturally she was delighted, and I had an in
vitation to a party she was giving. One thing led to anothe
Rosanke was definitely in the news and getting bigger pul
licity every day.

"If you smile on the press, the press smiles on you," I sai
to Kenneth, "and once they're on your side the world's you
oyster."

This was at a tiny party I was giving for them, on th
understanding that Vernon Miles would be there to mee
them. I'd told them how well I knew him, and they hope
to dress his next play. Unfortunately he never turned up—
another attack of asthma, his secretary said.

"What a go-ahead girl you are," said Kenneth. "I've neve
met anyone like you." And he finished off his fifth martini
He drank too much, even then.

"I'll tell you another thing," I said. "You've got to sto
316

letting your sister push you around. Rosanke's pronounced all wrong. You want the accent on the *ke*."

He sobered up at that. He lowered his glass and stared at me.

"What makes you say that?" he asked.

I shrugged my shoulders. "I hate to see a man kowtow to a woman. Especially when the man has the brains. It's laziness, that's all. One of these days you'll find the *ke* dropped out of Rosanke, and you'll only have yourself to blame."

Believe it or not, he took me out to dinner, and I heard the whole story of his childhood and how Rose and his mother had always preyed on him. They were devoted, of course, but, as I pointed out, the very devotion was the worst part about it. It had turned possessive.

"What you need," I told him, "is to stand on your own and beat the big drum."

The result of that dinner was rather extraordinary. Kenneth had a big row with Rose. It was the first they had ever had, he told me afterwards, but it must have cleared the air, because things were on another footing inside the business from that time, and Rose realised that she hadn't got it all her own way. Some of the model girls said that the atmosphere had changed and was spoilt; but that was just because discipline was tightened up and they had to work longer hours.

Kenneth proposed to me in a traffic jam. He was driving me home after a party—I still had the house in Victoria, Aunt Madge had left it to me in her will. We came to a block where the lights had stuck. There must have been something wrong with them.

"Red for danger," said Kenneth. "That's you."

"You flatter me," I told him. "I've never thought of myself as a *femme fatale*."

"I don't know about *fatale*," said Kenneth, "but here we are stuck, which is pretty much the same thing."

Of course he had to kiss me—there was nothing else he could do. Then somebody must have cleared the lights from a main switch. I saw them first.

"You know what green stands for, don't you?" I asked him.

"Yes," he answered, "all clear. Go ahead."

"Well, I'm not married either," I said. "The way's clear."

To be perfectly honest, I'm not certain that he wasn't the teeniest bit taken by surprise. You know how cautious some men are, and maybe he wanted another day or two to bring himself to the point. However, of course word got round in no time that we were engaged, and once that kind of thing creeps into the papers it's so difficult to deny. As I told him, it makes a man look a cad and it's very bad for his business. Besides, it gives people all sorts of ideas when a dress designer is a bachelor. So we were married, and I had a lovely dress on the firm. The only unromantic thing about the wedding was having to become Mrs. Sawbones.

Kenneth and I were very much in love, but I had an uneasy feeling, right from the start, that the marriage wasn't going to work out. For one thing, he was so terribly restless, always wanting to move on from one place to another. We had flown to Paris after the wedding, intending to stay put, but when we'd been there a day he said, "Dilly, I can't stand this. Let's try Rome." So off we had to go, there and then, and we hadn't been in Rome two days before he suggested Naples. Then he had the wild idea of wiring for Rose and his mother to come out and join us. On the honeymoon! Naturally I was hurt, and I told him that if it got into the press that he'd had to take his family on his honeymoon, Rosanke would be the laughingstock of London. I suppose that shook him, because he didn't suggest it again. But we didn't stay in Italy long, because the rich food disagreed with him.

Married life . . . what I could say about it, from within! I don't suppose I remember one night, during the six years we were together, that Kenneth didn't have too much to drink. He got so that he couldn't stand and he couldn't speak. He had to go off on a cure three times, but they never did any good. He would seem quite all right in the Home—he tried a different one each time—and then, as soon as he got

318

back to me, off he would be on the bottle again. What I suffered!

No, it didn't make much difference to the business of Rosanke, because once Kenneth started drinking Rose dropped him from the partnership and put a paid accountant in his place. She made Kenneth an allowance—she had to—but it wasn't safe to let him have anything to do with the finances.

I had given up my job, naturally, when I married, but with Kenneth always in and out of nursing homes I had to do something towards expenses, so I kept in touch with my friends in Fleet Street. Nothing official. Just snippets now and again. It helped, being sister-in-law to Rose. You wouldn't believe how much goes on in the fashion world. The buyers hear a lot of backstairs talk, and the model girls too. If customers only realised that every little slip of the tongue gets repeated, they'd cover their lips with sticking plaster every time they went near a fashion house. Anyway, I knew several of the buyers, and most of Rosanke's model girls too. Rose herself wasn't particularly discreet when she was discussing customers inside the family, so I heard a number of stories one way and another that afterwards broke in the press and made headlines. I can't bear gossip, but whispers have a knack of coming true. What's wish fulfilment today is fact tomorrow.

"I think you're a saint," my friends would say, "keeping up a home for Kenneth Sawbones, when he's an alcoholic. Why don't you divorce him?"

"He's my husband," I told them, "and I love him."

I believe I could have kept Kenneth off the bottle if only we had had a family. It was not for want of trying, heaven knows. Each time he returned from the Home I would do my best. But it never worked out. . . .

Finally, and this was the heartbreak of the whole tragedy, he wrote from the nursing home he had gone to for a fourth cure—away up in Yorkshire it was, too far for me to go and see him on a day trip—and said he loved one of the nurses there, and she was pregnant already, and would I divorce him?

I went straight away to Rose and his mother with the

news, and they said they were not surprised. They had fe
something of the sort was bound to happen in the end. The
said Kenneth was not responsible for his actions and it wa
very sad, but the best thing for all concerned was to let hi
go.

"How am I going to live?" I said. I was nearly out of m
mind, as you can imagine. "Six years I've been a slave t
Kenneth, and this is his return for all I've done."

"We know, Dilly," said Rose. "It's been hard on you, bu
then it's a hard world. Of course, Kenneth will have to pa
you an allowance, and I'll look after you too."

She couldn't afford to quarrel with me, you see. I knev
too much about her private affairs and the affairs of Rosanke

"Very well," I said, wiping my eyes, "I'll put a brave fac
on it, but it comes heavy to get all the kicks in life and non
of the sweets."

There was Rose, rich and famous, fêted by everyone, an
I was only Dilly Sawbones, who had helped to put her an
Kenneth on the map. It was a hard world, as she said, bu
she seemed to ride on top of it all right. A penthouse i
Mayfair, and lovers by the score, that's what came throug
being the first half of Rosanke. The second half, or what wa
left of it, had to make do with a few shabby rooms in Victoria

Naturally I didn't see so much of Rose once my divorc
came through, though she kept her word and made me
titbit of an allowance, enough to redecorate my poor ol
house. I always got my clothes free, too. After all, everyon
knew I'd been married to Kenneth and he had treated m
shamefully, and it wouldn't have done the name of Rosank
any good if I'd gone about in rags.

She had a bad streak in her, though, just like Kennetl
and these things always come out in the end. Although I wa
careful never to say anything against her, she began to los
popularity about that time—there were a fair number of dig
at her in the press—and word got about that the fashio
house of Rosanke was not what it had been, that it had ha
its day.

Of course I had to find myself a job. Rose's allowance an
the alimony from Kenneth weren't enough to keep me, so

pulled a few strings, and the next thing I knew I was working for the Conservative party before the General Election. I doubt whether the member for South Finchley would ever have got in but for me. You see, I knew a thing or two about his opponent. He used to go about with one of the models from Rosanke, and if there is one thing South Finchley hates, it's promiscuity in a member. I felt it my duty to drop a hint here and there, and our man got in with a slight majority. I'm a great patriot, and I put Queen and country before sentiment or any kind of personal considerations.

Anyway, working hard at the Conservative office helped me to get over losing Kenneth, and it was at one of their meetings that I met Lord Chichester.

"Who's that stiff-looking man with the eyeglass?" I asked someone. I was told at once he was Edward Fairleigh-Gore, whose father had just died, which meant that he had gone to the Lords.

"One of our ablest executives," said my informant. "In the running for Prime Minister if the rest of the Cabinet die."

I managed to get on the fringe of the group surrounding Lord Chichester and was introduced to his wife, a grey-haired woman who looked several years older than he did. It seemed that she was very fond of hunting, never out of the saddle if she could help it, so I asked her what on earth she did about clothes when she came to London, and wasn't it a nightmare wondering if she looked right. Lady Chichester seemed rather surprised, and admitted that the dress she was wearing was two years old.

"You ought to go to Rosanke," I told her. "She's my sister-in-law. You need never worry again, once you're in her hands."

"I don't think I do worry," said Lady Chichester.

"What about your husband?" I said, and raised my eye-brows. I didn't emphasise the point, and moved out of the group soon afterwards, but what I had said must have made an impression, for I saw Lady Chichester glance in the mirror once or twice, which, without wanting to be unkind, was probably a thing she didn't often do.

The upshot was that I got Rose to send her a card for her

next show. The fish were biting that spring, and Lady Chichester went. I was there. I sat beside her and advised her what to order, as she had no sort of taste herself.

I telephoned her every day for a fortnight after that, and finally she invited me to lunch. Lord Chichester came in late, and I only got a word with him when we had coffee afterwards in the drawing-room, but I made myself felt.

"Did you see the bit about you in last night's *Courier*?" I asked him.

"I can't say I have," he said. "I never read gossip."

"This wasn't gossip," I told him. "This was the truth, or, if you prefer it, prophecy. 'There's only one man who can make the Conservative party into a Fighting Force, and that's Lord Chichester.' "

It's a funny thing, but even the most intelligent men fall for praise. It doesn't matter how thick you lay it on, they revel in it. Lord Chichester smiled and made a sort of brushing gesture with his hand, to pretend it was all nonsense, but I pulled the clipping out of my bag and gave it to him.

That was the start of our affair. It took him over a year to admit that he was lost without me, and when he did he broke down and cried, but then he was not very fit just then and had only recently got over a bad attack of shingles.

"What you need," I told him, "is feeding up."

He was at my house in Victoria at the time. Lady Chichester had broken her leg in a fall out hunting and was laid up in Warwickshire, so Edward—we were Edward and Dilly by then—was on his own in their London house. I was worried that he wasn't feeding himself properly, and it was the worst possible thing for his digestion, as I told him, not to eat, especially after shingles. So one day I waited for him in a taxi outside the Lords and insisted on taking him home so that I could cook him a decent meal. And that was how he came to spend the first night in my house.

"Now, don't worry," I told him next morning. "No one will ever find out what's happened. It's between you and me. Of course, if those sharks in the press should get hold of a story it's all U.P. with your career," I went on with a laugh. I've never seen a man look so frightened—but then, a sense of humour was never his strong suit.

Poor darling Edward . . . Looking back on those years we had together, I realise that I was the great love of his life. I persuaded him that being married to Mary Chichester was no life for a politician; he might as well be married to a horse.

"It's not fair on you," I said, "all that stable talk. It won't help you to be Prime Minister."

"I don't know that I want to be Prime Minister," he said. "Sometimes all I feel like is going down to Warwickshire to die."

"You'll have to take me with you if you do," I said.

I don't know how it was, but he never seemed to pull his weight in the Conservative party as he should have done. He reminded me at times of Father in the old Eastbourne days. He looked hag-ridden, and when I tried to make him talk about what went on behind the scenes in the House of Lords —because, of course, I still kept contact with my friends in the Press and supplied them with news from time to time— he would try to change the subject and talk about his wife's horses instead.

"You ought to see Ginger," he would say. "She's a wonderful mare. And Mary has the lightest hands of any woman I've ever known."

"The trouble with you is that you've no ambition," I told him. I couldn't help being bitter at times. There I was, cooking delicious suppers, putting myself out to look after him, and all he could do was to complain of indigestion and rave about his wife's horses.

I never said a word against his wife. After all, she had the money, and it was only a matter of time before she would break her back out hunting, and then darling Edward would be free. It worried me that he made such a fetish of Warwickshire, neglecting his work in the Lords.

"You ought to get the farmers to build their fences higher," I would tell him. "If your wife's horses are as good as you make out, they'd leap a haystack."

And then I'd try to change the subject, get away from

Warwickshire, and put out a feeler or two about his brother peers, or better still the real bigwigs in the Cabinet. It seemed such a waste to have Edward coming round to see me, when it would help him so much to discuss foreign policy and what the Government intended to do about the Middle East, if his brain was going to soften, as it looked like doing. A word or two from me in the right quarter, and the political repercussions might be staggering.

"If you'd only met me ten years ago," I used to say to him, "the pair of us wouldn't be sitting here now."

"You're dead right," he agreed. "I'd be in the South Sea Islands."

He liked to pretend, you see, that all he wanted really was a quiet life.

"No," I told him, "you'd be Prime Minister. And I'd be entertaining at Number 10. It makes my blood boil when I see how you let the others pick all the plum positions. You want someone to stick up for you, and the person who ought to do it spends her time gossiping with a lot of grooms."

I really began to wonder whether the future of the United Kingdom would be safe in his hands after all. There were one or two Labour men who looked as if they had more backbone, and they had more money too. I never had a penny out of Edward—not that I'd have taken anything if he had offered it to me—but I did get rather tired of the framed photographs of horses which he sent me from Warwickshire every Christmas.

No, love stories don't have a happy ending. Not in real life. Mine finished with a bang, and when I say bang, I mean it.

The crisis came when Parliament dissolved at the end of the summer recess, and I was waiting as usual in a taxi in Parliament Square to pick up Edward and take him home. That was another thing—he was getting so absent-minded that sometimes he went straight home to his own house unless I caught him first. To my horror, I saw him come out of the Lords and make a dive into a car that was drawn up alongside the pavement. The car shot off before I could take its number or tell the taxi to follow it. There was a woman in the back of the car—I could see her through the window.

Here we are, I said to myself. This is it! I went straight back home and put through a call to his wife in Warwickshire. It was only fair to tell her the truth, and that her husband was going out with another woman.

But do you know what happened? The servant who answered the telephone said that Lady Chichester had sold the house in Warwickshire and was up in London, and that she and Lord Chichester were going to Kenya for six months, perhaps a year. In fact, it was very possible that they were going to settle in Africa altogether. Lord Chichester was tired of political life, and he and Lady Chichester both wanted to shoot big game. As far as the servant knew, they were leaving at once, perhaps that very night.

I tried his London house. No reply. I tried every hotel I could think of, without result. I tried the airport and drew a similar blank.

Then it all came out. Lord and Lady Chichester had left for Kenya under assumed names. I read the whole thing in the morning paper. The reason given was that Lord Chichester had had another attack of shingles and wanted to get away from it all. Poor darling—I suppose he was drugged. Handcuffed, even. These things can happen today, in a free country. It's a fearful reflection on the Conservative party, and at the next election I'm going to work for Labour. They at least are honest.

Meanwhile, here I am on my own again, with a broken heart. I did everything for Edward Chichester, just as I did for Kenneth, and what did I get out of it? Nothing but ingratitude. I don't suppose I shall ever hear from him again—she'll see to that. If I do, it'll be a buffalo's head on a Christmas card, instead of a chestnut mare.

What I want to know is this: where have I gone wrong in life? Why is it that no matter how kind I am to people, how truly generous, it never seems to pay dividends? From start to finish I've put myself last and the happiness of others first. And yet, when I sit alone now, in the evenings, I seem to see faces around me, Father, Mother, Aunt Madge, Kenneth, Edward, even poor Vernon Miles, and their expressions aren't kind at all but somehow hunted. It's as if they want to be rid of me. They can't bear to be shadows. They'd like to get out of my memory and my life. Or is it that I want to be rid of them? I really don't know. It's too much of a muddle.

My doctor says I live on my nerves, and he's given me a bottle of sleeping pills. I keep them by my bed. But, do you know, I have the impression that he's more worn out than I am. Yesterday, when I telephoned for another appointment, the voice at the other end said, "I'm sorry, Doctor Yardley is on holiday." But it wasn't true. I recognised his voice. He was disguising it.

Why am I so unlucky and so unhappy?

What is it that I do?